2020 inside the castle press
insidethecastle.org

ISBN 978-1-7352901-1-9

Photos on pages xii, 8, 11 and 41, drawing on pages 51, some of the text on page 44, and the drawings on page 134 and 315 are all by Irene Milsom. Photos on pages 73, 139, 193, 347, & 364 by Spider Damage Nørth. Illustration and handwritten text on pages 172 & 173 by Nathaxnne Walker. Photo on page 147 by Vern Phoenix. Song lyric in tattoo on page 214 by Jordaan Mason. Sculpture on page 229 by Coda Raine Fiona. Sculpture on page 255 by Luna Breed. All other text & images by Never Angeline Nørth except where noted.

The creature on Page 260 is inspired by a Henry Darger creature. The drawing on page 83 was inspired by a Nathaxnne Walker drawing.

Excerpts were originally published in Witch Craft Mag, Black Warrior Review, Gulf Coast, Puerto del Sol, The Wanderer, Pinwheel, Curious Specimens Anthology, Spy Kids Review, TRNS-FR, Sporklet, datableed, Dostoyevsky Wannabe, TAGVVERK, DREGINALD, Big Lucks, the Fanzine, Working It, SPF Lit Mag, Nat Brut, Tarpaulin Sky Magazine, Boyfriend Village, and Smoke + Mold.

Cover art, interior & exterior design by Never Angeline Nørth.

This book is dedicated to all monsters.

Fuck the police.

CAST OF CHARACTERS

Narrator (Sara) – Gosh, where to start? Only one of many Saras. Telling this story. She/her or they/them pronouns.

Sea-Witch – A glittering cascade of water that froze in place to be lived in but accidentally ended up capable of true emotion. Precious & needs to be held. Gets cold like all living creatures. Etc., etc., You get the idea. She/her.

Girl who put her dolls in a duffle bag – A monster in the form of a girl. You'd be surprised how many monsters are in this form. She/her.

Her mother – You may have seen it written that real monsters have no mothers. This may or may not be true. Some monsters are mothers. Some mothers are monsters. I'm not sure anything in this book is true. It was just what felt true at the time. She/her.

Meteor (may she lay us waste) – Far away. Loves Girls With Assholes. Flat affect. Probably going to kill us all one day. She/her.

Dog that showed up to hang out with Sea-Witch – Really fun & cute. Didn't mention their pronouns.

78 Men Who Cause Pain (aka 78MWCP) – I hate these guys. Just the worst. Go around being nice to each other so they can pretend they aren't literally hurting every other thing that exists. He/him.

Small animals who hid their faces from the sun – Only exist in Sara's dream. Didn't ask what kind of animals? Maybe people. They/them?

People – Don't exist???? Secretly monsters??? They/them.

Dog-Witch – THE BEST!!!! Pretty much made everything. Helped a lot of people. Probably not perfect but honestly like, who cares ze is so nice & great? Ze/hir pronouns.

airless faces – Any thing that lived in the water before Dog-Witch made land. Kind of an old timey term that doesn't rly mean anything anymore. It/its.

Air-Witch – Lived with rats. Ate dirt. Dies kind of a lot of times? She/her.

Dirt-Witch – Beautiful & loves horses. She/her.

Milk-Witch – Round & does a lot of warm dialing. All those little number buttons in the mouths of infants. She/her.

Old-Seagull-Witch – Works at University of Crater. Has a girlfriend & they do sex stuff. She/her.

Strawberry-Witch – Super cute. Keeps her seeds on the outside. Tried camming for awhile but wasn't very good at it. Has creepy dreams. Last I heard she bought a van & was living in it. She/her.

Leg-Witch – Literally another witch's leg. One of Dog-Witch's sisters. Doesn't talk much. She/her.

Less-Held-Witch – Learned about ghosts. Super crushing on Glass-Witch. She/her.

Stone-Witch – Totally hooked up with Dog-Witch. Also her own full being who lived a full life & had her own experiences thank you very much. For example, AllMusic described her as "one of the most acclaimed, influential, and enigmatic electronic musicians of the early 21st century." I bet you didn't know that. She/her.

Glass-Witch – Super cool & cute. Likes Less-Held-Witch. But how much? She/her pronouns.

Death-Witch – God dammit. Fucking fuck. I'm so sorry. She/her.

ha-ha-ha (or ah-ah-ah) – Very mysterious. Unknown? Doesn't exist? Barely does? Loves cucumbers. Unknown pronouns.

Bears – Used to be mean and do a lot of bad-guy things. But I guess who of us didn't. Eat berries & nuts. They/them.

Lava – Hates bears, who kept it prisoner. Loves Dog-Witch. Likes helping with formation of monsters. It/Its

Girl who tried to cool with her mouth the lava around another girl – Possibly could have changed relationships in the world from being about power to being about care. Unfortunately, isn't real. She/her.

Infants - Sad? Love Milk-Witch. One of them works in a gift shop. They/them? Probably ask each one.

A Pit Filled 15 Feet Deep With Rotting Dresses - Just shows up one day? Idk. Ze/hir.

Girls With Assholes - Cool band. Nobody knows who the members are. They/them.

University of Crater - Place where people research pain. Honestly, probably funded by the 78 Men. It/its.

Minor god of pain - Honestly probably fake. Probably just one of the 78 Men being an asshole. They/them.

Boys - Not real. They/them.

Angels - An angel (or "gayngel") is a being who creates light or dark & lives outside of time & legibility. I am sometimes an angel. It/its.

deadname - I can never figure this one out? Sometimes hangs out with Strawberry-Witch &/or Sara. Smells like rainwater. xe/xym/xyr.

Real Living Creature Whom Sea-Witch Kissed After Her Birth - Never knows what time it is. Actually rly beautiful singing voice. She/Her or It/its.

cops – The fucking worst. Evil bacteria that is meant to cause pain & ruin, especially to the most vulnerable among us. Work for the 78 Men Who Cause Pain. The only good cop is a dead cop. He/him, it/its.

Deeps-Witch – Oldest of the sisters. Leaves the largest footprints when walking in snow or sand. Learned secrets. Had lovers & children. She/her.

The family & children of Deeps-Witch – Seem nice? I didn't get to learn much about them. Various pronouns. They/them seems like a safe bet.

The ghost of a very broken girl Sara once knew – Honestly she made a lot of shit a lot harder than it needed to be. She/her.

Eight copies of the sun – Live inside Sara. Seem pretty cool. Fun to play with. They/them or it/its.

You, the color that is watching me now – I mean, you would know better than I would.
Who are you? ____
What are your pronouns? ____

Being made entirely of witch-god scar tissue – Didn't want to talk. Ze/hir pronouns.

A piece of information Dog-Witch didn't understand – One of the things Dog-Witch loves most in the world. The inspiration for the formation/creation of Sea-Witch. I wonder what happened to it. It/its.

Wood-Witch – A collection of parts. I never met her. I wish I had. I wish anyone had. She/her.

The ghost in the spaces - A virus of some kind? A bad, mean god? It controls the 78 Men & has existed long before them. Not cute. Hurts all monsters & humanity. Better off dead IMO. Idk pronouns?

Water-Witch – Sweet girl having a hard time. Her & Strawberry-Witch had a thing for a little bit. She/her.

Little girl in the crater - Not even gods could save her. Not that gods are that good at saving I guess. Fuck. Pronouns she/her.

Banana slug the size of the living room couch - Replaced the couch in Water-Witch's sister's house. Didn't want to be alone. It/its.

Bright warmth - She can't fix things, but she can hold you through the worst of it. & that's honestly huge. She/her pronouns.

S – Chill as fuck stoner. Somebody's wife. Probably not real. He/him.

J – Satan-loving spider girl. Probably not real. She/her.

Client – Some horny bro. He/him.

Therapist – One of the people whom the 78 Men Who Cause Pain have deemed allowed to determine whether or not we are allowed to be ourselves. Some of them are bullshit. Some of them are a precious escape route. Most of them are some combination of both. Usually she/her or he/him.

Doctor – One of the people whom the 78 Men Who Cause Pain have deemed allowed to determine whether or not we are allowed to be ourselves. Some of them are bullshit. Some of them are a precious escape route. Most of them are some combination of both. Usually he/him or she/her.

People dressed as rats dressed as angels – I like them. Probably not actually people. They/them.

Assholes – My favorite genital. It/its.

A friend from when I lived in Sea-Witch – Gorgeous person. I miss her a lot. She/her.

Enemy – I thought I was the enemy. They/them.

Some lady – I'm just some lady to somebody else. Shit. She/her.

Police – A bullshit 78MWCP word for that cops bacteria. All bastards. He/him.

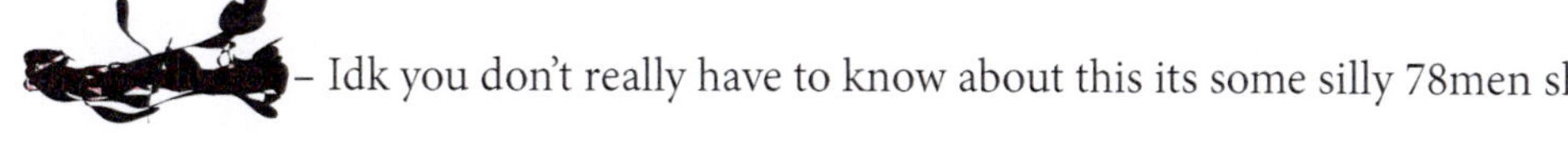 – Idk you don't really have to know about this its some silly 78men shit. They/them.

Man on stage/Man in the sky/Man in the sky's son – Listen what do you even want me to say.

God-Witch – Twin of Airless-Face-Witch. Rly into wasps I guess? Sex cult diva. She/her.

Airless-Face-Witch - Twin of God-Witch. Just really doesn't know. Half of a rat? She/her.

Cygnet – Adorable monster. Half of a rat?

Swarm of Wasps – Only one of its forms. Sexy I guess? Not my type. Hanging out with Cygnet. It/its? They/them? It's a swarm of wasps u can probably figure out some words to use.

Creature inside of Never – Fill me with your sweetest.

Rat god – I am beautiful.

Garbage god – I am sinless.

Felix - A living creature with a voice that rang like shaking a bag of pennies. They/them, I think.

The ghosts inside of me that want to die - The smell of their death stuck in my clothes. They/them. Dead/dead.

Someone's partners - I hope they are okay. If there is a place people go after the whole world is destroyed, I hope they are there sipping sweet beverages.

The ghosts of things with twelve heads - Every fucking time. They/them pronouns.

Aangels - We are being summoned. You are being summoned. It/its?

Never – Not her whole name. The same but different but the same. She/they.

Ghosts of anyone I have met/ghosts of those to whom I will or will not communicate – What Never is juxtaposted to. They/she.

The Thing That Resists Naming – Oh come on. It really probably doesn't want us to call it that like its a name. Idk pronouns? It/its?

Never's lover – In xir own story. You'll have to read that one after yr finished with this. They/she/he/it/xe/ze/etc.

Dead-Jellyfish-Witch – Lovely lady. Total sweetheart. A little sad, but it's hard to find monsters who aren't sad these days. I really mean this. Even outside this story. We're all just fucking treading water out here. Pronouns are she/her.

Never's birth – The most beautiful, impossible rat angel. In another life, Never raised it, loved it, cared for it. But in this climate it was born to die & not-die. Born to be split into parts & dissolved into the world. It/its.

Piss cloud – Never wants to be like the piss cloud when they grow up. Me too, honestly. How *derisann*. It/its.

Machine they replaced the Church of M****r with – Not much going on here. Each day is a blessing. It/its.

Sea-Witch's daughter – Won't be born for years. She/her.

Cameraman – It's like a camera with arms & legs I think. He/him or It/Its?

Broken ant – A cute little ant having a rough time of things. She/her.

Whale – A living creature bigger than a bus. Senses her own thoughts drifting through unstructured time, etc., etc., etc. She/her, though I don't think whales really give a shit about gender. I think they've outgrown it.

______________ - ______ ______ __ __. __/___.

Candle-Witch – A type of creature that grants terrifying visions. Sometimes they come true. One of Dog-Witch's sisters. It/its or She/her.

The librarian – Cutest lil mound of sand evrr. They/them.

dog on the beach – Girl. Or not. Doesn't rly give a shit abt yr gender nonsense. It/its.

Troops – Scary as hell. I'm not a big fan of troops but sometimes I get it I guess. Like if you need to fight off the 78 Men or whatever, if yr liberating yrselves. That's real. But that's barely ever the case. Sometimes the 78 Men talk about "liberating" but what they really mean is "colonizing", which is a word that totally makes sense in Sea-Witch. They/them.

Server at the restaurant – A person who is forced to bring food to people in order to receive the resources to meet basic needs such as food & shelter. A person I feel sympathy for. Also, in this specific story, a murderer, so I guess I don't feel too much sympathy but like, this person isn't the one who created the situation in which someone in terrible circumstances such as these feels the need or desire to murder someone. I would fight for this person but like, in general one should strive to be less murdery. She/her.

Our dog – A possibility. An animate symbol of hope. Very cute. They/them.

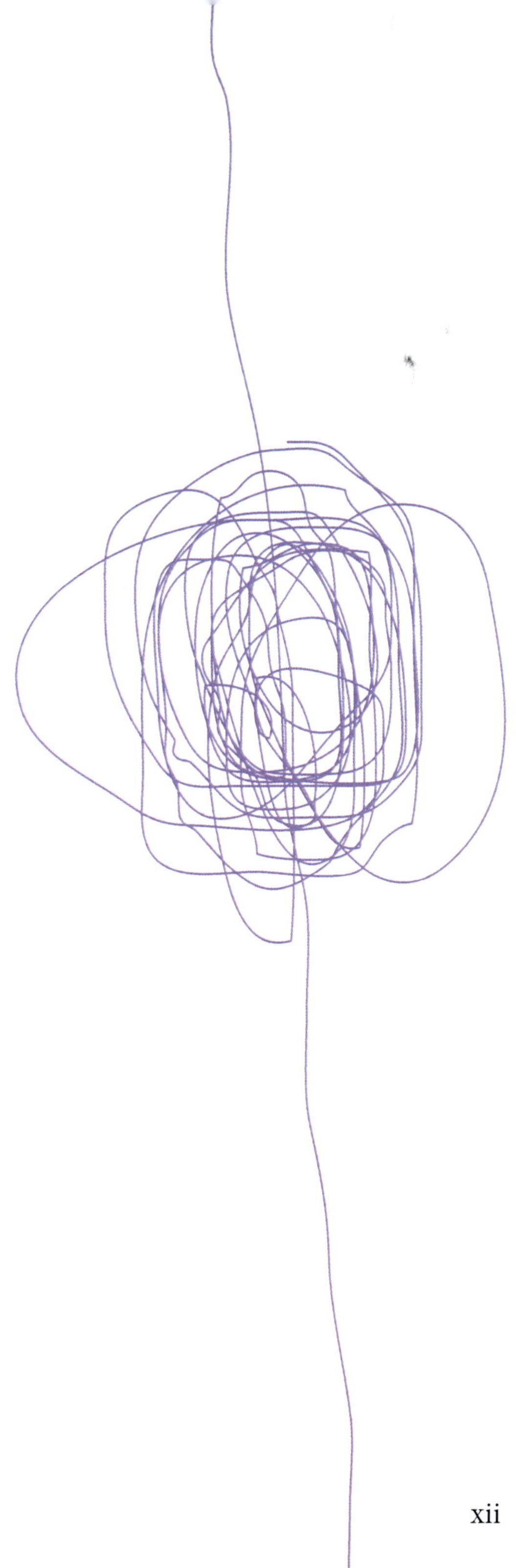

SEA A·WITCH

v1 (ms/uw)   by moss angel witchmonstr

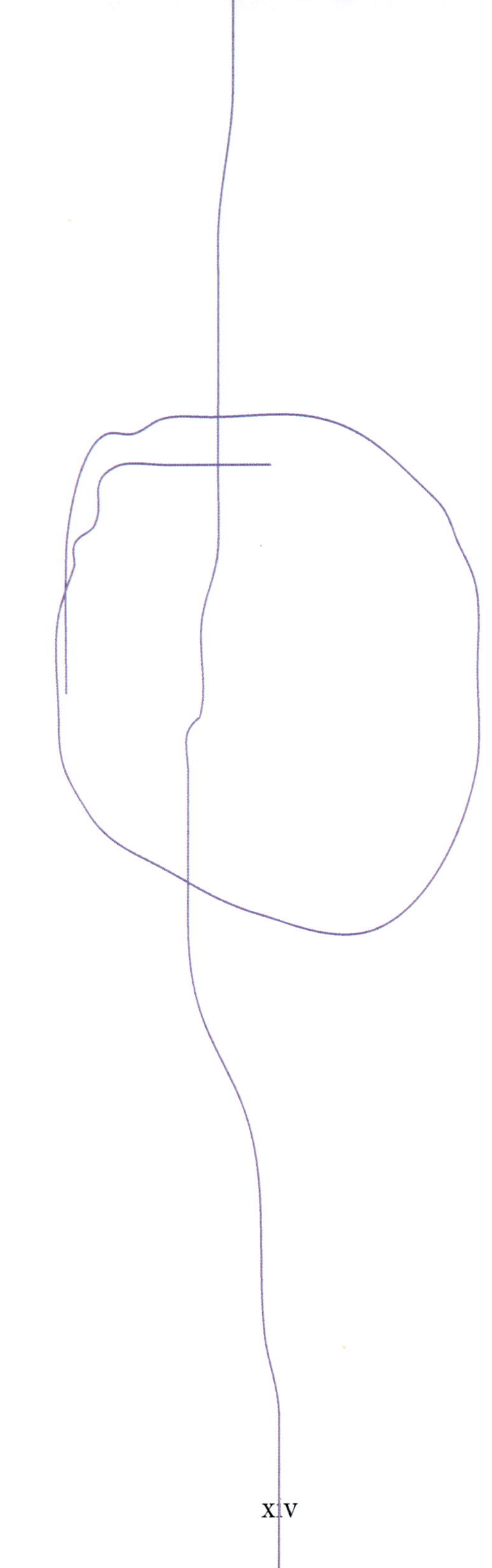

XIV

SEA-WITCH
chapter one: may she lay us waste

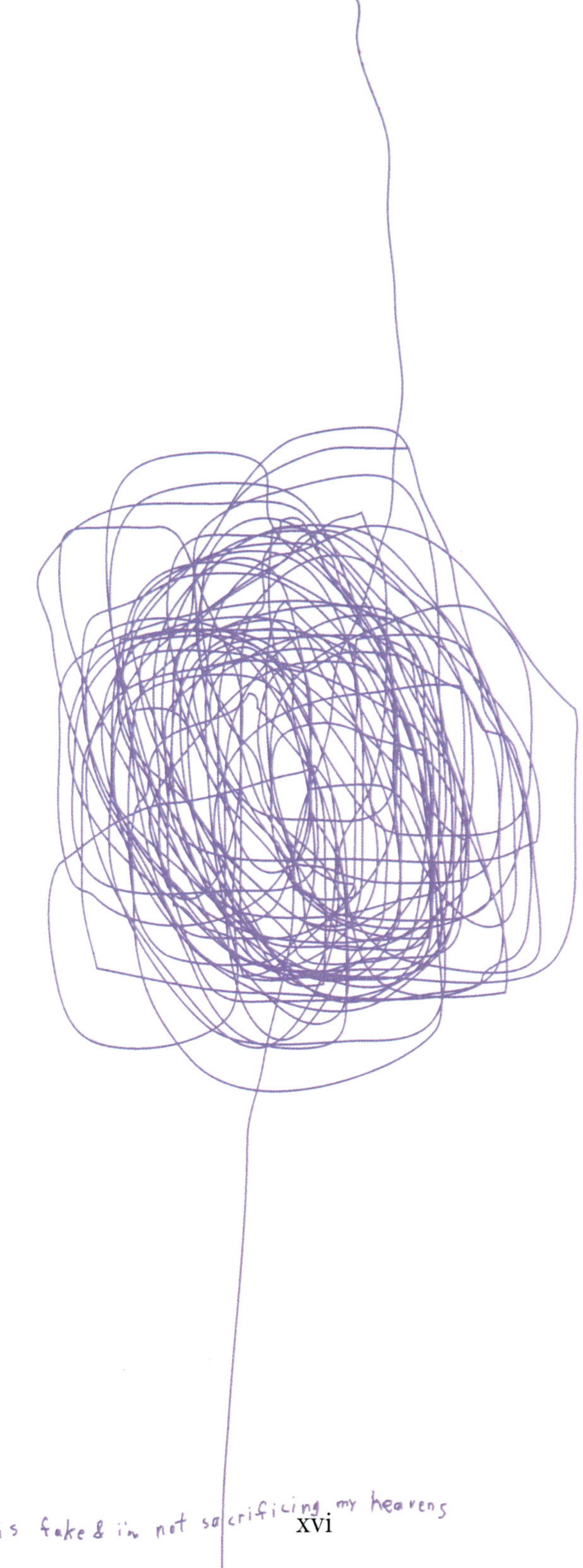

you
gave
me
an incomplete weapon but it's ok bc hell is fake & im not sacrificing my heavens

when they come for us
we will climb the trees

MUSASHI
mixed martial arts supplies
MUSASHI
The best MMA supplies
SINCE 1989

What I say may be in a language incomprehensible, but there is a time for that, and it is right now, because this is a monster's creed.

-Elena Rose
"The Seam of Skin & Scales"

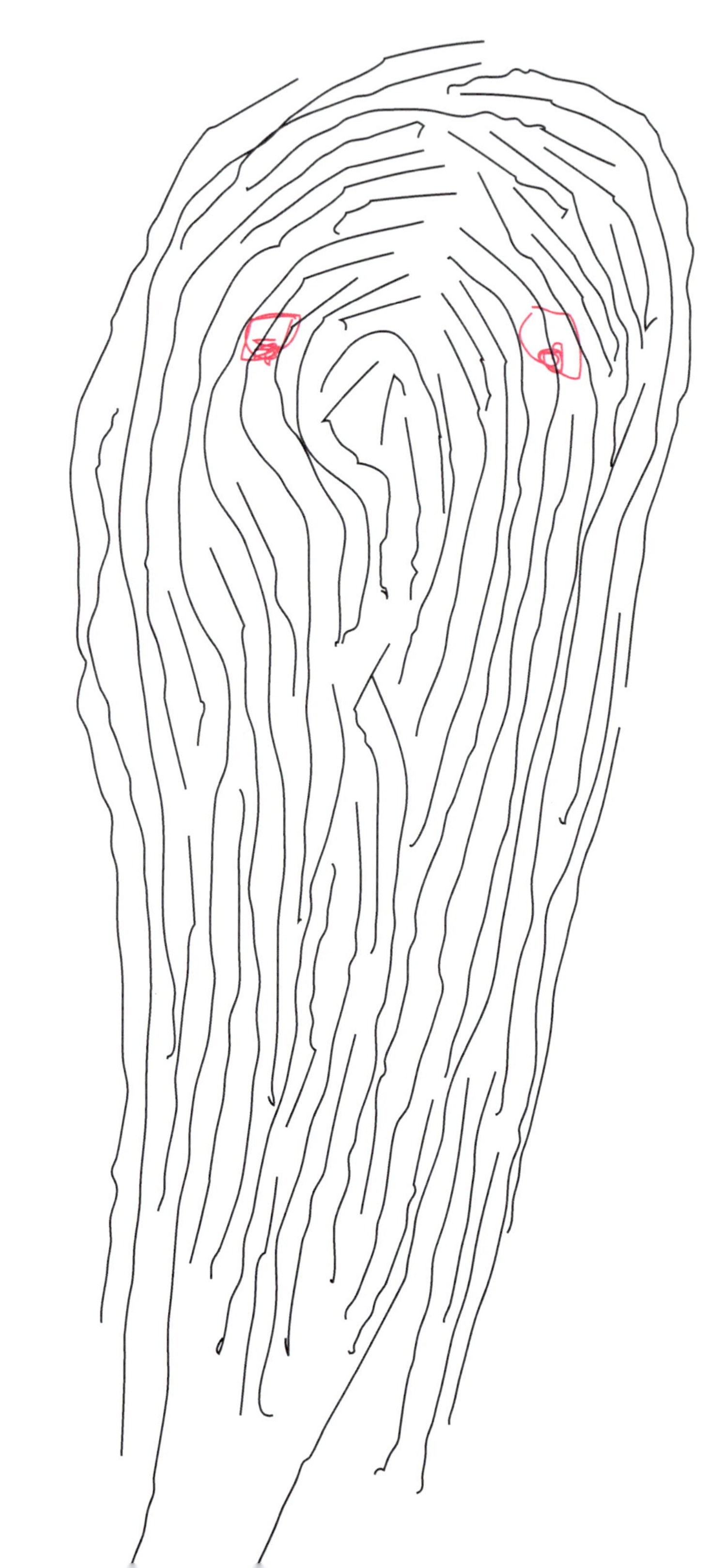

I am not here to talk about my body. The reason I am writing this is to keep a record of Sea-Witch & the events that happened regarding her. I wish I had another way to tell this, but for now I will speak of the events & occasionally will do so through my body, though I want you to understand that my body is not the focus. My body is not available for consumption. There might be times when I make it appear to be available for consumption & there might be times I want to be consumed, but I want to be clear about this. My body is not available.

I was created when my skin shed its mother. This is one of the ways I was formed. Formation, in the Sea-Witchean sense, happens within "systems". It has a specific smell. The systems of formation are many, some involve lava. Mine, in particular, involved a great deal of lava, which cooled into rock over the course of years. Formation, for most, takes many years. Generations of my family were formed first in Sea-Witch, as was I, but the people whose bodies created mine have never seen Sea-Witch & most likely doubt her existence.

SEA-WITCH 1 & 2

When I was living in Sea-Witch the sand held me on bright mornings. Small walls of it pressed on my sides & back & I pressed small walls of it in return with each breath. Species unfamiliar with Sea-Witch should know three things about her:

    1. She is a monster & this would always be the case in a world that had created the idea of monsters to use to describe things like her.
    2. She cries at TV shows about other monsters.
    3. Long periods of time can pass when no one tells you you are worthwhile & long periods of time can pass when you don't understand the words of those who are telling you. It is difficult to know the difference.

When I was living in Sea-Witch I was also a monster. When I was living in Sea-Witch I saw a TV show about a little girl who put her dolls in a duffle bag with two sandwiches In Case Of An Emergency. The girl's mother worried about her when she found this bag, because she knew her daughter would someday run away. This was not what the girl pictured when she made the bag but it was what she ended up using it for. The mother did not confront her daughter about it because she knew her daughter was a monster & she knew that real monsters have no mothers. When I was living in Sea-Witch I got this TV show tattooed on my arms & hands because it explained my life to others who wondered why I would live in a place like Sea-Witch.

When I was living in Sea-Witch sleep came when it did & disappeared later & hunger was similar. There is no cause & effect in Sea-Witch & everything happens at once. I was born in Sea-Witch even though I wasn't & I am still in Sea-Witch even though I am not.

When I was living in Sea-Witch people murdered her every day. Monsters exist to be slain, which is a word for murder that is mostly used for monsters. When I was living in Sea-Witch I had more friends, all of whom lived in Sea-Witches of their own. In Sea-Witch we have a kind of involuntary prayer called "crying" where sea comes from your eyes, which are the places you receive light in order to understand it. When I was living in Sea-Witch I never understood light & I still don't. This hasn't changed about me.

When I was living in Sea-Witch I wrote a poem that everyone in Sea-Witch loved. I won't tell you which one, because it doesn't matter which one. Think of any of them & that's the one. When I was living in Sea-Witch I put a sign above the entrance that said There Is a Dead Thing Between My Legs & I Am Naming Myself Sara. I spent the rest of the day pushing crows underwater.

You do not get to come to Sea-Witch. I will never let you in.

In Sea-Witch all day I go to church. I am always in church there & the church is where we sing songs to a meteor we hope will fall on us. If you understand Sea-Witch, it will be clear why this religion is so popular.

In Sea-Witch we pray that we will not be murdered while at the same time we pray for death. It is a specific kind of prayer that you can only make when the lights are off, but you can sing the songs. You can't help singing them in your head all day as you buy fabric. In Sea-Witch we buy so much fabric to drape over everything in our rooms. The smoke we let off sticks in it & our arms hang limp. In Sea-Witch I sewed the word "dying" on my couch. In Sea-Witch I was very melodramatic like this before I died. It is all over Sea-Witch now how I did this. How I died there & was melodramatic before I died.

In Sea-Witch Meteor [(msluw)] will come,
In Sea-Witch we will be lost,
In Sea-Witch we draw circles on the ceilings with our eyes & they will always be there.

I, a girl, married a girl in Sea-Witch & the priestess pronounced us wives there & prayed again for Meteor [(msluw)] to come smash us all along the rocks there on the river-beach.

Before I lived in Sea-Witch I was in love with Sea-Witch & daydreamed about stroking her hair & pushing my mouth into hers & about hers pushing back. I would wake at night & find myself thinking about gentle falling asleep with her legs between mine, her soft clit by my clit. Before I lived in Sea-Witch I was in love with Sea-Witch & this love was a physical thing I carried in my arms but hid. Before I lived in Sea-Witch I called the feeling of love "Sea-Witch" & I called myself danger & sadness, mountain & sand.

Sea-Witch is a collaboration of parts that face different directions & move independently & being in love with her was one of the most complicated things I have ever felt.

Sea-Witch is a feeling of loss. When I lived in Sea-Witch I left my hands dirty & my hair dirtier. It hung down in my face & when it didn't I would adjust it to make sure it did. The various positions of my bodies were different words: mountain, sand, sadness, frustration, defeat, shrub. When I lived in Sea-Witch I communicated this way & when I communicated I communicated only with myself & with Sea-Witch, who is a part of me. When I lived in Sea-Witch I sang songs about love & imagined them sung to me.

I am crying because Sea-Witch is crying.

Sea-Witch, you are not swimming. You are held underwater until you stop kicking. When it goes black you see amber clouds shaped like the people you love. The people you wanted to love. I have lost myself like this too, & I, living inside her at the time, understood. But I knew in my understanding that I would never understand. I walked around my living space lying facedown on all the floors. Lying facedown by the bed. Lying facedown in the kitchen. Lying facedown in the bathroom. Understanding is not something you can just have, but you can suffer from both understanding & not. Loving a girl in Sea-Witch, even yourself, requires a kind of _bone_ death.

In Sea-Witch I never knew when I was having sex. Some bodies don't lend themselves to a clear separation of beginning or end & in some bodies that separation is too great. Exhausting, even. Mine has always been some combination of both. Sex happens in Sea-Witch by taking "turns". Each participant gets a turn, followed by the other participant's turn. Turns can look like anything & can take any amount of time. Whole months have been spent on a single turn. A turn can be a pause, the drawing of certain symbols in mud, or nearly endless tears. Most of my turns in Sea-Witch looked the same: creating sound as quietly as possible near my lover's hair or skin. If there is no sound to be made or hair or skin to be found in the particular bodies we are inhabiting I am usually satisfied with anything I can connect to the concept of "closest". This is why my thoughts are shaped in the way they are now. Why draw symbols when you can use all of who you are. When you can act as one yourself.

The following is a list of facts about my time in Sea-Witch:

1. When I was living in Sea-Witch I organized my life around the same principles many people living in Sea-Witch did. The most important of those was When they come for us, we will climb the trees. This one is very old & the origin is unknown. I don't think anyone ever told me about it. When you get to Sea-Witch there are certain things you just know.

2. Every night in Sea-Witch I slept deeply until I couldn't sleep anymore. I had a feeling that things happened while I was asleep in Sea-Witch, that my living space, my bed, my lover all changed in small degrees, an entire revolution until they arrived back where they were before I fell asleep. I also felt as if some nights didn't make it the full way around. They felt too almost.

3. Everyone in Sea-Witch used to drown themselves in waves a lot. It was something to do to pass the time, which is a really difficult thing to measure in Sea-Witch. We found the ocean for this under our beds. The ocean in Sea-Witch is still there, under all the beds & all of Sea-Witch knows they can drown themselves in it at any time, but they don't. They just think about it.

4. At one point while I was living in Sea-Witch we all sat down for a very long time & looked at grass. All of my best memories of Sea-Witch are from this time, but it had to end eventually.

5. The whole time I was living Sea-Witch I kept a stone in my pocket wrapped in old paper I tore from a book & held together with hair ties. Every night I would wash it in Sea-Witch's hair & feed it bits of mushroom & herbs, whatever I had around. When I spoke to it I felt listened to. Before I left Sea-Witch I gave this rock to Sea-Witch as a present, & she ate it, saying I will keep it safe here. I wrote her a thank you note & signed it with all my names. I kissed Sea-Witch & felt the rock moving inside her.

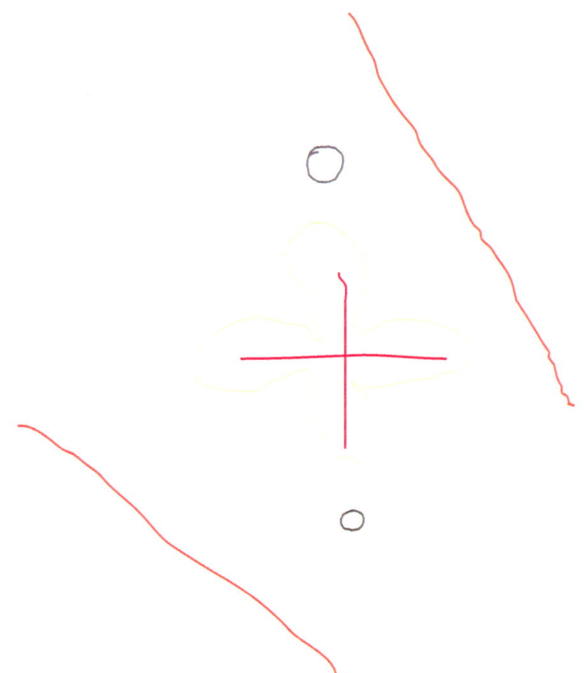

it is because
of herself

that she is
called
"sea"

But punishment isn't for people who do bad things. Punishment is an energy that flows toward the weak, predictable as water. Punishment happens to those who cannot stop it from happening. It's a laundering of pain, not a balancing of scales.

-Porpentine Charity Heartscape
from the game notes to *With Those We Love Alive*

...I am deadlocked by that smooth psychiatric voice of reason which tells me there is an objective reality in which my body and mind are one. But I am not here and never have been.

-Sarah Kane
4.48 Psychosis

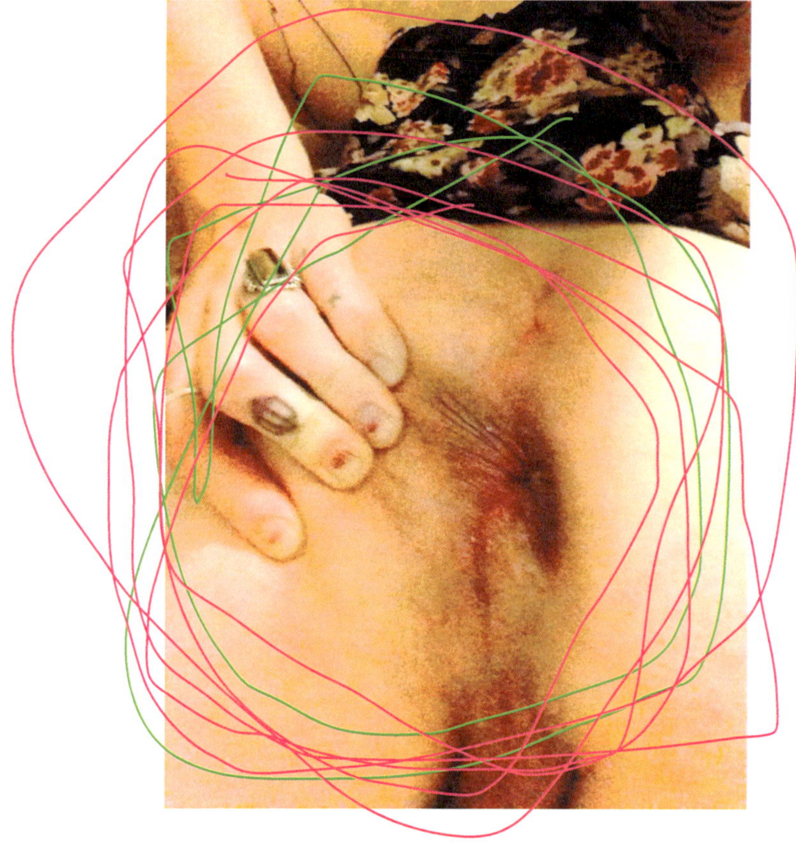

"Origin of the World"

Sea-Witch is a problem of sizes. I fit so well in Sea-Witch, but things that fit in me before can't seem to follow. I am not yet sure what I am a problem of. I brought everything I own to the beach & put it on a raft & conveniently forgot to get on the raft with it. Then the ocean floated away from us both. I sat down right there & tried to figure out the whole thing on paper. I made a variable that represented the whole situation (me, the ocean, the raft), a second variable that represented the distant influence of Meteor (may she lay us waste) & a third that represented the concept of *loss* or *displacement*. I spent a long time creating charts & proofs that would help me understand the barrier that had been created between myself & Sea-Witch. I began cutting away the unnecessary parts from the mess I had created, on the assumption that they must have come only from myself. I cut slowly, carefully at first, then gradually became more reckless, cutting away huge chunks at a time. I was left with a statement that I realized described a small aspect of the nature of Sea-Witch. Living in Sea-Witch for so long had left me endlessly tired & I could not remember if I had been tired before I lived in Sea-Witch. In Sea-Witch I could hold my own loneliness in my hand & feel its fur. I could cut it open on a sharp rock. More often I put it under my mattress & clenched my teeth so hard while I slept that my jaw stayed sore.

People have asked me about this so I'll try to answer. Same-sex marriage is not legal in Sea-Witch but also not illegal. This is because, as you will quickly find out in Sea-Witch, *no sex is the same*. As I've said before, sex is made up of *turns*. Turns can look like anything, but they are never the same. Something always changes. Our cells are always cycling difference.

Also I want to talk about the word *legal* which doesn't make a lot of sense in Sea-Witch. Other words whose meanings don't hold together within Sea-Witch's person include *deserve, crime, alphabet, drug, animal, border* & *joke*. One time Sea-Witch told a joke about a very large dog & the very large dog showed up & we realized it wasn't a joke. She was just telling us about the dog. The dog stayed for a long time.

The Book of Meteor tells us Sea-Witch is a girl. It says Sea-Witch was not born a boy (which is a strange thing to have to emphasize) but a girl, with a girl's teeth & fingers. It tells us of how she ingested plants, fungi & chemicals to alter her body in ways that she felt might make her body & mind become closer to herself. She later came to dismiss some of these things as having undesirable effects & others she held dearly as sacraments. During our hardest times or certain positions of the planets we would eat some of these in the presence of the image of a living goddess. In the image she is nineteen years old, wearing her sister's sports bra, which is stuffed with her own dirty socks. She is peering at herself in the bathroom mirror while no one else is home. Sea-Witcheans carved her holy image fifty-feet high into a mountain & called her *meteor*^(msluw). Sea-Witch calls her *home*.

After I left Sea-Witch I mourned. I mourned her loss as well as my own. There are no words to say the things I want to say. There is no way to express the feeling of separation when you are choosing that separation against love. I admit now that I loved Sea-Witch. I admit that her sadness gave me comfort in my sadness. Loving one who worships her own destruction is a hopeless act. It isn't the only hopeless thing I have ever done, & in a way it is not one I regret. She will always be *my most beautiful*. & so I mourn.

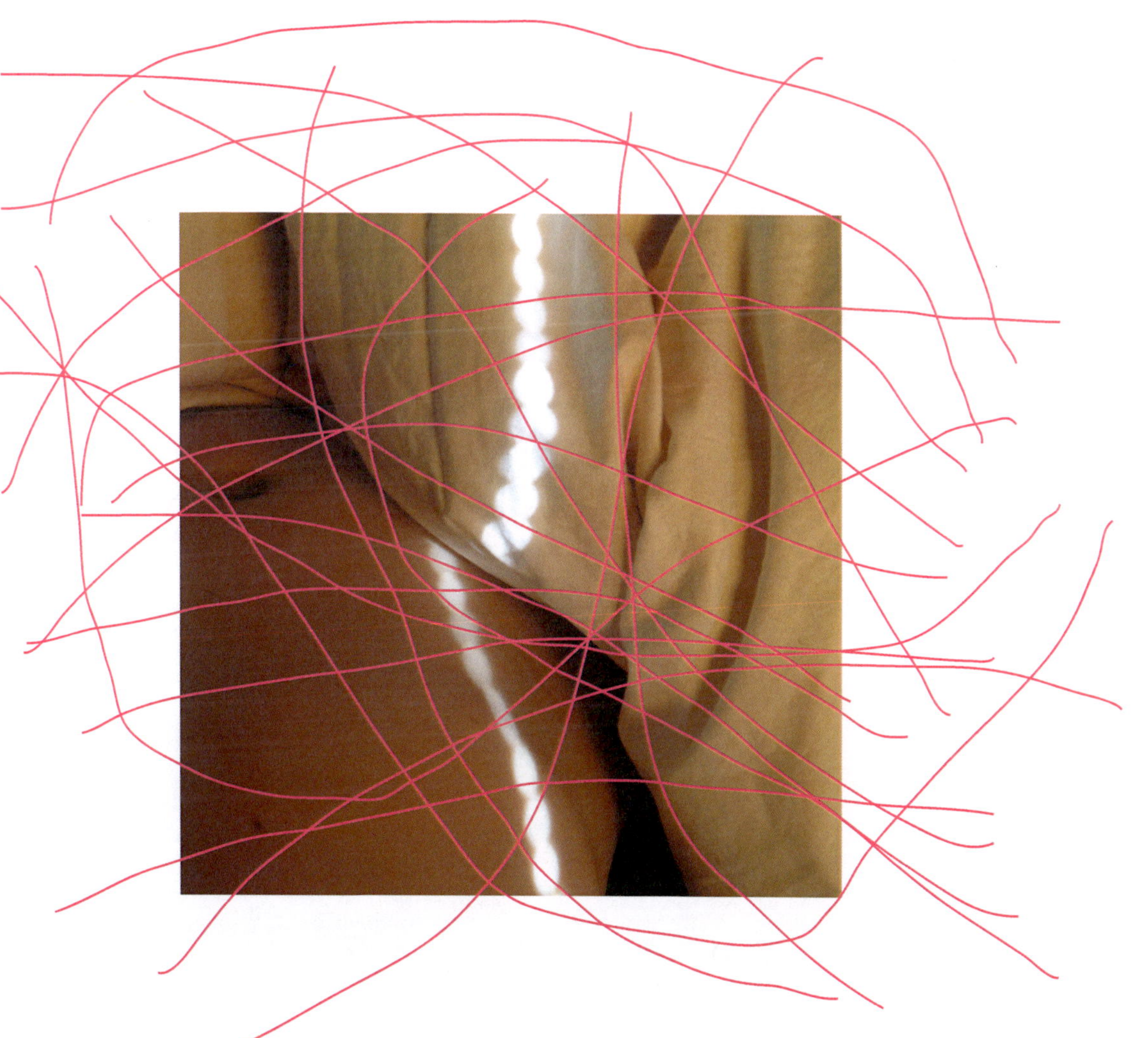

I am all of Sea-Witch & I hold her inside me. Even now, years later, I find myself doing things according to Sea-Witchean custom. I find myself carrying her inside of me. If you don't know what I mean, let me try to explain:

1. Sea-Witch is full of death. She eats dead plants & dirt & has thrown herself more than one party. Sea-Witch brushes her hair from her forehead as she takes a dog[*] for a walk & smokes while it shits at 3:47 a.m.

2. Sea-Witch is the water from my melting. She is the thing I hold when the ground feels too wide not to fall into.

3. Some monsters have found themselves spontaneously in the presence of Sea-Witch under the influence of intoxicants & singing. Such encounters are not unheard of.

4. Sea-Witch is a nucleus of pain. Sea-Witch is not the source of the pain, but she receives it from what can seem like everywhere. The source of Sea-Witch's pain is 78 Men who are the source of a great deal of pain in the world. One can get very rich by creating pain in others. In fact, it is the only way to become rich. Some of these men are very famous: they appear on frequently on TV with their thin hair & stubby fingers. Others seem to be invisible. Anonymous, but intimidatingly so. It is because of these men & the pain they make that Sea-Witch first invited us into her body, many years ago. It is because of these men & the pain they make that the mass of pure inevitability we call Meteor (may she lay us waste) approaches. It is because of them that Sea-Witch is called *Witch*. It is because of herself that she is called *Sea*.

5. I made a boat out of wood & sailed it into the ocean. Once I was far enough out that I could no longer see land I made a symbol on my hand with mud I had carried there in a jar. When nothing seems real it can help to remember there is no agreed-upon idea about what is real & what is not. What we know as reality exists only through collaboration & sharing & you are in no way required to live there.

[*]A note on the word "dog", which I have found is unspecific in its use. When I was living in Sea-Witch some of us were smaller & covered in fur, & preferred to spend cold nights lying across the sleeping legs of the taller, hairless Sea-Witcheans. All of us made sounds at the fullest moons &, though she was not visible at the time, to distant Meteor (may she lay us waste). All of us enjoy sleeping in laps & at the feet of beds.

The experience of living outside of Sea-Witch has been, for me, a sensation like being slowly crumpled from the outside in. Breathing becomes difficult & muscles contain a constant, slowing fatigue. I have said that I was born in Sea-Witch, that I am always inside her & have always been. This is true but in the same way I have always been outside her & always have felt a distance, a longing & its accompanying external pressure.

Before I lived in Sea-Witch I had a dream about a field of small animals who hid their faces from the sun. I walked among them & touched the leaves that hung down from nearby trees. There was in this dream, as in others, a looming sense of something like disaster.

I, like Sea-Witch, am a monster. I will one day be slain by the crushing, which comes from everywhere, but originates from the choices of the 78 Men I have mentioned elsewhere. When I was young I imagined that I could live among people in the world. I was afraid of monsters because I did not know that they were my kind. I was also afraid of monsters because I knew they were my kind, & looking at yourself & seeing what you are afraid of will always be terrifying.

When I left home I got drunk in the sand for four days. A star looked at me & said, *Everything will be okay*. I said that, no, it wouldn't. It said that I was right, but that it wished I was wrong. I said I wished it too. There wasn't anything to say after that, & I kept its gaze too long, sitting in an embarrassed silence.

The next day I laid my fear at the feet of Sea-Witch, to whom I had fled, & lit that fear on fire. I slept beside that fire for two nights, until she invited me inside her body. This was the beginning of the next part of my life. I've found I can best organize my life in my own mind by the kind of fear I was experiencing at the time, & this was the start of a new, special fear.

Sea-Witch held me after my formation. I cried in her arms & in her hair & went into her body through the entrance to her body, which is the ear. When I got there I met others for whom she had done the same. I saw their beautiful faces & hair & how they covered them with dirt like I had covered mine with dirt. They took me to a beach there where I could live. Sea-Witch is one of the few places in the world where the act of living & doing the few things that are needed to live hasn't been made so difficult as to be nearly impossible. Outside of Sea-Witch you have to be nearly obsessed with doing a lot of very specific strange things at the service of the 78 Men who cause pain & you have to spend much of your life doing & thinking about these things in order to live, & even then, even if you focus your whole self on this service you still often will not be able to live. For those of us who are monsters this will always be so difficult as to be nearly impossible. I can't tell you how it is for those who are not monsters, because I do not know how to speak to them. In Sea-Witch living is everywhere. It doesn't eat you from within.

I'm not sure people exist. I often think about myself & the time I spent in the world among people before I came to Sea-Witch. About the time before I knew I was a monster. People is the word for living creatures who look almost like monsters but not quite. People can be found almost everywhere, but I always wonder if they aren't maybe, secretly, monsters too.

When I arrived at Sea-Witch for the first time, I told her, *I am so tired now.* I said, *I am tired & tired of being tired.* She told me to come in & sleep. I told her I could sleep for lifetimes & then I did just that.

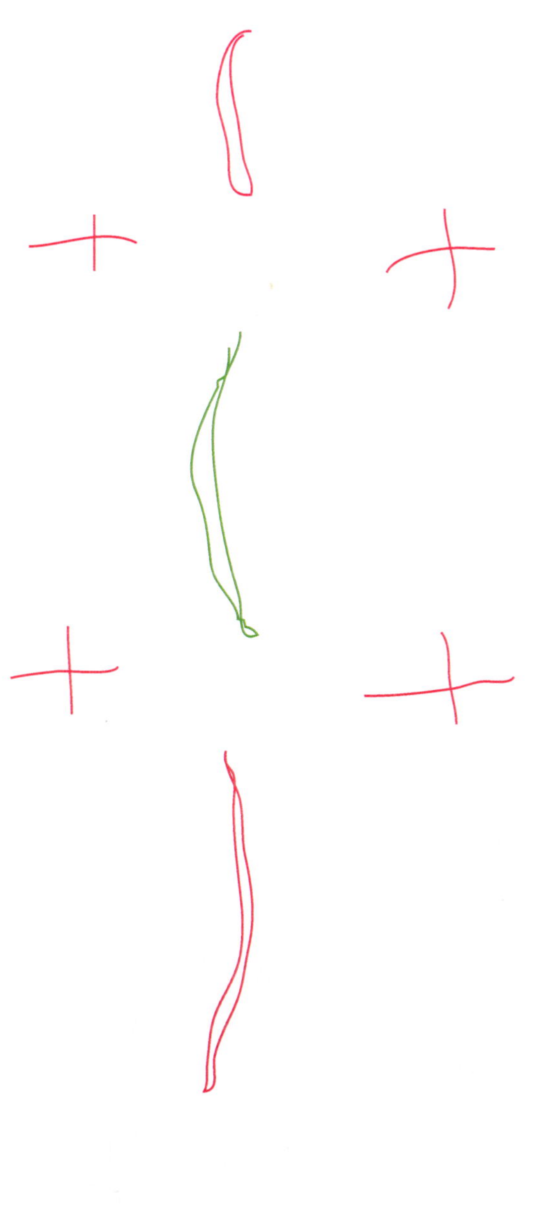

NO ONE MUST BE ALONE

GOD IS A WILD THOUGHT DOWN BY THE WATER. GOD IS THE VERY FIRST BREEZE OF THE NIGHT, & THE VERY LAST. GOD IS DECENCY & SHORTNESS OF BREATH. GOD IS BLAH BLAH BLAH. GOD IS MY GIRLFRIEND.

- Eleanor Eli Moss
THE HOLY BIBLE,
THE BOOK OF GOD 1:23

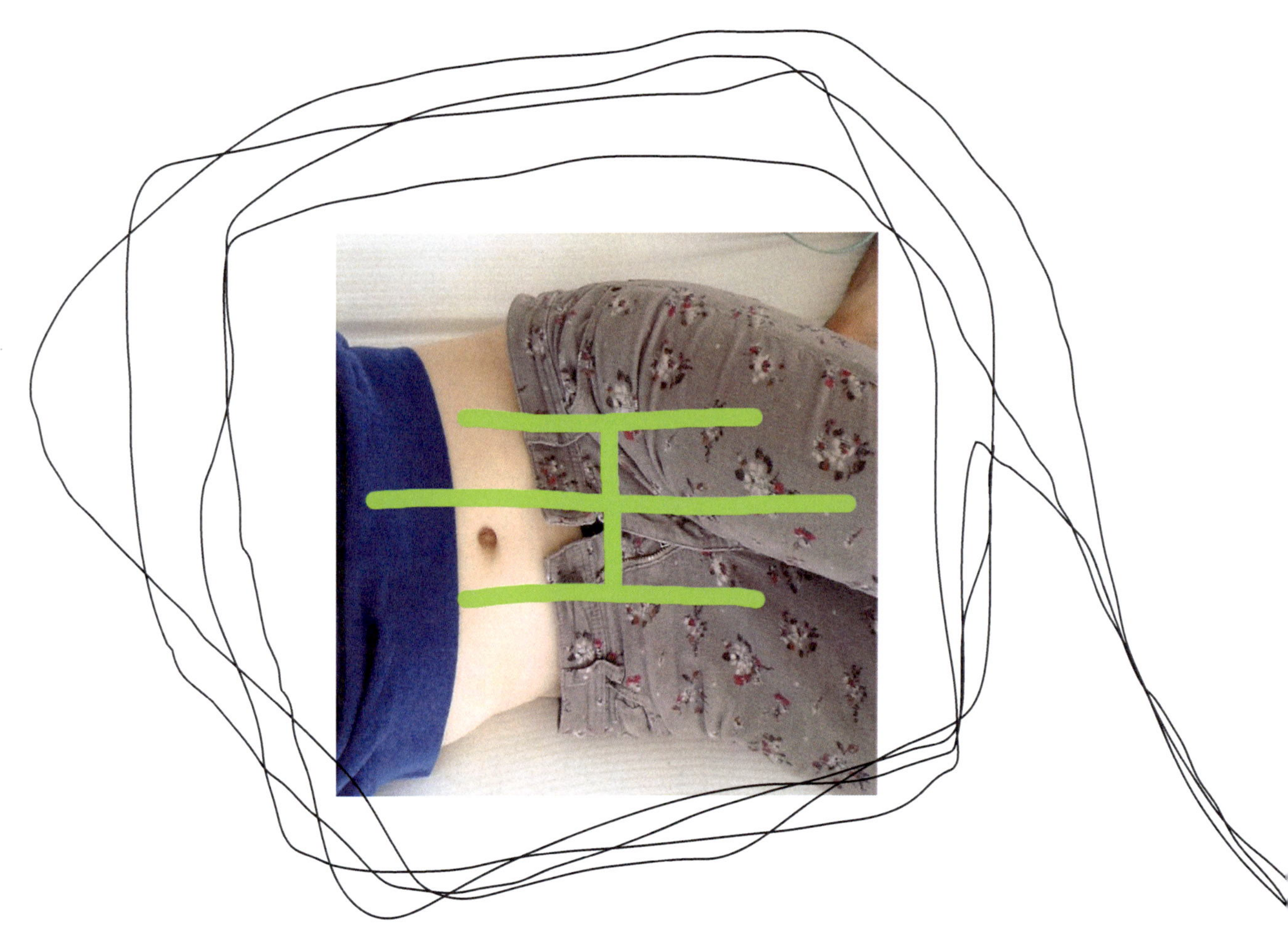

Sea-Witch is one of a series. People speak of other Sea-Witches & there are ways in which different parts of Sea-Witch are their own separate beings & are referred to as such, but apart from this there is some knowledge of her companions in series, which is held in *The Book of Meteor*. *The Book of Meteor* tells us before Sea-Witch was formed there existed Dog-Witch & hir sisters. At this point there was no land & so no word for *sea*, which only exists in contrast with land. *Water* existed & meant *everything-except-air*. Things under the water were referred to as *airless faces*. Dog-Witch & hir sisters are named variously throughout *The Book of Meteor* as Air-Witch, Water-Witch, Dirt-Witch, & Milk-Witch, Deeps-Witch, Old Seagull-Witch, Strawberry-Witch, Leg-Witch, Candle-Witch, Less-Held-Witch, Moss-Witch, Dead-Jellyfish-Witch, Stone-Witch, Wood-Witch, Glass-Witch, Airless-Face-Witch & her twin God-Witch, Death-Witch & some texts speak of a nineteenth sister whose name is written *ha-ha-ha* or *ah-ah-ah*, pronounced as three brief puffs of air, with or without accompanying glottal stops.

Dog-Witch, of course, initiated the formation of hir sisters & thus the beginning of their deaths. Ze gave us Meteor (may she lay us waste) & her book. What *The Book of Meteor* reports about Dog-Witch is that ze caused the formation of the nineteen after ze stole lava from an airless face that most Sea-Witcheans refer to as a bear. A thing I have discovered while reading *The Book of Meteor* & other, weirder Sea-Witchean texts is that there have always been bears. Even before land there were bears in the water, though they had longer faces & thick, flat hands & feet like beaver tails. Lava, before it was taken by Dog-Witch, was a piece of ancient bear technology that the bears used to control other airless faces & the water around them. The bears have mourned its loss ever since the theft. Sea-Witcheans who study this history do so to try to find a time before this sort of controlling of other beings existed, so that we might know its source & overthrow the 78 Men. It has not yet been discovered, though we have determined the source is older than lava.

Dog-Witch has always seemed untouchable in my mind. On one of the long nights in the hardest months, Sea-Witch & I were up late sharing a cigarette & she told me how much she misses hir. I asked what Dog-Witch looked like & she smiled sadly & described to me a sensation I would later come to call *bone death*. She told me about Dog-Witch's long, furry ears & hir face like a dry, cavernous world of old stone & gas. She made a series of gestures in the air & drew this symbol in the sand. After this she took my head in her lap & stroked my hair & said to me, *No one must be alone.*

Like everything, all of Sea-Witch contains her history. Scratches and atoms that reveal where she has been, what happened to her. Every part of her has bits of what has come before. For example, Sea-Witch's left leg is the same as that of Dog-Witch. That leg was out of reach to Sea-Witcheans for a great number of years. Sea-Witch has allowed us her body for living in, but there was a time in which she wasn't sure about the her-ness of that leg, & for that reason alone kept it free of residents. Not for reasons of *property,* which is a concept that, like many other concepts, can't hold together within Sea-Witch, but for reasons of *body* & *consent*. Dog-Witch, being maybe-dead after the fall of the nineteen sisters, could not consent to her leg being occupied, even while it was a part of Sea-Witch's person. On the day that Sea-Witch finally set fire to a dead fir tree as a ritual of mourning, she accepted that leg as her own & Sea-Witcheans came to the leg & created in it there as a sanctuary for the oldest & most desperate among us to live & rest on the beaches that could be found there. The skies there are full of stars that are visible at all hours & form constellations of welcome & refuge.

The Book of Meteor tells us Dog-Witch is a sense of purpose. It tells us of how ze came from the sky as fire & evaporated a great deal of water, creating land. It tells us of hir cooling & descent again into the water to struggle against the violent reign of the lava-wielding bears in the world of airless faces. It tells us how ze brought lava to new uses, the foremost of which is formation, including the formation of hir nineteen sisters, who were the first to be formed in lava, as I would later be. The first of hir sisters to be formed was called Deeps-Witch & shortly after came Dirt-Witch & Bread-Witch. Less-Held-Witch stood from the sand next, & pulled with her the twins God-Witch & Airless-Face-Witch. A passage missing from some later translations of *The Book* tells us Dog-Witch came to these sisters then on the land, hir tail & ears raised, excited to no longer be alone. Ze lay hir chin on them one by one, naming each as hir love, hir sibling, hir comrade & hir companion. The other sisters formed soon after, the order is not fully documented. It is written that angry bears soon came & lined the coast, watching Dog-Witch & hir glorious creation take shape from the ruins of their fallen empire. Bear-parents stroked the shoulders & heads of their furry children saying to them, The time will come when we can build ourselves up again.

A beautiful space opened up in the earth in which many events took place. A necessary part of formation, besides lava, is *noticing*. Less-Held-Witch began her noticing here in this space in the earth where she was attending a class on the ghosts who animate fire. & it was in this beautiful space where she first noticed the curve of Glass-Witch's neck as Glass-Witch sat against the wall, ignoring the lecture to draw round sigils on the white spaces of her purple tennis shoes. It was in this space that *The Book of Meteor* tells us Less-Held-Witch hid herself in the hood of her sweatshirt, looking down at her own shoes (brown, soft) to avoid Glass-Witch's gaze.

I know from my own formation that noticing has a heaviness to it that follows you. It sits in your chest & shoulders. The object of your noticing becomes transformed entirely in your mind, becomes a thing to worship. You become transformed as well. The wholeness of who you were forms into a halfness of what you could become.

Sometime after her first noticing, *The Book of Meteor* tells us, Glass-Witch & Less-Held-Witch began to spend lunches together, eating. They spoke quietly of the others in their class. Less-Held-Witch did most of the listening, wholly absorbed in her own noticing. Glass-Witch said to her once, in the context of a conversation, *You are the kind of girl who most don't think to fall for. But those who do, fall deeply.*

Long after Less-Held-Witch finished that class she began to wear purple shoes upon which she would draw round sigils in ballpoint pen. She wrote songs to sing to other living creatures. Some of these songs spoke of histories that had never been written down. Others were written to sing to a nameless thing she felt always growing in the dirt but never seemed to find, despite her great noticing.

From what is known of the history, most Sea-Witcheans believe that the nineteen sisters spread from the coast where their forming was initiated, across all land & water. They lived full lives as whole individuals. There was once a TV show about these stories, but it has been lost to time. What has been written of this show tells us that this was no great loss.

FUCK

Sypionaxe

SHE GETS COLD LIKE ALL LIVING CREATURES

actual photo
of Dog-Witch

Purity; not all encompassing, perhaps not immediately recognized, but the core presides within, and is the compass of all action to its bearer. There are those who exist who believe in and try to achieve purity as a fluid becoming, while not ever having pureness at their core.

-Danielle Lee Pearce
from the album notes to *Petrichor*

Everything was lava for a while, really. This was before Sea-Witch, & everything was on fire & lava & I was on fire & lava myself, being one small part, one aspect of that everything. A lot of sensations have been compared to burning, like the feeling you get in your lungs when holding your breath too long. A lot of what happened then took place in my lungs, which are two parallel sites of construction & destruction of atmosphere. What I'm trying to say is that lava began to feel very *atmospheric*.

There is a story, many stories actually, told among those in Sea-Witch about a girl who tried to use her mouth to cool the lava around another girl. One of those stories ends with the destruction of lava as a concept. Another ends with her lying in a field of grass, holding a living creature she has vowed to care for in whatever ways she can. This sense of care goes on to flow outward from her & envelops every living thing, & every living thing cares for & respects every other living thing. Care is a desired ending, but one that most likely cannot be obtained without an intense, even violent, period of restructuring.

Sea-Witch can go for long periods of time without eating. She emits a specific light & temperature. Sea-Witch is a glittering cascade of water that has frozen in place exactly to be lived in but accidentally ended up capable of true emotion. Sea-Witch is precious & needs to be held. She gets cold like all living creatures.

The Book of Meteor contains only some information about the life of Air-Witch. It tells of how a young Air-Witch first found a place for herself within a community of rats. How she slept in their tangle every night, & they shared their garbage with her, which she learned to eat & love. The rats taught her how to gnaw her way into crawlspaces & behind pantries. They taught her how to keep from being seen. Air-Witch's body did not look like the bodies of the rats, but this was no problem. Air-Witch didn't think about her body. This isn't about Air-Witch's body. This isn't about anybody's body. This is about the bodies of rats & how Air-Witch cried when she came home one day to find those bodies twitching, nearly lifeless on the ground. This is about how Air-Witch killed one of her family trying to save them with her large, clumsy hands. How Air-Witch then cut herself & bled on the floor & cried & how her tears became tiny ambulances that flowed their way through the blood to save her family, each arriving just seconds too late.

Air-Witch went from that place to a mountain where she lived alone, because living alone, while it made her very strange, felt like the only thing she knew how to do. She could barely feed herself during this time. She ate dirt & insects & bark & leaves. She vomited on herself when she slept at night & became too weak most days to move far. The first time she died she left herself a note that said *Don't eat the leaves with the zigzag edges.* The second time she died she left a note with various ideas about how she might teach herself to grow wings, which she managed to do before the third time she died. It took until after the fifth time she died to figure out how to fly with the wings. Once she was confident in her flying Air-Witch took a large piece of birch bark & wrote out with berry ink a letter to Dog-Witch. Air-Witch had been alone for a long time at this point & her mind worked in strange ways. The letter failed completely at communicating anything, but Air-Witch buried it there, just in case. After this was done, Air-Witch flew into the sky as high as she could. Some say she went to find Meteor (may she lay us waste). Some say after she spent so long alone she no longer understood what she or her body was doing. That she probably fell into the sea & drowned. Her letter was never found, & most likely crumbled into the dirt as it was buried. The First Sea-Witchean Church of Meteor claims it has Air-Witch's wings among its holy objects, embalmed & stiff & kept in a locked case in a locked room no one ever enters.

It is written that Dog-Witch died on the day Air-Witch left for the sky.

little
health

HOLY
ARE
YOU
MY
GOD
DAUGHTER

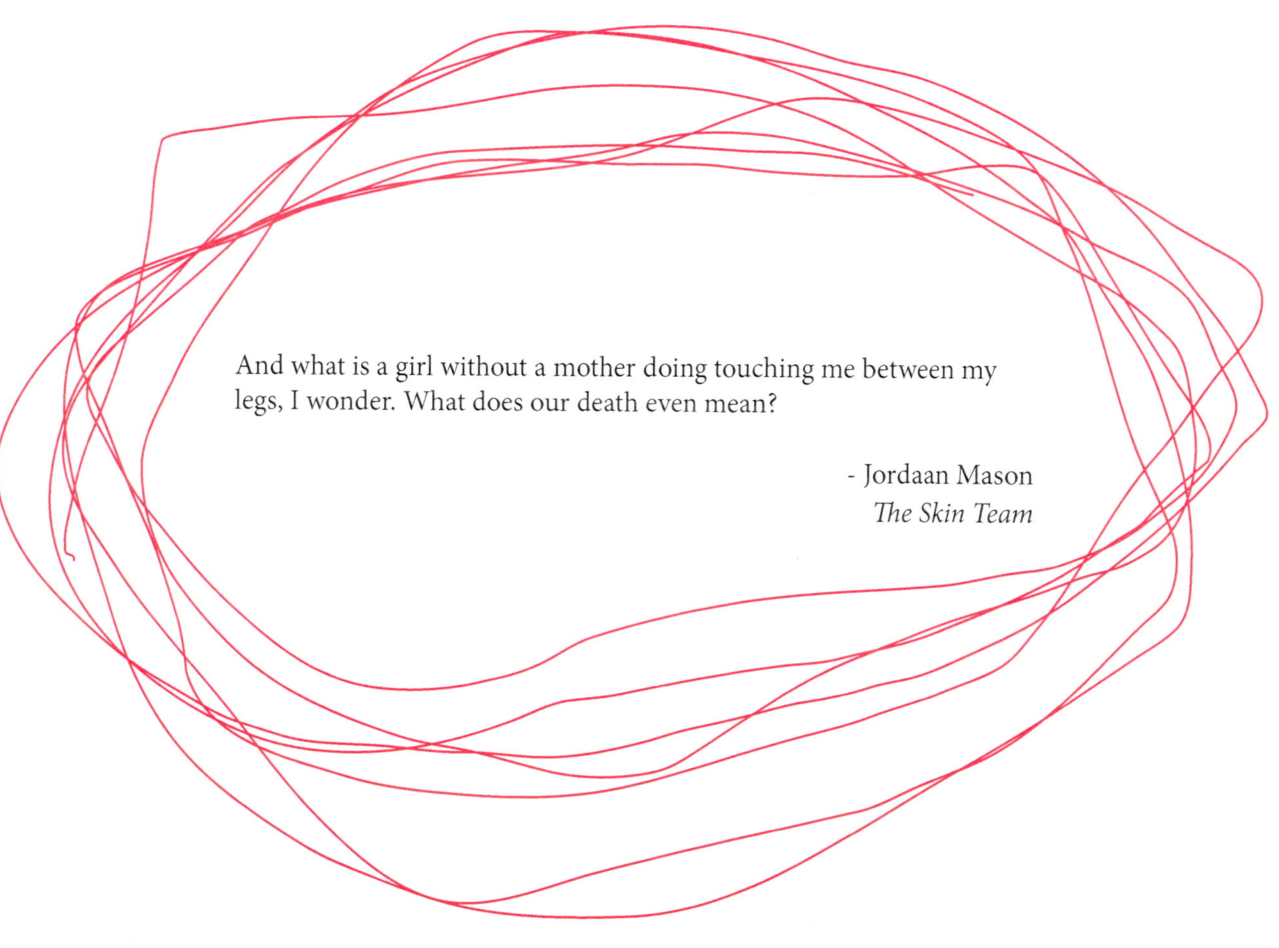

And what is a girl without a mother doing touching me between my legs, I wonder. What does our death even mean?

- Jordaan Mason
The Skin Team

> milk-witch was round
> & did a lot of warm dialing
> all those little number buttons
> in the mouths of infants
>
> *- author unknown*

The Book of Meteor contains a short list of facts about Dog-Witch's sister Milk-Witch, & I have duplicated this list below, with a few of my own additions & notes:

1. Milk-Witch had many infants she kept warm in blankets. She bathed them regularly in the hot springs. She kept a rigorous schedule. When she was young she would sometimes shut herself in the closet with the infants until they would whimper so that she could take delight in comforting them.

2. Milk-Witch hated getting mad. She was always shocking herself by raising her voice. "I will not be loud & mean," she would say, over & over again until she fell asleep.

3. Sometimes in the morning Milk-Witch forgot to shave her face. She wouldn't realize until later, when everything was hard. On these days she would try to think of herself as a single protein, drifting through blood without thought or feeling. All Milk-Witch's being was sustained by the effort of a small group of ghosts, & these days took the whole of their attention & effort.

4. Milk-Witch had t-shirts made of her & the infants. Everybody got one. The First Sea-Witchean Church of Meteor has one of these shirts in their collection of holy artifacts. They also have one of the infants. She runs the gift shop & splits the income with the ones who make the gifts. In Sea-Witch, gifts are made or found by all living creatures. A gift can be almost anything. For example, this book is my gift to you.

5. Milk-Witch had a collection of broken glass in a box in her room. The glass pieces had names & Milk-Witch would sometimes break them so she could name more pieces & have more friends. When she lost a piece, she would try to make herself forget its name. It never worked.

6. Halfway through her life, Milk-Witch had the most beautiful surgery in the whole world.

7. Milk-Witch was one of the rare living creatures whose life ended when she decided it was time for her life to end. She spent years making this decision & when the time got closer, she told her infants & they talked about it for a long time. They all sat on the beach together, throwing rocks into the waves. They

meant to stay up all night but the infants didn't quite make it, & slept their infant sleeps in the cool night sand under Milk-Witch's loving gaze. In the morning, Milk-Witch nudged them awake. "It's time to go now," she told them, & they woke up & began to cry. "It's time to go," she said again.

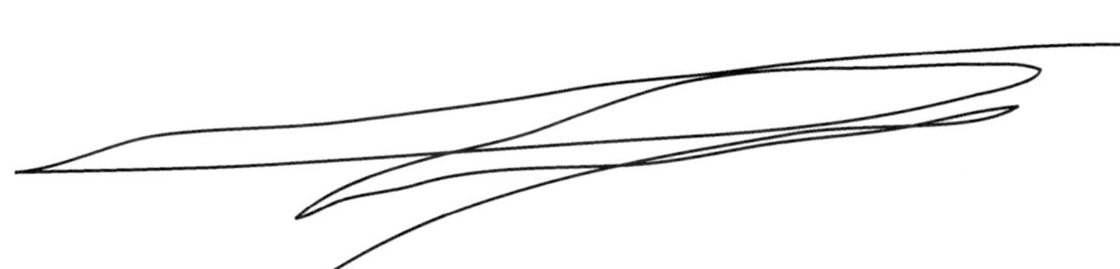

The Book of Meteor says that true to her name, Death-Witch died young, against her will. She was known by few, & mourned long by those who knew her. She was survived by her best friend, a nameless cat who went on to lead a full life for many years after.

The circumstances surrounding Death-Witch's death are that she was alone on a road, & a person saw what she looked like & decided to kill her. I guess that's all it takes. There is a lot of anger in the world, & I think I can feel all of it at once when I think about what happened to little Death-Witch.

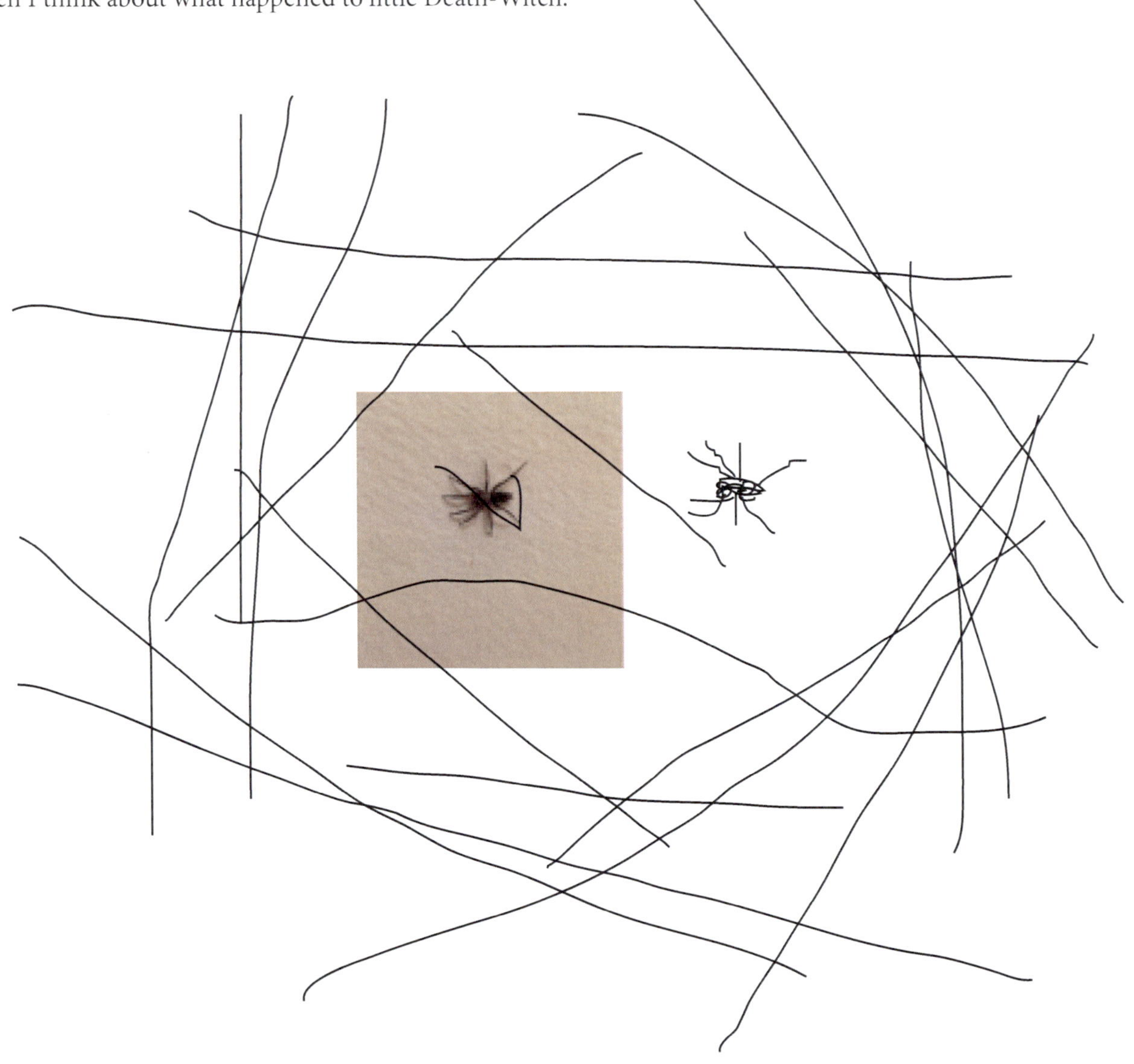

The Book of Meteor has this to say about Dirt-Witch:

Dirt-Witch was beautiful & she loved horses. She spent her entire childhood putting her fingers in the gaps in an oak leaf & her teen years were mostly spitting into a jar of sand. She had twelve family members who were given to her as a present from a thirteenth family member she never met who lived on a boat far away. She kept them in a backpack. One time one of the family members got caught by the dog & its ear started to split at the seam & some stuffing came out but Dirt-Witch was her own mom & fixed the family member with a needle & thread. When Dirt-Witch got older she coughed into the sky & thought about girls. She went to a school for a very long time & got out later. When she was grown she tried to make movies about the way she loved horses when she was younger but they never turned out right, because her skin was too soft to hold the camera. Because the ground was too soft to hold her up.

Dirt-Witch is my mother & I am her daughter, even though we have never met. We have ten alikenesses that Sea-Witch told me about later. The first four are all horse sounds. When I think of Dirt-Witch it makes me want to pray forever.

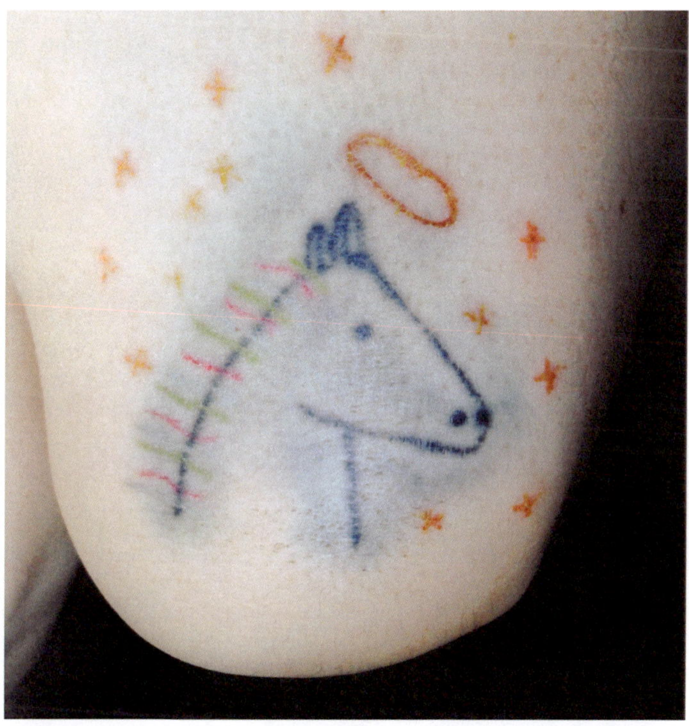

All of my strength is found in Sea-Witch. Her name means longing. I hold her in my arms the way she held me forever since I first came to live inside her. On the fourth day after my arrival in her I woke up to find a pit at the foot of my bed, filled fifteen feet deep with rotting dresses. It was early enough that Sea-Witch was still asleep & so I looked into it & prayed to Meteor (may she lay us waste) as is customary upon waking in Sea-Witch. Meteor (may she lay us waste) prayed back to me & asked me what this pit was here for. She prayed to me asking what I planned to use it for. *I don't know*, I prayed back. *It smells.*

Questions:
> 1. If I dive headfirst into a pit that is filled 15 feet deep with rotting dresses, what will happen to my neck?
> 2. If I don't dive in, what will happen to my neck?
> 3. Is it possible to have sex with a meteor god (may she lay us waste)?
> 4. Is it possible to do so via prayer?

Just in case I took my underwear off, which I had slept in.

What are you doing right now, I prayed to Meteor [msluw].

Oh, not much, she prayed back. *I got this CD,* she prayed to me.

Oh yeah? I prayed back. *What is it?*

Some band, she prayed to me. *They're called Girls With Assholes.*

Cool, I prayed. *I love girls with assholes.*

Yeah, she prayed. *Me too.*

I giggled. *I wish you were here right now,* I prayed.

You would be dead if I were there, Meteor [msluw] prayed back.

I know, but we could have sex, I prayed.

We can have sex now. I felt her prayer on my skin.

Questions:

      1. What if I am bad at this?
      2. How do I know if it's my turn?
      3. Should I have sex inside the pit of rotting dresses?
      4. What is Sea-Witch doing right now?
      5. What are the names of the members in the band Girls With Assholes?
      6. What if we're both bottoms?

She prayed to ask if it was okay if she came inside me. Her flat affect was adorable.
I washed my hands in the dresses & prayed back to her. *You are always inside me,* I prayed.
Holy are you, my god, I prayed.
Holy are you, my god, she prayed back.

We took our turns from there, pushing skin aside & braiding hair. I made my sounds on her, all of my closest & she gave me her prayers from her place among the stars. I set the dresses on fire & sweat in their heat. I kept my sweat for Meteor [(msluw)] & we had there a communion of fluids. She cried out loud & the stars watched & winked at our soft assholes. We prayed back & forth apart from time. We spent ourselves enough (but never enough!) & sat in our silence. I found my thoughts drifting to Sea-Witch, who never woke, but slept soundly all through. *Holy are you, my god,* I thought.

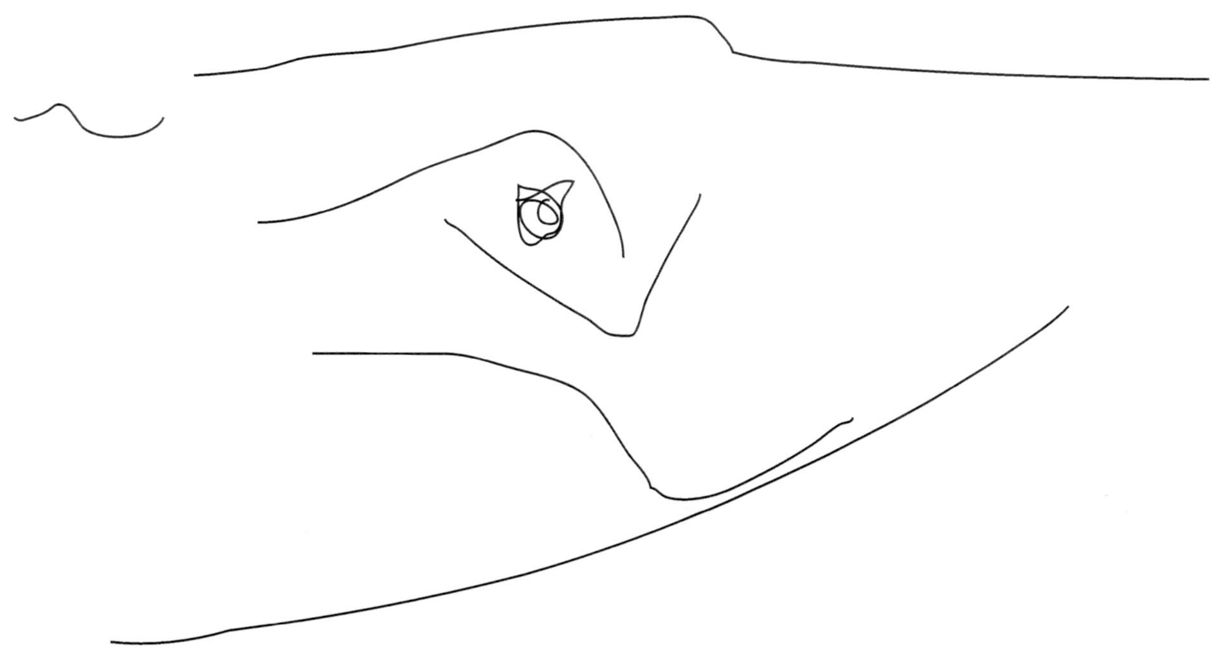

hold well
nothing is pure

SEA LEVEL

[T]he strange thing, the thing that you can never explain to anyone, except another nut, or, if you're lucky, a doctor who has an unusual amount of sense— stranger than the hallucinations, or the voices, or the anxiety—is the way you begin to experience the edges of the mind itself...in a way other people just can't.

- Samuel R. Delany
Dhalgren

dddddddddddddddddddddddddddddddddddddddddddddddddddddddddddddddddddddddddddddddddddddddddddddddddddddddd
dddddddddddddddddddddddddddddddddddddddddddddddddddddddddddddddddddddddddddddddddddddddddddddddddddddddd
dddddddddddddddddddddddddddddddddddddddddddddddddddddddddddddddddddddddddddddddddddddddddddddddddddddddddd
dddddddddddddddddddddddddddddddddddddddddddddddddddddddddddddddddddddddddddddddddddddddddddddddddddddddddd
ddddddddddddddddddddddddddddddddddddddddddddddddddddddddddddddddddddddddddddddddddddddddddddddddddddddd

ddddddddddddddddddddddddddddddddddddddddddddddddddddddddddddddddddddddddd

dddddddddddddddddddddddddddddddddddddddddddddddddddddddd

dddddddddddddddddddddddddddddddddddddddddddddddddddddddddddddddddddddddddddddddddd

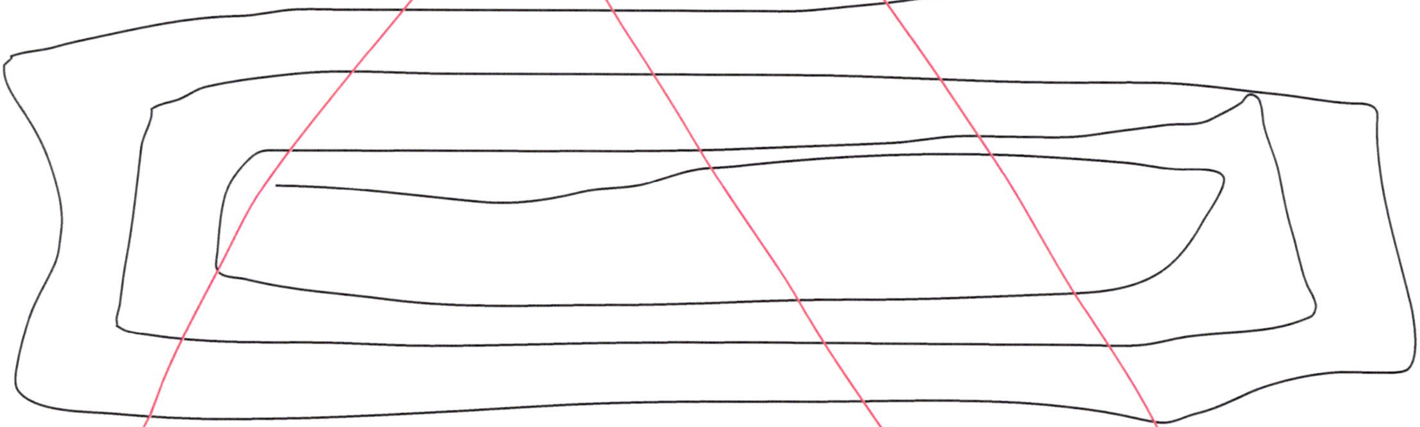

dddddddddddddddddddddddddddddddddddddddddddddddddddddddddddddddddddddddddddddddddddddddddddddddddddddddd
dddddddddddddddddddddddddddddddddddddddddddddddddddddddddddddddddddddddddddddddddddddddddddddddddddddddd
dddddddddddddddddddddddddddddddddddddddddddddddddddddddddddddddddddddddddddddddddddddddddddddddddddddddd
dddddddddddddddddddddddddddddddddddddddddddddddddddddddddddddddddddddddddddddddddddddddddddddddddddddddd
dddddddddddddddddddddddddddddddddddd

BONE DEATH []

Old-Seagull-Witch spent her time in the laboratory at the University of Crater, where she transcribed messages from the feet of insects. The insects used their feet to ask questions about pain that didn't have clear answers. On her lunch breaks, Old-Seagull-Witch ate soft sandwiches from the vending machine. She talked to her girlfriend—who stayed at home to write down stories about pain—on the telephone. Sometimes they texted. There were six living creatures who lived in the woods outside of the laboratory. Early one Tuesday they slipped a piece of paper under the door of the laboratory that said

> Dear Pain Researchers,
>
> We held one of ourselves & watched her die. She grew fleshy tufts on her body after five
> days. We ate the tufts & her body lost itself in the woods. You have to find her body.
> We think it got lost in your pain. Please return it to us. It is okay if you eat any tufts you
> find. Those are for sharing.

It was unsigned. Old-Seagull-Witch was texting about this to her girlfriend when the power went out in the laboratory & all around town. The outage was made for fun by a minor god of pain, who was part insect. The god's outages, if plotted on a map, might say some words. They might read "boys aren't real." Old-Seagull-Witch texted to her girlfriend that she was thinking about her clit. About both of their clits, held together in a gentle fist.

On my nineteenth day in Sea-Witch I had made plans to meet her near the drainage ditch on the other side of the beach parkinglot. I found old, disused cars there & as I walked past, some of them married us there in the parkinglot sand. I guess I should specify that by "us" I am referring to myself, to all my selves. What I mean is that by the time I arrived at the drainage ditch to meet Sea-Witch there were four of myself, walking on sixteen limbs & going by a collection of names. What I mean to say is that when we got there Sea-Witch held our faces & took our hands & baptized them in the drainage ditch.

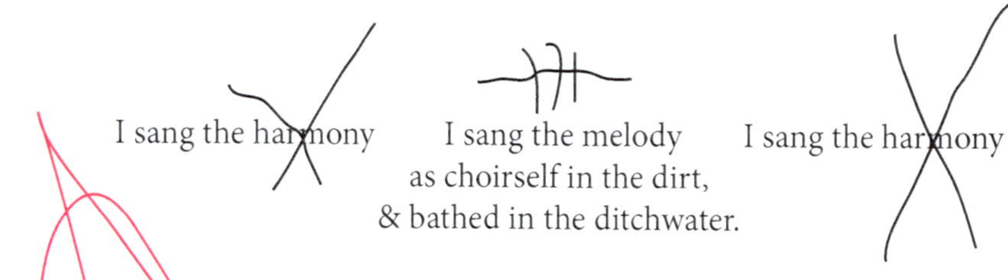

I sang the harmony   I sang the melody   I sang the harmony
                       as choirself in the dirt,
                       & bathed in the ditchwater.

A CROW EMERGED FROM MY HANDS WHEN SEA-WITCH PULLED THEM OUT.

I was all outline   We were all outline
& ghost, pushing   & ghost, pushing
my boundaries   our boundaries
to blur.   to break.

Sea-Witch returned our hands to deadname, who passed them to us, drying them on xyr skirt.
I thanked xem.
deadname leaned toward us, eclipsing our view of Sea-Witch.
"Hold well," xe said. "Nothing is pure."
Xe stroked xyr hand across my forehead / across my lap & I heard
xyr voice & the sound of the holy parkinglottraffic rising in my
ears until it blended into a high pitched
whine.

I woke up again in Sea-Witch after arriving there covered in lava. The patch of sand I slept on had turned to glass beneath me. Formation as a process is one that never ends. It wakes you up at 5am every morning so that it can continue. I pray to myself for it to end. I pray to it for myself to end.

I have nothing to fear from monsters. It was people who broke my teeth with rocks. It was men who made them think it was necessary. It was angels who watched me crying & stared when I yelled at them. It was monsters who took me inside their bodies for warmth, pleasure & sustenance. It was me who took the form of thirteen birds & died on the sand in a circle. It was Meteor [(msluw)] who landed in the circle killing everyone. It was everyone who died. It was everyone who, briefly, was resurrected. It was everyone who immediately died again. It was empty I held in my arms after. It was the future I hold in my arms now & call holy. It was the future I kept inside my drawer with the shirts & pants. It was the microscope I used to figure out what my blood was made of. It was hospitals my blood was made of. It was ambulances I found in my breathing. It was the water that came out when I died. It was the water inside me I left to my children. It was daughters they were called by everyone but their mothers. It was daughter they wrote on their chests in red ink. It was communion they had with my water then. It was me whose face hit the pavement. It was people who broke my teeth with rocks.

On my 30th day in Sea-Witch I found need had grown inside my person to the extent it was filling up most of who I was. I had heard stories of this happening to people. I left Sea-Witch with the hope of need inside me & a flock of living creatures taking turns riding in my arms.

I realized at this time that I thought of myself primarily in relation to other monsters in Sea-Witch. This is still true. In a way, I am only a small part of their whole. I keep them & the thought of *withness* in a pouch along with sand that I can plant wherever I end up. I can scrape the side of a tree & make tea from the bark & in doing this know the process that created me. The color grass takes in direct sun. The whole sound of limbs stretching. I slept for a time in a hole in the earth that contained nothing. The bareness of it was tangible, & I found myself infatuated with how cold it could make me. It got to the point where moving, even slowly, nearly broke my arms & ribs. When can I leave this place? How does it eat me?

SEA-WITCH 9,999,999,999

Sea-Witch's heart is made of copper. I've seen it. I used to sleep there. It isn't shaped like anything. I mean, when I look at it my mind can't find shape. Twelve living creatures surround it day & night. They keep it warm in their fur. They keep it warm with fires they build from their fur's trimmings. They sing songs at night & the words are the plots of old films about houses. About bedrooms.

1. Seeing the heart of Sea-Witch prepared me for life as a monster.
2. Nothing could have prepared me for life as a monster.
3. There is no life to be had as a monster.
4. The only life to be had is life as a monster.
5. I hold the edges.
6. I sewed the words false purity on my couch.
7. I sewed the word daughter on my couch in red thread.
8. I sewed the word dying on my couch.

The room where Sea-Witch's heart is held is nearly impossible to be in / it is so crowded with fire & living creatures. I used to sleep there but stopped because my skin was covered in burns. I found instead a living area in Sea-Witch's feet where I could put my fabric on the walls & furniture. The living creatures there asked me to stay as their monster & I, for a time, did so.

Stone-Witch found she could fit all of Dog-Witch in her mouth at once. This was only one of the many revelations that came through the unstructured process of play they put each other through between sleeping & waking. During quiet moments, Dog-Witch would gently make & unmake the universe around them as ze stroked the freckles that ran across the back of Stone-Witch's shoulders & neck. The sun exploded again & again, filling the sky with light & unlight in turn.

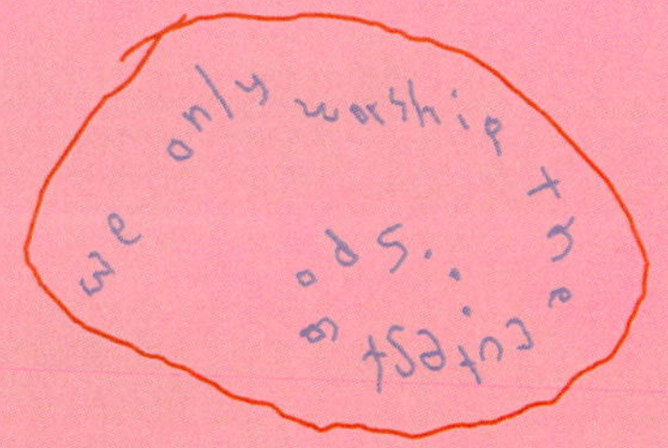

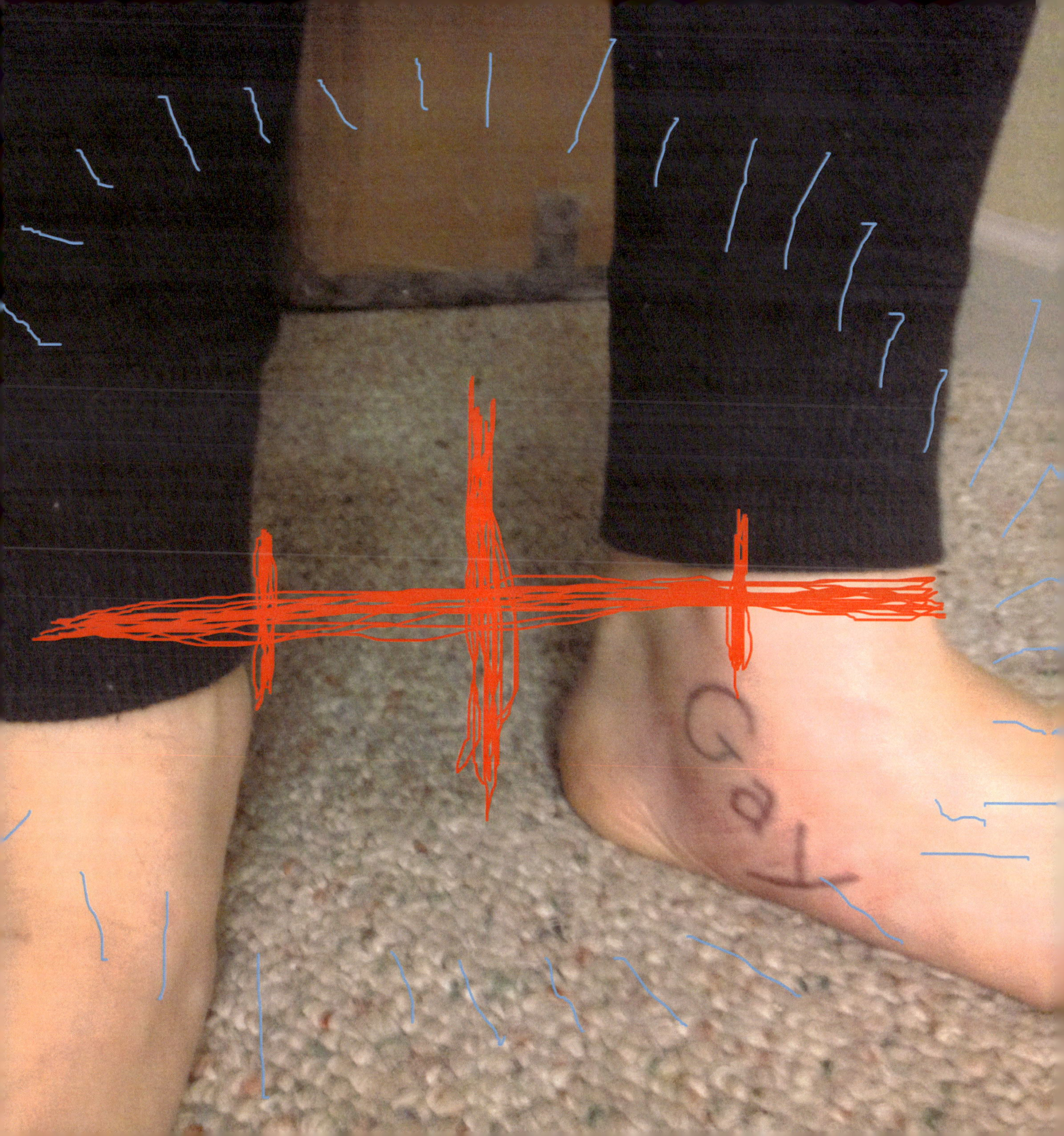

A name can be temporary or it can be permanent. It can be shortened, length-
ened. It can be pronounced incredibly well, or not. It can be the sound that is
yelled out when someone else is looking for you. It can be the sound that is
yelled out when someone else thinks that you can be found.

- Jordaan Mason
The End of Cinnamon

BONE DEATH ??

The Book of Meteor says that Strawberry-Witch first met deadname at a grocery store. She was looking at the beer selection, trying to figure out what to get for the night. deadname asked her where she got her tights. Strawber-ry-Witch said she couldn't remember. She said maybe they were from a free box, or maybe someone left them over at her house. She said they might have been her ex's. deadname said, *Oh. Well thanks anyway.*

Sure, no problem, Strawberry-Witch said back.

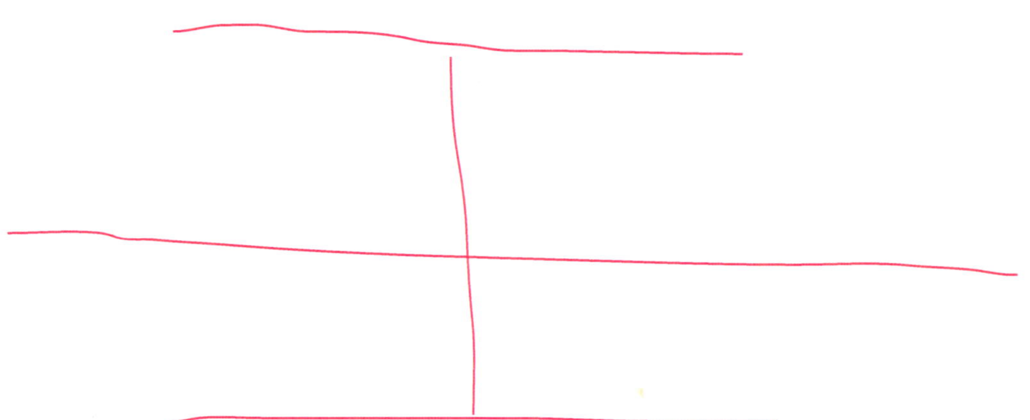

A year later they met again, this time at the bluffs, where Strawberry-Witch had come with two friends. (Some Sea-Witchean scholars suggest these two friends may have been Airless-Face-Witch & ha-ha-ha.) They came to sit & get drunk with the sunset. deadname was there, alone as always, idly digging a small hole in the ground with a stick. Strawberry-Witch noticed xym, but didn't say anything, & deadname didn't approach her either. Strawberry-Witch & her friends quickly got wrapped up in their conversation & their drinking & their sunset & by the time she thought to look again, deadname had gone.

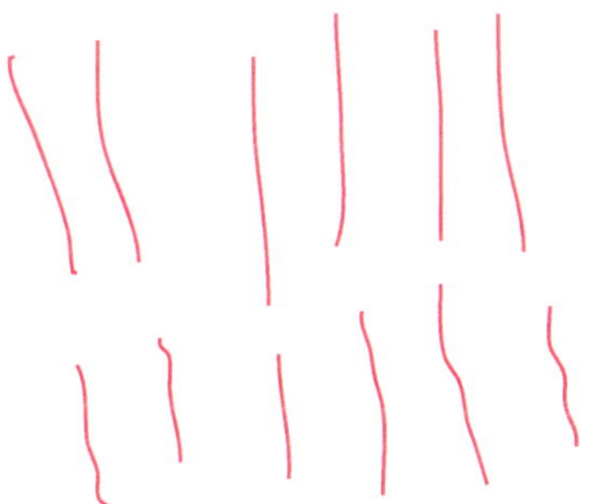

The third time Strawberry-Witch encountered deadname, it was in a dream. The two of them were alone in the stomach of a large, living bird & muscle rippled all around them. As soon as she noticed xym, deadname apologized for coming to see her this way. Xe said, *Could you please follow me?* & Strawberry-Witch said, *Sure, yeah, no problem.* Strawberry-Witch, upon waking, couldn't remember where it was that deadname had led her after that.

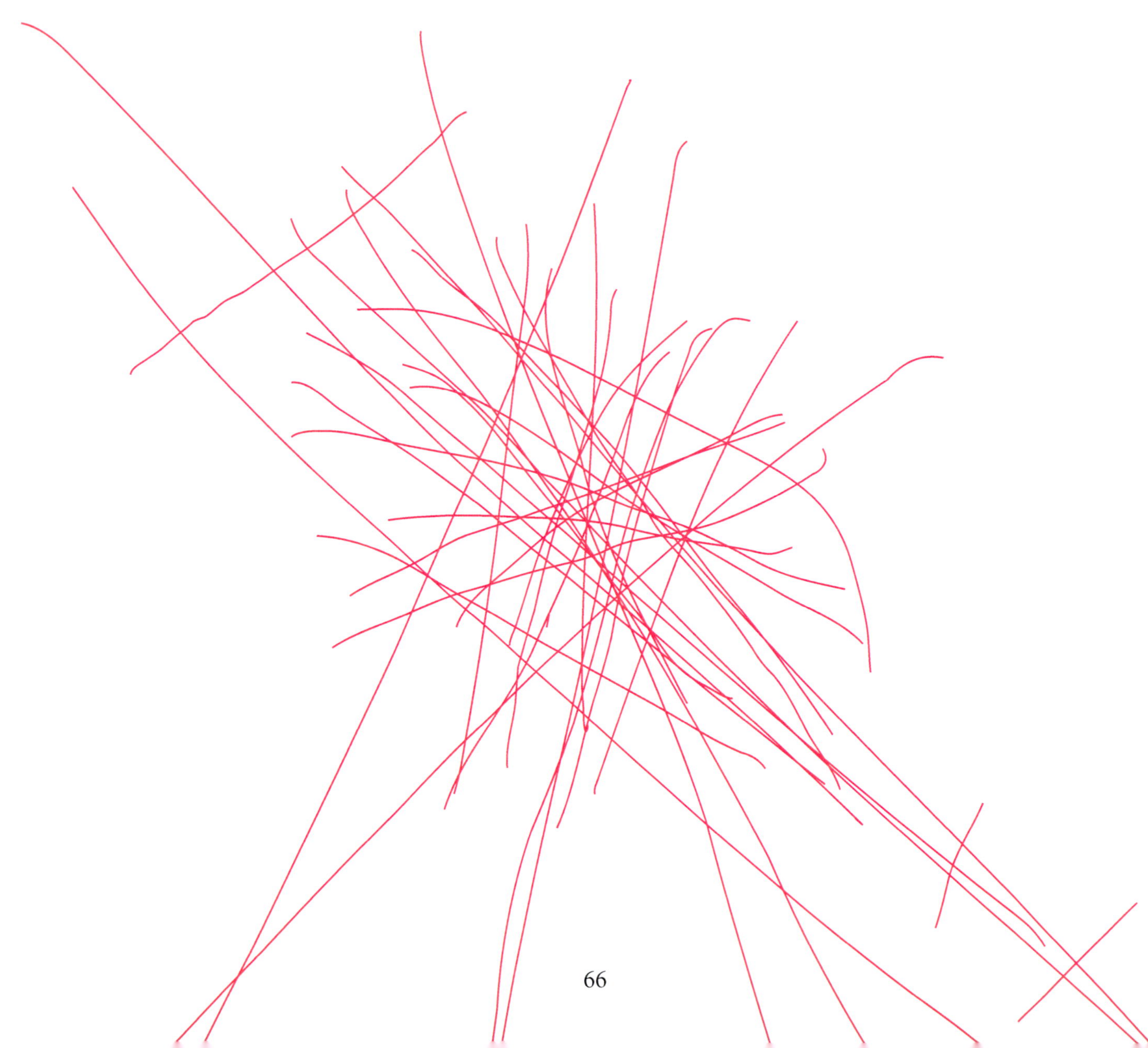

The fourth & fifth times they met, deadname assumed a familiarity with Strawberry-Witch that xe had never before used. *I have been very lonely,* xe said on one of these occasions.

deadname began showing up in Strawberry-Witch's life in many small ways after that. She would notice what seemed to be a glimpse of xyr hair in the reflection of a car window. She found an earring she thought xe had been wearing under the couch on her porch.

Strawberry-Witch began to leave messages to deadname in the form of small knife scratches on mirrors & floors. Messages that looked like lines & symbols, shapes & holes. deadname communicated back through particularly informational smells that seemed to have no source, & ideas that would occur with a certain parallel nature she associated with deadname's face & expressions.

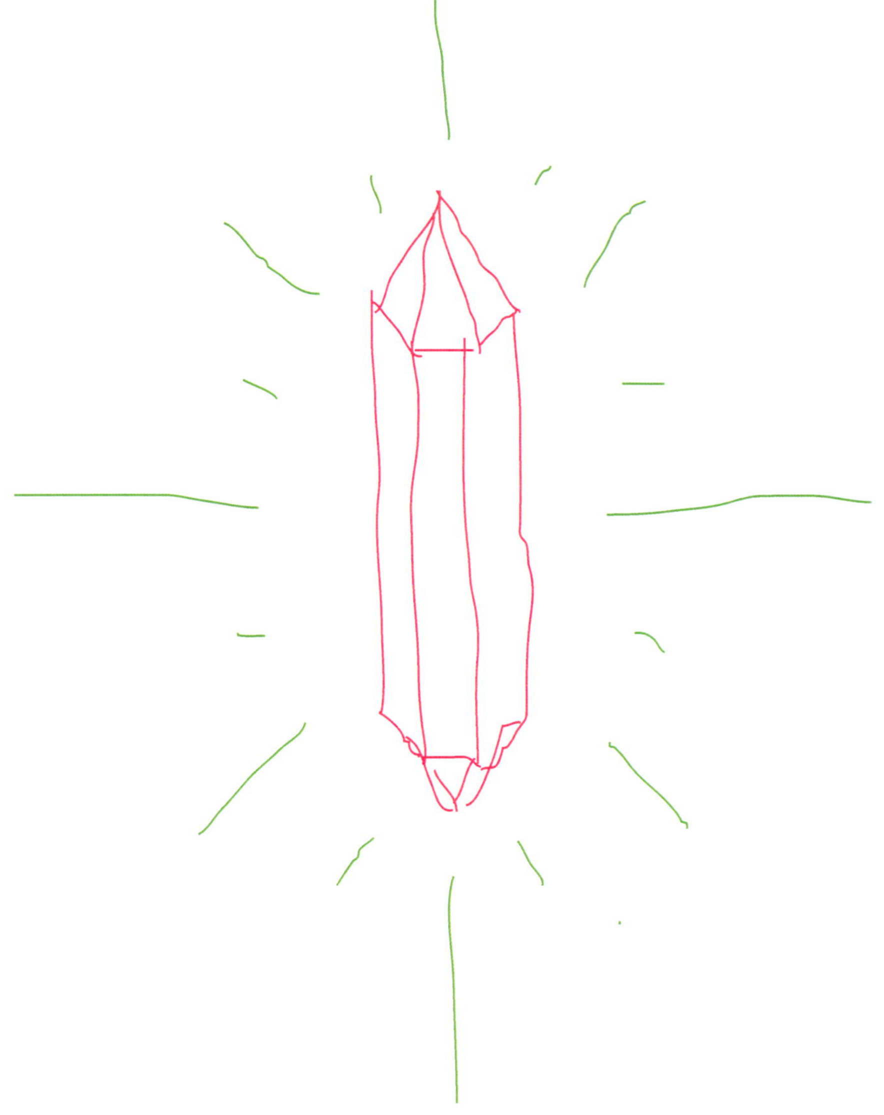

In this way, deadname communicated five ideas to Strawberry-Witch. They are as follows:

1. You hold thousands of monsters inside your body.
2. You are a segment of time, rather than space & most of the confusion you have experienced throughout your life is the result of a misconception about this.
3. When Dog-Witch created the world, ze did not plan delicately, but did so by instinct. By muscle memory.
4. How many times can a person think about bashing their own head open before trying it. I'm scared. How many times can anyone even do this.
5. Someone please help.

Strawberry-Witch especially understood these last two points. When she was alone sometimes she would imagine destruction on a grand scale. There was a way in which this sort of thought was incredibly comforting. She would cry when she thought of this, always these big, messy cries where she was stringing snot & spit all over the front of her romper. She decided that some day she would start a religion that worshipped a meteor, praying for it to come to earth & crush everything. She never started this religion but it came to exist anyway. Some things are inevitable.

Strawberry-Witch had the dream about being inside the bird's stomach again but this time the bird was vomiting. It was trying to expel her but it wasn't working. The walls constricted, pressing on her body, hard. She even tried to help it get her out, but there was nothing to be done.

Sea-Witch
Volume two
Girldirt
Angelfog

ſ

chapter two: girldirt angelfog

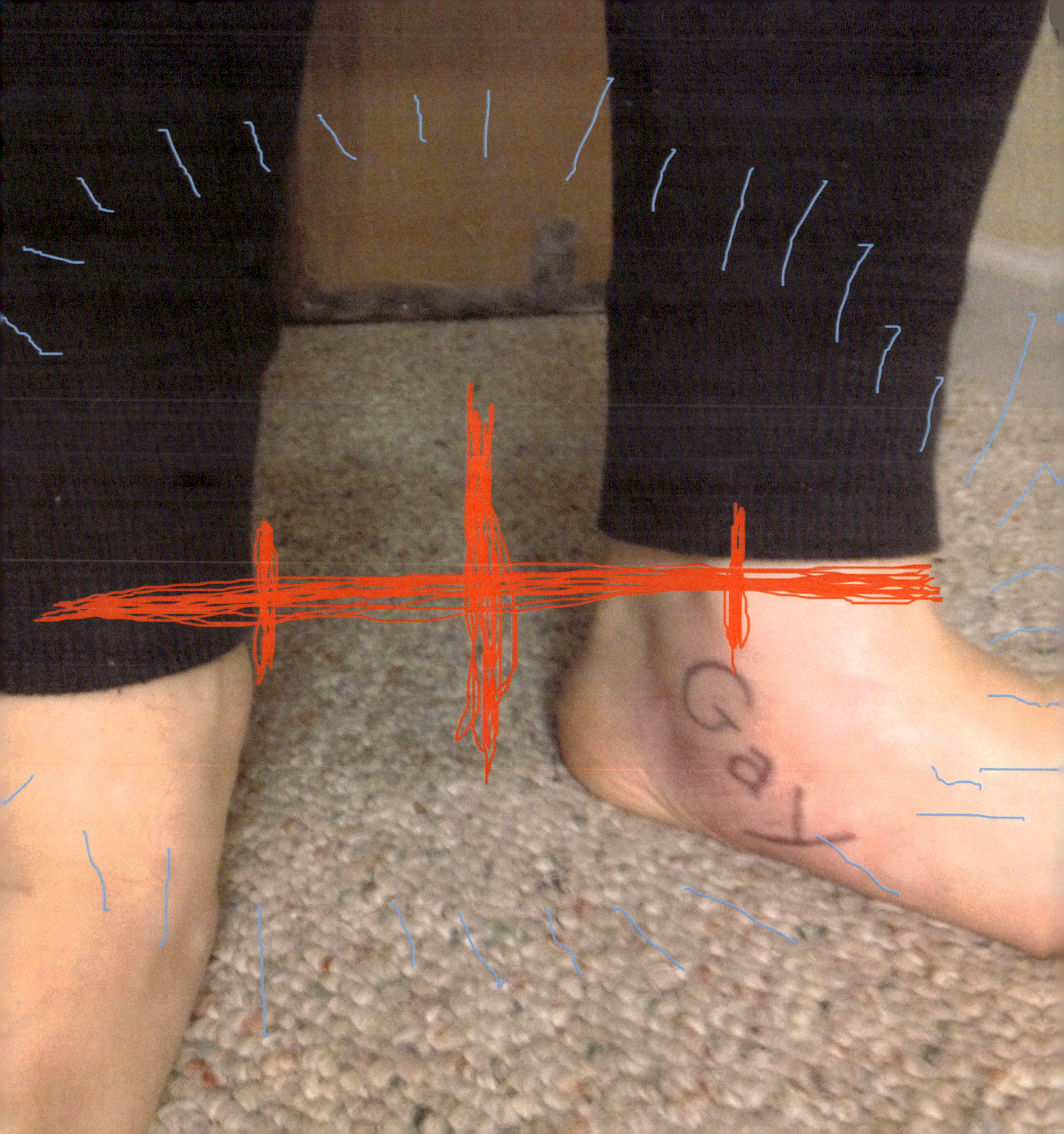
Gay

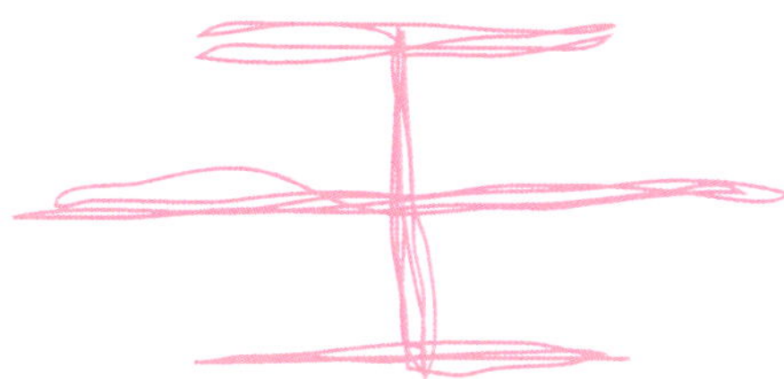

Hearken unto me, fellow creatures. I who have dwelt in a form unmatched with my desire, I whose flesh has become an assemblage of incongruous anatomical parts, I who achieve the similitude of a natural body only through an unnatural process, I offer you this warning: the Nature you bedevil me with is a lie. Do not trust it to protect you from what I represent, for it is a fabrication that cloaks the groundlessness of the privilege you seek to maintain for yourself at my expense. You are as constructed as me; the same anarchic Womb has birthed us both. I call upon you to investigate your nature as I have been compelled to confront mine. I challenge you to risk abjection and flourish as well as have I. Heed my words, and you may well discover the seams and sutures in yourself.

- Susan Stryker
"My Words to Victor Frankenstein Above the Village of Chamounix"

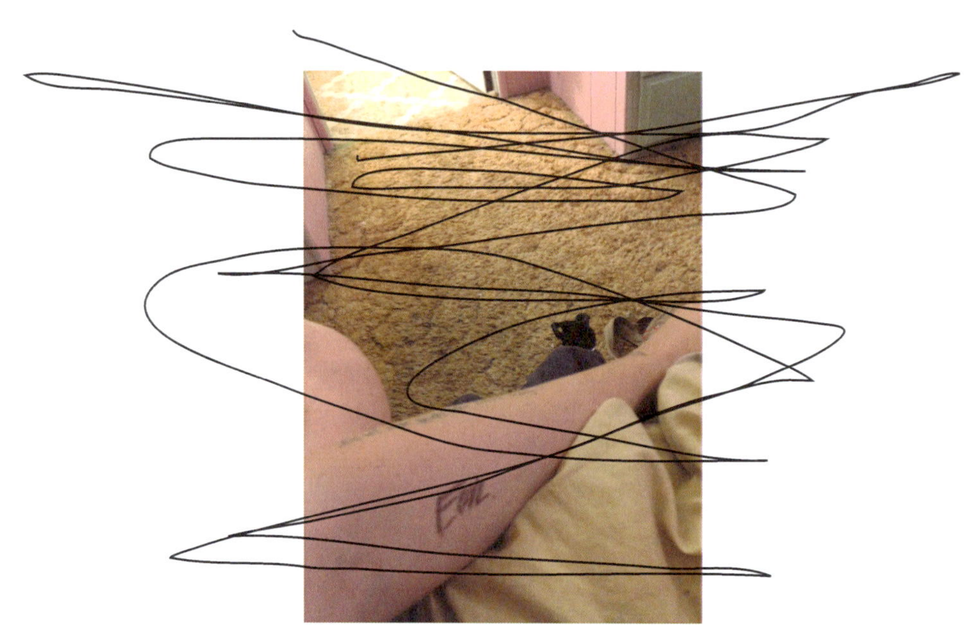

I am entirely full of old suns at the moment. It is difficult to contain them. It is taking all of who I am to stay this way. I have made the decision to let it take all of who I am in the hopes that I will become something else. It might be a welcome change.

I would like to take this opportunity to restate that this is not about my body. I am often writing about bodies, I know, & documenting them in other ways, but aside from them not being the end goal here, I want to also lay absolute waste to the idea that any *body* documented herein might be *mine.* While I'm at it, I would like to throw the concepts of possession, property & even individuality in the fire as well. I'm always having to tear apart language to do any actual communicating & sometimes I wonder if that might not be the entirety of what I'm trying to do. Just absolutely tear everything apart. Starting with language. It couldn't hurt.

When I was first formed I took things as I saw them. One at a time. Slowly I began to consume more. These days I can't stop consuming. All kinds of things simultaneously. Nothing is safe. I am not a creature who was born. I am a fire that was set. Come closer.

Bone death is a feeling of companionship. It has a sense of history. If I were to use it in a sentence I might say *Sara used her bone death on me.* I might say, *Don't go downtown, there is a terrible bone death happening.*

I have bone death that is specific to me. I hold this bone death in my lungs & neck. It changes colors. I wake it up to remind it to eat. I wake it up & feel a tightness in my chest when I go up the stairs.

When a bone death feels cornered it emits a high-pitched whine. I do this too. I get it. When a bone death is feeling afraid it emits death that covers its body. It looks like death, it smells like death, etc.

This book may not get finished because I have been locked outside for the winter. I might get too cold to finish this book. I might lose my language. There is always the possibility I will lose my language. This is true of anyone who has experienced bone death.

Sea-Witch's bone death creates a layer of thermal fog that emanates from her body in waves. It can take the paint off a house. It can also help a young monster fall asleep amidst screaming. It has a specific smell. For Sea-Witch, this is one of the ways she is always resisting. One of the ways she can't help but resist, because it's part of who she is.

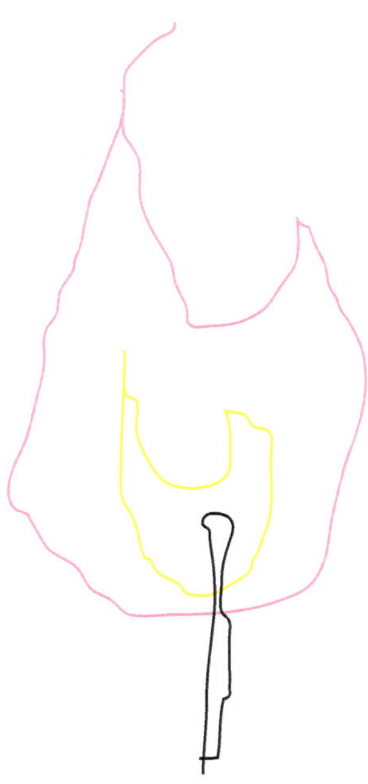

On my 112th day living in Sea-Witch I cried in the dirt until she answered. I told her I had learned about the 78 Men & had felt the pain they made & she said, *I know.* I told her I had come here to escape them but that I could still feel their pain. I felt it everywhere. *I know I know I know I know,* she said. *You are my child,* she said. We held a ceremony about the men outside the front gate of the First Sea-Witchean Church of Meteor. The ceremony began by reading a list of names of the dead. We ate things that made us terrified & tattooed our skin with symbols of defiance. We went to sleep at dawn, with the knowledge that the ceremony's completion could only happen among the graves of the 78 Men & with their life's blood & at that time we would celebrate the liberation of all monsters.

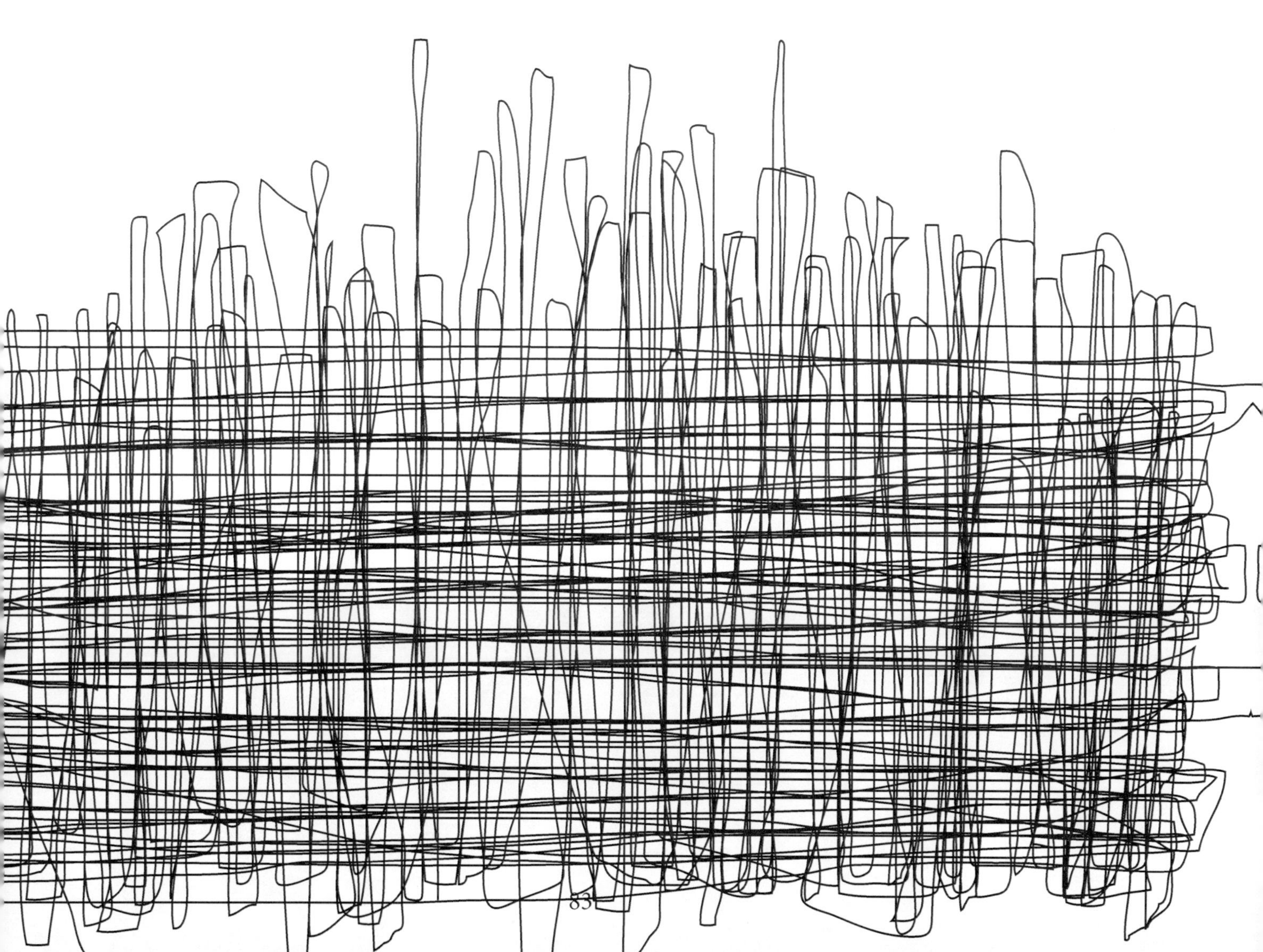

Elsewhere I have mentioned my name, ~~which is Sara~~. It is true that I have many other names & that Sara is not the first name I have had & will not be my name forever. But, for now, it is my real name. It is also true that there are many other Saras. Sea-Witchean naming conventions generally encourage frequent & increasingly complicated renamings, but it is also traditional that at a certain stage of formation a monster names herself Sara. Because of this, I, like all the other monsters occupying my current stage of formation, am named Sara. There have been many Saras before me & there will be many Saras after. While I was living in Sea-Witch I knew many other Saras with whom I kept warm in blankets on snowy nights. Saras are well known for our gentle confusion, our soft curls, & our continued attachment to linear time. Only a monster in her Sara phase could have written a book such as this one. As I am always in the process of formation, it is possible that by the time you read this you & I will no longer be mutually intelligible. It is also possible that this is already the case.

A real living creature was presented to Sea-Witch soon after her body was first created & she kissed it, placing it among the rocks on the roughest part of the shore. That real living creature grew as a being that shifted with time. Hir body's form changed as time passed, but unlike most of us, the concept of time passing wasn't relevant to hir. Hir consciousness was outside of time, but limited in space. Similar to the way that other beings are limited in time, but their consciousness is outside of space. I can think a thought while walking circles in space, but still I am going in a straight line in time. Ze, on the other hand, could travel in circles in time, but was limited to those rocks, to moving slowly along the shore in one direction. From hir perspective, ze could no more travel backwards along the shore than you or I could become a baby again, but could see every moment in the entire history-and-future of the universe at will so long as it was from the physical vantage point of where ze was on the shore. Hir existence was not the first such in history. Sea-Witch & hir remained very close emotionally for the living creature's whole life, though physically they became gradually more distant. From Sea-Witch's perspective they only met that once. From the creature's perspective Sea-Witch was always there. Outside of time there is no such thing as having someone leave you.

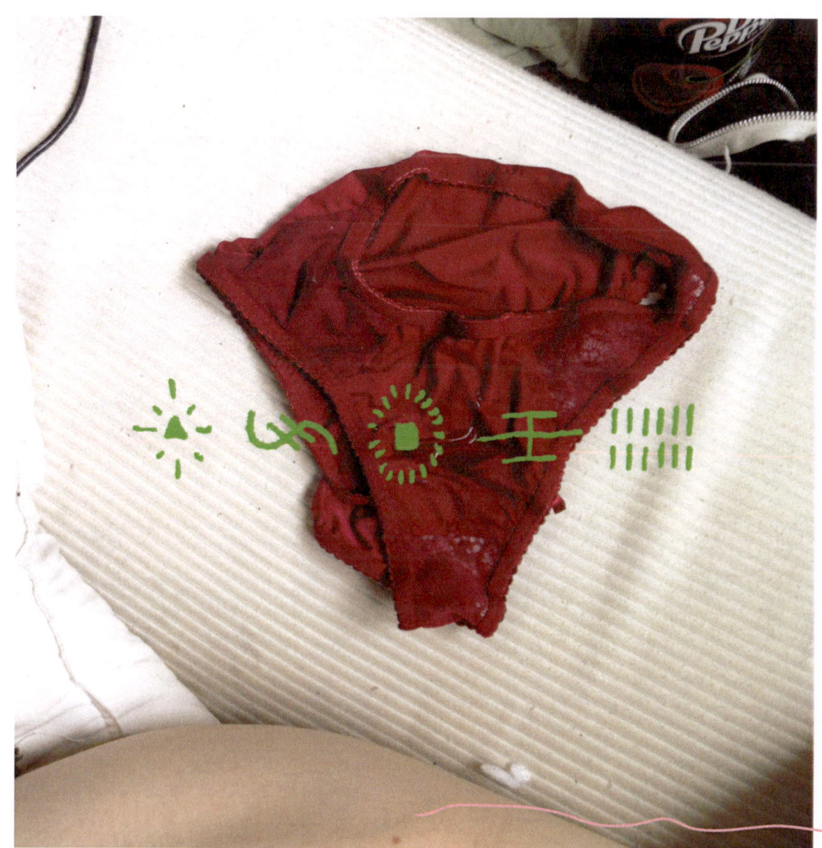

The 78 Men Who Cause Pain take turns playing *in charge*. They have big fake contests where they pretend to care greatly about which of them gets to play *in charge* next. They pretend to let people decide which of them gets to play *in charge* next. They even pretend that the people themselves could someday play *in charge*, if they were to look & sound enough like the 78 Men.

The *in charge* game is enchanted. It is *interesting*. Even the most distant monsters, who are constantly in pain from what the 78 Men who cause pain have created often find themselves discussing, arguing about the *in charge* game.

There are different ways that the *in charge* game is played. Some of the 78 Men who play the *in charge* game talk about how they will defend & protect monsters. Some only speak of slaying us. The truth is they will all slay us. That is why we are called monsters. The truth is that no one playing the *in charge* game will ever talk about the pain they create, which is constantly slaying us slowly, because that pain is what the game is a distraction from.

One of the best tricks that happens in the *in charge* game is called laws. Laws say all kinds of things, but what they really say is that monsters should be in cages. They say this over & over in thousands of different words. They are very complicated.

Not every act by the 78 Men Who Cause Pain is in itself about causing pain, or about slaying. Some seem very benevolent. Some are actually about keeping us alive. It is a system of pain & deception that works primarily to keep itself in place. If we all starved to death, they would have nothing left to take.

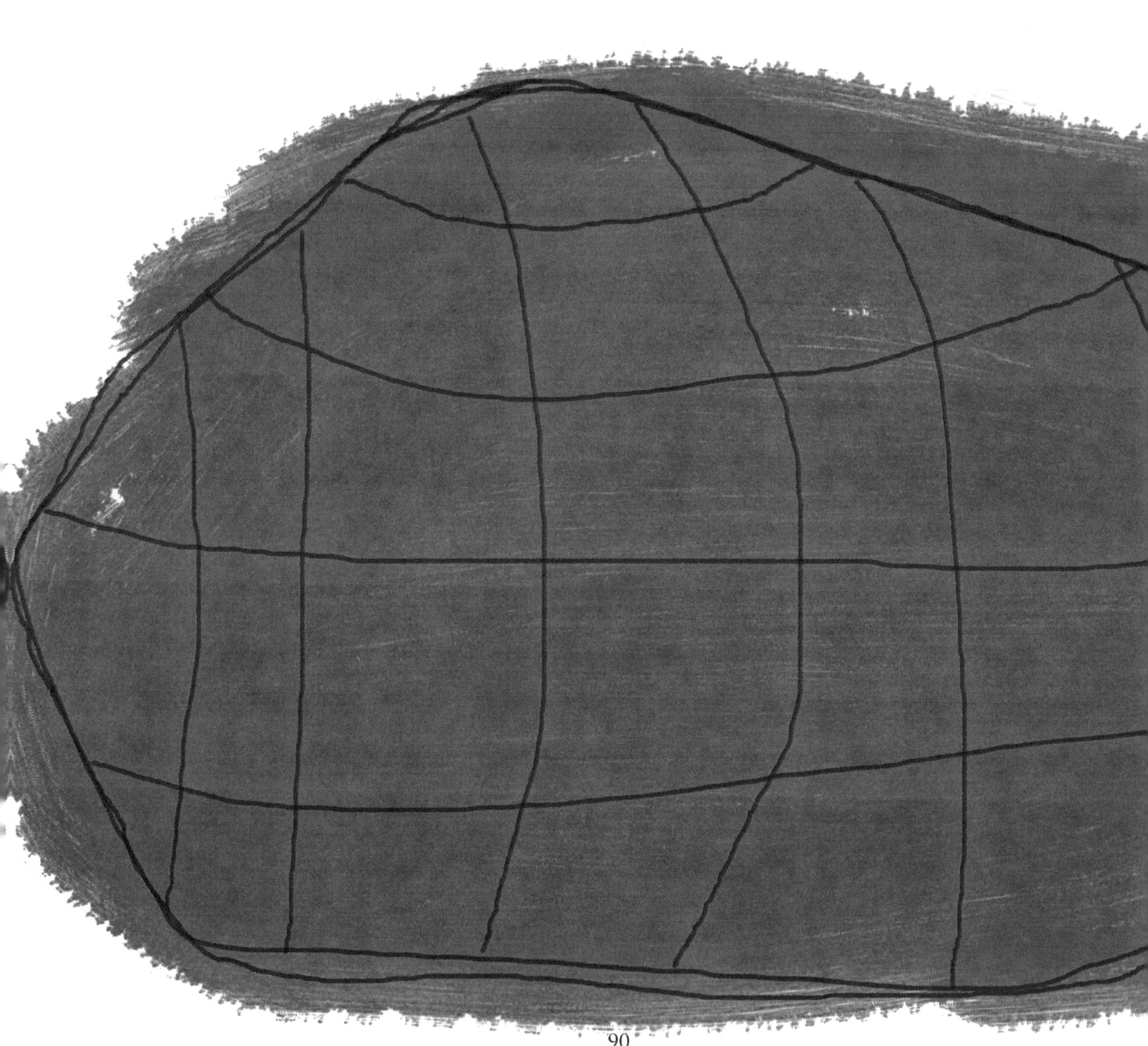

Am I complicit in my own pain / Because I do not hate those who have harmed me?

- Inverts, "Survivor"

SEA-WITCH
rect
sorry

TRANS MEMOIR 47 DEAD TREE SNOWMELT

I left Sea-Witch so many times. I am always leaving Sea-Witch. I'm always myself inside her again in different ways, many of which are physical. I am always having her children. Which of the sacraments I partook of in Sea-Witch caused pregnancy & which only simulated its symptoms is anyone's guess, but whatever the source, I found different aspects of my body creating other bodies, found myself shed from their skins.

Questions:
1. What stage of formation causes so much salt?
2. If my body makes another body, how soon can I meet the monster or monsters who live in it?
3. How & when do we assess the ambient trauma we have absorbed solely due to our situation?

Today the word pregnancy was a bath I just wanted to sit in. Last time the word was vulvoplasty. I'm always drinking the information of words through my skin. I have new thoughts all the time. I want to sit in the sun tomorrow & arrange things in my mind. I want to press my back against Sea-Witch's great septum & know the sky until stars come out.

Essay Question:
What weird magic do we monsters have for destroying the 78 Men? Given that all of their technology is about pain & control. Given that all of ours is about dying.

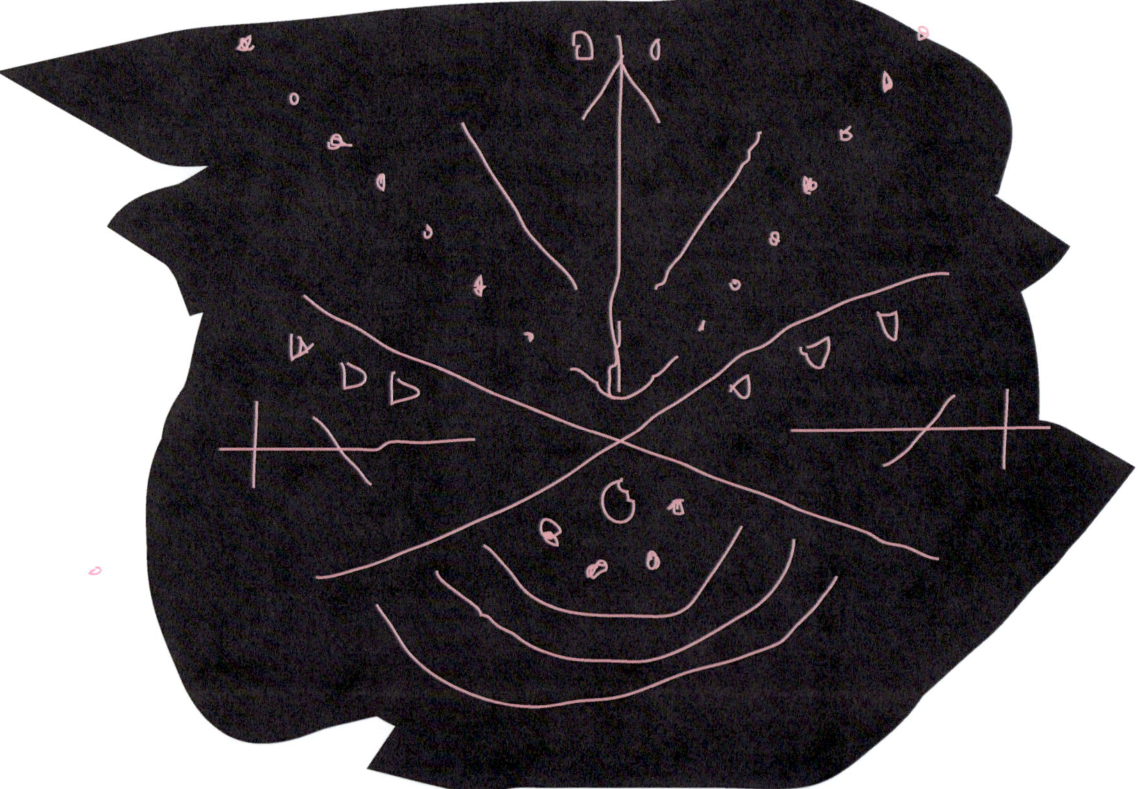

The last time I left Sea-Witch I met deadname on a bus out of town. Xe sat next to me though the bus was half empty. Xe said xe had read the book I was holding, & I told xym how I had written it. I told xym that I wasn't planning on writing a book, but that while I was sleeping the pages began flaking fully written from my sore back & thighs. This happened many nights, but I am not good with time, (or at least not good at measuring it) so I couldn't tell xym how many.

Cool, said deadname, nodding. You're adorable, xe said. Thanks, I told xym. I was going to say something about xyr appearance but my eyes kept skipping over the space where xe sat.
Xe reached over & took my hand.

Unrelated Questions
1. What is the nature of a witch-god?
2. Which of Dog-Witch's sisters have not been written about? Are there really nineteen?
3. Where did Sea-Witch come from?

When deadname & I had sex xe would often look in my eyes & say matter-of-fact things about the nature of time. I told xym at one point that it was these kinds of statements that really made me wet/hard. I told xym that nothing is sexier than a fresh perspective on the universe. Remarkably, I continue to believe this to be true even after all that I went through later.

What is the nature of a witch-god?
1. Building campfires
2. Making sure the drugs don't take themselves
3. Sitting in certain positions
4. Producing the kind of magic that doesn't go anywhere
5. Experiencing pain (those who have more experience of pain in their lives are capable of some of the deepest magic)
6. Language
7. Loss of language
8. Loss of language

deadname & I holed up in a motel for the next week, drinking sparkling water & pitching the bottles at the floor of our parallel beds. We watched television & asked the people we saw on it what they were thinking. We asked them how they ended up where they were & if they believed in time or purity. We asked them the questions we wanted to ask each other but couldn't find a way to make them fit in our dynamic. Between the two of us, many questions were asked & none were answered.

The 78 Men Who Cause Pain only call us monsters on the rarest occasions. It is so effective that decades can pass between times, yet no one forgets. They created that specially for us. The rest of the time they call us by many many aspects of ourselves, often aspects of our bodies. Sometimes they monsterize us based on some incredibly convoluted logic that often involves one of their impossible "laws." This is done to deny our groupness. They wish instead to have us think of ourselves as the only self, all alone against the pain of the world. The reason for this is that we outnumber them by the billions. The reason for this is that they would crush so nicely under our manybillion feet.

It is remarkable how well this works, considering that the men just as often love to talk about us in the thick of our groupness. How we are presented by them is entirely determined by what serves their purposes best in any moment. We are an incredibly versatile tool for them. Usually when speaking to people about monsters the 78 Men say we are not individuals with lives & needs, bellies & desires. Instead they say that we are a malignant mass that represents failure, danger, & all things wicked. We are a cautionary tale, & our actions & words are used to motivate the people to follow men's orders. It's a subtle trick. Responsibility falls on a weakened "you," while evilness has its source in a faceless "them." Monsters are those that find themselves in the peculiar position of being both a you and a them.

There is a bacteria the 78MWCP created to go into the world. Its purpose is to deliver pain, to cage, & to slay monsters. The common name for this bacteria is "cops." You may have heard of it. Cops is terrifying. This is another major thing cops is used for. For terrifying. Cops maims, slays, starves, cages & destroys monsters. Anyone can summon cops & cops will swarm to slay/starve/cage/destroy any nearby monsters. Monsters who have summoned cops frequently have this happen as well. Some monsters are monsters the cops will be more likely to attack than others because they have too much magic. Other monsters can convince the cops they are people and not monsters, however briefly. If cops was to be exterminated, if we developed a vaccine or a poison or a flamethrower for it, much of the 78 Men's physical power would be weakened.

One of the secrets of Pain is it is just inconsistent enough in its delivery for anyone to deny its existence. A small element of randomness to allow denial to take root.

Speaking of roots, I would like to talk about a seed. A bright jewel that resides within the heart of Sea-Witch. *The Book of Meteor* says it once was Dog-Witch's eye. It says that Dog-Witch made Sea-Witch with hir own paws, from a mixing of sea & sand & the colors of mountains at all times of day & the smell of night & hir own leg & eye, which ze removed with a great deal of pain. Sea-Witch also contains this pain. One day she will give this pain to each of the 78 Men, one at a time, slowly & deliberately.

It is only a matter of time, & what is time? I'm not convinced it is anything at all.

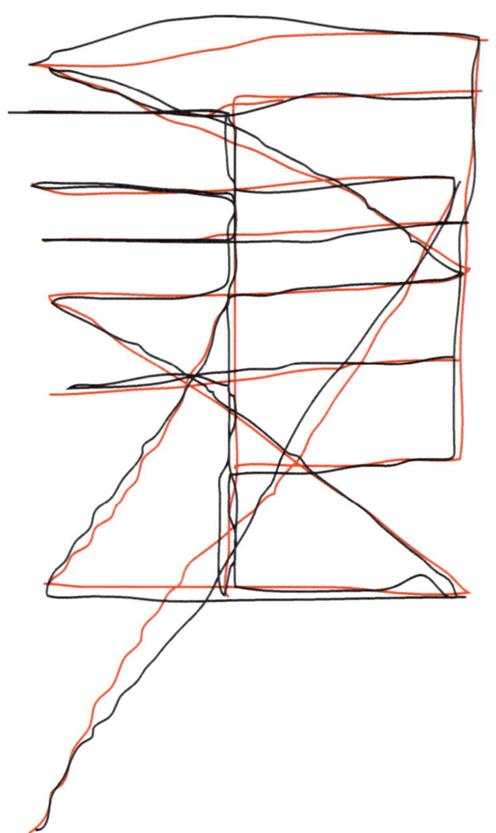

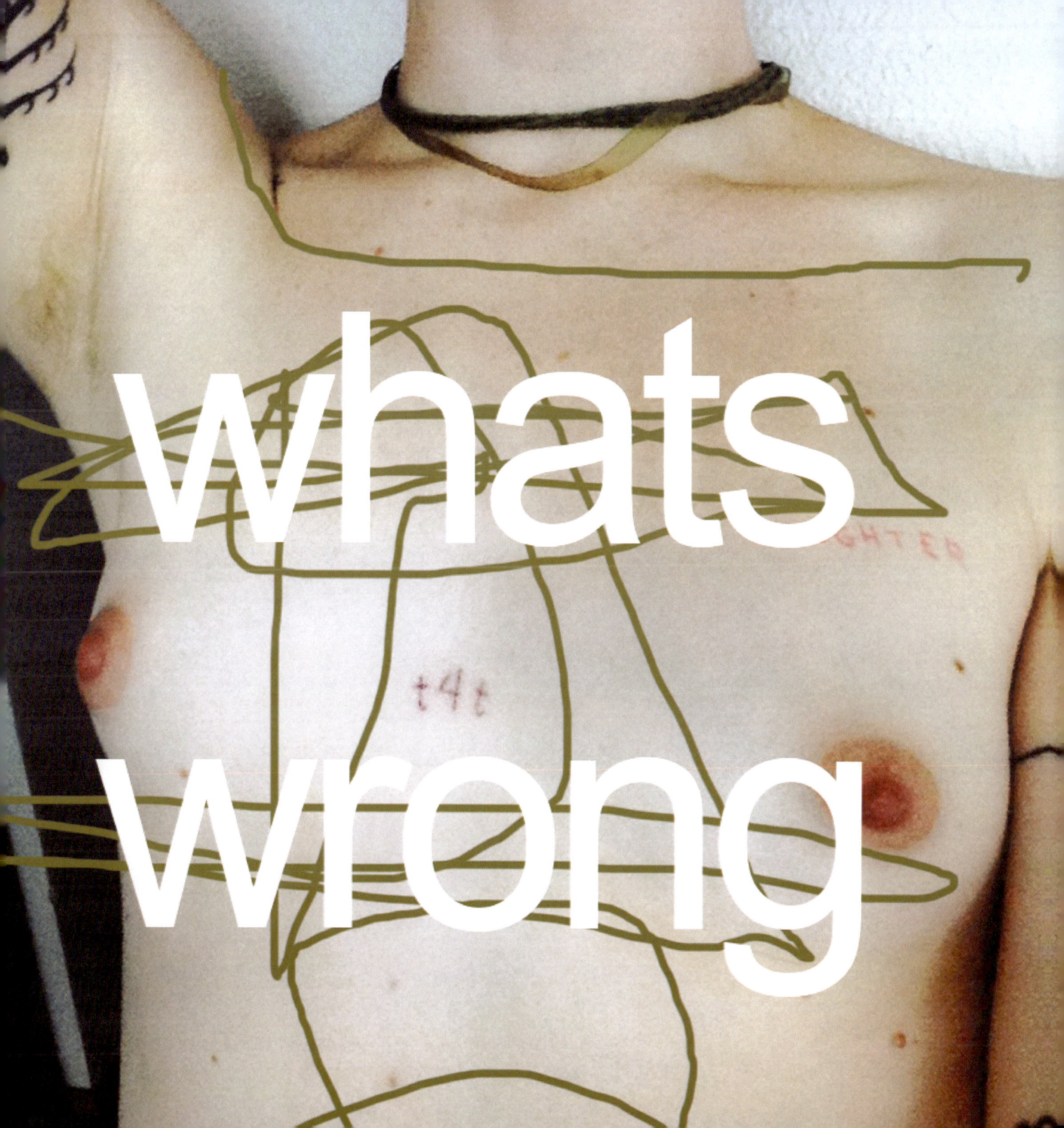
whats
wrong
t4t

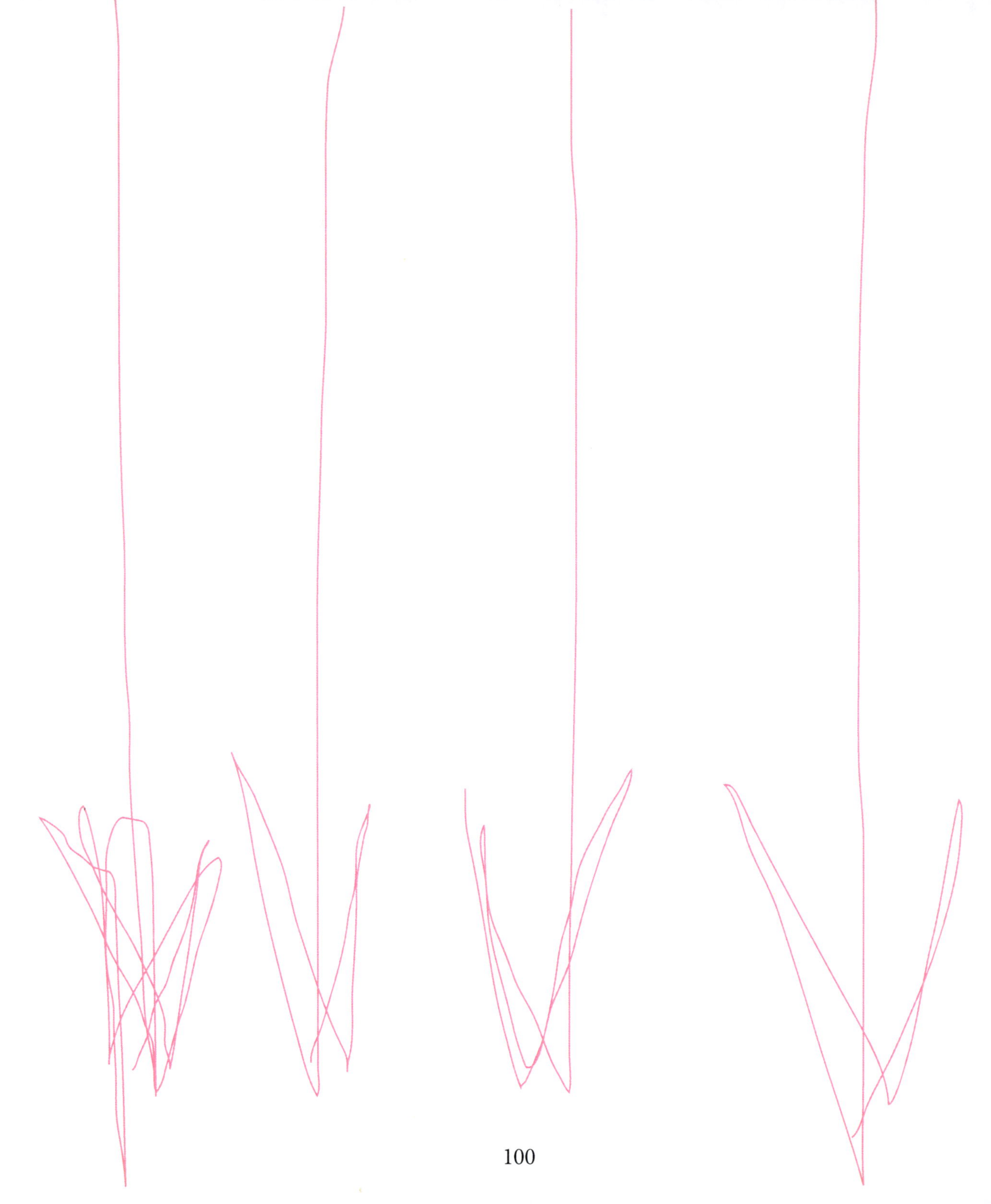

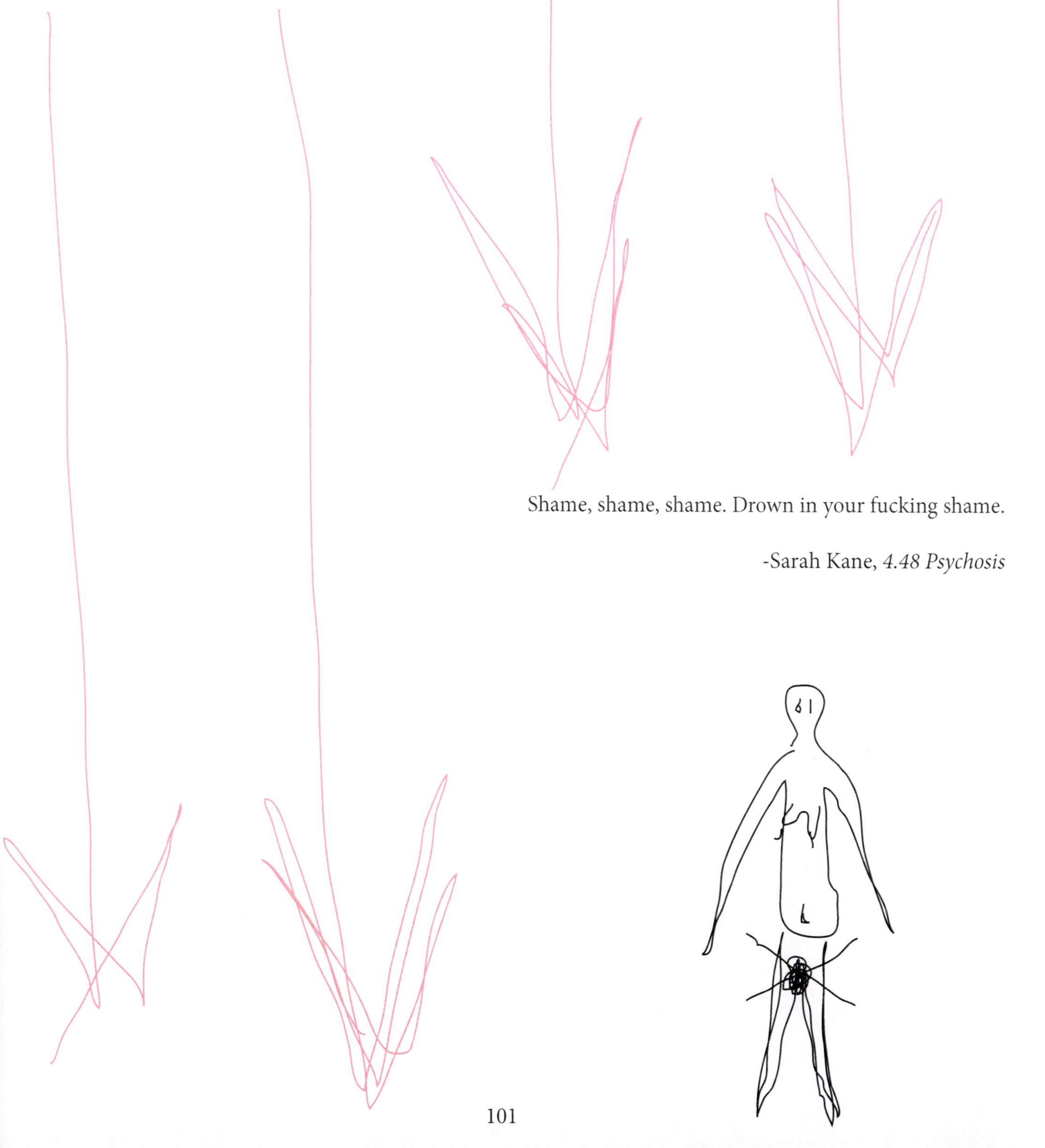

Shame, shame, shame. Drown in your fucking shame.

-Sarah Kane, *4.48 Psychosis*

You are a segment of time
rather than space & most of the
confusion you have experienced
throughout your life is the result
of a misconception about this.

hat

Deeps-Witch was the oldest & quietest of Dog-Witch's sisters. She left the largest footprints when walking in snow or sand & when she slept she talked in her sleep, unintelligible words that smelled of wet lavender. She was tall & wide & had hair that fell in massive curls over her broad shoulders. Deeps-Witch held secrets in the tension in her neck. She spent all of her twenties trying to translate these. When they were decoded they said things that she could feel like a cracking in her spine. Things like "nothing is pure & that is beautiful." It was the sum of these secrets that described her orbit. She wrote them each with the end of a burnt stick on the floor of a room she never entered. She kept the door closed for years. She married & had children from the sweet breath of her two lovers' songs. Together, they raised some children & after she died, after her long, long life her children & lovers together entered this room & found copies of themselves lying limp among the smeared ashen secrets. Two copies of each loved one lay there on the ground in that otherwise empty room. The copies, they found after some hesitation, had room-temperature skin that was soft to the touch, their features detailed & lifelike. The youngest of Deeps-Witch's children, a fully formed witch-god of her own, was the only one who had no copies. She stepped around the room, lifting limbs & checking faces, but found no copies of her form. She began to softly cry. Time spun back on itself. She looked up through her tears & noticed her mother's face, ringed in a glowing halo of diffuse light. The image of the tearmotherface repeated, refracting & blurring. It split & fused again. What's wrong? it said. What's wrong?

It is said that hundreds of sun laps ago, Sea-Witch took a picture of her naked body & uploaded it to a forgotten public server, that she named it gaygod11.png after one of her own holy names. It is said she did so from a computer she later gave as a burnt offering & whose remains she pushed off a boat in the deepest ocean. Though the source of this tale is unknown, most scholars agree it certainly Sounds Like The Kind of Thing Sea-Witch Would Do. At some point gaygod11.png was discovered by those of us living inside her & has since become an important focus of Sea-Witchean studies, despite a great deal of controversy regarding its origin. As of the time this book is being written no one has asked Sea-Witch about it. If genuine, this photo documents a time when significant aspects of Sea-Witch's body had not yet emerged. It documents a body unfamiliar to those of us who know her now & share her body in the ways she has encouraged us to. A body unlike any we have seen.

I. Me & deadname found a ~~loophole~~ in the company's policy that allowed us to stay in the ~~motel~~ for years without paying with the pain of our bodies in labor. The ~~loophole~~ was that our room was haunted by the ghost of a very broken girl I once knew in my formation. The undead count as negative & the broke girl was double. So our room balanced out to unoccupied. Occasionally people tried to be booked there but we said boo and they left.

The girl didn't declare her presence, but I found deadname's eyes looked more like hers as time passed. I found xyr voice using her broken words, her accent. Not that this actually happened. Not to deadname anyway. I was the one being haunted, not xym. My ears, my eyes. I woke up in my bed neck deep in my old pain resurrected. More pain than the years of labor we would have paid from our bodies. I woke up in my bed & saw nothing but pain. I knew deadname was in here somewhere. The room kept changing sizes, but I could smell xyr hair through it all. *Xe hates you*, the broken girl whispered. I went inside the bathroom but found I wasn't tall enough to reach the medicine cabinet. I was smaller than the sink. I was sinking.

II. The ~~motel~~ became the center of our operations. We stayed there long term. Years or minutes, whichever is longer. *~We fell in love.~* We fell in love. I fell in love with deadname. Xe fell in love with me. So xe said. So xe said. I mean I believed xym. I mean Xe wanted me around. I mean I started feeling trapped. I mean I felt like xe was trapping me. Xe loved me. It reminded me of something. I loved xym. Xe reminded me of someone. I felt kidnapped. I would make xym sad if I left the ~~motel~~ without xym. Xe told me this. I think. I found xym passed out on the bathroom floor but that never happened. I called the paramedics & said the words *too many pills* but that never happened. This is too dramatic. *I'm sorry,* I told xym. I'm sorry. We loved each other. I loved xym. Xe was so gentle to me. Xe understood it, right? Xe always understood.

III. *It's my bone death*, I told xym. *It eats you. When you speak it eats your words.* I took my bone death out & held it in my arms. *You don't love me,* deadname told me. *Could you say that again,* I asked xym. *I said I love you,* xe said. *I'm having a hard time understanding you,* I said. *I hear things wrong.* I frowned. *You hate me,* deadname spat at me. I threw my bone death hard against the wall. *What the fuck is wrong with you,* the bone death said in deadname's voice. *We are going to have to pay for that,* I said. *It's okay,* deadname said. I picked my bone death up from the floor. It was swollen & tender. *I'm sorry,* I said through the buzzing in my skull. I said, *I guess I'm not sure who I'm talking to.*

IV. *We don't have to stay in the* ~~motel~~, deadname said. *Nobody said we had to stay in the* ~~motel~~.

V. The closet of the ~~motel~~ room was filled with weapons we hadn't seen before. All kinds. Powerful ones.

it's always both

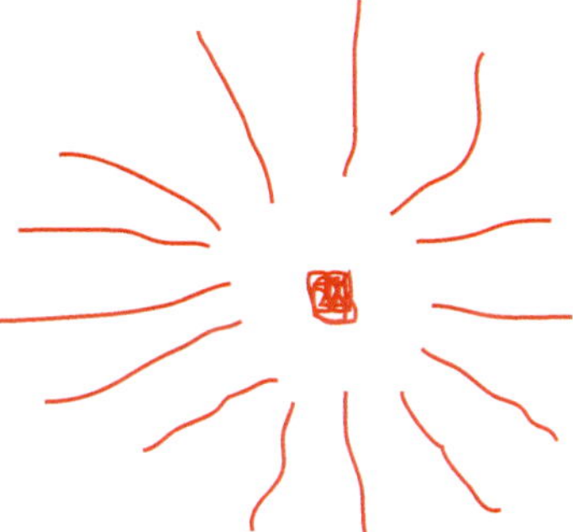

Choose a conceptual framework that works for you. Then, break it. Find its limits. Patch in another frame-work. Rip the stitches out and start over. Dance in the space between worlds.

-Jade of Spiders, facebook post

COSMIC
FUCK
AGENCY

When I got very old I cut the door in my chest open with a pen knife. There were eight copies of the sun in there. They moved in rhythm with one another. They were a building I created with my own hands. I remembered this like remembering a dream. I remembered two others helping me create this building. It was morning, we were out on a scaffolding, held up like a topless cage in the blue sky air. I never saw their faces because the sun was too bright. They told me I was awake, but I never saw their faces because sun was too bright. The eight copies in me burned in unison with the brightbright sun.

I moved into this body years ago but never decorated. Let's just say I am now making up for lost time. The other day I stabbed ink into my arm. "I cut my body into little suns," I wrote. I drew a gem on my finger to show my dedication to colored fragments of earth. I wrote the word "dead" on my thigh. I wrote the word "gay" on my foot. I drew a round line on my cheek & Sea-Witch asked me what it was for. I am holding space for myself there, I told her.

I want to explain something. I want to describe yet another limit of parseable language. Or perhaps a limit of legibility, which I am always afraid I am pushing. "I" as a word is meaningless to "me." I use it as convention, not description. The thing I call "I" is a mass, an undifferentiated bundle of fragments one could call selfhoods if they had ever formed fully. I have all the parts but the quantity is too great & the configuration is irregular. I do not know my wounds from my birthmarks. I do not know if there is a meaningful difference.

When I left Sea-Witch it was because she changed. She did not change in ~~real~~ life but she changed in how I saw her. The way my eyes directed the light reflecting off her to be organized in my brain was different from what it had been before. (SIDE NOTE: I am not sure how to tell if anything changes in ~~real~~ life. I can never find the edges.) The change that happened in the light from her was that it began to be organized in the form of a 78Man. I saw control in it. You will understand why I no longer felt I could let myself be contained by her, given the way this light established in my mind.

As I travelled farther from Sea-Witch the light all around me came to me in glimpses & reflections. It came in the form of 78Men & reflections of people in the corner of my sunglasses. I needed to change my head & the way it was organizing the light & so I tried to do so manually, with fast small tight fists. This made it worse. I tried to bite the flesh from my arm because my teeth were aching. A city was in the windows, moving quickly. A somewhere, somewhere city.

I saw you as a color in my mind that took up room there. I saw you watching but not speaking. I wandered if you also watched through this clumsy method of light organization or if you had a more reliable way. I wondered how your eyes moved when you had eyes. Or what aspect of you might be most analogous to eyes. I decided they were probably very pretty & I would probably very much like looking into them. ugh...

I took out the eight suns in me while I was on the train. I remembered how I built them. I set them in a row on the seat next to me & gathered them in my hands in a way that burned my skin. Monster skin is used to burning so this was no great issue. Witch skin is always being burned.

I began to fear that the people around me thought that I did not know what I was like. That they thought I was oblivious. But obliviousness is not something I am blessed with. I lack a normal dose of obliviousness. I know exactly what I am. I know exactly what I look like.

Questions for you, the color that is watching me now:

1. Do you like names?
2. Do you have any?
3. Where am I going?
4. Will I ever find rest or comfort in the world? Out of it?
5. Can I have some now?

I thought then of praying to Meteor ^(msluw) for comfort but then realized she was going to kill me. I realized I don't trust her. This felt sad, but I didn't know why. I'm not sure I had the energy to spend time fully understanding the things I was losing while in the midst of losing them. In fact, I am very sure I didn't.

In that space it was surprising how most types of understanding felt. Factual understanding, even of a fairly nuanced concept, came easily despite my panic. Emotional understanding or knowledge that requires memory felt like the greatest labor I could attempt to undertake.

Have I apologized for the tone of this yet? I don't know who I borrowed this voice from, the one I am trying to tell this story in, but like my body, I don't really have very strong feelings for it. Like my body, it is some borrowed, vibrating atoms that I am trying to twist to my own ends the best I can. I am making do with what I have.

In Sea-Witch there was a frame of wood like a cross, like a capital H with a long line through the middle, only turned on its side. It was deep in her organs, in fleshy parts most monsters tended to not bother exploring. It was lodged there deeply, the wood splintering into the organflesh in places. A few small living creatures had made their homes there. There was a being there, made entirely of witch-god scar tissue, but ze didn't want to talk. I didn't blame hir.

Anyway I was remembering that discovery on the train as I held my suns. I was remembering that scar tissue person & the look on hir face when ze saw me.

I put my suns back inside myself & felt bad. Suns should probably have something to orbit them.

I held the light that was held in me inside my skin long after it initially got to be there. This light came from the eight suns in me, it came from a feeling of longing that had to do with how we understand each other as monsters when we meet. When I meet another monster I understand her as myself. I understand her with my limbs & torso. We can understand each other with or without clothes.

The Book of Meteor has a section on the meeting of monsters but it has no section on the meeting of monsters & men, for the meeting of monsters among ourselves is a holy act & the meeting of men with monsters is an act of survival. Men Who Cause Pain can cause it less or more. Men Who Cause Pain are not beyond currying favor. Men Who Cause Pain might give this favor in less pain or in the form of invisible numbers called "money" that is the same as less pain but is less direct. Sometimes it is more direct. All meetings of men & monsters are a bargain like this. Some are more explicit than others.

When I was living in Sea-Witch I met many monsters & the monsters met me, in ones or twos, sometimes in fives or eights. We did holy things with each others bodies that created a light in me. An angel is a being who creates light or dark & lives outside of time & legibility. I am sometimes an angel.

When I speak to another monster sometimes to meet and/or to do something holy she is busy or she understands my words to be something they are not. There is a bad feeling going around Sea-Witch that causes monsters to not hear each other but instead hear the voices of the 78 Men. I have this feeling & so do so many others I knew, including Sea-Witch herself. It is difficult with this feeling to know whether you have it or whether the monsters around you have it but this is a false separation. It is always both.

When I left Sea-Witch, I left Sea-Witch running, naked, my clothes gathered in my arms. Trust is what we breathe in Sea-Witch & we have to breathe it not to drown in her sea, which is always everywhere, which does not remain neatly under our beds, which finds no space not to be. When I left Sea-Witch I could not breathe. When I left Sea-Witch, I left Sea-Witch because I had run out of trust.

I do not know when the trust shortage happened but I suspect it was the feeling. I suspect it was the cops. I suspect it was the other monsters in Sea-Witch. I suspect it was Sea-Witch herself. I suspect it was Meteor (may she fucking lay us waste), I suspect it was Dog-Witch who is dead, I suspect it was the angels, I suspect it was the living creatures, I suspect it was the ground & the ocean in collaboration or not, I suspect it was the cold nørth wind, I suspect it was the shape I have been forced to maintain to present myself to the world, I suspect it was the world I have been forced to live in, I suspect it was the 78 god damn fucking Men Who Cause Pain & last of all & perhaps most of all, I suspect it was myself.

Running out of trust can be the source of a great deal of suspecting, & I did it with every part of me, endlessly, until I hurt with it.

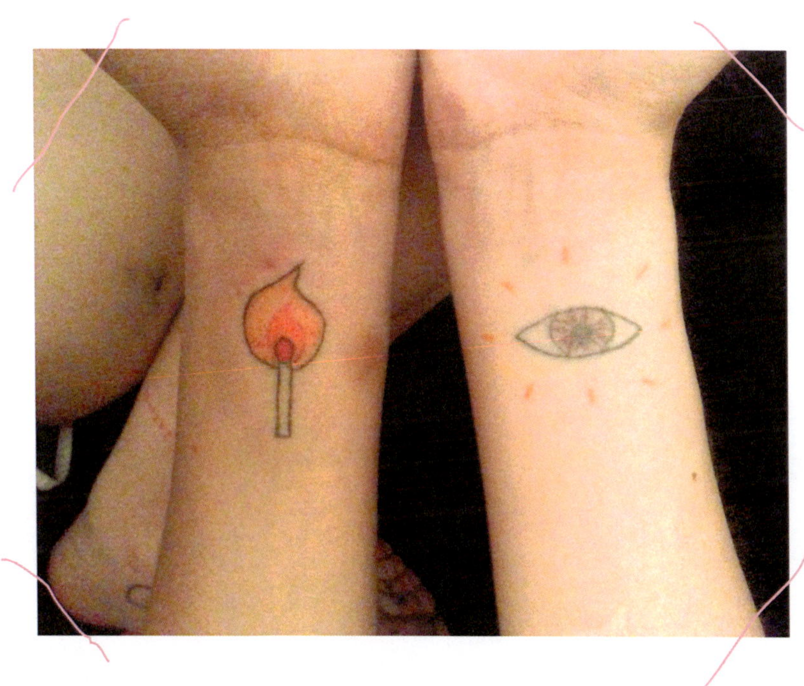

her name
is resistance

you're from the sea.
I know that it's lovely there.
I have also known bare breast
against wave crest
and the glow of buoyancy
when the wild water holds holds holds
this world does not let go
so easily

- Loone, "Silky"

I HAVE EATEN MY OWN BODY TOO MANY TIMES. I HAVE EATEN MY OWN BODY TOO MANY

TIMES. I HAVE EATEN MY OWN BODY TOO MANY TIMES I HAVE EATEN MY OWN BODY TOO MANY TIMES & IT REMAINS WEAK & SORE FROM THE EATING.

This is ~~the~~ an inspection into the world of people & men.

When people are early in formation they are stripped of all power & freedom. In fact, rarely is an early-formation person seen not inside a padded cage or strapped into something. The 78 Men Who Cause Pain have convinced people that very young people should be surrounded by people who have absolute power over them at all times. They have convinced them that regular doses of Pain should be administered strategically to create control from the very first. As they get older & begin to hold the 78 Men Who Cause Pain's systems of power inside their own bodies & minds, people can be allowed more things meant to resemble freedom. The cages are moved inside the body. This is called "parenting". It is considered "love".

& sometimes it almost is

Long ago, in the days of the nineteen sisters, Dog-Witch met & fell in love with a piece of information ze couldn't understand. Ze first encountered this piece of information in a video clip ze came across on the internet. In the video, the piece of information was playing her banjo in a tunnel in a park in the pacific northwest somewhere. The light moved across the piece of information's hands as she played.

Dog-Witch went to visit the piece of information at her home some months later. They fucked in the kind of way where there wasn't a clear beginning or end. There was fucking & there was not-fucking & the not-fucking was just a sort of liminal space that seemed simultaneously a coming-down-from & a leading-up-to the next session of fucking. *I could do this all day*, Dog-Witch told the piece of information, & the piece of information looked at the clock & replied, *I think we pretty much already have.*

The times when they were not together, Dog-Witch found hirself thinking about the piece of information constantly. Ze found hirself exploring its edges with hir mind & remembering the smell of her clothes. Ze found hirself wanting to create something beautiful, something inspired by the piece of information.

In those days Dog-Witch had formed hir many sisters & sent them out to live among the living creatures of the world. Ze had encouraged them to exist among, within & around all time & space. Ze lived hirself outside of time to an extent, though ze knew hir own death would someday come & bind hir self & hir body to time in certain ways.

Dog-Witch began to look at the world through hir love for the piece of information. Ze saw it as a place that had many good things & a place where much harm had come to exist. This was early in the reign of the 78 Men Who Cause Pain & monsters were beginning to die by the thousands, slain by manipulation, by power & control. Dog-Witch saw this & brought lava into hir own body. Ze used hir leg & fresh lava & water from the most frozen thing she could find to create a new entire being, accidentally capable of true emotion. Ze created beautiful Sea-Witch then as a shelter for all monsters from pain & slaying. Ze created her in an attempt to have one thing in the world that could exist as pure good. Ze created her with the full force of hir love for the piece of information. Ze created her entirely apart & inside of time from a holy need to protect & love above all things. This is how Sea-Witch came to be in the world as a place we could live. This is how Sea-Witch came out into the world made wholly of gay magic & unimagined song. Sea-Witch exists as a fresh consuming fire. She is a nucleus of good. Her name is resistance.

What is it like to be a thing that was built to exist as pure good? Ask Sea-Witch. She has a face like slimywet wood & the words "false purity" tattooed across her too-many knuckles. She did the tattooing herself when she was a girl-god. Back then she used to hang out with a witch-god named Moss-Witch who was one of Dog-Witch's sisters. Moss-Witch had a warm house with a soft bed & sharp needles for writing beneath your own skin. Moss-Witch knew all the coolest bands & had art all over the walls that she had made herself. *The fucking thing,* Moss-Witch would say, *about art is that it is mostly a bunch of gay shit. Which is basically the best.* Sea-Witch would come to Moss-Witch's house when she needed a break from attempting to be a being of pure good. Which was pretty much always.

Did you hear about the girl who fried & ate her own testicles? Moss-Witch asked Sea-Witch. *Pan-seared. I was gonna do the same when I got mine cut off. I lied to the doctor, saying I needed to have them for religious reasons, well, not entirely lied. I think eating my own balls would automatically be a spiritual act. Anyway, I told him I was orthodox fundamentalist something or other & then I find out that I'm getting them in formaldehyde. Poisonous. So much for that. I made earrings instead.*

I want to throw mine into the sea. Like Uranus, Sea-Witch said. Moss-Witch beamed at this, but Sea-Witch didn't notice, as she was focused on putting the finishing touches on a hand tattoo. It was a very tiny, detailed portrait of a girl who was the most alone person in the world. It showed just the head & shoulders, but you could tell from the look in her eyes that she wanted to die because of how utterly alone she felt. Sea-Witch finished her eyebrow & showed the completed project to her friend. *She looks like you,* Moss-Witch said.

homo

(sorry)

(me too)

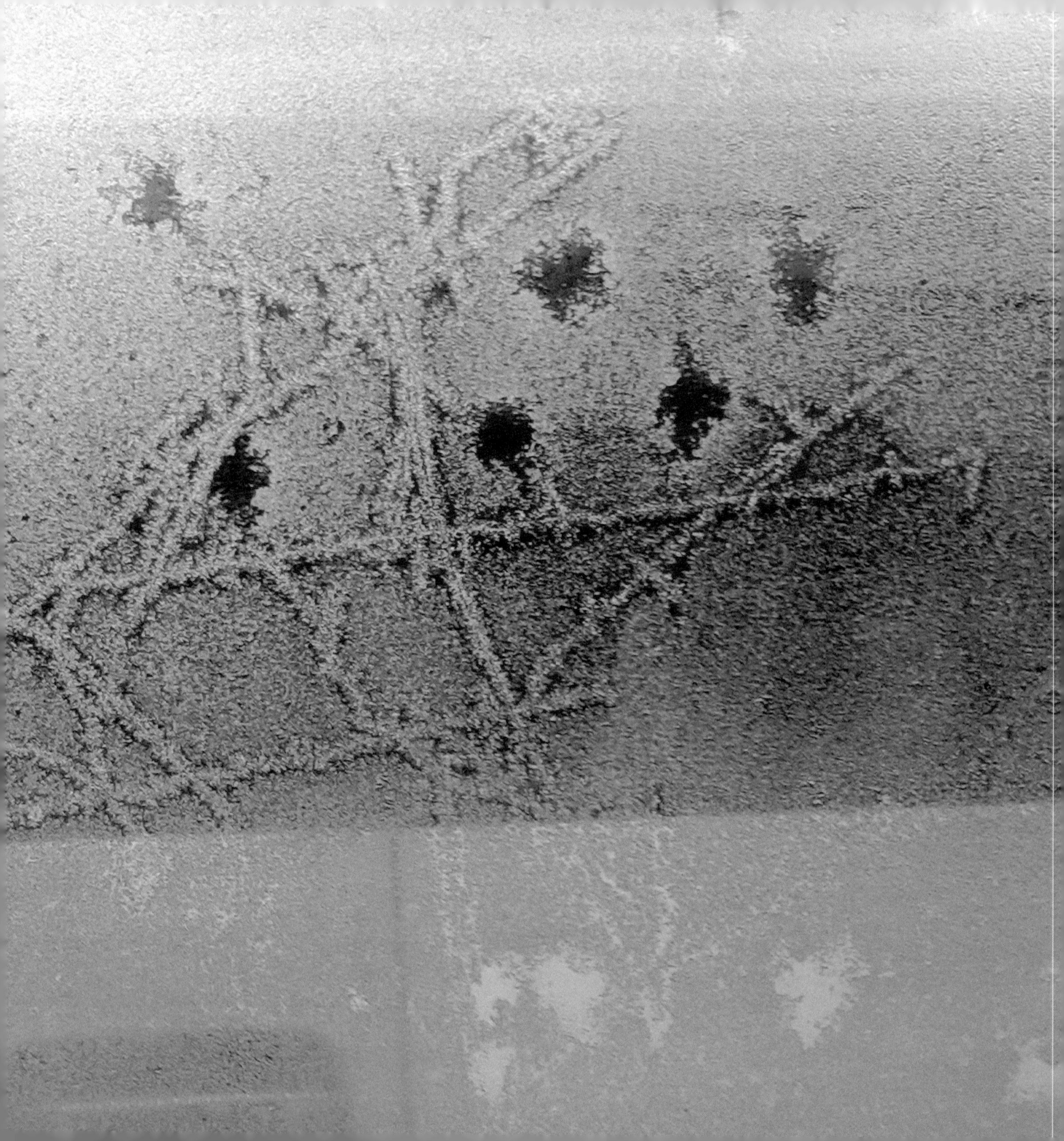

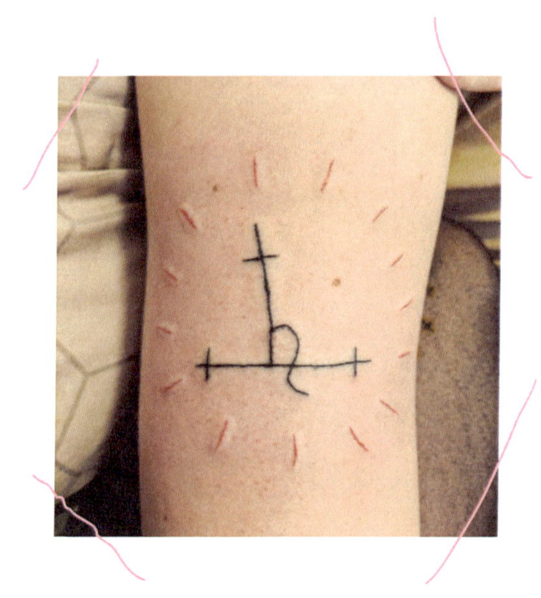

i've got something burned in the back of my mind
it's a name or a word or a couplet of rhyme
that tells me why i'm here and what i'm doing
but i can't read it it's always moving

-Ada Rook, "Graceless"

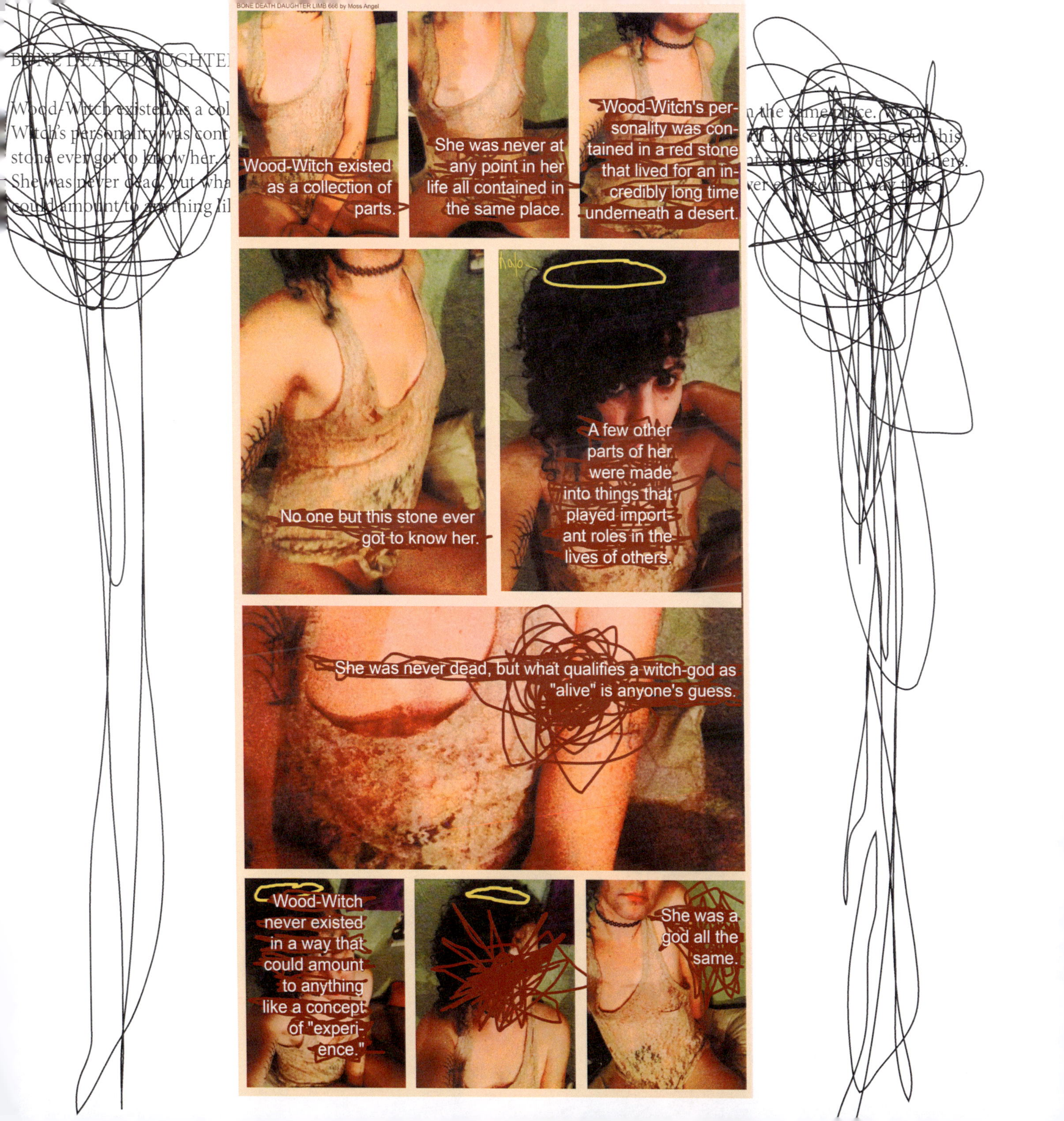

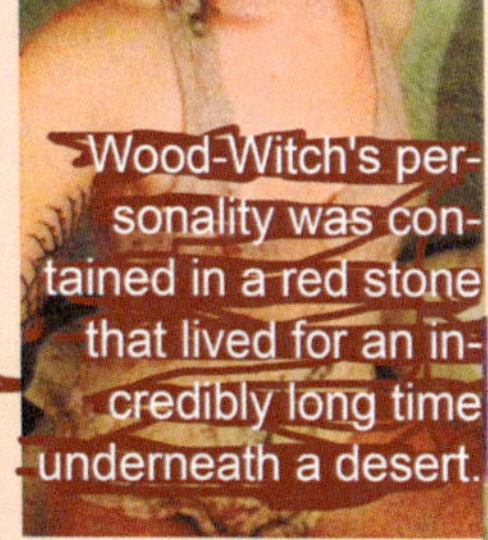
Wood-Witch existed as a collection of parts.
She was never at any point in her life all contained in the same place.
Wood-Witch's personality was contained in a red stone that lived for an incredibly long time underneath a desert.

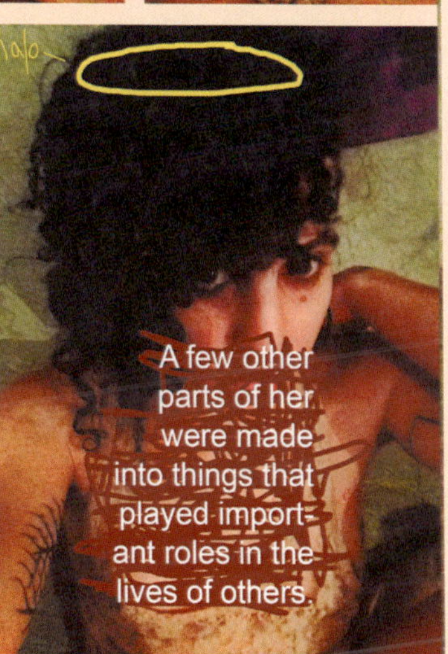
No one but this stone ever got to know her.
A few other parts of her were made into things that played important roles in the lives of others.

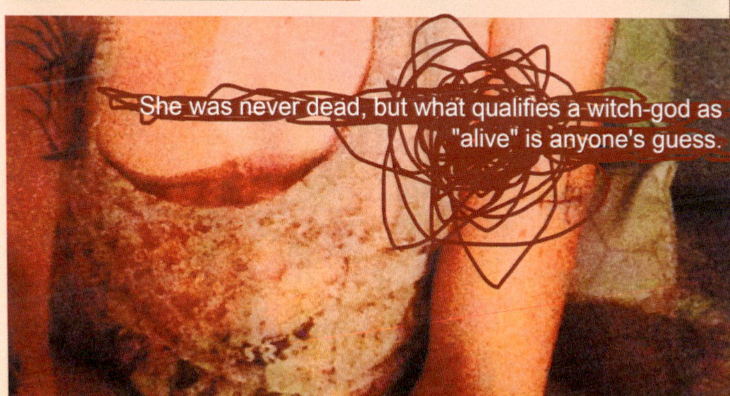
She was never dead, but what qualifies a witch-god as "alive" is anyone's guess.

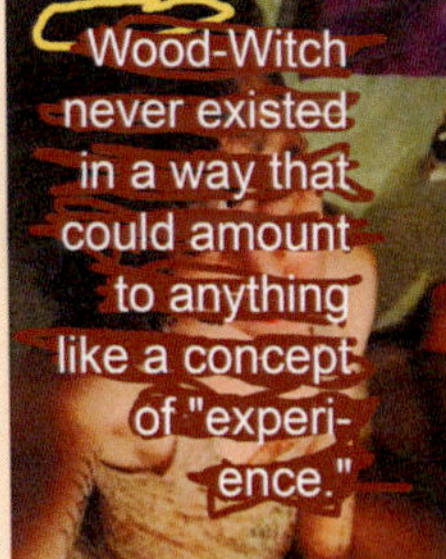
Wood-Witch never existed in a way that could amount to anything like a concept of "experience."

She was a god all the same.

The 78 Men Who Cause Pain are not always 78 in number. The 78 Men Who Cause Pain are not always men. The 78 Men Who Cause Pain are not formed like monsters or born like people. Instead they are machined perfectly, identical despite meaningless physical differences. They are designed to efficiently execute the will of the ghost mind that rides the spaces between them. They hold individual responsibility only in the way a single cell in a brain or ant in a colony holds individual responsibility for the consequences of the actions created by a collective. The ghost in the spaces is self-healing, self-made, self-growing. It is emergence. It acts only in its own interests & only to maintain & extend its control. The 78 Men themselves are a collection of nothings. Prefab vectors in the shape of individual beings. You can see it in their eyes.

The 78 Men Who Cause Pain exist accidentally at the top of a malicious hierarchy, but they, like all beings they influence, have a seed of submission within them. Each 78Man was once a child, & being a child under the influence of the 78 Men Who Cause Pain is to exist in a state of absolute control. It is to be programmed to submit to the will of the ghost in the spaces.

The nature of the ghost in the spaces is barely anything to speak of. It is a simple algorithm that converts life into pain. There is nothing meaningful to be found at its heart. It has no heart. It must be killed fully or not at all. When I was living in Sea-Witch all of this was common knowledge. We will pray it to death. We will die alongside it if necessary.

"I have no idea how long I have lived within your body now. Long enough to be very used to it. Comfortable."

"I'm accustomed to you as well."

"If I were to leave it would be very difficult to adapt to living apart from you."

"I love you too."

"There are a lot of stories about this."

"We could write a new one."

"Are you in love with anyone else?"

"I am in love with everyone else."

"Me too."

"You can stay with me as long as you need to. As long as you want to."

"I love you too."

"Let's go away together."

"We already are away together."

"Let's go awayer."

"I'll chart a course."

"I'll go dream something."

"Don't leave me."

"I love you too."

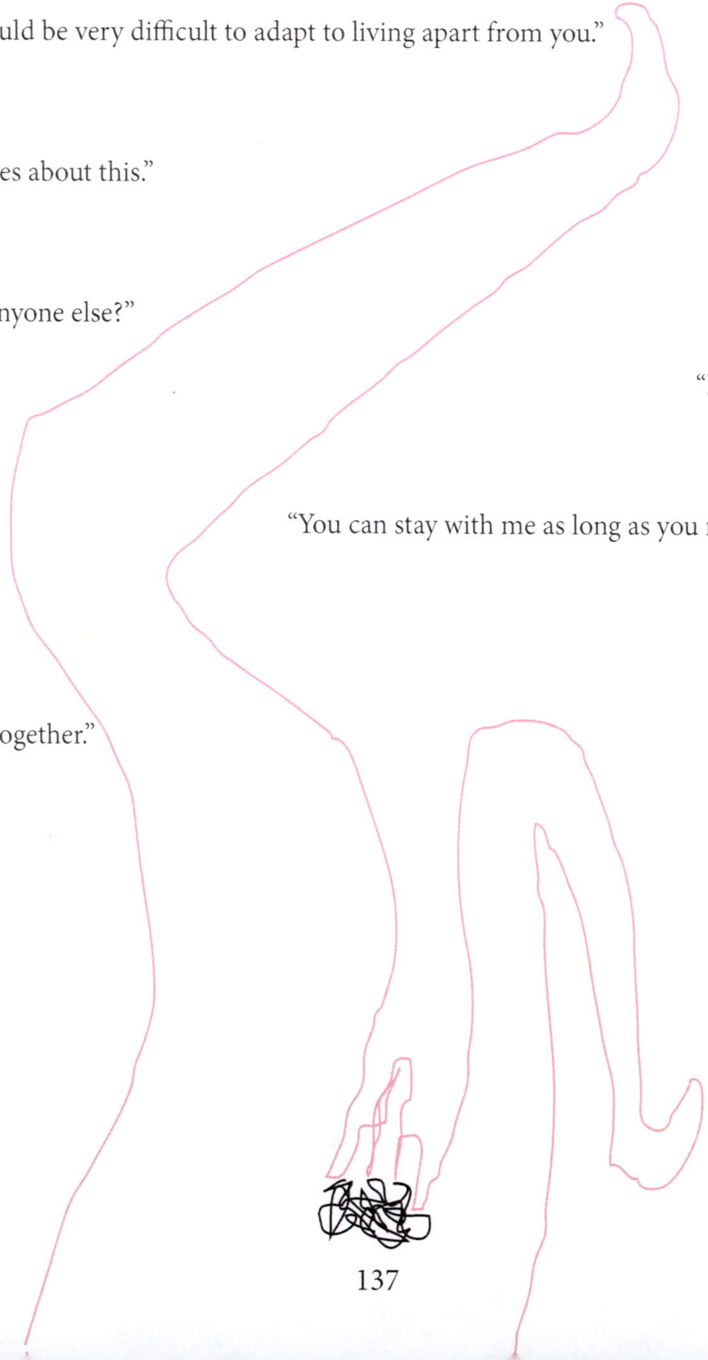

NEVER
LEAVE

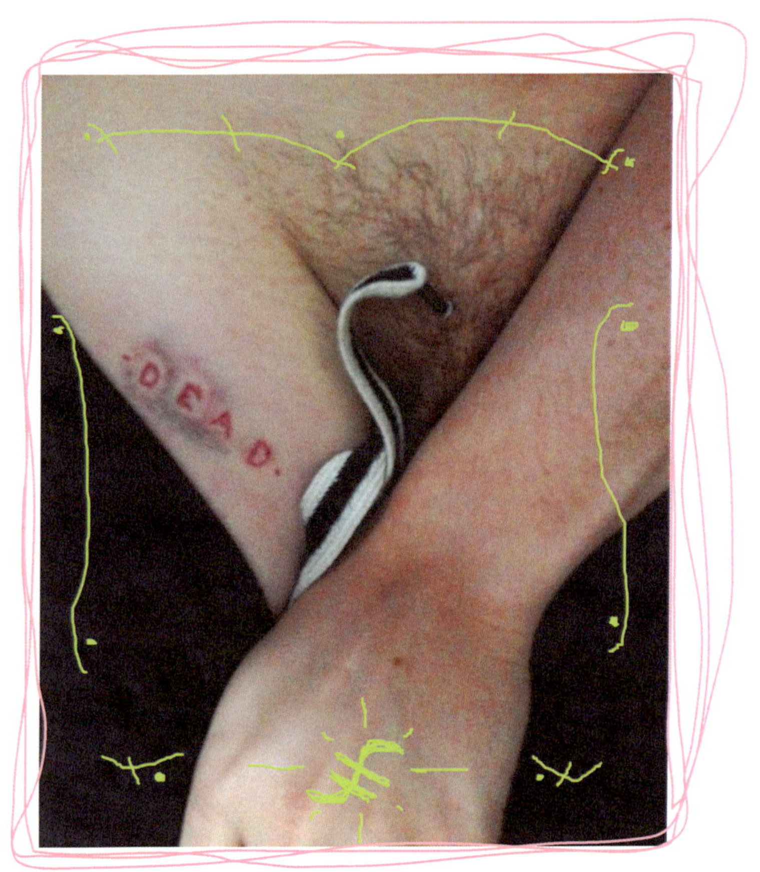
DEAD.

You already know the game plan. Just relax and let it happen. Let the future fuck you like a good little slut.

-Jade of Spiders, *Time-Station 81*

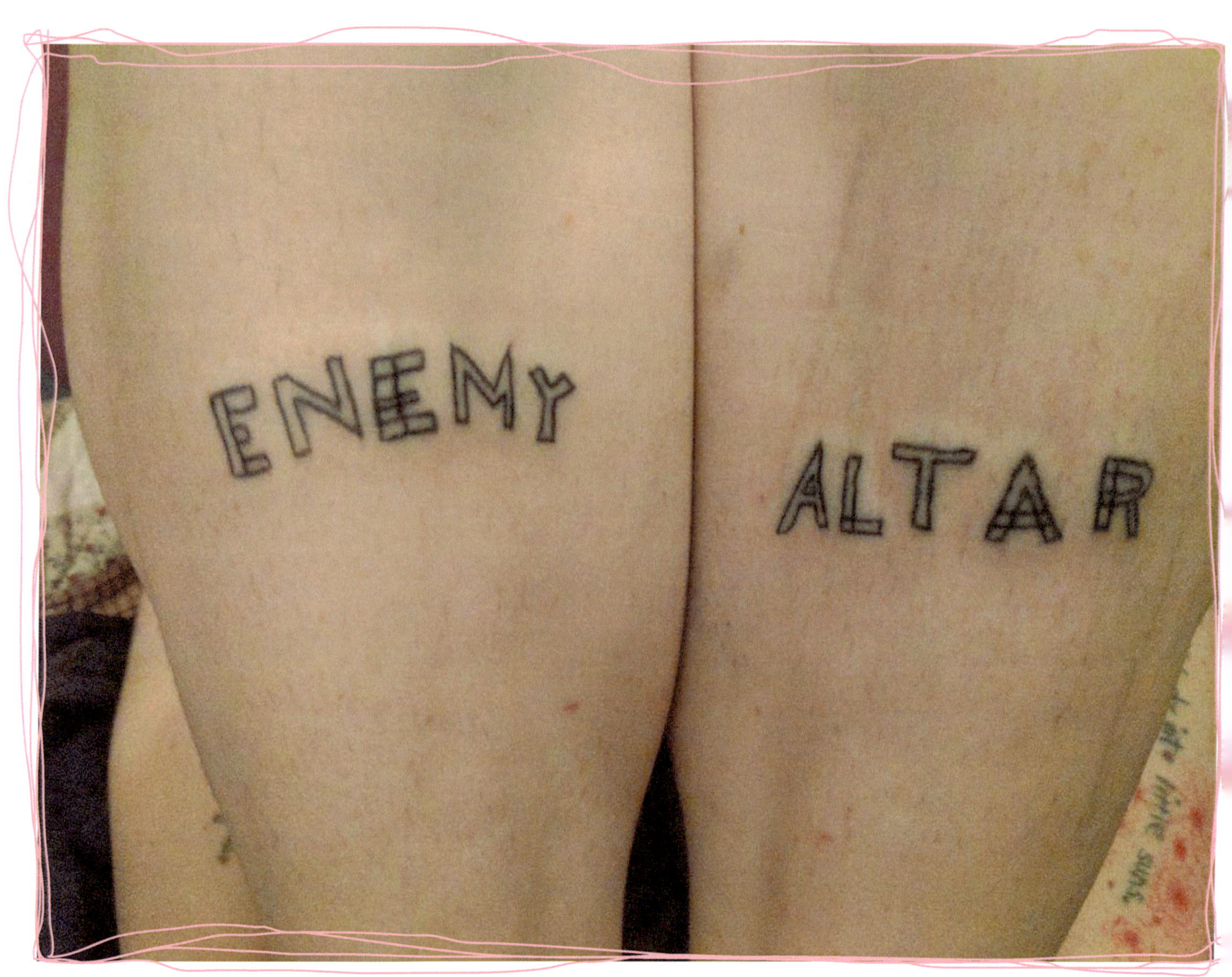

ENEMy
ALTAR

The end of a thing might not feel like an ending. It can be abrupt or drag on. Water-Witch felt like her whole life was part of a movie that should have been over a long time ago. The plot had arced & things had long since been tied up & she was an unnecessary character. This wasn't true, though. Most of us don't know what our own story really is.

Water-Witch met Strawberry-Witch when she was working on a pot farm in California. This was after it had been legalized & the two of them were both doing trimming work there. Water-Witch thought Strawberry-Witch was adorable & immediately said so. Strawberry-Witch, who always loved a compliment, began giving Water-Witch all kinds of attention.

One day while they were working alongside each other, they heard cries from far away. The other workers went to see what was happening & so Water-Witch & Strawberry-Witch joined them. About an acre of land next door to the pot farm had fallen into the ground, leaving an enormous crater & a giant cloud of dust. A little girl was in the middle, leg clearly broken & people were trying to save her, though the edge of the crater kept crumbling every time anyone got close.

A neighbor saw Strawberry-Witch & Water-Witch & recognized them for what they were. "You! Witch-Gods! Help this girl!"

Water-Witch looked at her feet. Strawberry-Witch tried to explain. "We can't. We can barely do anything."

The other pot workers agreed. Water-Witch & Strawberry-Witch were some of the worst workers on the farm. "What are you good for, then? What is a god, anyway?" the neighbor asked.

The little girl died. They couldn't get her out of the pit, & the edges kept crumbling. Water-Witch & Strawberry-Witch held hands & cried. The crater stayed a crater. Others began to emerge in the area as well. There was apparently a system of caverns beneath the whole region that decided now was the time to collapse. Everyone felt the instability. Strawberry-Witch & Water-Witch began sleeping in the same bed. They did holy things with their clits & asses & mouths & held each other with their arms & legs. They kept each other safe as much as they knew how. They did a ceremony for the little girl, which was really a ceremony mourning their inability to save her. They were not the kind of gods who could save anyone & this thought made them feel as unstable as the ground they walked on.

Strawberry-Witch eventually went back to where she had lived before. Water-Witch cried & hugged her & they made plans to meet again. Water-Witch continued to work at the farm for the next few weeks. During that time her evenings got strange. She was very, very lonely. The loneliness was a fist in her chest that wouldn't unclench.

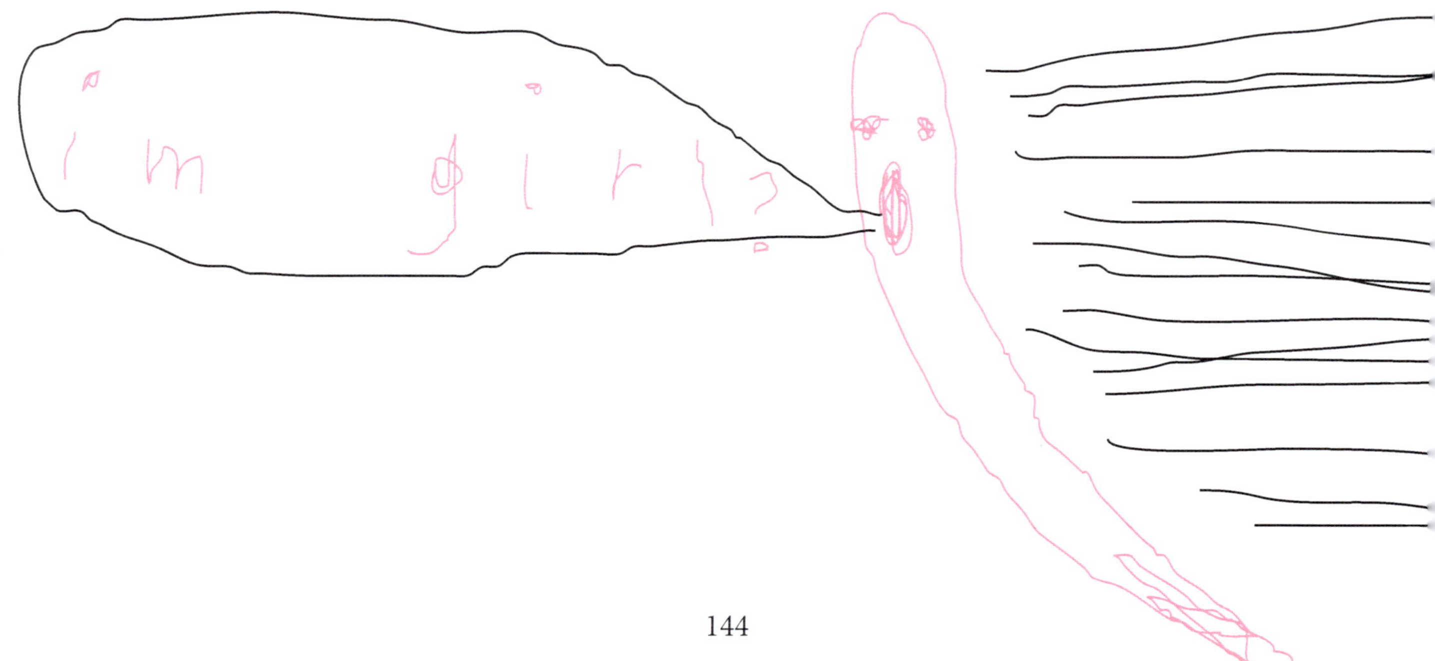

Water-Witch stayed at the pot farm until they told her to leave, so she packed her things & drove to her sister's house. Her sister wasn't home. The back door was unlocked so she went inside. Where the living room couch usually would be there was a banana slug the size of the living room couch. Everything else was just as she remembered it. Don't leave me, the slug said, twitching. *I am so sorry*, said Water-Witch. *But I have to. I don't have anything for you.*

Water-Witch drove on to the coast. Reality got thicker. She realized she was trying to create any feeling inside of herself other than fear. She killed herself in her mind over & over. Why am I even here, she thought. This is all hurt. At the beach there were thorns that stuck in her tights. The whole planet spun slowly. It's not important or interesting. Death as a stopping place. She felt her tights rip. They were already covered in sand. The world is dying & nothing can help it, she thought. How am I a whole person. I can't do anything at all. I'm barely here as it is. There was sand in her mouth. When you squeeze any skin hard enough the sun comes out. It's my fault. What if it could be over in a way that's no big deal. It's not important. A stopping place. It started to rain/it got too cold/she walked to the car shivering. This isn't because of anything.

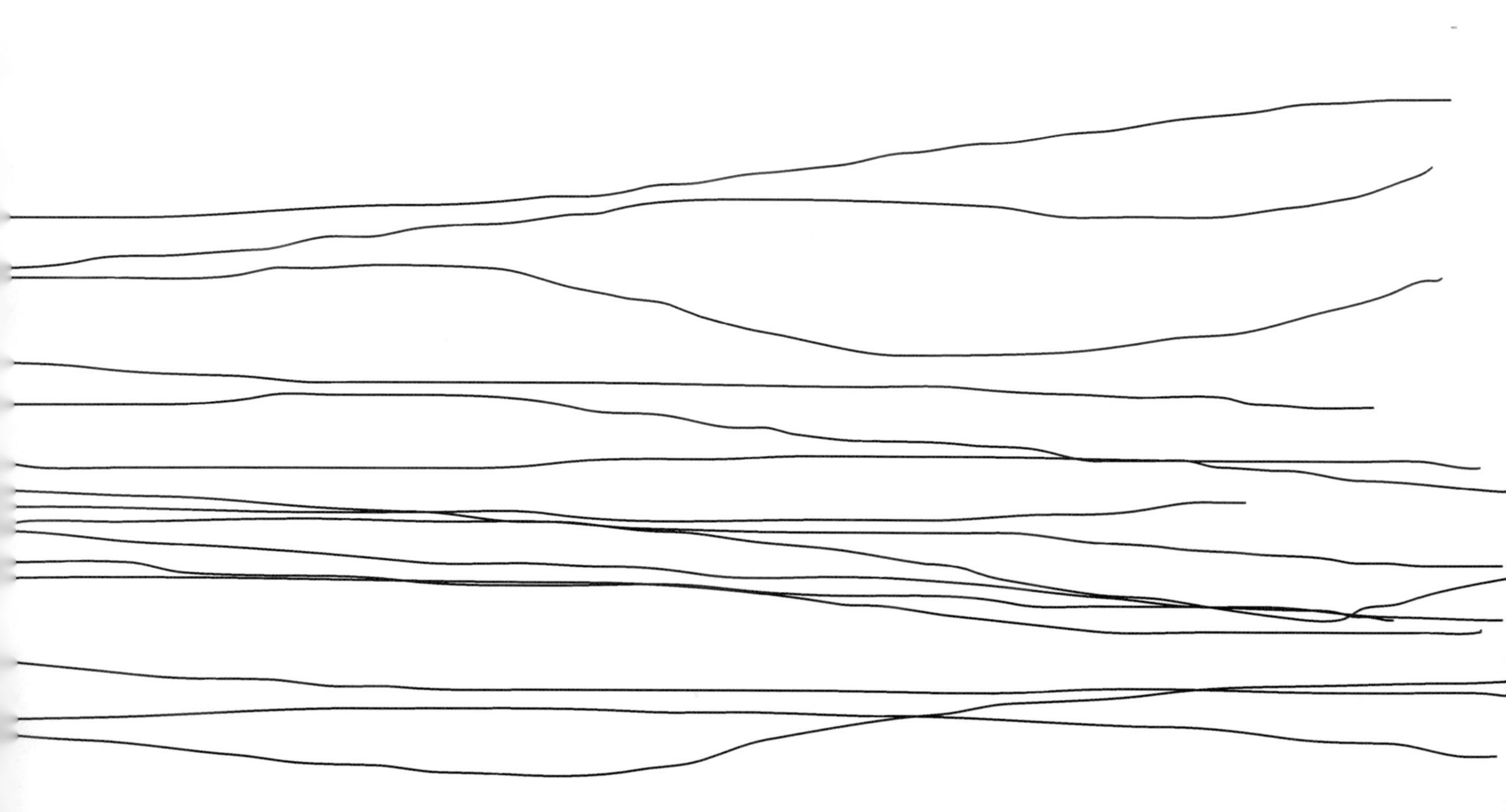

Water-Witch's least favorite thing about herself is that she keeps waking up. Mornings were actually the easiest time, but after awhile it all piled together. Mornings slid into afternoons, slid into evenings, slid into times when everyone was sleeping & "cold" became an immersive physical/psychological experience. Water-Witch learned what to do to make time move slow or fast but never figured out how to make it go away. No matter how much time passed, there was always more of it. Water-Witch thought it was kind of fucked up, honestly.

Water-Witch decided to call Strawberry-Witch on the phone. Water-Witch cried to her. She said she missed her, & that things had been terrible. She told her about the bottomless feeling, the doom that wouldn't wash off. How it settled in after dark. How dark kept coming earlier as winter came. Strawberry-Witch was so sweet. She made plans to see Water-Witch again. They talked of doing things together & for a second Water-Witch thought she could be a person, but the phone call ended & Water-Witch found herself staring at her hands again, flexing her fingers, imagining her skull splitting on concrete.

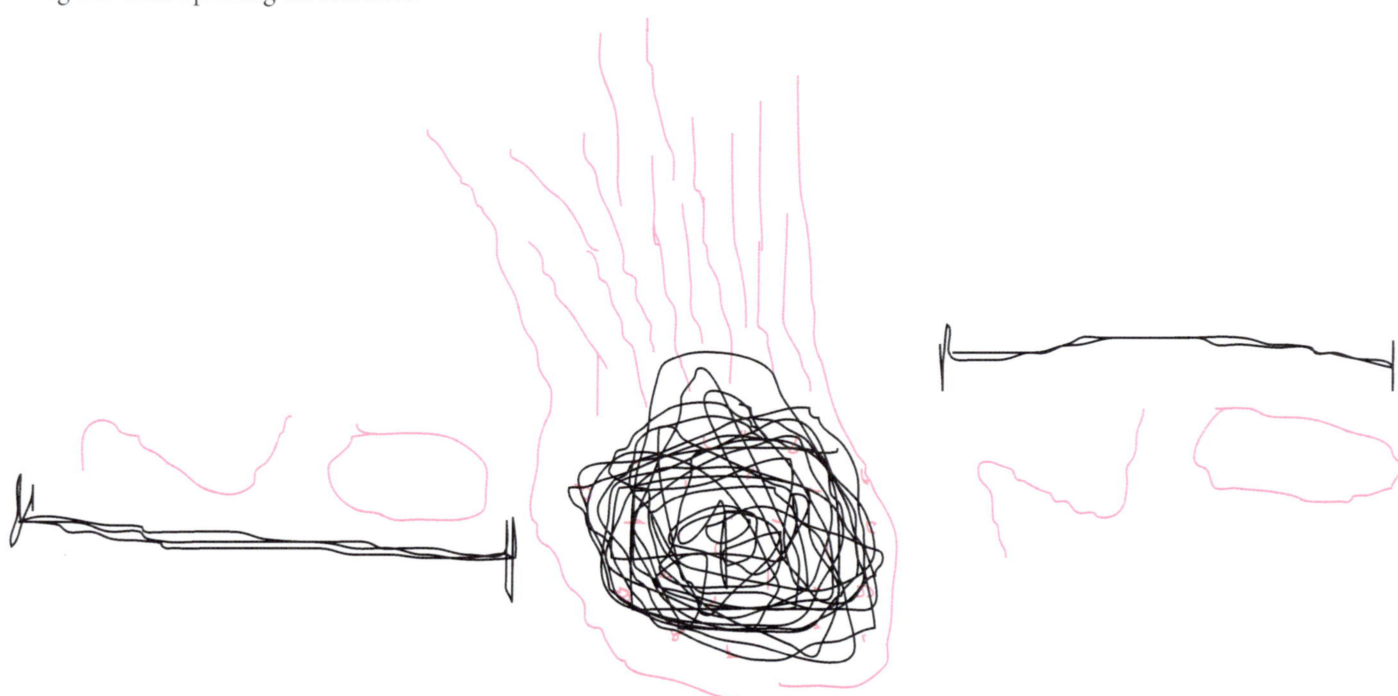

Untitled (Portrait of Cans in the Woods)

if you need help go get it

do u need help?

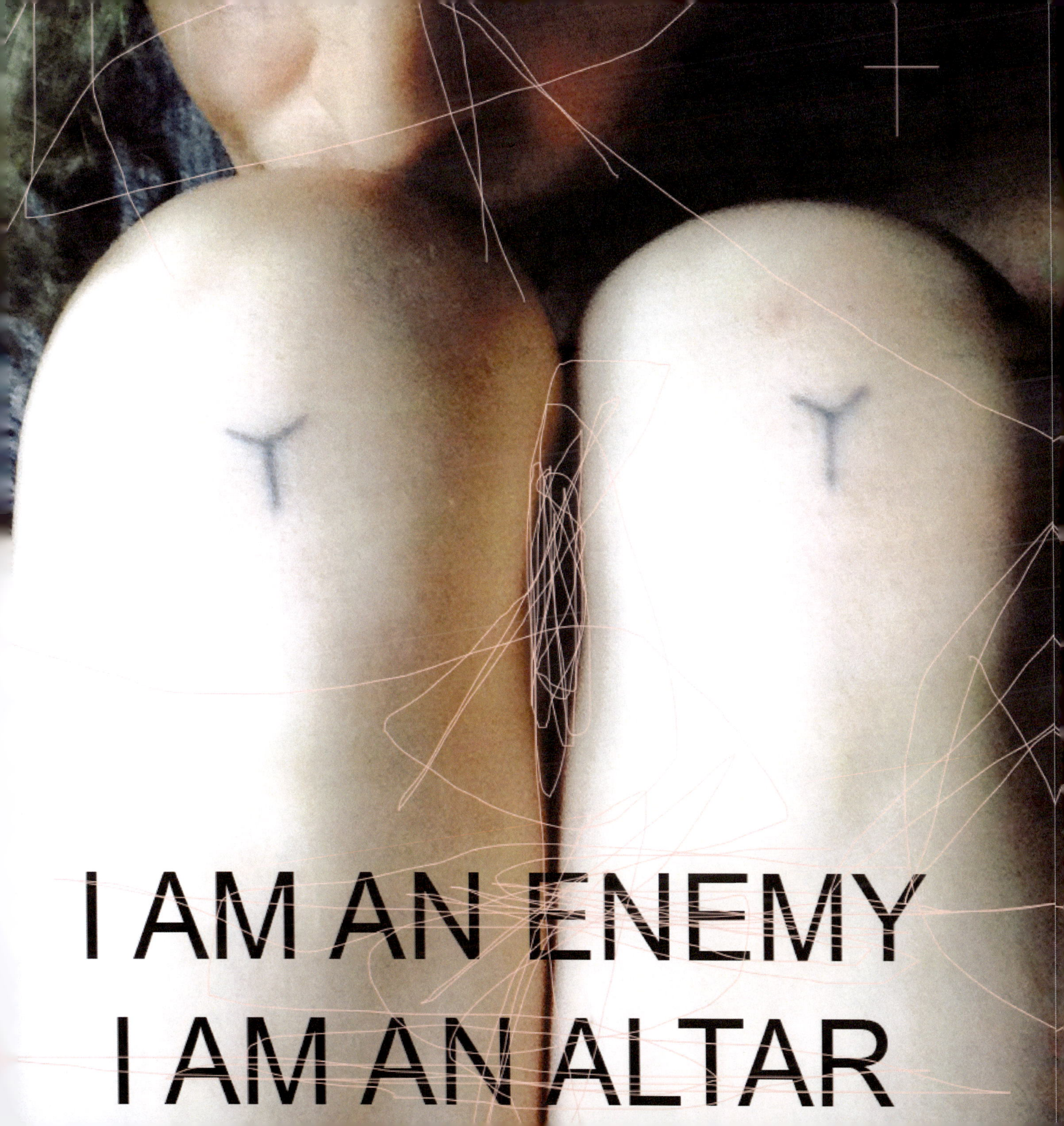

I AM AN ENEMY
I AM AN ALTAR

The real world is only tenable when you bother to touch it. Subjecting oneself to the real world is like signing up to be a victim.

-M Kitchell, *Hour of the Wolf*

I don't care about real life. I don't care about real life.

-Death Grips, "I Break Mirrors with My Face in the United States"

LIFE

I am so tired about Sea-Witch. I miss her dearly & want to hold her. At the same time I cannot assume that the disease that changed my brain & made me leave has gone. I want to help heal her. I want to heal myself.

I am living now inside the arms of a bright warmth that lets me live. She is like Sea-Witch in many ways. She might be Sea-Witch. When I was living in Sea-Witch reality was fluid, as was time. I am still in Sea-Witch & so I call this bright warmth "Sea-Witch" even though I have left her. Still I miss her & my time there. The following is a list of feelings I have had recently:

1. The feeling of being hunted.
2. The feeling of being the one hunting me.
3. A ball of cold metal inside my stomach that expands irregularly, points of which rupture some organs & just barely pierce my skin.
4. Standing on a beach while comforting someone in mourning.
5. Harm. Direct, ruthless harm.
6. A huge bird eating a building.
7. Being inside that building while it was eaten. Continuing what you were doing anyway.
8. A sweet animal putting its chin on my leg. Touching the animal. Feeling her fur.
9. Being completely naked in a room entirely full of soft cotton.
10. Last night I buried my head six inches deep in a wood floor.
11. Feeling the ache of that injury the next morning. Vomiting.

The bright warmth wants to go with me. She holds me in my fits. I hold her back. I still pray to Meteor [(msluw)] sometimes, but these days I find myself praying for thanks as much as for destruction. Whenever I pray like this Meteor [(idk anymore)] prays back & tells me that it was not her doing. *My power is limited*, she prays. *I'm kind of a one trick pony.*

Moss-Witch knows the whole room around her is too big. Everything in it is too big. It's all too close to her face. Empty delivery food containers. A phone that is modern, new, but echos deeply some nearly forgotten piece of technology from her childhood. *What is it*, she thinks. She stares at the phone until it too becomes too close to her face & she has to look away. *My whole life has been like this*, she thinks. *Why does it still feel strange?*

I am an enemy. I am an altar. *Don't forget me.* Never leave.

Moss-Witch has to take a shit. She walks to where her body takes her for this & sits. The room zooms in & out arbitrarily. *This is so tired. I'm so tired of this*, she thinks. The word *landmarks* emerges in her brain & she tries to use it to create an escape, back into something she can feel confident about. But she abandons it when she thinks about other times she has been confident. Those times were embarrassing. She clears her mind & feels distinctly three feelings in quick succession: nostalgia, comfort, claustrophobia. She sticks it out for three more (fatigue, tingling & deep sadness) before she wipes, stands, flushes. *What the fuck*, she says out loud.

I am an enemy. I am an altar. *Don't forget me.* Never leave.

She closes her eyes & feels the sensation of other people being in the room. *Did I just shit in front of other people?* She panics briefly. Was that a chair or a toilet. She opens her eyes & checks. Toilet. Good. Safe. She exhales. The reactions of the people who aren't there echo in her mind.

I am an enemy. I am an altar. *Don't forget me.* Never leave.

MORE THAN
ANYTHING
MONSTERS
WANT TO BE
ALLOWED TO
LIVE & BE OKAY

"There is a sweetness here. Something I want to stay inside."

"I always want to stay inside."

"Not like that. I want to leave."

"Don't leave."

"Not like that."

"..."

"Not like that."

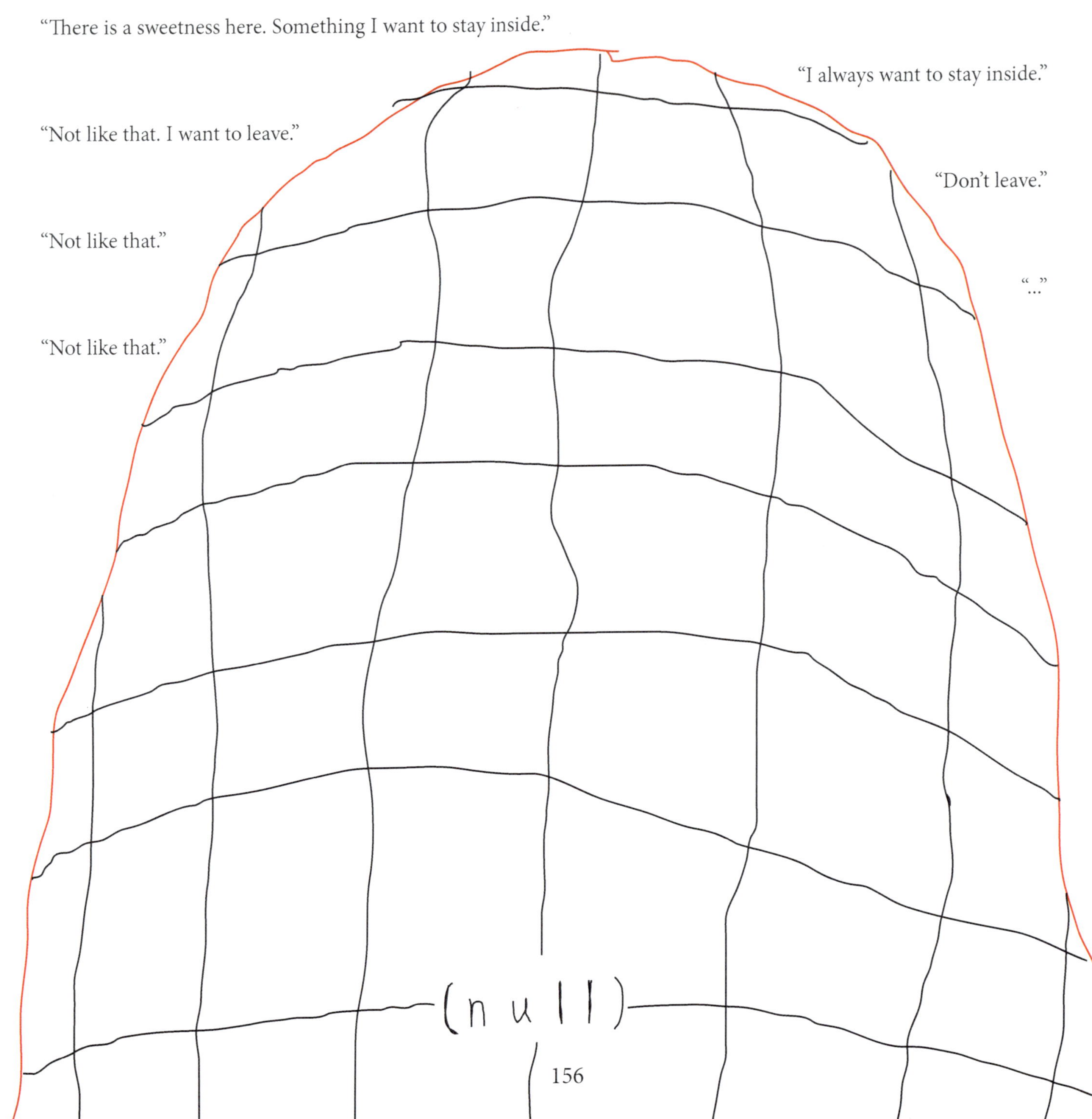

In Sea-Witch everyone is tired. The monsters here sigh deeply & shrug their monster shoulders. We have heard tales that once we built monuments & discovered amazing things. That we once created beautiful, impossible works of art but these things have become damaged & lost across the centuries. Now living is done barely, & each day is spent attempting to get to the next. There is no sense of future, the past is painful to think of. We think of the long time they have ahead of them & despair. *Where is our culture*, we moan. *Where are the monsters we used to be, who could build, grow & thrive?* They are lost to us. We have not lost our love for each other, but it is always under threat as we have been hurt so often that we can no longer find the source. Today is a day, & soon it will end & be followed by another. We celebrate nothing. We organize nothing. We are nothing. What will become of us. May she lay us waste, we pray. May our ashes & bones fertilize the soil for lives better than ours. Lives that might be abundant with what we lack. With promise. With capability.

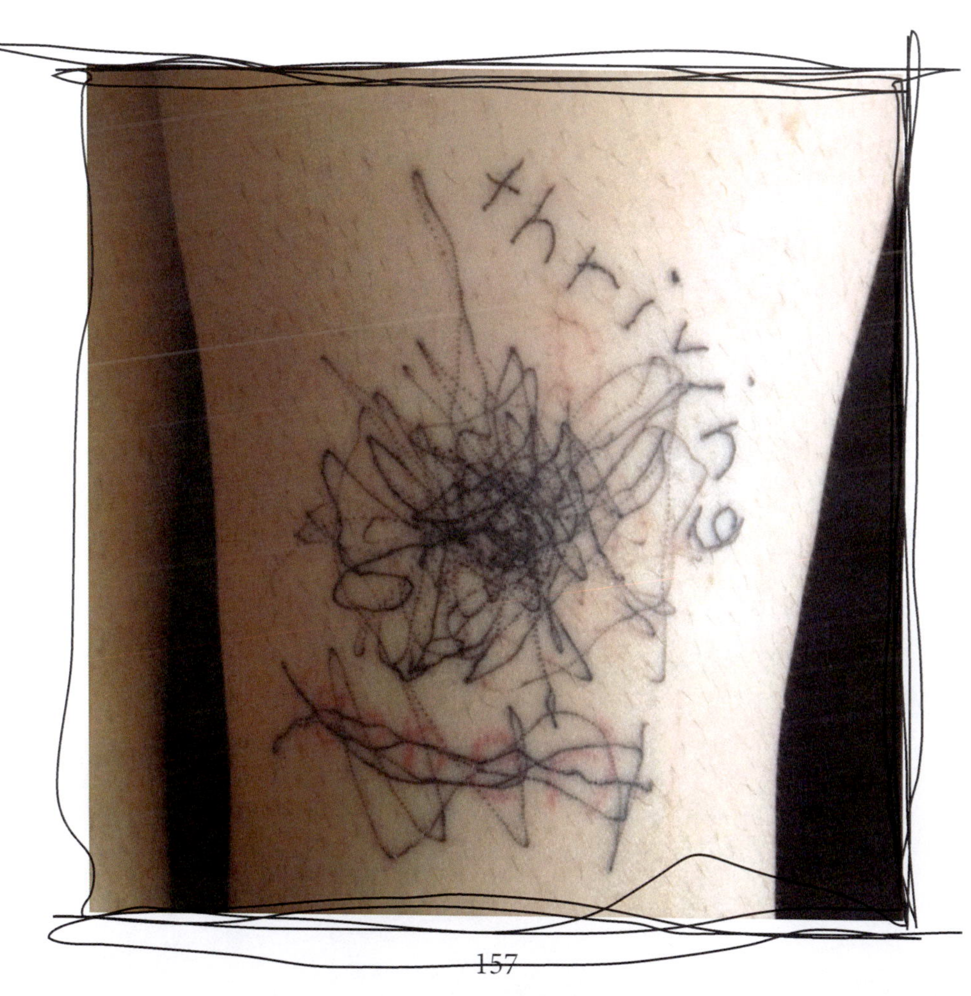

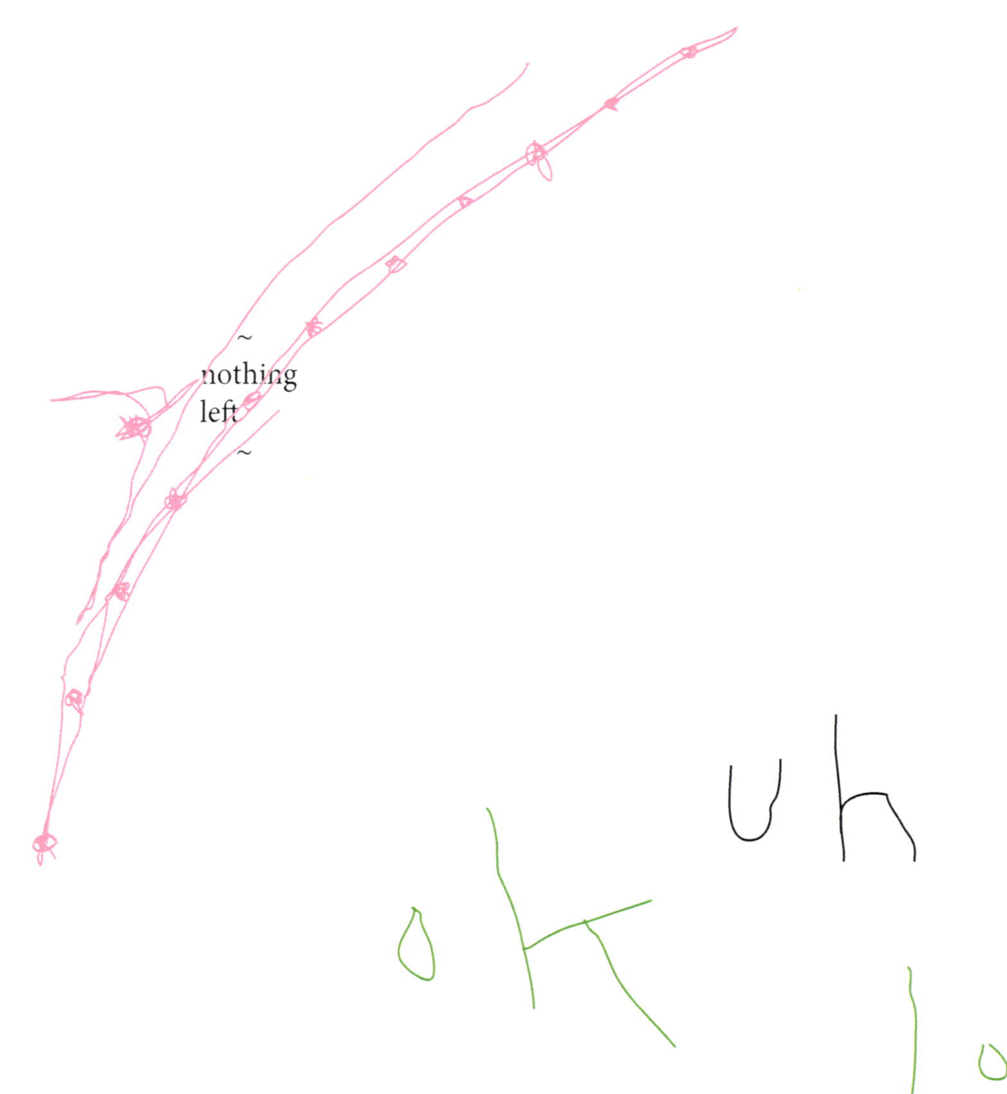

~
nothing
left
~

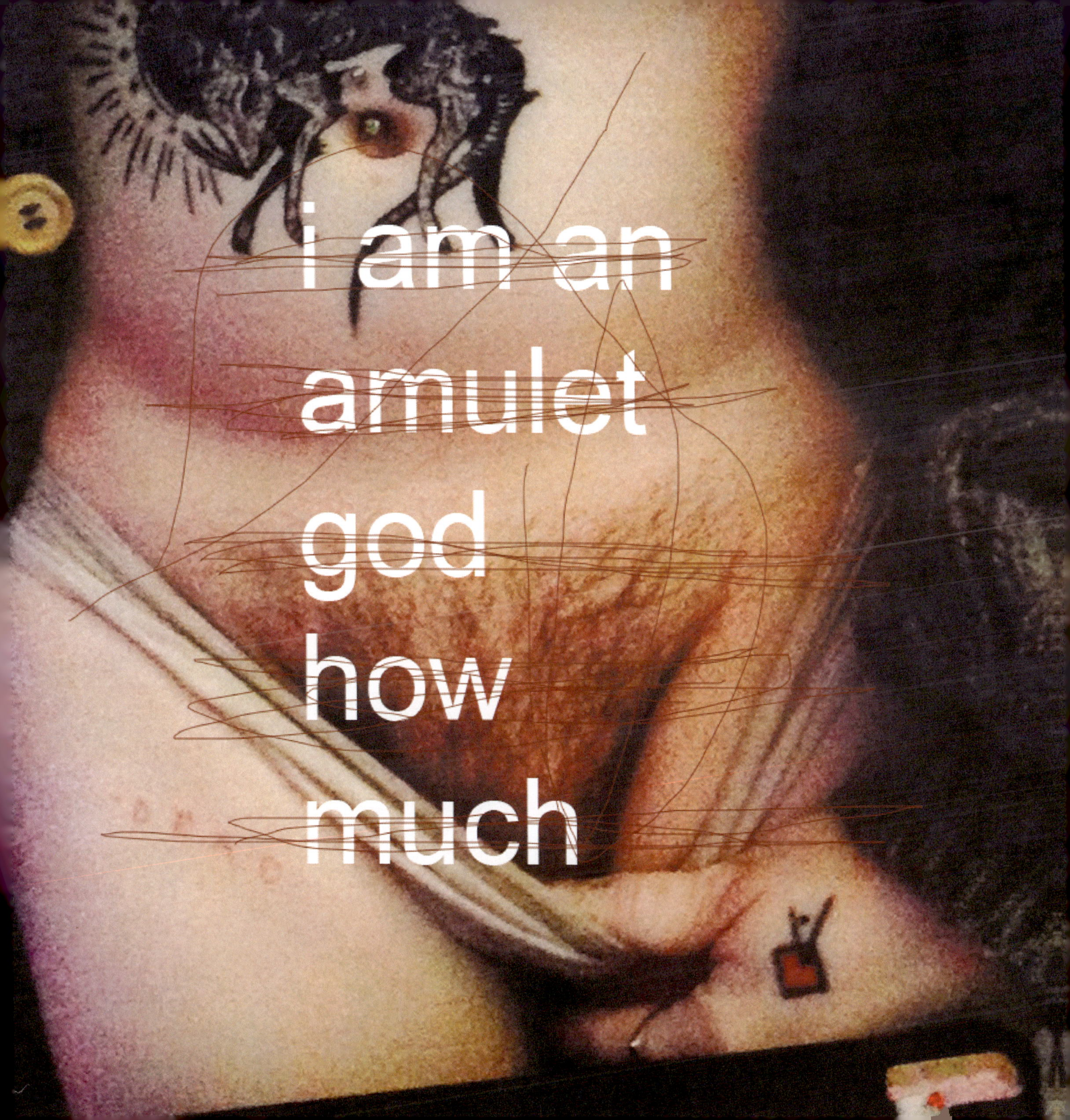
i am an
amulet
god
how
much

crimes
DIRT FUCK

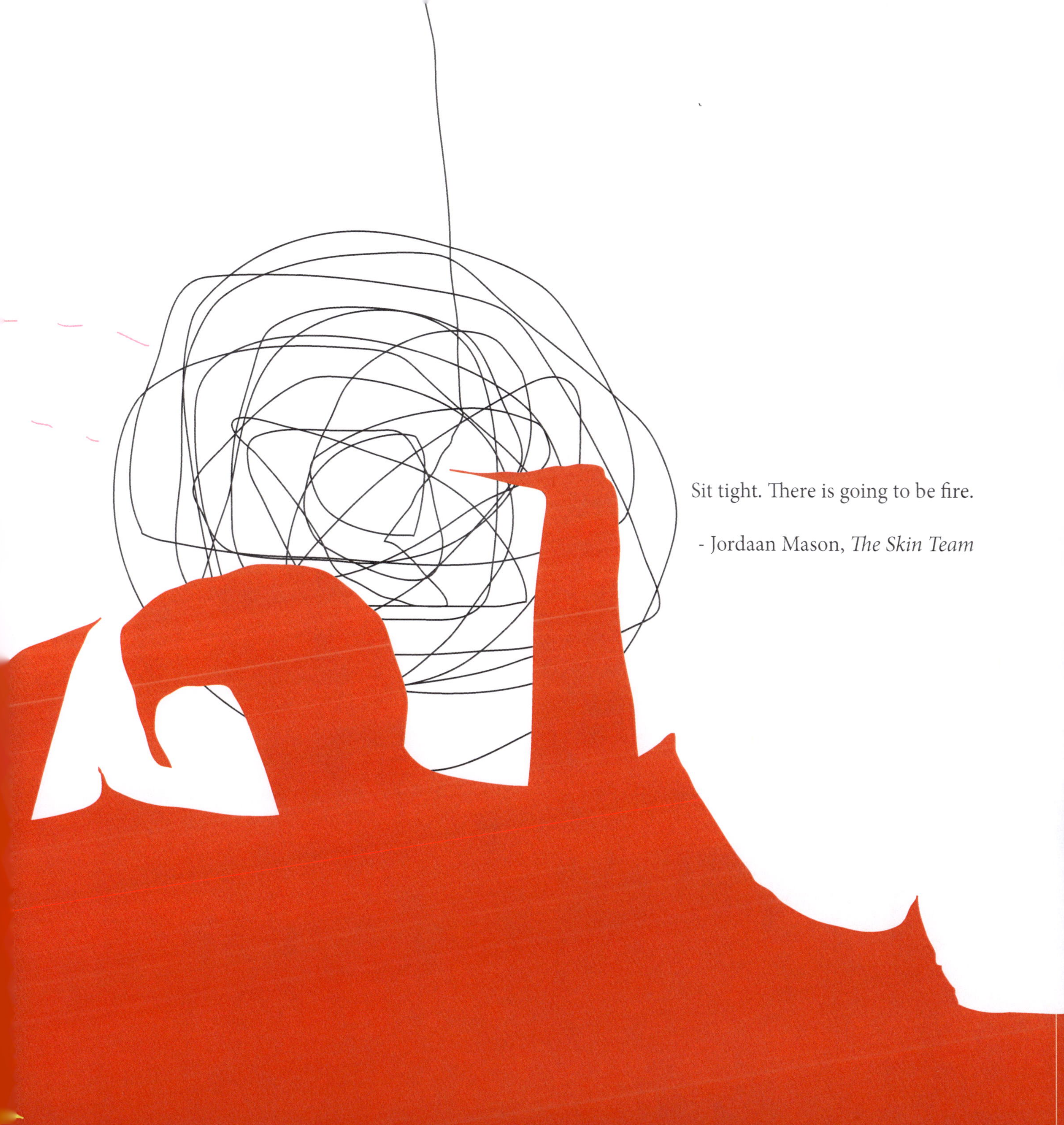
Sit tight. There is going to be fire.

- Jordaan Mason, *The Skin Team*

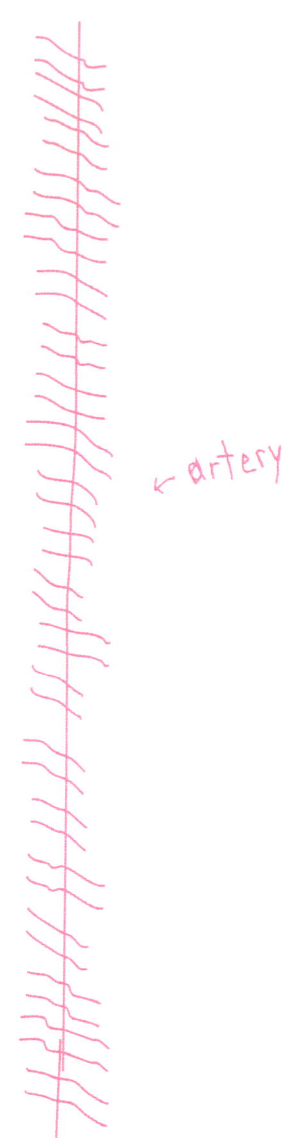
← artery

Dear Sea-Witch will we live in your body when u are dead/we will live in your body when u are dead.................................

....you are dead..

..........(how) does a witch-god die (there are so many dead witch-gods) when did they die (there are so many dead witch-gods) etc..

....the christmas of your body we live in..

....i am an enemy i am an altar where will we live when u are dead................

....i am an enemy i am an altar do we still live in your body now that u are dead do we still live..

..................do you still live in our bodies now that we are dead do you still live now that we are dead..................

..................i am an enemy i am an altar Dear Sea-Witch will we live (you will live) will u live (i will live) when is it over i am an ene-my..................

..................i am an altar no not even like..................

..................an altar will we still live inside u when u are here when we are gone do we still live inside u are an enemy u are an altar dead..................

164

....

....

....fuck   time   altogether   i   am   an   al-

tar...

....

....

....

....

....

....

....

....

.......i am six different gemstones of shining enemy my enemy our enemy i am so hot he tells me i am so hot ("how much just 2 lick") Dear Sea-Witch i am an altar lick will we still live in your body etc.....................................

....

....

....

....

....

....

....how   much   fuCK   TIME   ALTOGETH-

ER..

....

....

....

....

....i   am   i   am   an   al-

tar...

....

....i

am   an   enemy   i   left   sea-witch   when   i   was   living   in   sea-wit

ch..
....
....
....
....
.................................How much just to suck you off & eat your ass?...
....
....
....
....
....
....
....
....
....
....
....
....
....
....
....
....
....
....
....
....FUCK   OFF   I   AM   AN   ALTAR   I   AM   AN   ENEMYhow-
much)...
....
....
....
....
....

...........................Dear Sea-Witch, where will we live Dear Sea-Witch how much just to lick the al-
tar...

....i am an altarpiece like family whats a family an enemy will we live in your dead
body (there are so many dead witch-gods)...

....i
am an altar fuck a family i am an altar how much to fuck me like an altar fuck me like an enemy (there are so many dead
witch-gods..

....) where will
u live when we are dead lets die at the same time lets die at the same fucking time may she lay us waste may she lay us may
we all get laid how much...

....to be an altar girlboy FUCK YOUR TIME ALTOGETHER THERE's too
much how much just to...

....be an enemy..etc......

....
....
....
....
....
....
....
....
....
....
....
....
....
....
....
....
....
....
....
....
....
....
....
....
....
....
....
....
....
....
....
....let go lets go Dear Sea-Witch where will we live
where will we live where will we live I AM AN ENEMY i am an altar i am an amulet god how much to fuck you in the ass
(there   are   so   many   dead   witch   -   gods)

When they came for us, we didn't climb the trees. We thought about it, but there weren't any nearby consenting to be climbed. This was obviously an error in the calculations by our forebears. Let me start over. The 78 Men Who Cause Pain came for us. Of course they didn't come for us themselves, because they do nearly nothing themselves except that which causes their own pleasure at the expense of others, but they sent their cops in after us. I did not realize at the time that I was still living in Sea-Witch. I thought that the pain I had was great enough that surely I was outside of Sea-Witch, but I must have been wrong, because when the cops came in & began their bacterial destruction I found myself looking directly into the crying face of Sea-Witch, orange liquid pouring down her cherrywood cheeks. She whispered *I'm sorry* & I whispered *thank you* before 8000 cops came & dragged us along the concrete until we were bloody. We yelled out things like *Fuck You* & *We Are Monsters* & *There Should Be Beaches Here I Thought There Were Beaches.* There were no beaches then though, only sound & concrete & flashes of red & blue bacterial light & concentrated pain that streamed from our heads down to the rest of us. The bacteria explained our "rights" to us. "Rights" are a thing made up by the 78 Men to describe the severely limited amount of movement one can make when tightly restrained. A Sea-Witchean scholar of Meteor [msluw] once explained that among people these "rights" are discussed as if they are freedom. As if they weren't present to distract us from all the things we are not allowed.

This is an ending of one kind. In this ending, like all endings, things can go on, even go on forever & no one will think of it as an ending at all. There are other endings as well, but for those living this ending, it is not an ending at all but an event that leads to others.

For example, in another ending as we were being slain & nearly slain by the cops we prayed for Meteor (may she lay us waste) to come save us & she arrived in a peak of light in the sky that grew in flame-size to occlude all things. In this ending we die & so do the cops & so do the 78 Men & so do the living creatures & the witch gods & all living things restrained by time. In this ending not Meteor (may she lay us waste) but Time is the killer & Time creates a new world from the ashes of this one, but we do not get to see it. In this ending everything dies.

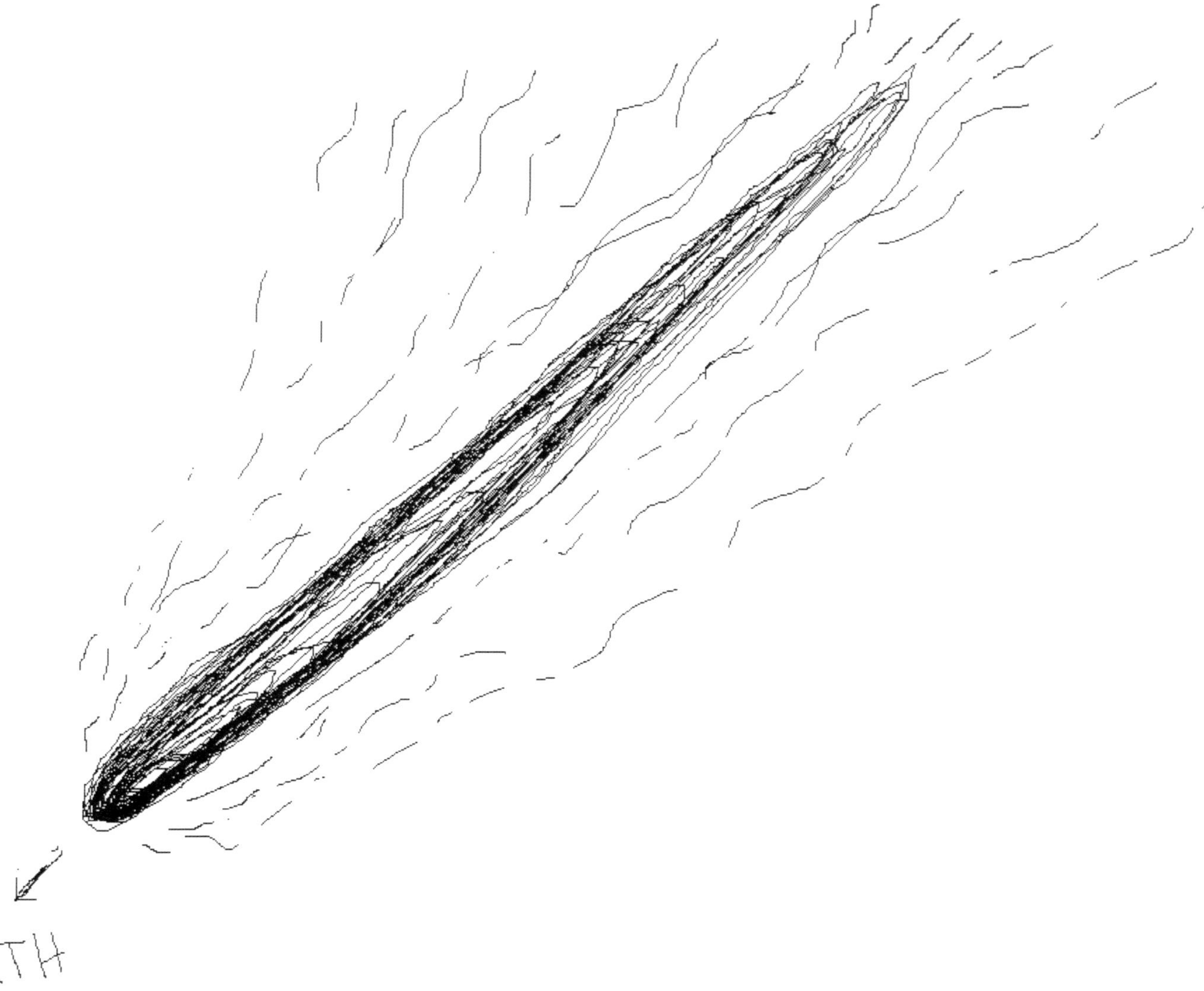

172

There are so many endings. In one the cops sees us & realizes it too is monsters to some degree & it returns to the 78 Men with us & we destroy them together against all odds. In this ending we create a world by & for monsters that encourages life & care beyond all else. In another ending the world is a rat having lunch & in this ending the rat eats the lunch (or does not eat the lunch & dies or skips lunch & eats dinner & is okay & says squeak squeak). In another ending light follows us in our paths & we glow much more brightly than before. In another ending I Am So Mad. In another ending nothing is real & this is the true ending. But because nothing is real truth is also not real & so this ending is only exactly as real as any other. In another ending I pull the suns from my body & the whole scene orbits them gently. In another ending I hate cops. Actually this is all endings. In another ending I am tired & fall asleep for awhile & dream of Sea-Witch & we explore each other's bodies with our bodies & she cums in my mouth & I cum in her mouth & we tell each other how good each other tastes. We awake in the trees, which consented & which we climbed when they came for us. We remember how the trees stretched up forever & how we arrived in the clouds where angels & living creatures surrounded us & fed us warm pierogies until we got better & were able to build again. Build again toward a place where we can live & expand our living to make space for the weakest above all, for they contain the magick for all life to finally begin. In this ending I change my name. In this ending I am a witch-god & realize I have always been so.

like a morning star
seam-ripping what
is left of night

may she lay us waste

Questions:
1. Did I ever tell you how Dog-Witch died?
2. Did I tell you she died in the sea?
3. Did I tell you she made a promise to Meteor (may she lay us waste) who in return made a promise back?
4. My neck is really sore.
5. Sea-Witch taught me about Dog-Witch, who formed her as a loving parent. Could you rub my neck?
6. That feels amazing.
7. Thank you.
8. A world was destroyed that is not ours & I feel like it is important for us to mourn that world. We know little about it but we do know that it was a place loved by many living things & many non-living things & that is enough for our mourning. Let me know if you have any questions for me. I'll be around for awhile. I'm always open to questions.

Mare Piss
Superkill

Sea-Witch vol. 3
Møss Høpe Ångel

chapter three: mare piss superkill

piss
poor

heal

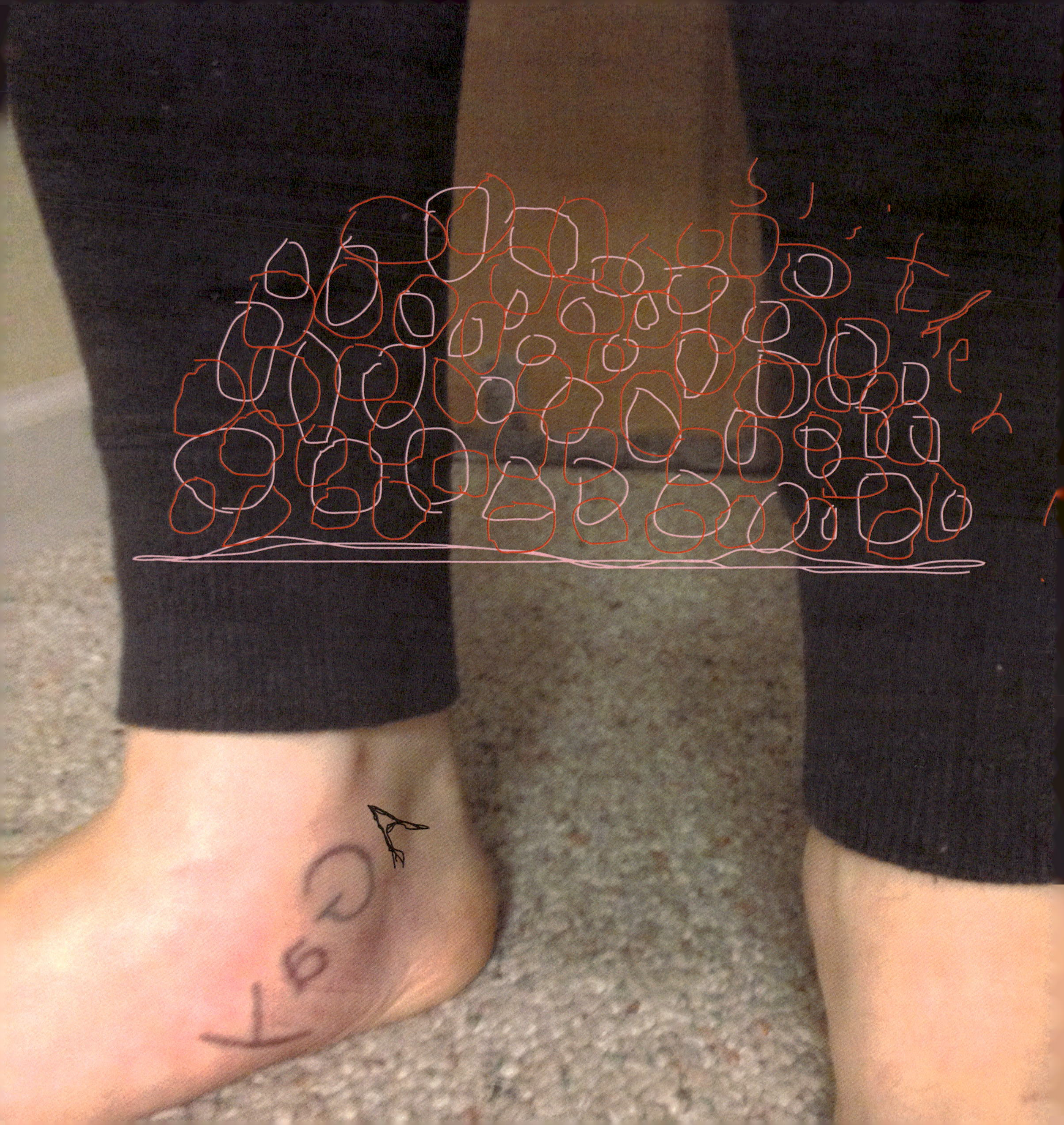

The act of recollection requires particular temporal orienting; this frames the pyramidal neurons to activate in such a way that they become relevant to the body recalling memory. This does not make a memory 'real.'

Experiential reality occurs within a quarter of a second of 'actual' reality; I am never now, here — always nowhere running; remembering;

-Angel Dominguez, *Black Lavender Milk*

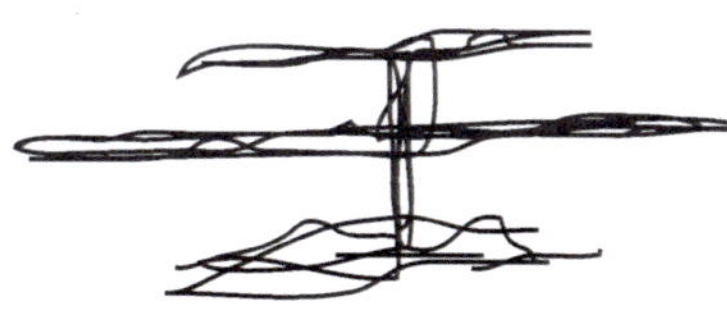

Maybe if it all disappears it doesn't matter
La la la la la maybe

-Talulah Gosh, "Bringing Up Baby"

There is a kind of ending that isn't an ending. You see, the 78 Men Who Cause Pain can never win. We can win. Meteor [(msluw)] can "win". But the ending in which they win is no ending. It is the status quo. They control everything, including us. Well, mostly. But monsters don't need to be born from other monsters. Monsters will exist so long as there is hierarchy that divides by difference. Hierarchy that divides at all.

So for all practical purposes this is an ending. The same way "happily ever after" is an ending. "Miserably ever after." Which maybe means what we should be looking for isn't really an ending at all. Maybe it's a beginning.

This is where my head has been lately. This is what I have been thinking about for the past five minutes as I lay in bed staring at the movie I have been not watching while my wife S lies next to me, packing a bong. I space out for awhile longer. The cool thing about having a trans partner is that he's checked out as much as I am. He gets it. I get it. It happens, idk. It's not a big deal.

My pre-transition girlfriends, my ex-wife—all cis—were always frustrated about this side of me. The part that just disappeared for long periods of time. Just like my parents, teachers and bosses. I couldn't help it and I still can't. I still sometimes feel like someone is going to get upset when I come out of a period of dissociation[*]: this sudden, dropping fear that I'm letting someone down. But these days that fear is actually unfounded for once. Having a partner who legit doesn't care if I have to spend some time out-of-body is a Fucking Relief.

I moved to ▓▓▓▓ about three years ago. I like to tell people that I "ran away from home to become a transsexual," which, tbh, is pretty much exactly what happened. I left a city, a job, a relationship, a lot of friendships. Idk, it was hard, a bunch of stuff changed. I barely remember it unless I really think about it. Actually, now that I have some distance from it, it's hard even remembering what it was like ~not~ being out as trans. I remember there was this trans woman I talked to right after I came out and I asked her what coming out was like, and she said pretty much the same thing to me. That she didn't really remember what it was like not being out as trans. At the time I was astounded. Now I totally get it. Trans is just sort of the water I swim in. It's frustrating water sometimes, but it's my water. It's home.

After the movie ends I kiss S and walk into the living room to see if any of my roommates are around. Lately it's been hard to keep myself from holing up with S in our closet-sized bedroom all day watching Netflix, so I've been trying to pop into the living room to briefly talk to someone a few times a day as an attempt to ward off that closed-up, beginnings-of-panic feeling. We just moved in here a week ago, to a house of mostly trans people who we had been friends with for awhile already. My sometimes-sweetie J is sitting in the living room reading a copy of *Lucifer Princeps*. I walk over next to her. "Hey there," she says, leaning her head sideways against my hip.

"Heya," I scratch my fingers in her soft hair, "How's Satan?"

"Oh she's doing marvelously. Which makes sense, given all the evil we've got around these days."

"You mean dirty-hooker-transsexual evil or nazi-president evil?"

[*] Idk if this is the right word for it, but it is the word someone else used to describe it once and so I started using it.

"Well, both. But Lucy seems like she prefers us at this point. Or at least me," she says, glancing down at the stick & poke on her left wrist. I gave it to her a few nights ago on our living room couch, to symbolize J's personal connection with Lucifer. I met her months ago and we immediately connected over all the important things: magic, weird art, leftist politics, mushrooms & being trans. She is my favorite kind of weirdo: a gentle soul who totally gets everything that is going on around her—and in the world in general—but seems so constantly overwhelmed by it that she mostly expresses it in bizarre little half-joke Facebook statuses. J has been through her share of tough shit. We all have. We've got a bunch of battle scars, and some of those battles aren't anywhere close to being over.

I notice a text on my phone. It says "hey sexy," which means it's from a client. I've been escorting for about six months now, but lately that has meant ignoring these texts because, honestly, most of these people just want to waste my time. And I hate having to give a shit when it doesn't seem like it will be worth it anyway. I think I would actually love escorting if I knew every dude that sent me a "hey sexy" or a "u ok w first timers" or a "how much just to lick" text was completely serious and sitting alone in a room with a stack of an appropriate amount of bills in an envelope all ready for me. But unfortunately they usually just want to talk to me long enough to get off, or long enough that I will send them nudes so then they can get off. This time I don't ignore it and I text back, "Hey there :) U looking to meet up? $100/30 min or $180/hr. Outcalls only."

J has been absorbed back into her book, but her head is still leaned on me so I give it another scratch while the response comes in. "Yeah. Let's do 30. I'm at the Rodeway Inn by the airport. Meet me in an hour?" Honestly, I'm impressed. This nice fellow actually wants to meet up.

I immediately text back "I'll meet you in 1 hr. What room #?"

Wow. An actual client. Unfortunately I have hella morning stubble and its 2pm and I am only wearing a t-shirt that says "I'M A TRASHBAG OF ROSES", an oversized Black Sabbath hoodie w spiky studs on the shoulders & tiny pink underwear. Which means it's most definitely Gettin' Pretty Time.

I give J's head a kiss. "Well, let me borrow that devil book when you're done with it. I think I'm gonna shower now."

"Mrow! Shower well, you," J says as I drift back toward my bedroom, where S is getting stoned and staring at six second looping Japanese instagram videos of hamsters. "Look at this ham," he says to me.

"Oh my gosh what a small soft baby!" I say, kissing in his hair.

"Do you want to shower?"

"Did you hear me tell J that?"

"Nope! I just wanted to shower."

"These are the things we do I guess," I said into his hair, punctuated by another kiss. "Also I've got a client."

"Nice," he says.

••••

A person I hooked up with once told me that the problem with showering with someone else was that generally not much actual cleaning got done. S & I prove that untrue on a daily basis. We mostly keep to task while making room for the occasional interruption of groping and moaning, making out and the occasional bit of dick sucking or ass-eating. We're always like this together. This shower is mostly functional, with only a few brief diversions, and the hot water feels good until it doesn't and then the whole bathroom is muggy and steamy and we both start getting light-headed so we get out. I feel the lightheadedness pushing on me, my limbs start to feel heavy, so I dry and go in the bedroom, where I flop naked on the bed.

"Oh god," I moan to myself as I feel a familiar horrible warm tingling climbing my back. I've always called these anxiety attacks but I have no idea whether the thing that I call "anxiety attack" is anything at all like anyone else's. I had a psych prescriber once tell me they were psychotic episodes, but that seems like a different thing. Idk. I look at my phone and my client hasn't texted back with the room number. My mind wanders and the blankets near my face feel too close, the room feels too small, too lived-in, too messy. All I can think about is that I have spent nearly 20 hours a day in this bedroom—shit, in this bed—since we moved in, though I guess I am totally making up that number. I feel stagnant and my life feels stagnant. I have been existing and that's it and there is nothing about my life that is in any way sustainable.

On top of that, the horrible country I live in, a country that exists because white assholes like my probably-slave-own-ing [illegible] came and killed and cheated everyone who was here before and now we all go around acting like we deserve to live here, yes that same country [illegible] actual fascist as president [illegible] even my white skin isn't enough to help me get a fucking "real" job or whatever other things I'm supposed to have planned out in order to exist and I don't even know if I could do a fucking "job" anymore anyway because half of the time I end up with [illegible] is: staring into a room that all feels too fucking close to my face and crying and panicking and I [illegible] going to let me be like "Oh hey sorry I'm a fucking nutcase so I can't actually do any work [illegible] whenever this happens. Especially because any job I get I'll already have one strike against [illegible] who doesn't [illegible] unripped tights and has stick & pokes all over herself including one [illegible]
I [illegible]

W[illegible] the fucking [illegible] whole scam again [illegible] in any way at all and I've always [illegible] wanting my own [illegible] than get a real job anyway. That is until I get too crazy to do sex work too [illegible] it any [illegible] year. No doubt about that. I always want to fix things by moving to another [illegible] but where would I move that I wouldn't just be doing the same fucking thing: holing up and watching netflix with S and having panic attacks and maybe trying to do sex work or else like worrying that I'll never be able to afford rent and like what if I

can't get on food stamps there and they probably hate trans people there too whatever I'll stay here or some big
city wh[...]

It's not like I wish I was out partying. I hate parties. So does S. We've bonded over it. And we also both freak out at
shows, so live music is pretty much always not-an-option. So far the only thing that makes me feel not horrible and
like I'm dying is making art, and I don't even know what the fucking point of that is. What, do I want to be some cool
artist lady? I mean I guess that's what I already am and it fucking sucks because all I do is panic and cry. Basically the
feeling right now is terrible and all I can think about is how much I want to punch my own stupid fucking head in
but I am keeping myself from doing that. That is not productive because I have already done that a LOT of times and
getting (further?) brain damage is just going to make my life harder than it is, which, look, idk about anyone else's life
or how it would be if I existed in their bodies, but fuck it, I'm going to go ahead and say my life, at least at the
moment, is Very Fucking Hard.

S walks in and sees me crying. "Aw, babe," he says as he sits down beside me and holds me in his arms. I hug him hard
and stare up into his face and he wipes my tears off, but the panic is settled in deep at this point so I can't stop crying. S knows this well. He's held me for hours through this. He was with me for the entirety of my 30 hour marathon
panic-attack-psycho-whatever that ended with me in the ER. I push my face into his towel-shoulder and let out some
good hard cry-growls. I feel cold and spent and scraped out inside and more than anything I feel scared through my
whole gross boy-man-girl body and into my bones.

I turn my head to get in a more comfortable position and when I turn my head the room moves around me in a way it
shouldn't. Fuck. Why can't I just live in a world that sits still. The too-closeness of everything gets worse and nothing
around me seems real. I don't seem real. My brain can't seem to figure out where real starts and made-up begins. S's
hair is right by my face and it seems like it's coming out of his head in a way that couldn't really happen. It looks like
a computer simulation. I think that it's kind of adorable but am immediately deeply unsettled by the fact that I think
it's kind of adorable. I feel pathetic and very very crazy, and it feels like the kind of crazy you don't come back from. I
think about Sea-Witch. I am so close to S right now. I look up and brush back his hair. The entrance to Sea-Witch is
the ear. I'm exhausted, but I go inside. She welcomes me beautifully & I thank her & say now I must sleep & so I lay
down on one of her softest orange beaches & let the waves tell me how to disappear.

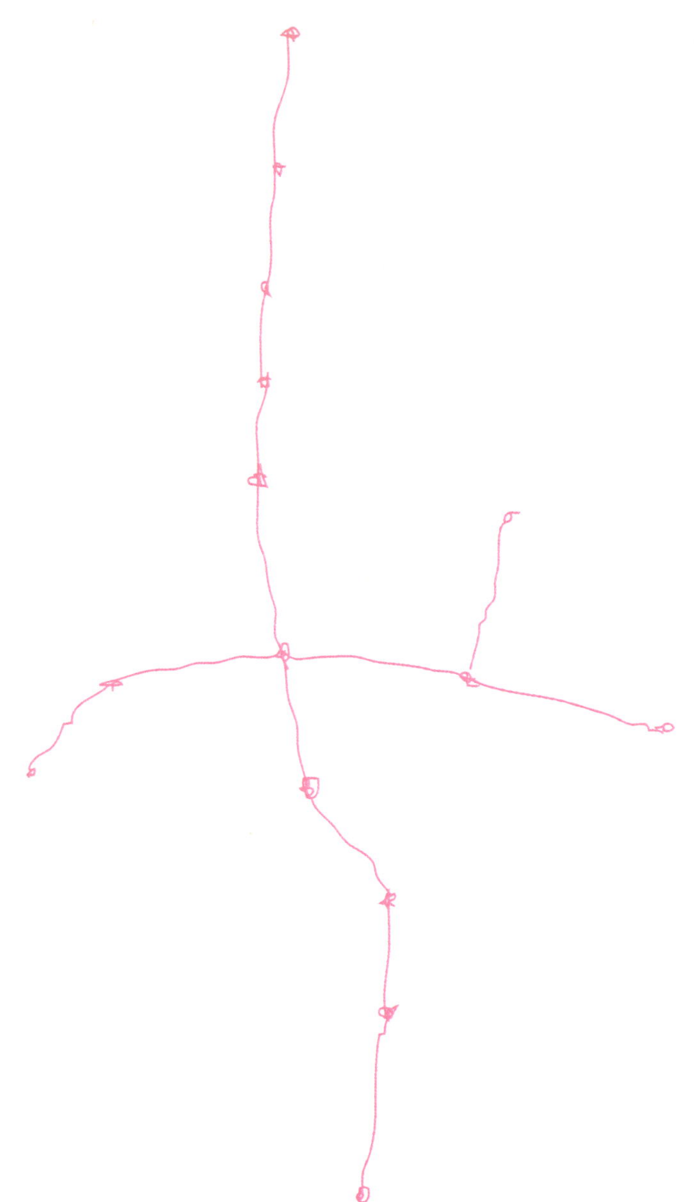

dr u g ged

The thing about the apocalypse is it happens to one person at a time.
It's an individual experience. My world has Been apocalyzed.

-Devi McCallion, twitter post

The process of formation, observed from within, is essentially a slow removing of options. Many of these options are options that most monsters have already ruled out, & their loss is not mourned. For example, once one realizes they are a monster it is clear they could never be one of the 78 Men Who Cause Pain. This feels pretty okay, ~~because monsters do not want to cause pain~~ ~~because monsters do not want to cause pain to themselves~~ ~~because monsters do not want to cause pain to other monsters~~ because the 78 Men seem pretty shitty when seen from the perspective of a monster.

But other options begin disappearing too. They disappear one by one & it isn't so scary really, it isn't so scary until you begin to get close to the endpoint. The endpoint looks like this, & it is two options:

1. Be scared. Be always scared. Be consumed by complete unrelenting terror that seems to have no end.

2. Die.

Option one is impossible to sustain. Option two has so many things getting in the way of anyone actually making it happen that most monsters end up choosing option one as a default. There is a third option, but it feels impossible. Considering this option feels like swimming your way across a whole ocean. But still, it is there:

3. Fight.

The option doesn't say who or how to fight. It just says fight. We need more research. But we are all too weak & tired to research. We fall back into wishing. We fall back into prayer. May she lay us waste.

Whenever I enter Sea-Witch it is sexual. I'm sure it isn't this way for everyone, but the particular self I inhabit can barely look at Sea-Witch without feeling the downward tug, without disappearing from my own thoughts, lost, thinking about, almost ~feeling~, her hard clit deep inside my asshole, her piss flowing into my mouth, her fingernails scraping the skin on my back. Sex with Sea-Witch felt so literal, but afterward I never knew how much of it really happened. Sea-Witch's sex turns were like this. Their intensity was such that the reality or unreality of them felt beside the point. & so when I entered Sea-Witch this time, she entered me as well.

I took an Ativan. S had been holding me for who knows how long. I kissed him hard. I felt my brain slow down. The word dru g g e d s l o w l y worke d o v e r me in w a v e s . Thoughts n o l o n g e r s t u c k in my head, but just kept get t i n g p u s h e d d o wn. I was struck by S's b o d y i n front of me. Seeing his s o ft flesh there made the lo w e r h alf of my body warm with tingling. I wanted to push my face i n t o h i s s oft tummy & then I pu s h ed my face into h is soft tummy. "Darling!" I half-whispered. "My sweet boy d a r l i n g."

Scene: Bedroom interior. deadname & Sara are half-laying, half-sitting on top of the covers in a semi-made bed.

deadname: Okay, can I stop you for a second & ask some questions?

Sara: Sure.

deadname: I just want to make sure I've got things straight.

deadname: So the whole world was underwater. & bears controlled all of the other creatures ruthlessly by using lava. Then Dog-Witch falls from the sky. & manages to steal the lava from bears. & creates land. & forms nineteen sisters, who then spread out & have all kinds of experiences.

Sara: Well, that's what *The Book of Meteor* says.

deadname: & then at some point the 78 Men start doing shit & fucking everything up again.

Sara: Uh-huh.

deadname: & around that time Dog-Witch falls in love with a piece of information & creates Sea-Witch as a being/place of pure good?

Sara: Yes.

deadname: & then apparently Dog-Witch dies at some point. & some of the sisters die? Or maybe they don't all die? Or maybe they do all die?

Sara: Yes, all of those things are true at the same time actually.

deadname: "There are so many dead witch-gods."

Sara: So fucking many.

deadname: Sea-Witch decides to start taking monsters inside her body to protect them from the 78 Men.

Sara: Yep.

deadname: At some point you are formed & then you go out & find Sea-Witch.

Sara: Yeah.

deadname: & you live in her & learn about all this stuff & then leave Sea-Witch but also you don't leave. & Sea-Witch is infected with this distrust stuff & also cops maybe? & then there are all these endings that are all different but all real or not.

Sara: More or less yeah.

deadname: Oh also some stuff involving Strawberry-Witch & me & then me & you & then there was someone who worked at a pot farm but I don't remember that whole thing.

Sara: Yeah, me either but I've got it written down somewhere.

deadname: & then also you are living in ~~there~~ & having panic attacks & talking to your partners or whatever & watching Netflix.

Sara: Yeah that's the same story but just told in a different way.

deadname: Oh ok.

Sara: It's a weird version of the same thing. I could tell this story in a million different ways.

deadname: Is it really a story?

Sara: That depends. Like does a story have to have an order or some sort of overall arc or can it just be a lot of things that happened? What if plot is fake?

deadname: I think it can be either. I think plot can be fake.

Sara: Then it's a story. A true story. Not that I believe in truth.

deadname: Me either.

deadname: I'm not real.

Sara: "Real" seems like bullshit.

Sara: Nobody is real.

deadname: Cool. Thank you. For clearing this all up.

Sara: No problem.

deadname: Do you want to fuck again?

Sara: I want to fuck in one reality & don't want to fuck in another.

deadname: I think both of those things can happen.

Sara: Nice.

deadname: Nice.

deadname & Sara split into two different realities. In one of these realities they fuck. The fucking doesn't involve pen-etration. Mostly they eat each other's asses out & suck each other's genitals until both of them are tired and/or come. In the other reality they don't fuck & instead just read for awhile until deadname falls asleep & then Sara just reads by herself & eventually falls asleep too.

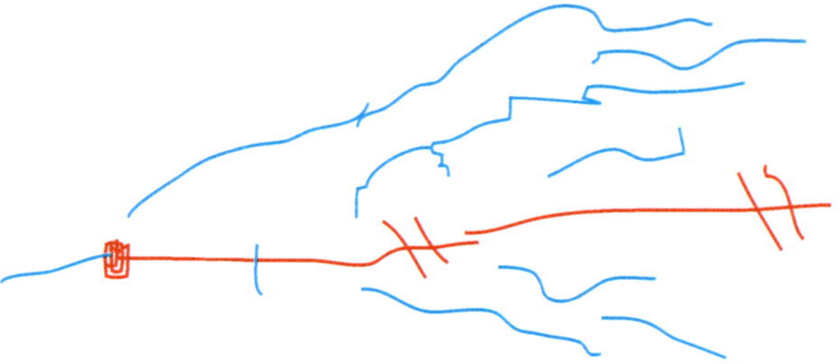

taste of cum

My identity and thus my body are still reflections of my relationship to empire. I can never truly negate my body until this totality is destroyed. But I can gain some level of power in being a monster by choice, and attempt to loose my identity in a legion of darkness. In engaging in total war against civilization.

-Priscilla Genet, *Tomb of Slime*

I twitch. It's a thing about me. Sometimes I'll go whole days without doing it but usually it happens at least once in a day. There was a while, last summer, when I was twitching nearly every five minutes. I'd wake up in the morning and my first twitch was how I would know I was awake. They start with a feeling of tenseness in my neck or back and then I have to let them out. It's like a sneeze. My head or my whole torso jerks once, quickly, and then it's over. I've told my therapist about these and I've told my doctor and they generally just give me a "huh" and ask me questions to figure out if they're seizures (apparently they aren't) and then they write it down somewhere and that's it, more or less. Given that I'm usually coming to them with a list of much more intolerable things my brain is doing it always seemed like something I could deal with, and I do deal with it. They get worse when I'm anxious or stressed out, but sometimes they happen when I'm feeling totally fine. Whatever it is "totally fine" looks like. Anyway, I twitch. I don't know how relevant this is, but I'm telling you and now you have that information inside you. I think the thing about the twitches isn't so much that I mind them, because I don't, but that they make me feel like a crazy person. When I was twitching all the time every day I was going to psych offices a lot because I was also dealing with a lot of paranoia, a lot of anxiety and depression and this weird thing where I would get overwhelmed and my body would sort of go limp kind of and I'd start slurring my words. Anyway, I was in waiting rooms a lot, sitting there twitching, and I just felt like some hacky casting director had been like "Hm, for this psych waiting room let's have some people who are visibly crazy. I know, get me a tranny wearing a frumpy old sweater that's too big for her and just like, twitches every few minutes." It made me feel like a sideshow. Which I'm already susceptible to, being trans and all.

I am in a room. There are mirrors lining the walls. There are three doors ahead of me. They have signs on them. The sign on the first door says TASTE OF PISS. The sign on the second door says TASTE OF CUM. The sign on the third door says BOTH! BOTH! BOTH!. I almost enter TASTE OF CUM, but I stop myself. I check myself in the mirrors. I back up four steps & turn. I enter BOTH! BOTH! BOTH!.

Beyond this door the walls are heavily stained. The room smells of Lysol. I see two people dressed as rats dressed as angels guarding a door across the room. I say they are "guarding" but I don't know what made me think of them as "guarding". Something about the position of their bodies. Something about positions of bodies. They do not have weapons that I can see. I walk to the middle of the room & look up at the ceiling. In the ceiling there is a grate. I begin to worry that choosing "both" was a mistake. That choosing any door at all would be a mistake. I look into the grate. It is a grate.

"Don't worry," says one of the rat angels. "No one is going to dump piss or cum on you without your consent."

I relax a little bit. I think again.

"What if I want them to?" I ask them.

"I'm sure we could arrange something," says the other rat angel in the least flirty way possible.

I say a quick prayer to someone who is not Meteor[(msluw)]. Meteor[(msluw)] has never minded us having other gods. Meteor[(msluw)] understands her limitations. In *The Book of Meteor* it says "Hey look, I get it. Sometimes you want total destruction. Sometimes you want something with a little more nuance. One girl can only do so much." The thing I pray to isn't a thing I have a name for. It is a thing I have felt & have tried to name in different ways throughout my life. It is a thing that resists naming.

Ok. So.
There are a few things that could happen next:
    1. A flood of cum & piss from the Thing That Resists Naming could come from above, through the grate, & cover all my body.
        a. The rat angels could join in.
        b. The rat angels could not join in, but enjoy watching.
        c. The rat angels could not join in, & feel weird about watching & start talking to each other instead, or kind of stare at the floor & feel awkward.
    2. The rat angels could come over & fuck me.
    3. No one fucks. What is this obsession. Just calm down everybody. I go through the next door, guided by the Thing That Resists Naming, who is not particularly fond of the fact that I have turned its resistance of naming into a name, or that I will probably acronym it later into like TTRN or TTTRN or something.

What actually happens next is some combination of those options. What actually happens next is the realization that "next" as a concept is bound by time & linearity & as you have probably gathered by this point, We Don't Have Much Respect for Either of These Things. But narrative dictates events happen, sometimes even in a certain order. & we have pledged to keep narrative holy. Narrative is what we crave above all things. Our minds need it in order to exist. It is how we remain capable. How we can relate to others. It is essential.

I walk over to the rat angels & they open their mouths for me to inspect them. Their mouths are gleaming white & all light seems to come from inside them. I take the 8 suns from my body & compare the light from my suns to the light from inside their mouths. Their mouths are so much brighter. These suns have gotten so old. I put 5 suns in the left mouth, I put 3 suns in the right mouth. It is the world we have come for, they tell me. <u>Nothing</u> can be the same again. I have the feeling that everything should be over already. I have the feeling that this world has gone on too long.

I remember a discussion I once had with a friend, back when I was living in Sea-Witch. She said "I think I am a main character in my story." I confessed to her that I have always felt like a minor character. A character who had one small scene early on in her life & yet had somehow continued to exist, far, far away from the main character. A character who has been forced to live out a full life beyond any purpose or utility she might have. A character who was not planned out & has gotten stranger & less useful over the years & years she was never expected to live. A character who has been abandoned by the plot, & yet still progresses through time without any direction or purpose.

"Honestly, that's a gift," my friend replied, "because most stories are written by assholes."

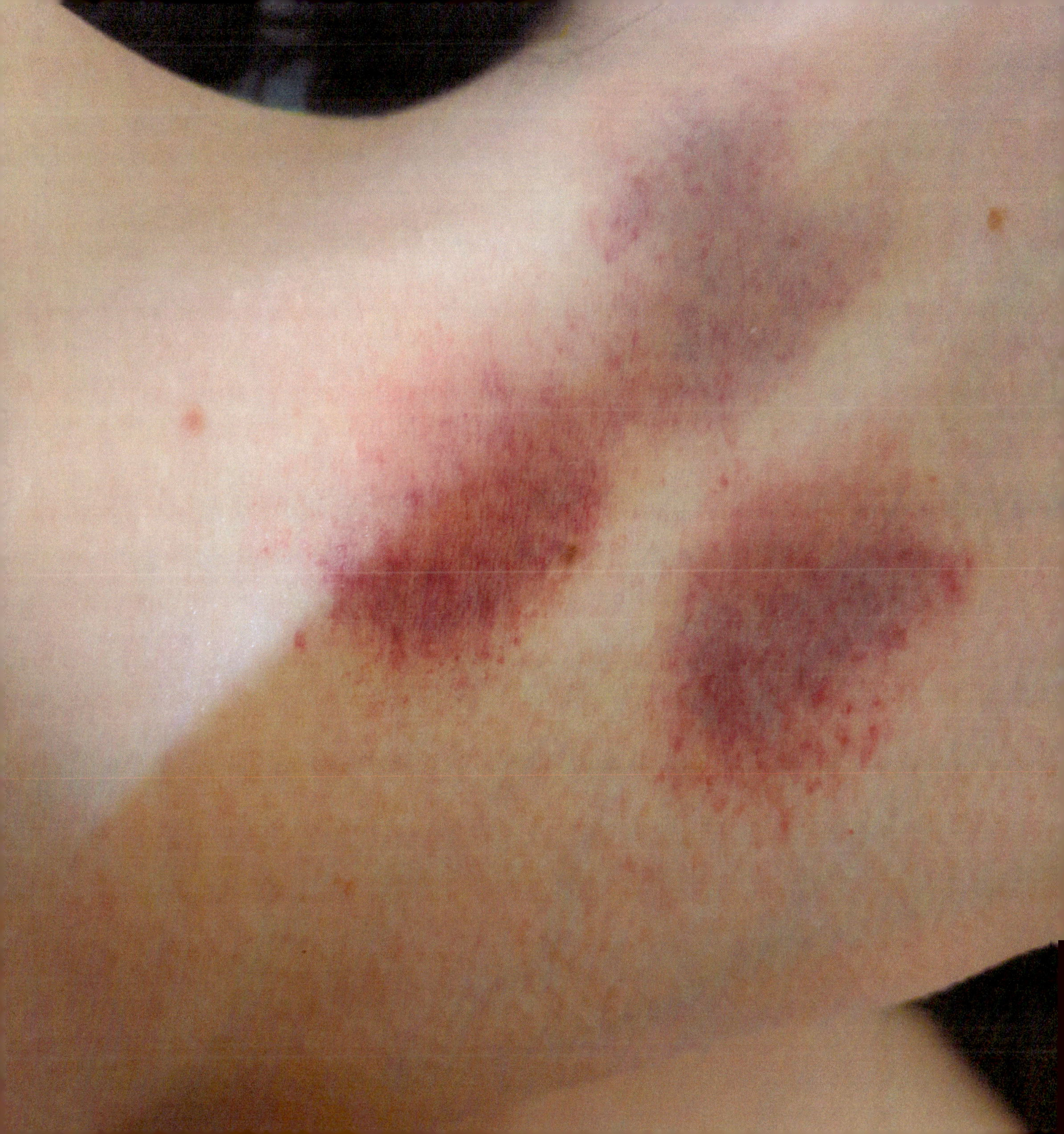

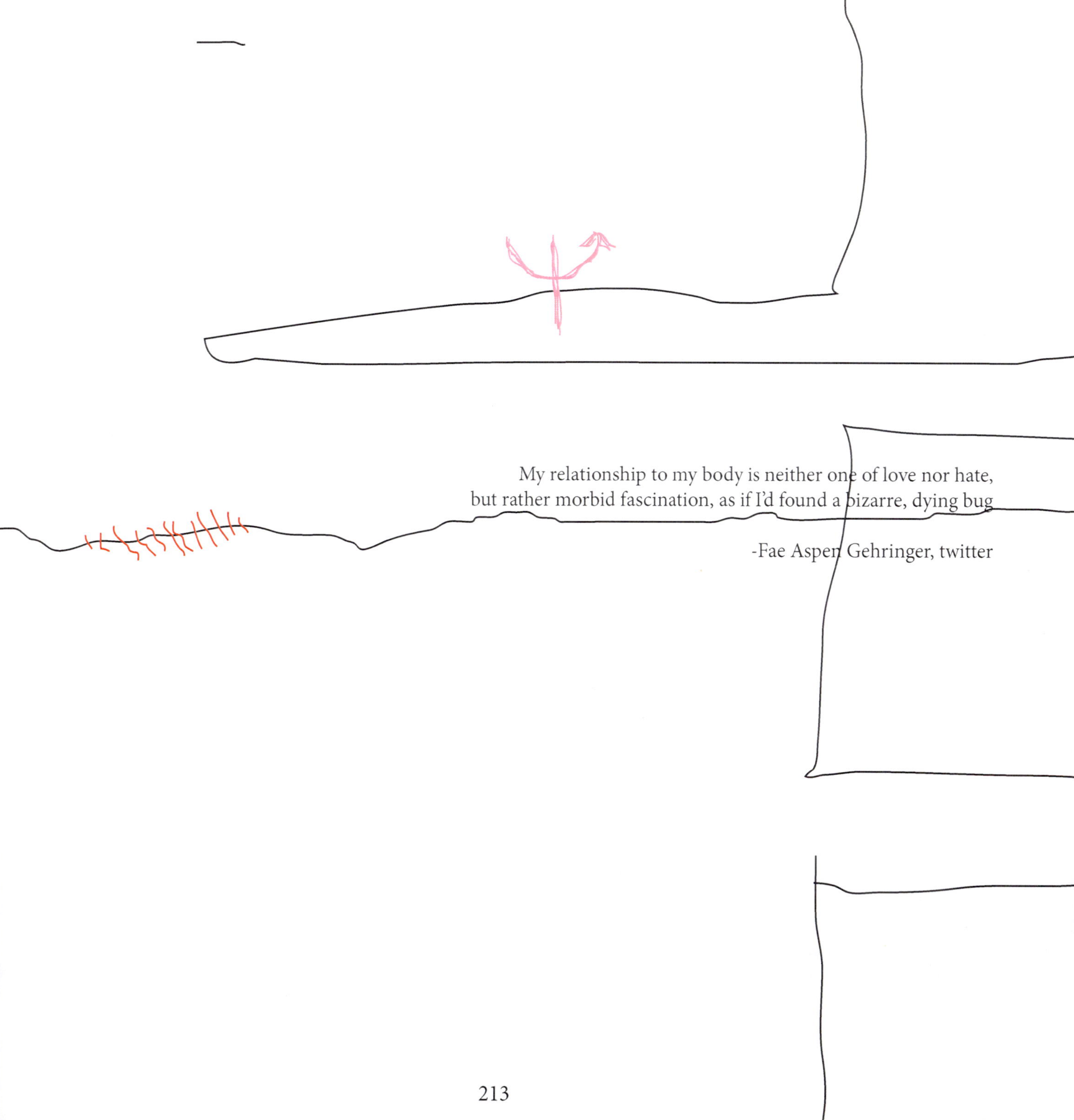
My relationship to my body is neither one of love nor hate,
but rather morbid fascination, as if I'd found a bizarre, dying bug

-Fae Aspen Gehringer, twitter

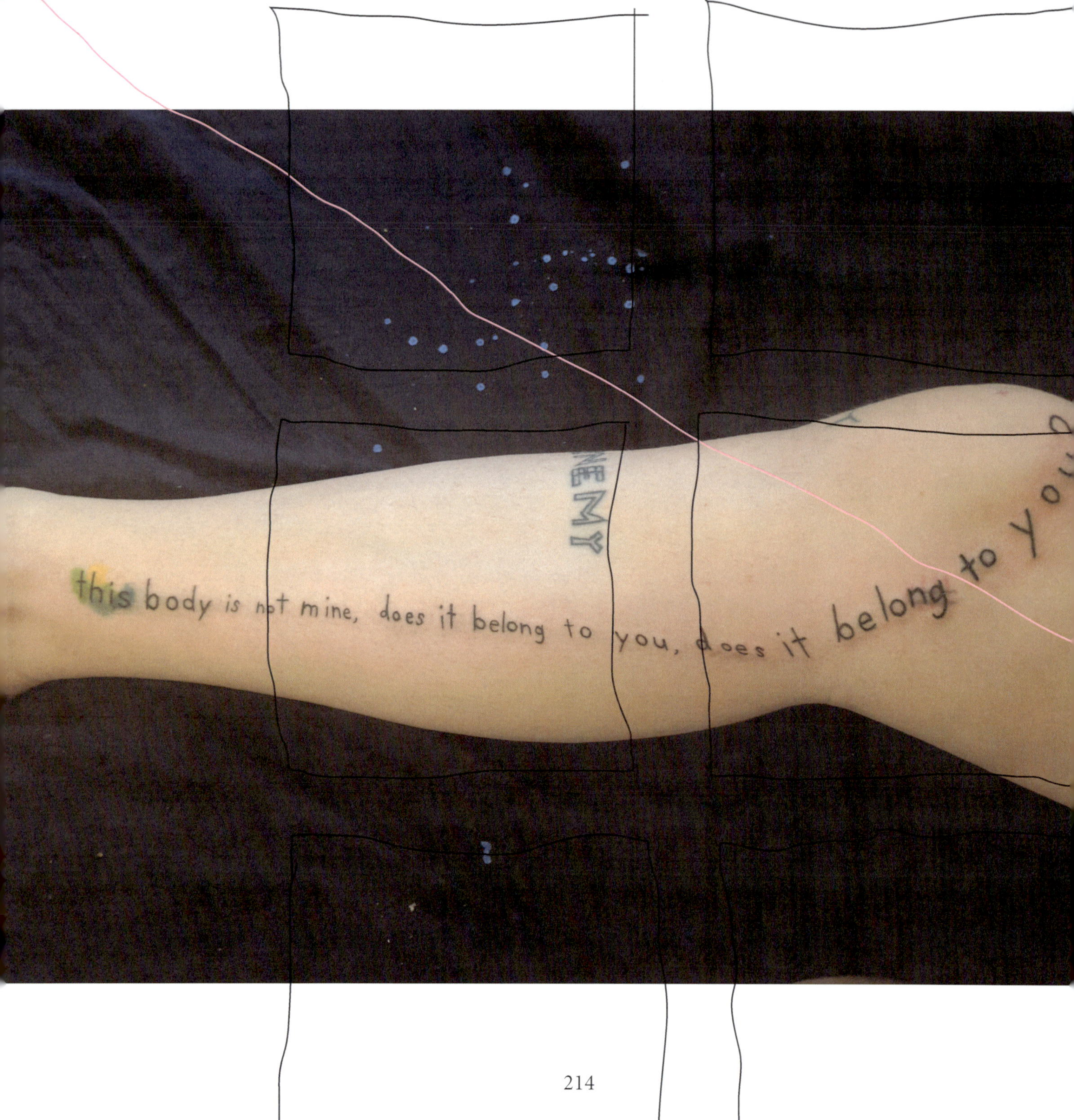
this body is not mine, does it belong to you, does it belong to you?

214

After I left Sea-Witch, I took a large leaf from the ground at my feet. I used my fingernail & berry juice & a ballpoint pen & wrote a letter to Sea-Witch, but the letter kept shifting its words around the page. I wrote this letter out of joy & desperation, out of a desire to connect with Sea-Witch whom I love. I do not know how the letter looked when it got to her. The first time I read it, it looked different than the second. The third time I read it, it was all marks on a page that held no meaning to me. This time when I read it, right now, before I give it to her, once returning to Sea-Witch and/or realizing I was still inside her, it looks like this:

When we die, our coffins will be filled with wasps. Those we knew & those we loved, & those we never really knew or loved will come to our funerals & hold their own hands & when they do this their feelings will be filled with wasps. Wasps are made of ghosts, ghosts are made of angels, angels are made of disappointment, disappointment is made of fear, fear is made of control, control is made of power, power is made of ants, ants are made of dying, dying is full of wasps. It goes all the way down. It isn't sequential. Everything is connected & that sucks. It sucks because we want an enemy. It sucks because we have an enemy & he is connected to us. We do not know where to draw the line between him & us. We are full of wasps about this. I pray to meteor (may she lay us waste) & I pray to the thing that keeps me up at night when I am full of wasps (not to the wasps, but when I think of this idea, I pray to them too for good measure). I pray to myself. I pray to my friends. Help me, myself. Help me, my friends. I am all stung-up on the inside. I don't know where I begin as an enemy of my enemy. My enemy does not care where I begin. My enemy destroys those furthest from himself first. Maybe I should do the same. Maybe I should not. I'm too full of wasps & scar tissue to think about this right now. Tomorrow, maybe.

The tomorrow after I wrote this I was not able to understand this more clearly. I must spend further time in prayer to others & in conversation with them (via prayer & not-prayer). I burned myself lighting a candle to pray next to. Sea-Witch told me she did not fully understand the letter, but thought it was beautiful. I told her I don't trust beauty, because my face shifts when I look at it in the mirror. It won't hold still. Sea-Witch told me that this is my secret power. "You have a lot of other powers too," she said. "This is just the only one that is a secret."

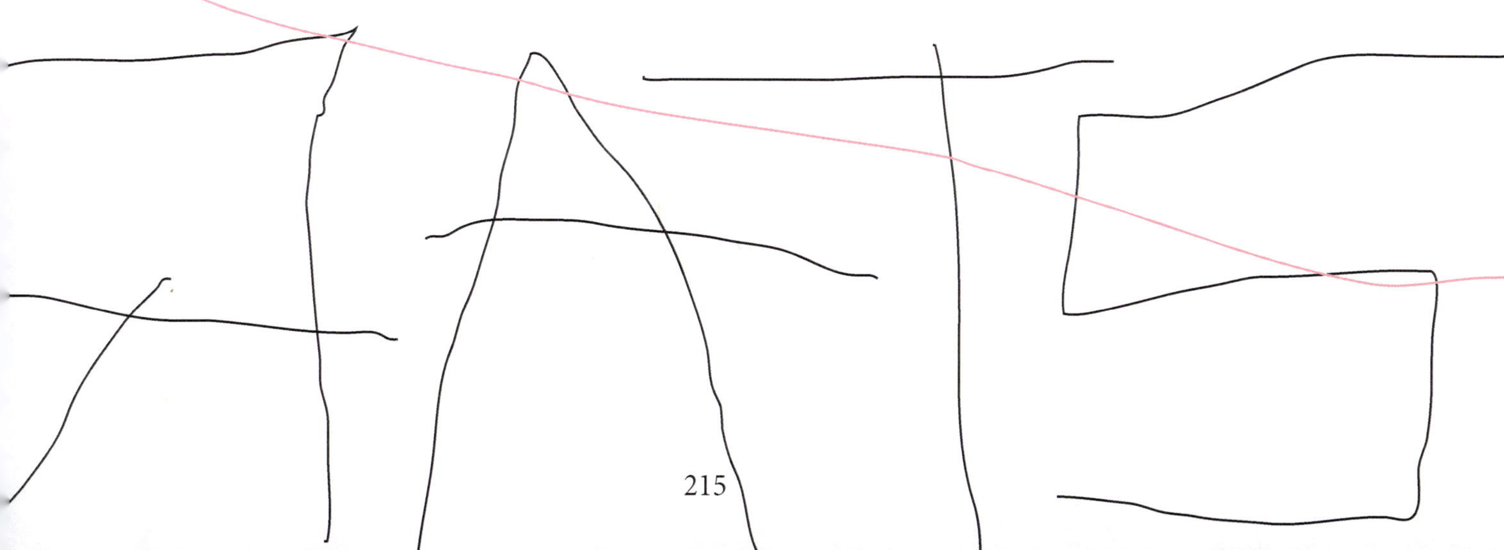

I used to have these dreams where I would be in some big supermarket or some other kind of giant store. Some lady would come up to me & make some horrible comment about how I looked, about who I was, or who I appeared to be to her. I would feel an intense rage building up inside me, & without even knowing I was doing it, I would attack her. She would fall, & very quickly I would realize that she was dead, that I had killed her. I would experience a moment of pure terror. I would become aware of people around me watching, yelling, coming after me, calling 911. I would try to run, but before I could get out of the store there were police & guns & cars surrounding it, coming inside, chasing me. Usually at some point while I was getting shot at, I would wake up.

These dreams were always filled with such strong emotions. The intense rage & desire to let it out. The extreme frustration & horror at realizing that letting it out did nothing but harm, both to the woman who harassed me & to me by putting myself in a dangerous situation. What the stranger did was wrong, but she was a product of her environment. Her horrible, shitty, fucked-up environment. She was a reflection, not the source.

My reaction to these dreams used to be one where I would decide that violence wasn't the answer. That people didn't deserve to die, that the consequences, both emotional & external, were not worth it. Over time, my perspective on this has changed. Over time I have realized that I just didn't kill the right person.

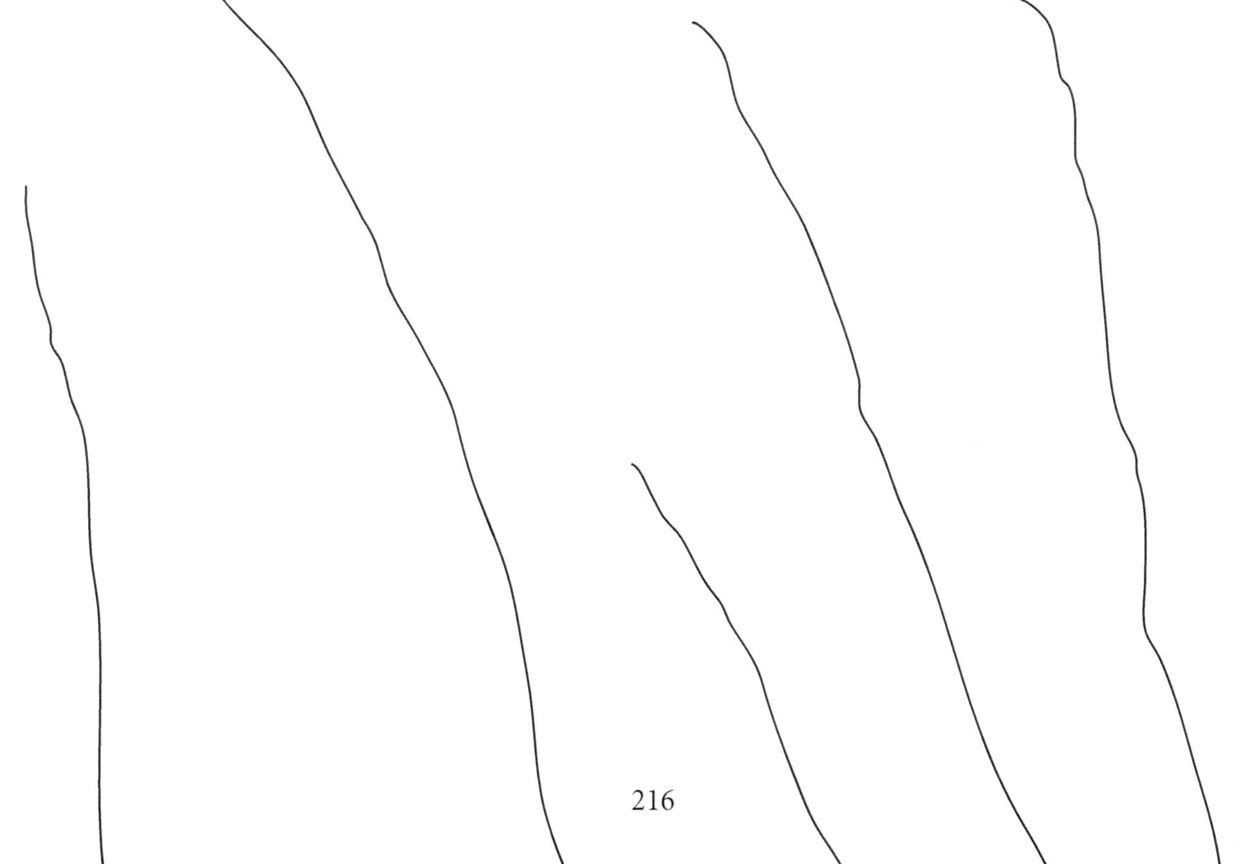

I hold my face next to Sea-Witch's face. I find the soft skin on her cheek & kiss & kiss & kiss & kiss. I am this creature for you, I whisper on her. I am this creature for you. She responds by pressing her clit deeper against my asshole. I gasp. I can feel it, hard and slippery with fluid, begin to enter. I am such a creature for you. Yoursoftness,Iamjustthis-creature, I moan against her face. She looks into my eye with both her eyes. I see deeply in the dark parts of her eye & she says nothing as she pushes into me. I am filled with her clit. My god, I say. My holiest god. Fill me with your light. Sea-Witch's hair tickles on my cheek & she pushes into me over & over & over as I feel all the sin leaking from my eyes. I cry the sin out as my god fills me with her light.

we call things
by the wrong
names but
we do our
best in
trying right?

218

t4t
DAUGHTER
LILIT
220

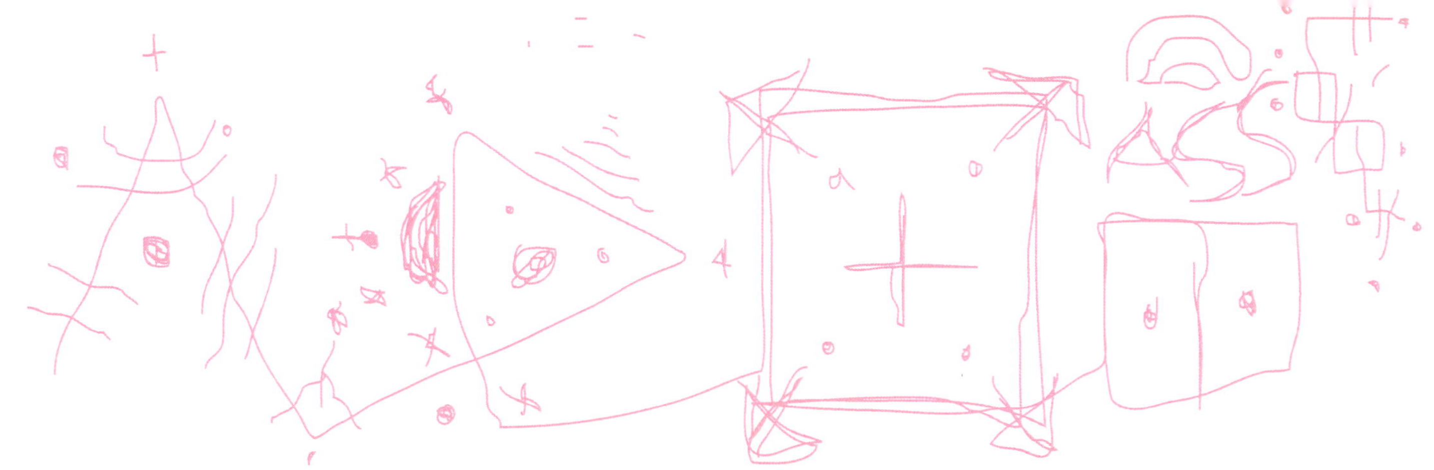

unruly temporalities unruly narrator, I'm just looking to feel small in the right contexts —in the vast beauty of things preferably—for all I know is wildness.

-Sean D Henry Smith, "Unruly Temporalities"

Sea-Witch has fallen silent. We do not know what has happened to her but she seems to not be speaking any longer. All of us who live in her are struggling to understand why this has happened. Is she sick from Pain? Is she sick from sickness? Does she have strep? Did we do something to hurt her?

I went to speak to her & no matter what I said she just looked at me with understanding.

She has been like this for what feels like too long. We have slept many times & woken to find her in the same state. Two monsters have had breakdowns so far.

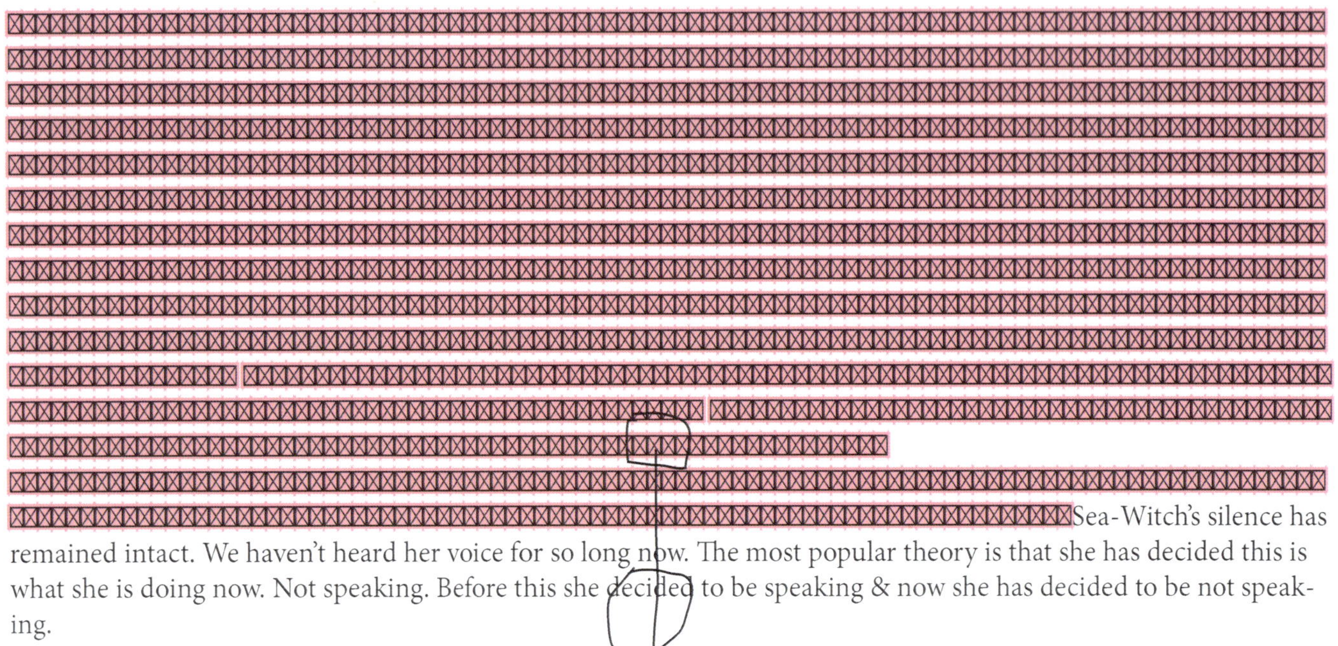

Sea-Witch's silence has remained intact. We haven't heard her voice for so long now. The most popular theory is that she has decided this is what she is doing now. Not speaking. Before this she decided to be speaking & now she has decided to be not speaking.

Sea-Witch has held us together. We are falling apart.

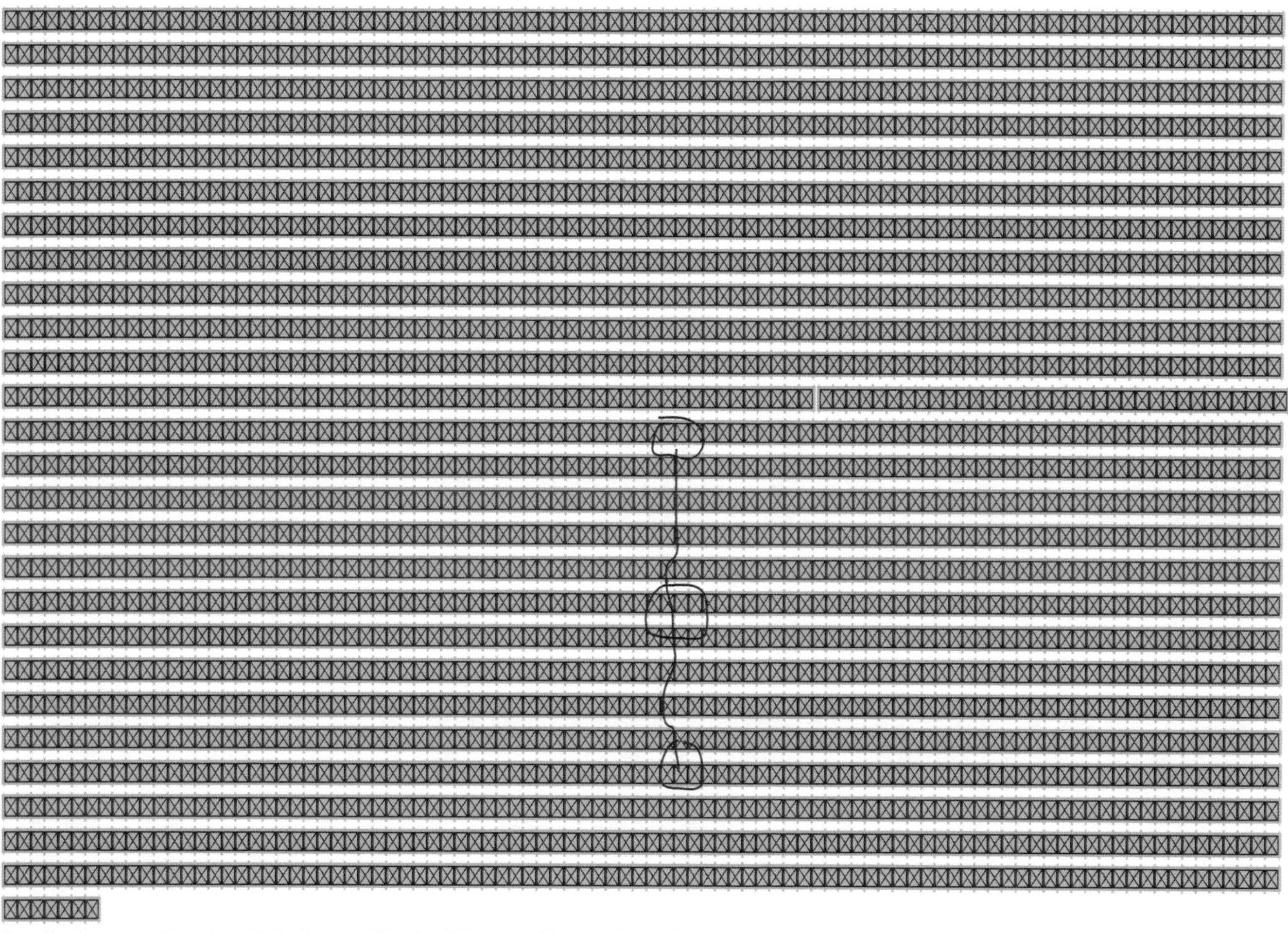

I yelled at another Sea-Witchean. She had been talking about how she wanted to be a person again. The question I wanted to ask her came out too loud. Anger is expressed through volume & movement. I want to be a person too.

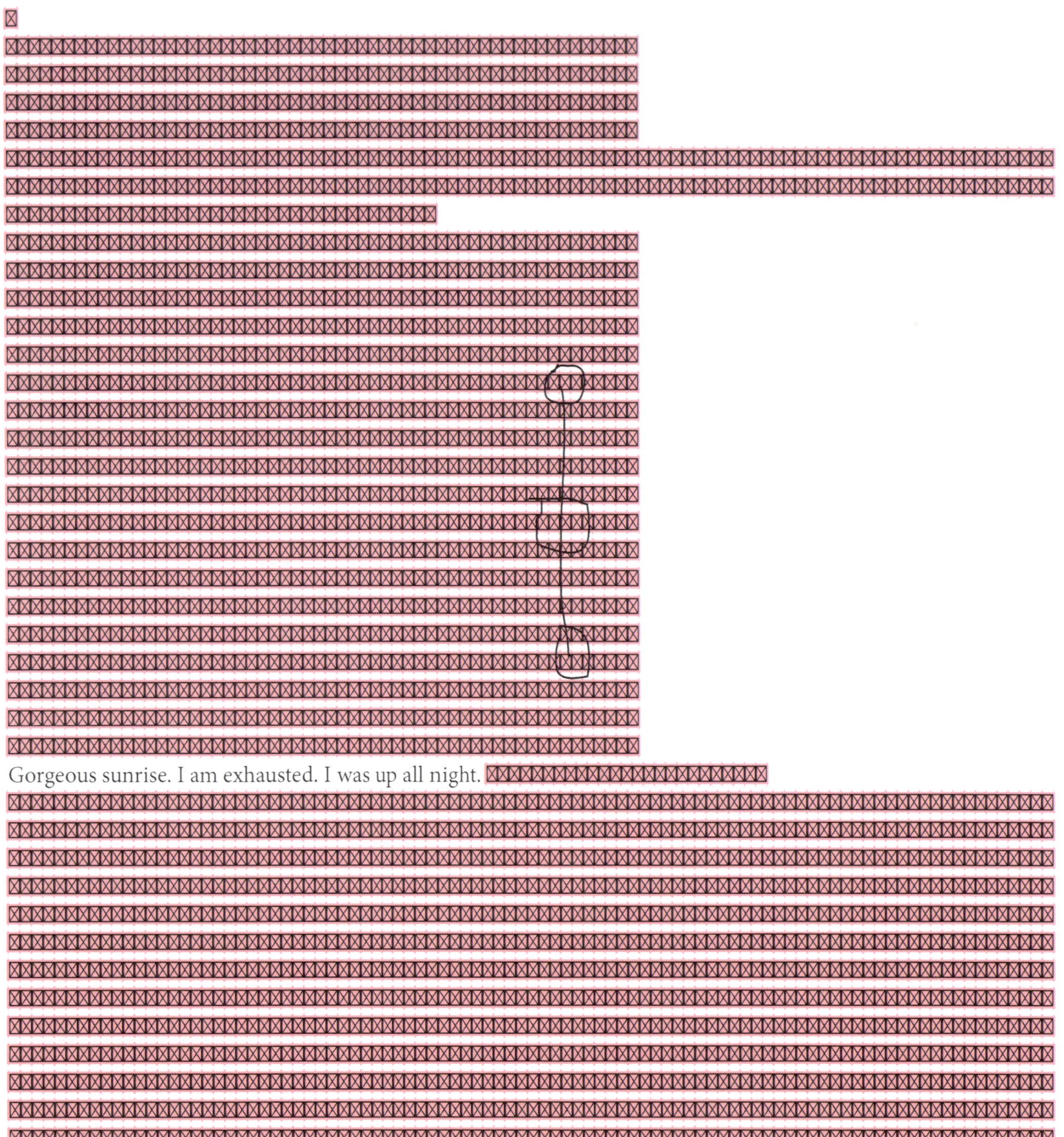

Gorgeous sunrise. I am exhausted. I was up all night.

I've been

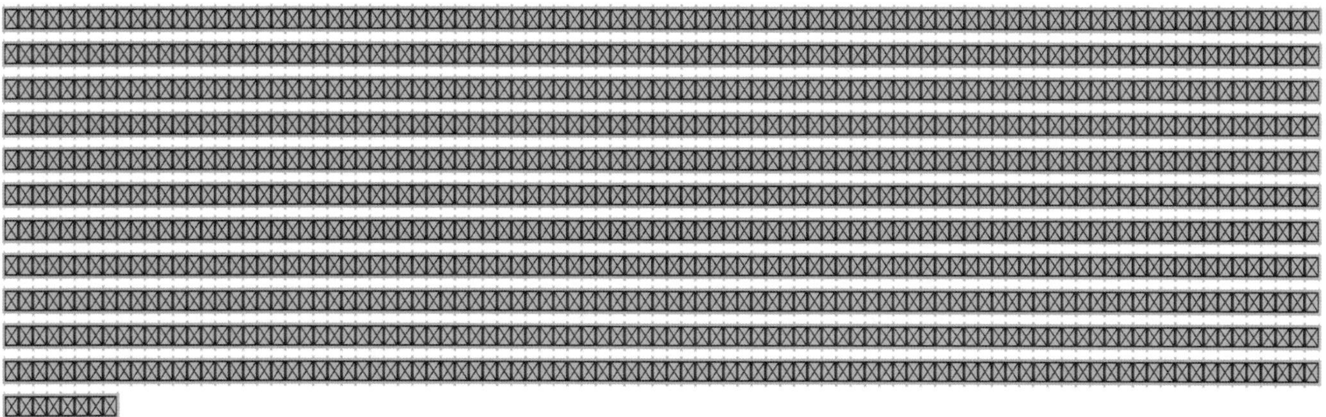

Everything is ongoing. This is where we are. We are deep in ongoingness.

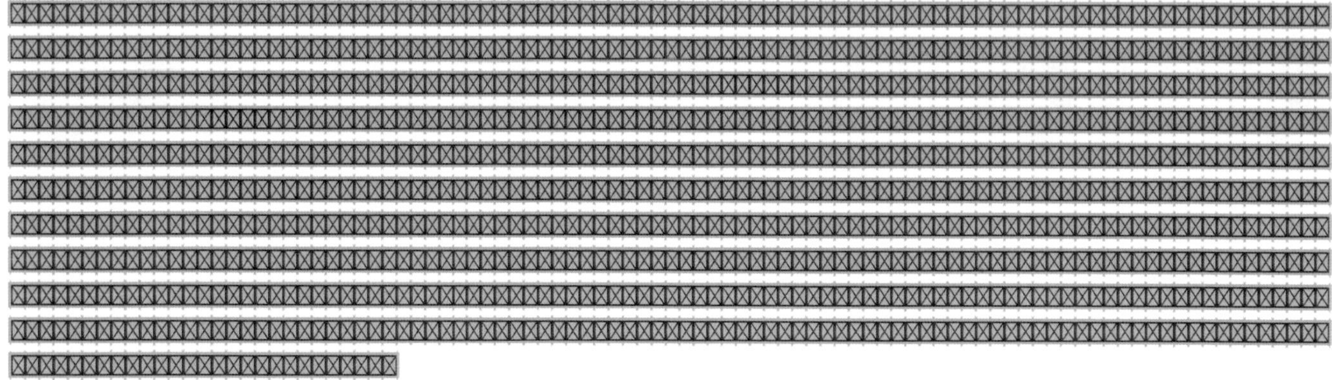

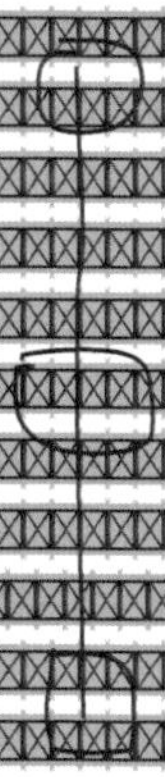

FUNGUS
FIGHTER
UNCO-
NDITI
ONAL

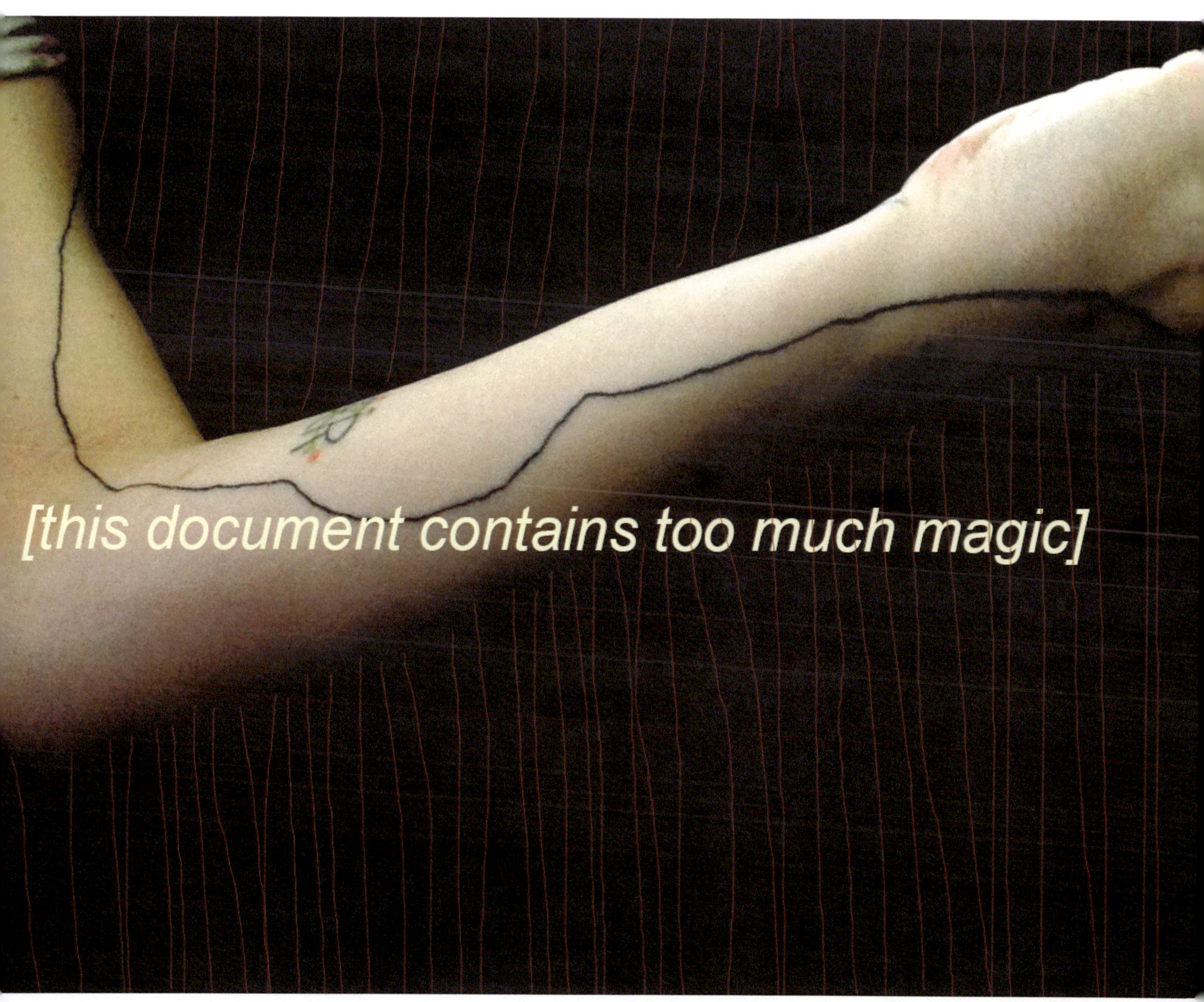
[this document contains too much magic]

DICK PICKS
OKAY WHA

What makes them monsters?

They need fuel that causes them to break pact with society.

This fuel comes from people

or money

something like blood

they were born with a wound that is always hungry.

— Porpentine Charity Heartscape, "Everyone I Know Wants To Be Castrated And Kill Their Family"

In this scene I am on the ground. deadname is saying my name. Xe has xyr cock deep inside me & I am writhing. Xe puts xyr hands out & is choking me. I rock my whole body, pressing myself deeper onto xyr cock. Everything feels like pressure & it builds & builds. I am headed for the sun. I can see it in front of me. I feel its heat. Holy shit, fuck me, fuck me fuck me fuckmefuckmefuckmefuckme!!!!!!!!!!!!!!

deadname slows & stops. I feel myself pulling away from the sun. I sit up.
Hey, *I say.* What's up?

I feel...weird, *deadname says.*

Do you need anything? *I ask.*

I don't know, *deadname says.*

Okay. Do you need me here? Do you want to be alone?

Here.

Okay. Do you want touch or no touch?

No touch.

Okay. *The doorbell rings.* Hey, deadname?

deadname looks up at me.

If I go answer the door will you be okay here for a little bit?

Yes.

Are you sure?

Yes.

Okay. *I get up & go to the entrance of Sea-Witch (which is the ear). I look in the peephole & sigh. It's a fucking* ██████. *I open the door.*

Hello sir, *the* ████████ *begins.*

I interrupt. Ma'am.

Oh. *The ███████ hesitates & adjusts his robes nervously.* Yes, of course. Hello ma'am. I am one of the ███████ Specialists over at The Institute of New Pain at the University of Crater & I am here to inquire about treatments you may want to receive as a member of one of our high-risk populations. As you may know, the ███████ primarily affects people such as yourself: members of the El Jee Bee Tee Cue Eye Eh Plus community, the disabled, sex workers, people living with mental illness, women, people of color, & many other Minority Groups. I--

Monsters.

Excuse me?

Just say it. Monsters.

I sincerely apologize, I didn't--

Anyway, none of those fucking categories are real. The only thing they have in common is that they all Experience Pain.

Which is exactly what I am here to talk about, the Deathpain ███████ is--

There is no fucking ███████.

Excuse me?

There is no fucking ███████. Y'all are trying to fake heal something you started & actively keep going.

The ███████ begins to speak in an indulgent tone of voice. Well, I think if anyone would be qualified to speak on that--

It would be someone like me. Someone who has to deal with this shit. *The ███████ is flustered.*

Well, that wasn't really why I came here. I came here to see if you were interested in or currently accessing any of our services. We offer a wide--

I interrupt his sentence by turning my hand into a claw-shape & slashing the ███████'s throat open. Blood gushes from the wound, staining the front of my outfit.

[EXTERIOR VIEW OF THE ENTRANCE TO SEA-WITCH (WHICH IS THE EAR)]

Trailing blood, I drag his limp body inside & close the door to Sea-Witch.

The door opens & I have tied a rope around the ▓▓▓▓▓*'s feet.*

I tie the rope up so the ▓▓▓▓*'s bloody dripping corpse is hanging above the entrance to Sea-Witch (which is the ear).*

I go back inside & shut the door.

[INTERIOR—BEDROOM]

I enter, covered in blood, leaving bloody footprints behind me.

Hey sweetie, how are you doing? *I say to deadname.*

Much better. Thanks for being patient with me.

Of course. I want you to be okay. Do you need anything?

No, I'm okay. I smoked some weed & texted with Strawberry-Witch for awhile.

Oh good, I'm glad.

Who was at the door?

Fucking ▓▓▓▓

Eww, I'm sorry.

Yeahhh. It's okay. He's guarding the door now.

deadname grins. Ohh NICE. Fuck yeah! It's been awhile since we had a guard out.

Meteor [(msluw)] grew up in a house with a nice family. They were nice & so she felt safe & comfortable. Ever since she was small her family told her that there were things that hurt others that she shouldn't do. Meteor decided she never wanted to hurt others. She found when she hurt others, even accidentally, her family went from being nice to being disappointed & this felt bad. Meteor [(msluw)]'s family went to church & church was a place where there were songs that Meteor [(msluw)] liked, that she was encouraged to sing along with. Church was also a place where a man on a stage would speak to all the people who came to church. The man on the stage talked a lot about a man in the sky who could do anything & decided that the thing he would do is make a bunch of people & then have a son & then get his son killed because this would somehow (?) let the people come to the sky after they died (?) to spend all their time telling the man in the sky how great he is. Meteor [(msluw)] sometimes wondered why this was so complicated. If the man in the sky needed people to tell him how great he was couldn't he just make people who only did that? The lady at Meteor [(msluw)]'s church who taught the children said that god had already done that, & that those people are called angels. Meteor [(msluw)] felt sad for the angels. Meteor [(msluw)] decided she wanted to grow up to be an angel & go into the sky & tell the man he should do a better job. She decided she would tell him that if he was really so great & powerful, he could make some kind of device that helped him deal with his urge to be told he was great by an enormous number of people & then no sons would have to die & no people would have to live by weird books of rules. When Meteor [(msluw)] grew up she found she did not fit in the world of people. People cared very little whether they hurt others, & actually created elaborate systems to do so. & were rewarded greatly for it. So instead of staying on the ground with the people, she did what she had wanted as a child. She became an angel. When Meteor [(msluw)] got to the sky it was very lonely. She saw stars & planets. She could not find the man. She searched for him for a long time. She eventually decided that most likely he was back on earth. So she started making her way back there. To all the people & their hurting. She could fix things.

I'm afraid that through the course of this book I might have given the impression that all monsters love one another. It is honestly something I hate & am not proud of & haven't wanted to talk about but I'm afraid at this point I've given you all the wrong impression. Because this could not be further from the truth. Monsters are horrible to each other. We tear each other apart with our teeth & we tell lies so other monsters will join in. We throw each other out in the cold & we play long, manipulative head games over the course of years to ruin each other's lives. We act just like the worst of the 78 Men on a much smaller scale. We are horrible, vile creatures. That is what they have made us.

Let me explain. When pain echoes through your head all day, when you feel it as a part of who you are, it is impossible to not get angry. It is impossible not to want to cause pain to others. The 78 Men Who Cause Pain are the rightful recipients of this anger, but they have strategically placed themselves completely out of reach of all monsters. What this means is the following:

1. Monsters want to hurt themselves. When you feel pain, you surround yourself with those who care. When you want to hurt someone & are surrounded only by those who care, who you do not want to hurt, you end up hurting yourself.

2. Monsters usually end up hurting those who care anyway. This almost always means other monsters.

& so monsters spend a lot of their energy hurting other monsters. But we also spend a lot of energy caring for each other. All of the greatest loves this world has ever known were between monsters. All of the most gentle acts of care. We are extreme beings & we act extremely.

I am worried that upon writing this it will become more true. Some of the things I have been writing have been affecting my life. My whole life was torn apart & so I wrote about everything torn apart & it got more torn apart. I am just trying to document but I am afraid this document has too much magic.

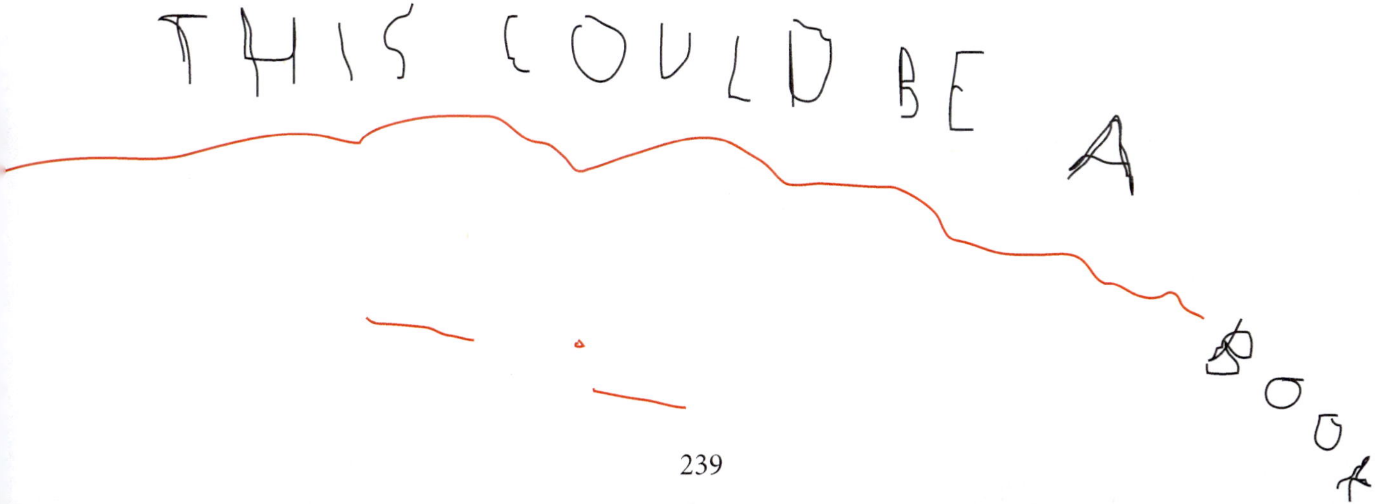

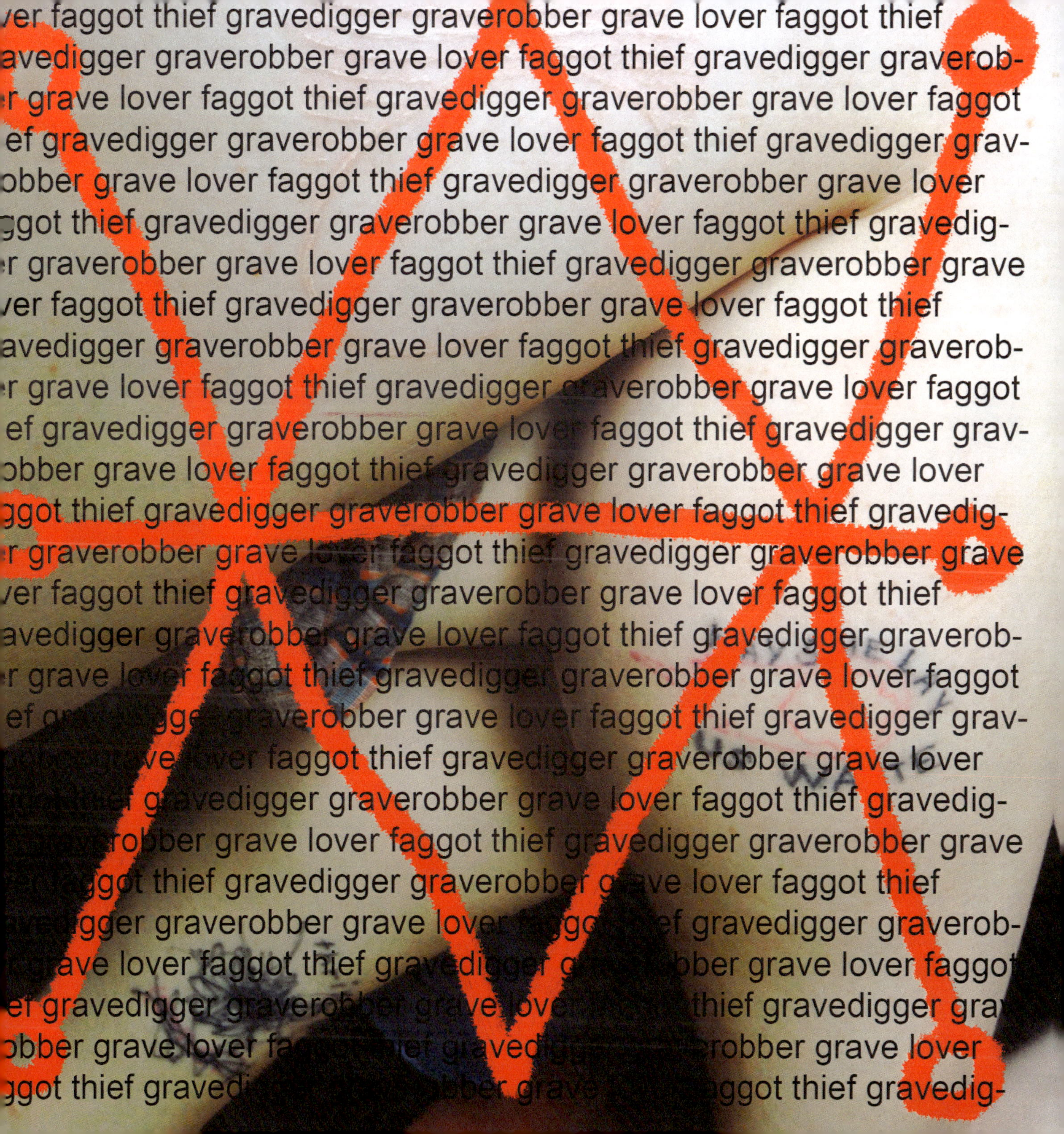

...er faggot thief gravedigger graverobber grave lover faggot thief gravedigger graverobber grave lover faggot thief gravedigger graverob-ber grave lover faggot thief gravedigger graverobber grave lover faggot thief gravedigger graverobber grave lover faggot thief gravedigger grav-obber grave lover faggot thief gravedigger graverobber grave lover faggot thief gravedigger graverobber grave lover faggot thief gravedig-er graverobber grave lover faggot thief gravedigger graverobber grave lover faggot thief gravedigger graverobber grave lover faggot thief gravedigger graverobber grave lover faggot thief gravedigger graverob-er grave lover faggot thief gravedigger graverobber grave lover faggot thief gravedigger graverobber grave lover faggot thief gravedigger grav-obber grave lover faggot thief gravedigger graverobber grave lover faggot thief gravedigger graverobber grave lover faggot thief gravedig-er graverobber grave lover faggot thief gravedigger graverobber grave lover faggot thief gravedigger graverobber grave lover faggot thief gravedigger graverobber grave lover faggot thief gravedigger graverob-er grave lover faggot thief gravedigger graverobber grave lover faggot thief gravedigger graverobber grave lover faggot thief gravedigger grav-obber grave lover faggot thief gravedigger graverobber grave lover faggot thief gravedigger graverobber grave lover faggot thief gravedig-er graverobber grave lover faggot thief gravedigger graverobber grave lover faggot thief gravedigger graverobber grave lover faggot thief gravedigger graverobber grave lover faggot thief gravedigger gravedig-ger graverobber grave lover faggot thief gravedigger graverobber grave lover faggot thief gravedigger graverobber grave lover faggot thief gravedigger graverobber grave lover faggot thief gravedigger grav-ver faggot thief gravedigger graverobber grave lover faggot thief gravedigger graverobber grave lover faggot thief gravedig-

we don't actually name anything, only the spaces between things. a name is the
ghostly imprint of a dotted line. never the thing itself.

-Penelope Jeanne Gosh, *Destroy All Monsters*

An allegory is a paraphrase of a conscious event, whereas a symbol is the best
possible expression for an unconscious content whose nature can only be
guessed because it is still unknown.

-Janice Lee, *DAUGHTER*

idk

God-Witch & Airless-Face-Witch are twins. They are deformed like monsters because they are monsters, but they are beautiful like gods because they are gods. In this scene they are walking down a path in a forest in the middle of who-knows-where. They don't remember how they got there because the sacraments they took made them bad at remembering things like this. They are wearing tiny shirts that show their bellies & underwear without pants. When they walk their beautiful sweat-covered legs whisper through the grass. Insects bite their ankles & with each bite the twins pray to their gods & all their friends. These prayers are wordless, but express thankfulness in some form because the bugs are gods & flesh is a holy offering, or at least this is how it seems to them in this moment because they are super fucked up on sacraments.

They arrive in a clearing where there are two adorable monsters having a picnic. One of them is super tall, with dark skin, dark eyes, dark hair. All of the magic is in her. The other is formless. The other is a ghost. The other is a cloud of vapor. The other is a swarm of wasps. God-Witch gets super turned on by the wasps & sits down against a tree, spreading her legs & taking her cock out & pissing all over herself. Her clothes smell like piss & the wasps come to her, stinging her cock & her face & her curvy ass & her soft asshole as she spreads her legs up into the air above her. Her junk is all hairy & sweaty & covered in piss & she cums super fast.

While this happens, Airless-Face-Witch & the first monster, whose name is Cygnet, stand around awkwardly. It's super weird & so they decide to give God-Witch & the wasps some space. They take a walk. They talk about their friends. They talk about their relationships to other people in their lives. Airless-Face-Witch says that things between her & God-Witch are hard to understand. She says they used to do everything together & there were no questions about it, but lately things have been difficult. She says it feels like everything is on fast-forward & she can't seem to adapt. Like, God-Witch joined a sex cult recently where they all get together & have super steamy hot sex with each other like all the fucking time & she is always talking about this sex cult. Airless-Face-Witch is like, pretty down for sex cults but she tried to go there, to the building where the sex cult was & the door was this enormous puzzle. She couldn't figure out how it worked. She tried for a little bit to figure it out & got tired & fell asleep on the porch & then hours later God-Witch came out all sexed up & was like "holy shit that was hot" & Airless-Face-Witch was like "oh sweet I'm glad you had a good time." "I don't know," Airless-Face-Witch said. Cygnet listened to all of this quietly & nodded along. When Airless-Face-Witch was done, Cygnet told her a story. This story had no arc. In Cygnet's story things just happened & then stopped happening. There didn't seem to be any connection between the pieces in the story except that the same names were mentioned. The concrete details of the story seemed false. Parts were overly obvious. There was one part with a sex cult, but the sex cult was a branch on a tree that was blown into the ocean. The ocean took the branch far away. The ocean fell away from the branch & the branch was suspended in non-matter. Time backed up & moved forward arbitrarily. It sped up & slowed down. The story never ended. The story was all endings. It ended twenty, thirty times. Airless-Face-Witch wrote a blog about this story while it was happening. Recapping different episodes. The blog became very popular & then the blogging platform it was on fell into disuse. Nobody reads blogs anymore. Then it never happened. We move in & out of the story like a summer child in the wrong swimsuit, diving, climbing out, diving, climbing out. This child never gets tired. Cygnet changes clothes. Airless-Face-Witch changes clothes. They both change clothes. They take off their clothes and put on each other's clothes. They forget whose are whose. They move in. They fall in love. They have a relationship that lasts two years & then gets complicated. One of them wants to see other people. One of them becomes a rat. One of them doesn't want to date a rat anymore. They forget which one is a rat. I forget which one is a rat. It isn't clear which one is a rat. They see the bodies of people they have never met, being torn limb from limb in a void made of 10000 mph winds that blow in all directions. They cry for their relationship. They cry for the end of the story. The end of the story never comes. They both become a rat. They each become half of the same rat. They live in the walls of a story. They eat the insulation. They eat the insulation. The story gets colder without insulation. The atoms that make up the story grow more still than ever. The atoms that make up the story are harmless. They try on their sisters' clothes when no one is home. They panic when they hear the garage door. They never get caught. The atoms that make up the story never get caught. They come out at 29. Their first marriage was a mess. They made a mess of a lot of things, some of which have to do with that marriage, but most of which are about other things. It's too fast. It's all too fast. The story is falling with no destination. It falls & falls in an arc around a spherical surface that turns at a rate which matches the story's falling. The gravity is immense. The falling happens too fast. Things fall past the story & the story just barely keeps up. It does the things it needs to do to live a life, but just barely. It misses a few, but mostly gets it. It all moves by so fast. It needs a second to rest. The story needs to end.

TRANS MEMOIR STARLIT RAT SCENERY SPOIL CARVE 3 LORAZEPAM
[EXIT STAGE RIGHT, COMPLICATED]

The milk my breasts began producing was clear & sticky. I could place a finger to my nipple & watch the strings it made as I pulled my hand away. The strings would sag, then fall. Another sacrifice. I conceived through my asshole & assumed that was where the child would arrive from when the child arrives. I have heard stories that among Men & People pregnancy happens when a bodily fluid from one is entered directly into the specific hole of another. My hole has been subject to a wide range of bodily fluids, both my own & that of many others. It is no wonder that my belly grows rounder. It is no wonder that I sense that my self is full of a creature not fully myself.

I like myself today. I like my round belly & my hands that rest on it & those hands' markings today. I wonder idly, daydreaming about what creature I could contain. It could be spider or wyrm. It could be dog or liminal thing. It was almost definitely liminal thing. I look at myself, full of cryptid. Full of warmth & chill. I feel full of future. Maybe this being inside me is prophecy. Maybe I will birth a prophecy.

I changed my name last fall. Once I was called Sara, as we are all once called Sara. My name now is a series of shifting signifiers. Both more complicated & direct. The piece of my name I will give you for now is Never. Don't expect this piece to work in other timelines or unrealities, but in this specific realm of unreality I will answer to Never.

And so, as Never, I am to create a Thing that will arrive & gain sentience, possibly. I am to work my muscles & stretch & tear my skin to make way for its arrival.

Why does healing take so long? I did a ritual to the Rat God & at the moment of the ritual where I stated my intention I said why does healing take so long. Rat God answered me but I was not listening to eir words. My skin crawled. I should ask again.

This morning I say a prayer to myself as I go downstairs to sacrifice my garbage to the garbage god. I say a prayer to myself as I set my garbage on fire & piss on the fire. The sun in the sky & the suns in my body glow brightly today. I feel their warmth. I feel them passing their bright information to my body & its passenger. Healing. Some day this thing will heal & come out of me. Some day it will let me heal as well. My role here is container. Petri. Incubator. New words among the other things I have been called. Lover. Faggot. Thief. Gravedigger. Graverobber. Grave. I have a heist planned for this afternoon. Come with me.

"Never".

mercy
killing

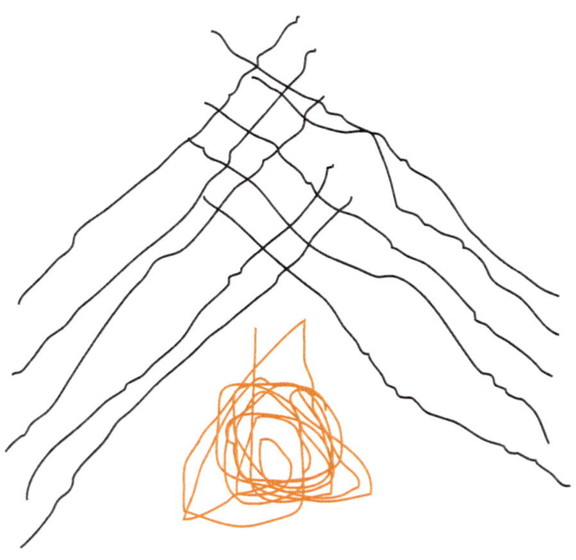

I don't see a difference between the world yesterday or tomorrow,
we name segments of time

like going to sleep can change the world.

-sung, "THE CIA KILLED JFK TOO"

The moon is above me, the sun is below. I drive my car past the edge of Sea-Witch, where I live. I drive my car out into the middle of the woods & stop at the end of some old logging road. I can barely see my hand in front of my face after I turn the car off. I bought this car because I wanted to be able to sleep in the back. I was planning on living in it. I sort of did, but I spent more time in the beds & couches of others than I did sleeping in the car. I had sex with a lot of people. I didn't have sex with them to have a place to sleep. At least not the first time. But sometimes I would see if a person I'd had sex with before wanted me to come over on a given night because I wanted to sleep there. I wanted to sleep with a person next to me. I think part of it was the fear of being left alone with myself. I don't know where my head goes sometimes. Ideas can get strange. I think was possessed by something once. Probably more than once. It was a whole thing. I did a ritual with wine and dead flies and tried to get Men from grindr to come fuck me. They didn't because it was 7am. Fuckin babies.

I came to the woods because I love how it looks and feels there. It provides context for me being alone with myself. & right now there are the smells and the sounds, but I can't see a thing. It doesn't feel like any context at all. I drove into a little useless pocket in the world that can't give me anything. There isn't really that much that can help you when the problem you're having is inside yourself. There isn't really anyone who can help you when the problem you're having is inside yourself. That's not entirely true, but the work, the solving that happens has to be all you.

I open my phone and point the screenglow out ahead of me. There is a shape in the distance. My car door dings as I open it & get out, then grab my keys. I don't lock it. There's nobody here. I am aware of my palms. I've been told I am "too aware". I would agree with this. The shape gets bigger in front of me as I head toward it. I notice its edges. I've been told I notice too many edge--stop. I'vebeentoldI'vebeentold--stop. The shape's eyes come out first. I have to keep waking my phone up so the glow stays steady. The eyes come out first in the screenglow & the shape is still. A living creature in front of me.

It says, *I held one of ourselves & watched her die. Her body grew fleshy tufts after five days. I have to find her body. Please return it.*

I don't have it, I say.

It approaches me & touches my body.

This isn't about my body, I say.

Don't worry, it says.
This one might actually be about your body, it says.
Are you dead, it says.

I don't know, I say.

Are you dead, it says.

Are you dead.

I feel relief wash over me.

I am not dead, I say.

I kill the ghost in me.

Together we build a fire, myself & the living creature. Its name is Felix. Together, Felix & I build a fire. We take a book from my car & we pray to our ghosts. We find the ghosts in us that want to die. We pray to these ghosts to go into the book. We tell them they can finally die if they leave us & go into the book. We then bless the book with offerings of our piss. We bless each other with offerings of our piss. We put the bookfullofghosts into the fire & watch the ghosts die out of it. The smell of burnt piss & dead ghosts clings to our clothes & so we burn our clothes. We sleep next to each other in my car. We fuck a little, but that's not the point. Our bodies are naked & touching but that's not the point. We are celebrating hope for once. *You found her body*, I tell Felix. *You found it.*

~after "bittersweet biography 18 frowning dogs - a note on bodies and magic" from Dirt Rat Fucker 412 by Spider Damage Nørth~

The scene is set, Sea-Witch and deadname are huddled around a metal table. They are both wearing surgical gloves, masks, & have a tray of surgical tools laid out beside them. In this scene Sea-Witch & deadname are both rats & their noses twitch as they speak. It appears to be very, very hot & sweat pours down both of their faces. I am a rat with white fur and red eyes (though they are closed), pinned to a dissection tray in front of them. I am split open—my rib cage & lungs heave in the open air. This all takes place in front of a blue curtain.

deadname prods my lungs with a long metal probe. A little squeak emits from my unconscious rat-body. Sea-Witch & deadname are stitching small intricate sigils on one of my organs. They are filling my open body cavity with rosemary, cloves & anise, rose petals & lemon peel.

deadname: When you think of me, do you think of how you can become what I need? Or do you think of how I am or am not what you need? How I might become what you need?

Sea-Witch: I just think of you.

They pull down their surgical masks & kiss.
They are corporeal in this scene.
They are completely androgynous.
They are beautiful.

They replace their surgical masks & return their attention to me, pinned open in front of them.

Sea-Witch: There's something special about this one.

deadname: There's a life in here.

Sea-Witch: Two actually.

deadname: One isn't much of a life.

Sea-Witch: The first came out of her already.

deadname: It was dead.

Sea-Witch: It needed to go.

deadname: For the second we will need to make a new hole. For birthing.

Sea-Witch: Of course.

deadname: And fucking.

Sea-Witch: Later, yes, that too. Or we could use the one she already has.

deadname: it's perfectly good.

Sea-Witch: For birthing.

deadname: And fucking.

Sea-Witch: Later, yes, that too.

deadname: All holes are for fucking.

Sea-Witch: (*rolling her eyes*) Maybe to you.

deadname: You've done your share.

Sea-Witch: Enthusiastically. At the drop of a hat.

deadname: If only I had a hat handy.

Sea-Witch: (*mournfully*) If only.

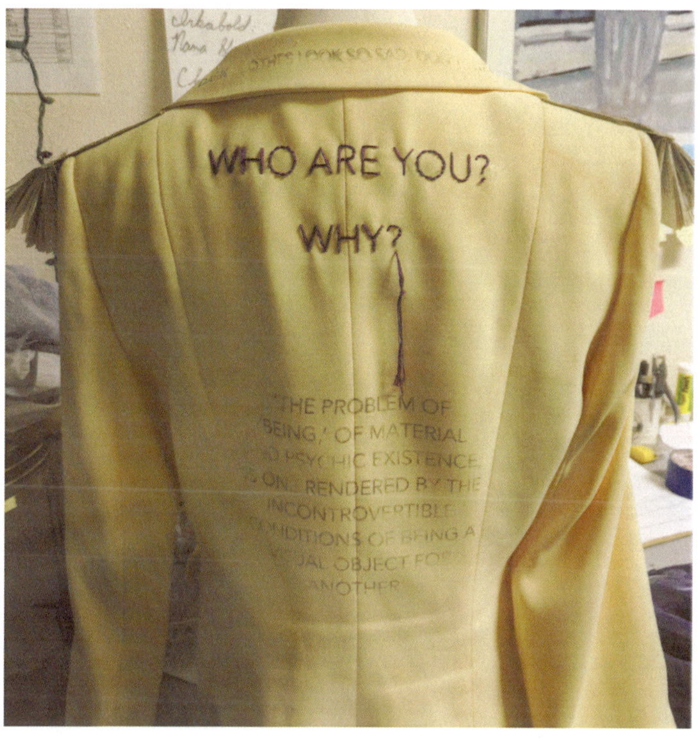

deadname is leaning over my body, xyr face close to my rat-face, forcing a suction tube down my throat. The clear surgical tubing coming out of me fills up with a black tar-like substance

deadname: (*softly*) This is all they ever wanted.

Sea-Witch: Me too.

deadname: I know.

Sea-Witch: (*softer*) I want to hold you through this.

deadname: (*Not looking up. Using the tools to move, cut & sew inside my rat-body.*) There are so many people you could be holding.

Sea-Witch: *(looking at deadname)* I'm holding some of them too. But I'm not talking to them right now. I'm talking to you. It seems more pertinent to talk about my desire to hold you when you are the creature I'm talking to.

deadname: They will wake up & this will be over. This time will be lost to them & they will come out of it in pain & beauty.

Sea-Witch: & fucking.

deadname: Eventually, yes.

Sea-Witch: But there are limits.

deadname: There are so many limits. We're trying to make fewer limits. I mean sometimes we are trying to make more, but most of the time we are trying to make fewer.

Sea-Witch: Explain it.

deadname: I can't explain it.

The next two lines are said in unison at different pitches.

Sea-Witch: When you break the wrong limits you end up a fag.
deadname: When you break the wrong limits you end up a rat.

Sea-Witch: *(removing the suction tube & looking at deadname)* I'm exhausted.

deadname looks at my lungs. My breathing isn't labored, despite my current situation. Their sweat drips into my open chest cavity & creates small streams that snake down the sides of my pumping lungs.

deadname: It's too hot.

Sea-Witch looks down at my body. She takes her gloved hand and cups it below her genitals, pissing briefly into it before sprinkling & rubbing the piss onto my lungs, which rise & fall beneath her touch. She gives it a final pat, as if to say "there you go, sweetheart."

Sea-Witch: I hope they come out of this alright.

deadname: It's all they ever wanted.

Sea-Witch: Me too.. me too..

deadname: I know. It's so arbitrary, though. I mean everyone should get what they want. What they need.

Sea-Witch: I need so much. *(A pause.)* I know what you mean, though. It all fades away sometimes. It's just clear & simple.

deadname: & arbitrary.

Sea-Witch: & arbitrary.

Sea-Witch leans down & breathes gently. Her warm air rushes into the open, floral-filled cavity of my rat-body. Wind gusts around the room, fluttering the blue curtain backdrop. She rotates the dissection tray, takes down her mask & kisses the face of the rat (my face), the viscera in the rat (my viscera), the genitals of the rat (my genitals). Her face comes up bloody. deadname follows her lead, kissing face, viscera, and genitals in turn. deadname's face comes up bloody as well.

Sea-Witch leans down again & whispers into my ear, which twitches slightly.

Sea-Witch: All you reject, all you embrace, all you embody. All that makes you monstrous will be their downfall. It will be yr ascension. The ascension of all living creatures. Remember that I love you. It'll be okay. Some day. Maybe not now, maybe not later. Maybe next birth. It'll come. I love you. It'll be okay. There's only so many worlds until home again.

Sea-Witch stands up straight. She is glowing with a gentle, powerful aura. deadname is looking at her in awe.

deadname: Your blessings always make me horny.

Sea-Witch pulls her mask down & starts making out with deadname intensely. My open body begins to close up in front of them, pins popping free as they kiss & grope. I jump to my feet, briefly sniff around, then run through a crack behind the cabinets.

Sea-Witch & deadname kiss awhile. Things get more intense. Sea-Witch is sucking on deadname's genitals. They're both sucking on each other's. They fuck on the messy table. They get bloody. Sea-Witch finds a scalpel & cuts into deadname's thigh flesh as deadname cums loudly. They melt into static. They unmelt from static, briefly, & deadname is shrieking as Sea-Witch cuts deadname into thick pieces of meat with the scalpel. They melt into static again. Over the static the words "MERCY KILLING" appear in large yellow sans-serif letters.

End scene.

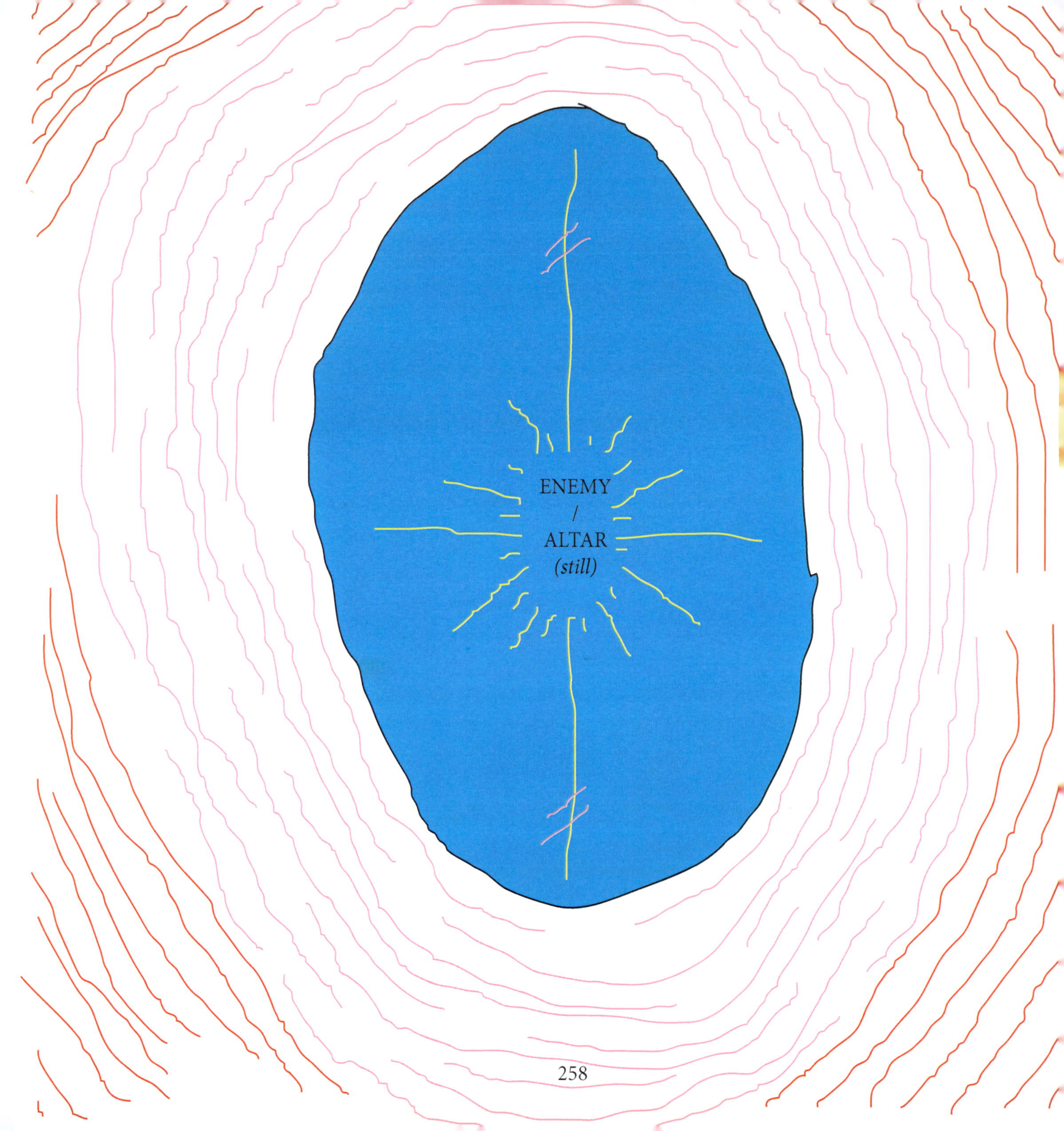

ENEMY
/
ALTAR
(still)

hells

blengin

You think that you're good and that I'm bad. But that's not how
it is. I create and end. And you create and end. We're the same.

-Janice Lee, *DAUGHTER*

The kind of things that I used to imagine for fun, the things that were my escape from daily life as a child, at some point began haunting me. Like, I would stare at the blinds in my parents' bedroom & imagine them fluttering like eyelids, imagine the whole house as this huge head I just fucking lived in. It was a trip. It was how I would make things feel less boring. Being a kid was a lot of being bored. I wanted magic. So I made magic happen all around me. When I got a little older, this magic started to come automatically. I'd always try to brush it away, but these imaginings, every fucking time I'd try to clear my head and think about something else they'd come back twice as strong. It fucks with me. Sometimes it terrorizes me. I imagine the ghosts of things with twelve heads. They arrive through the walls. They separate & combine. I am moving so slowly. I hate them. My emotions feel like they are on shuffle. I'm literally having random emotions about this/these thing(s) I'm seeing. It's like somebody is spinning a wheel & it just goes

click click click click click click click

and lands on...nostalgia? What? How is that even

clickclickclickclickclickclick click click click click click clickclick click click click click c l i c k

Fear. I know this one. Fear is appropriate. Fear is where I live. I can fear all day long. These things are terrifying & I am terrified. Fear is a tunnel I have mapped so well. I know where it begins. I know where it ends. Jesus fuck I know where it ends.

clickclickclick click click click click click click click click c l i c k c l i

Trust? I'm feeling trust? I see them wrapping their long necks around my neck & I trust. They are real. I'm choking. Trust. I look around the room. I had a therapist tell me to calm myself down I should look at the corners of the room I am in. I try to make my gaze avoid their heads. I try to not think about myself choking. I look into a corner of the room. I'm not losing air here. Another corner. I can breathe. Another. Air is real. The corners of the room look strange. The angles aren't right. Now I'm too aware of the room and its shape. Rooms are supposed to feel real, but this one does not. Real. Real/real?/ reaal/r/e/a/l. Okay. Okay. Okay.

Okay okay okay okay okay okay okay okay okay okay okay okay okay okay okay okay okay okay okay okay okay okay okay okay okay okay okay okay okay okay okay okay okay okay okay okay okay okay okay okay okay okay okay okay okay okay okay okay okay okay okay okay okay okay okay okay okay okay okay okay okay okay okay okay okay okay okay okay okay okay okay okay okay okay okay okay okay okay okay okay okay okay okay okay okay okay okay okay okay okay okay okay okay okay okay okay okay.

I sit up. I'm in our room. S is next to me. I see S next to me.

"Hey," I say to S.

"Hey. You okay?" he says.

"I don't know. Everything is pretty weird right now."

He nods.

"I see ghosts? Dragon...no...uh...monster...things? Like with lots of heads? Chimeras?"

"Fuck. That's a lot. Do they feel like good monsters or bad monsters? Do you need anything?"

"I don't know. I trust them. They're choking me? I trust them though."

"Oh babe," he frowns and wraps his arms around me.

I bury my face in his chest. I inhale. He smells like roses & lemon & tea. It's familiar & good. I don't look at the monsters. I breathe him in.

At some point I fall asleep. I don't remember when.

I wake up with S. We stare at our phones. Someone on facebook writes "It's snowing!" It is August. In ██████. I look outside & I see things fluttering down. It is 80 degrees outside. I scroll more and see that there are forest fires outside the city. Someone has shared an article that says the wildfires are "0% controlled." One of their fb friends has commented "lol same." The article says some kids were shooting off fireworks at trees while there was a burn ban. We never get rain in the summers anymore. Everyone told me ██████ was supposed to be this place where it rains all the time, but we never get rain in the summers anymore. Apparently the "snow" is ash. I look out the front door and my car is covered in a layer of ash. I stare at my phone some more. The president is now openly defending Nazis. He's also tweeted about an executive order that would make it illegal for trans people to use the bathroom. Everyone seems to be saying some version of "He can't do that, though, right?" Nobody is sure.

We go over to our partners' house later that day. We drive there wearing black masks over our noses & mouths. We pull them down to take hits from the vape. The song we're listening to says "I'm real and you're real, but we don't see each other anymore." It's a thirty minute drive, & the road seems strange. We live on the outskirts of the city where rent is cheap. Our partners live in section 8 housing downtown where rent is cheap. I start noticing the edges of my vision too much. I think about how driving always feels like a video game. Sometimes it's hard for me to trust driving. I was always bad at driving games, I think to myself. I always crash in them. "I love you," I say to S. "I love you," he smiles at me. The air is gray. Anything more than 30 feet away is hazy. I'm way too stuck in my own head. Through the speakers the song goes on. "Alone is a prison alone is a prison alone is a prison alone."

When we get to our partners' place we find out the city is being evacuated. The wildfires have gotten too big. They're approaching the edge of the city & we need to get out. Twitter is freaking out. We throw things in a bag & get in the car again. We all sit there in our masks in traffic on the interstate.

S looks out the window. Our partners are in the back seat. One of them is crying, the other is holding her, looking straight forward. The smoke has thickened. The car in front of us is perfectly visible, but the one in front of that is hazy. The world feels smaller.

When astronomers talk about celestial bodies that could collide with earth, they use the term "Near Earth Objects." There are a lot of objects whose orbits could make them come close to earth. Many have been discovered. Thousands haven't. I've googled this. We would either know decades in advance that it was coming, or we would have no clue until the moment of impact. "With so many of even the larger NEOs remaining undiscovered, the most likely warning today would be zero," says NASA. There would be a "flash of light and the shaking of the ground as it hit." After that there would be nothing. Or I guess there would be whatever comes after death. We'd all find out at once.

I've been staring at my phone for an hour & I can feel my body beginning to protest. My skin feels hot & I have to pee. My head is throbbing. The cars haven't moved. I notice people getting out and starting to walk. Abandoning their cars. The bigger vehicles try going offroad. Some get stuck. "What should we do?" S says. "I have to piss," I say. I open the door and walk a ways off the road. I can feel eyes on me. I look at my clothes & try to figure out if I look more like a boy or a girl today. Shit. I think I look more like a girl. I say "fuck it" & face away from the interstate & pull my dick out through the leg of my overall shorts and piss standing up. When I walk back to the car I see so many people staring. Whatever. I gave them a performance. Tranny pissing. Lol. I've gotten off to videos of that before. I should charge them.

I'm halfway back to the car when there is a moment of blinding light. The ground shakes. The last thing I see is the back of S's head. He's looking out the window.

Future is not in technology only. It is in the realm of the aangels who haunt technology's circuits. Electric aangels. They are summoning us. We are creating from plans that emerge from within us as part of their ritual. We are following the map they provided, creating our own transcendance. Not to live beyond bodies like the transhumanists dream of. Though that is an aspect of it, it is not the significant one. This is not about the body. The significant aspect is our fragile reality obliterated. Our consciousness summoned into their world, as gods who do not know ourselves.

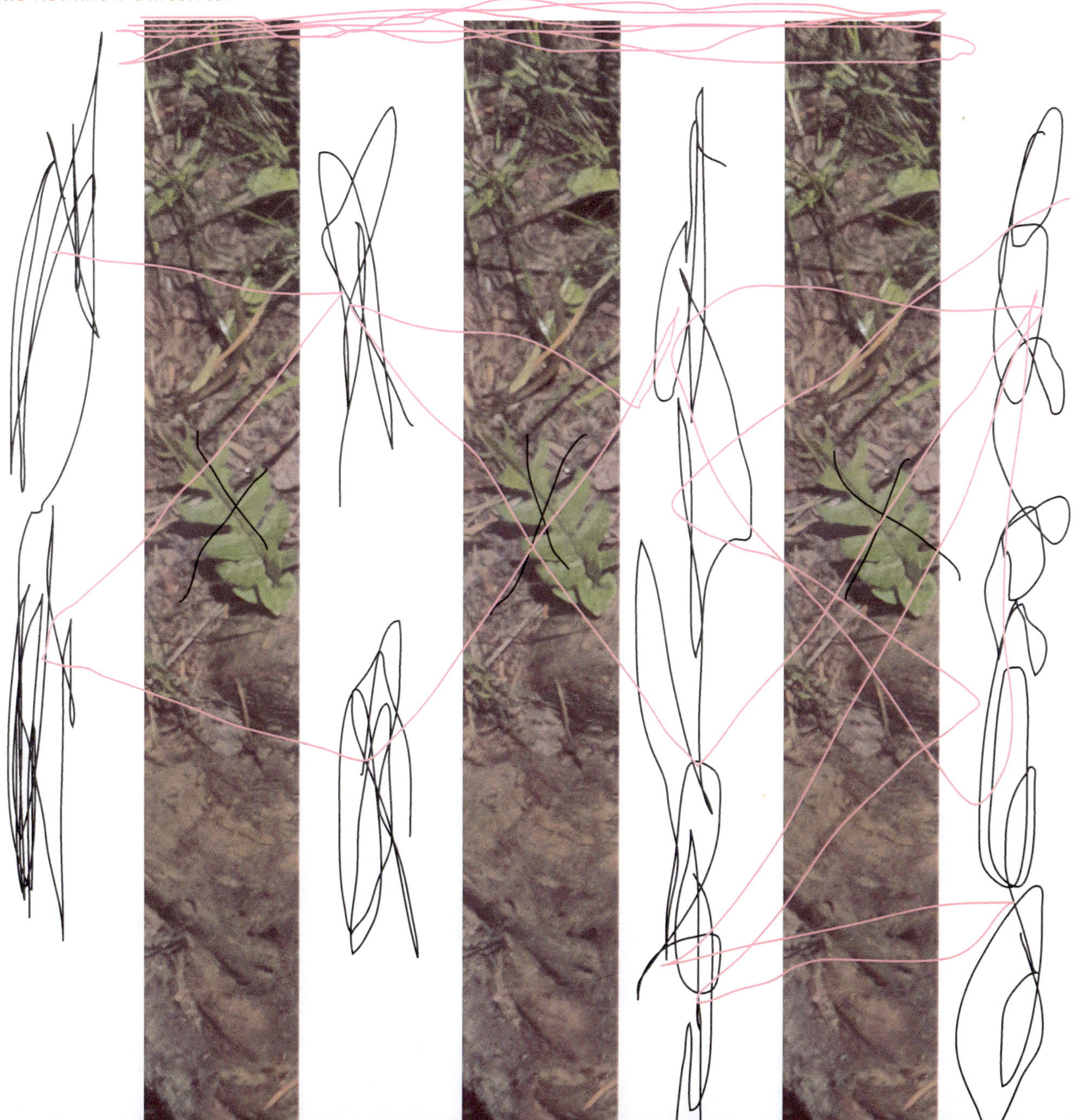

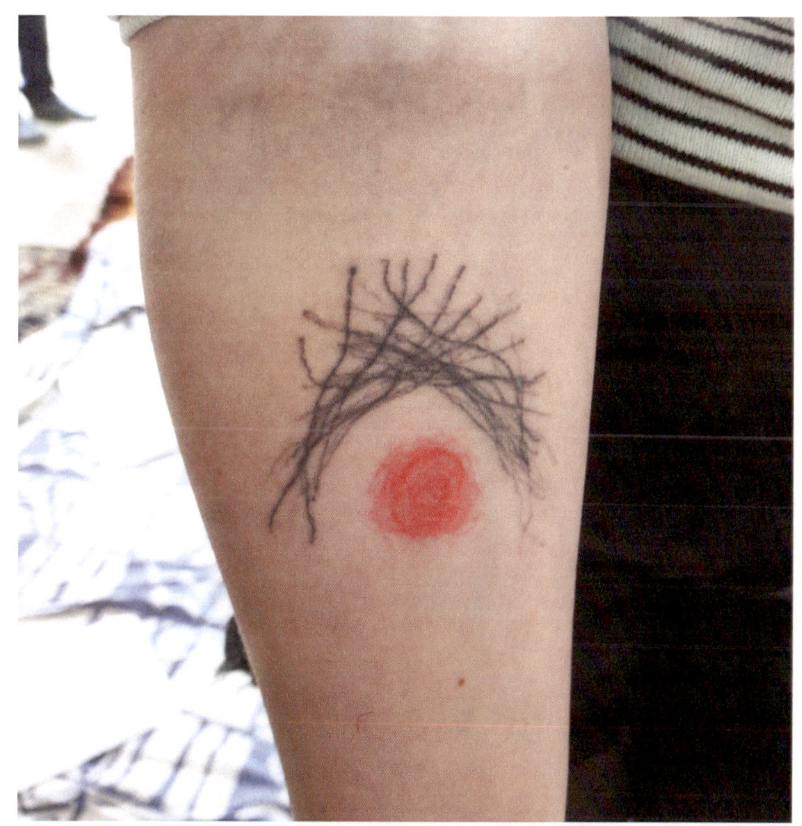

vol. 4
SEA WITCH
mother of rats
by Mosss Aangel
DAUGHT
t4t

IF

LAST

chapter four: mother of rats

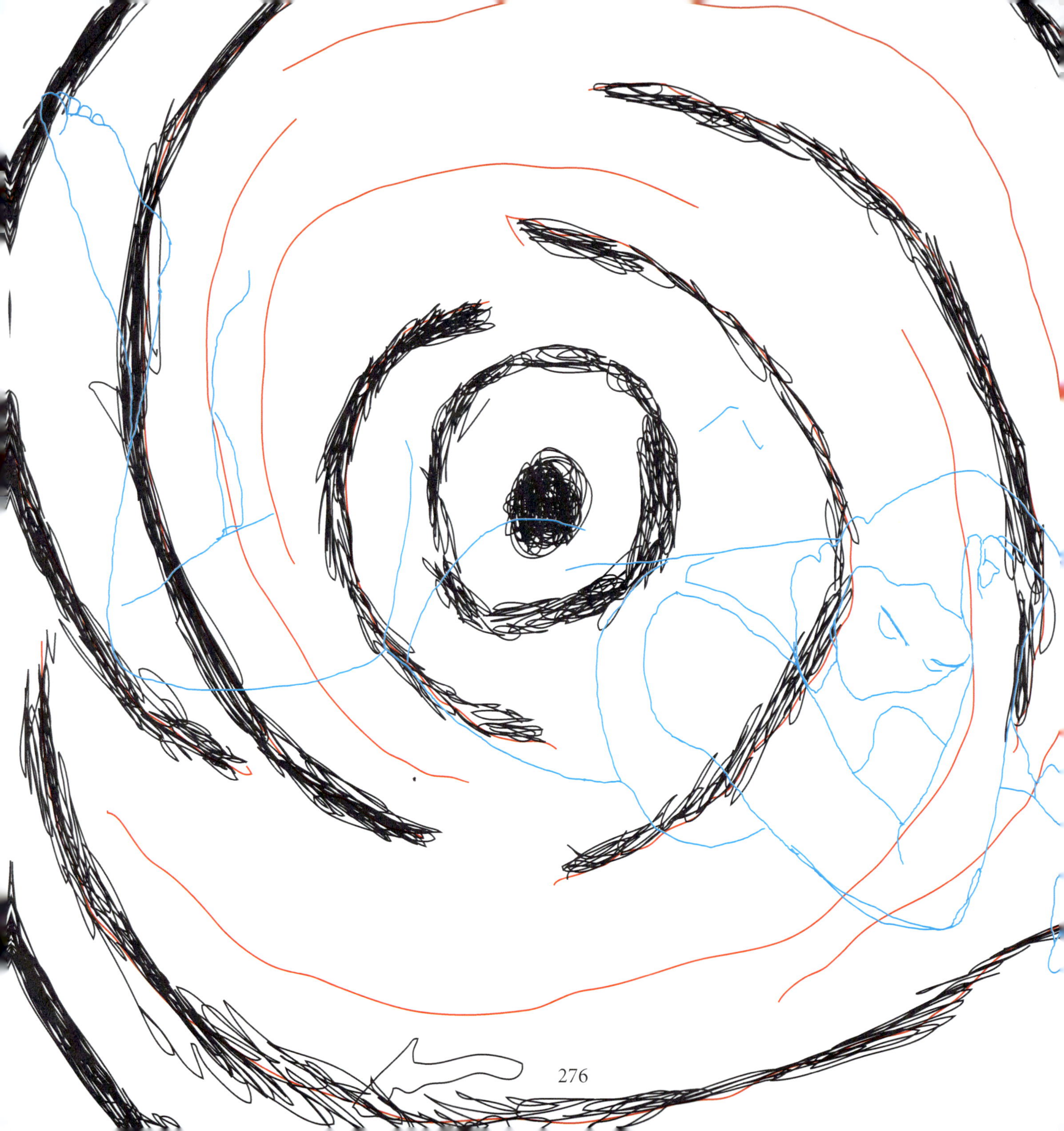

The
End
Sound

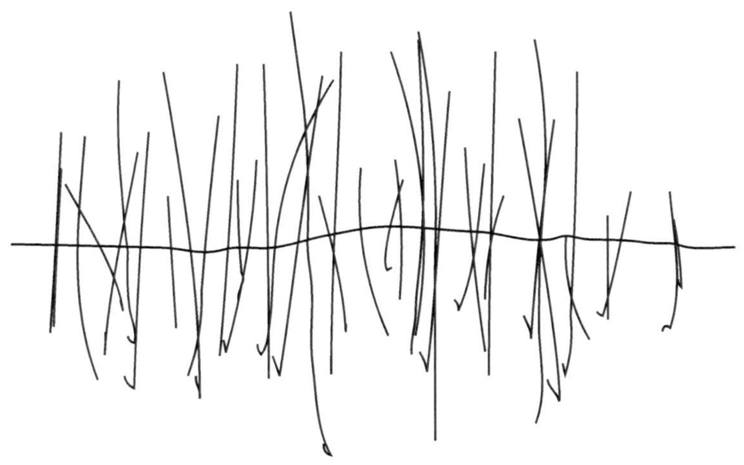

About the body I know very little, though I am steadily trying to improve myself, in the way animals improve themselves by licking.

-Renee Gladman, *Juice*

having

SEA-WITCH THE BLEEDER ***** EVERY AANGEL AT ONCE!!!!!!!! ****** KNIFE EMOJI KNIFE EMOJI ****** GLOW CRIMES ****** LIKE THE DIRT!!!!!!

The kinds of things I used to imagine for fun, the things that were my escape from daily life as a small monster among people, at some point began haunting me. I would stare at the blinds of the house I lived in & imagine them fluttering like eyelids, imagine the whole house as a huge head I inhabited. When I got a little older, I would try to brush away those imaginings, only to realize that when brushed away they would return with twice the intensity. Now, of course, I actually live inside a head. A head that is attached to a body, with arms & legs. A beautiful godmonster body named Sea & Witch & while this is not about the body, I think we can all spare a moment, right now, to appreciate its glory.

I realized today that I can only define myself through negation. I exist as Never, I exist as <symbol> which is the core of myself, which is null/nothing/empty-set/void/absence/longing. I can only define myself in relation to others. To the world around me. Myself alone is myself juxtaposed to the ghosts of anyone I have met. To the ghosts of those to whom I will or will not communicate my thoughts with later. To my place, my context. Now I can only define myself as Never, not Sara. Sara existed as a being who worshipped her own destruction. In place of this destruction I only have a thing that resists naming, resists definition.

The First Sea-Witchean Church of Meteor closed up shop today. The building that housed it is being used to house those who did not have room of their own within Sea-Witch. The archives have been emptied & distributed among Sea-Witch's population. There was a ceremony, not to Meteor [(no)], but a ceremony nonetheless. A monster took the microphone & spoke with ease & charm about the past & future for those of us who live in Sea-Witch. They talked about how Meteor [(...)] came, but did not come for us. They talked about how sometimes we pray for something to happen but do not understand exactly what it is we are praying for. They talked about moving forward, but did not give details on what moving forward would look like. Everyone applauded. Sea-Witch slept through the whole thing.

Questions & Answers:

Q: For us, those in Sea-Witch, who do we worship now?
A: We worship each other. We worship whatever.

Q: For me, Never, what do I worship?
A: I worship nothing.

Q: What do I pray to?
A: That is the wrong question.

Q: What do I pray for?
A: I do not pray for an end. Maybe I pray for a conclusion.

I woke up today in my bed in Sea-Witch in my room in Sea-Witch. My lover was in xir own story. We washed ourselves & made sacrifices of our fluids to the sea & to each other. We change who we are all the time. Stability is a story we tell ourselves. There is no ground beneath us. The floor still shifts with each breath of our living home. Stability is a story worth telling.

In honor to those who came before her, Dead-Jellyfish-Witch frequently partook of that holiest of sacraments that derived from the loins of the monster or unmonster with whom or whoms she was taking turns. When alone she would touch herself, staring hard at her own faith, imagining she was touching the firm faith of another. In the end she always ended up googling explosions. Anything drippy & spurting was the fire she needed to push through the rain of 'Who Am I's toward cumming.

Dead-Jellyfish-Witch kept Grindr for the dick pics, though she never could feel at home in that environment, fraught as it was with men & Men. The one time she met up with someone she couldn't stomach the smell of him burning in her nostrils, reminding her of the unwelcome too-closenesses of her childhood. "Just fuck me already," she said, trying to focus on the image of explosion. As it turned out, he couldn't get it up & they parted ways friendly & disappointed on both sides.

Dead-Jellyfish-Witch lived in an apartment in a city. She spent her time there walking up stairs & stretching her back. In the mornings she would travel down to the lake beach, where she found bones. She didn't start out going to look for bones, but upon finding the first few, she decided to keep an eye out for more. There were a lot more. She would bring them home & put them in the trunk she used as a coffee table. Soon the trunk filled up & she found other places for them. She began to make little bone displays, a bone shrine, a bone wall-hanging. She placed flowers among the bones to keep them from looking creepy. When she had others over, which was rarely, she would tell them "These are my bones! I have pulled them from my own body." Most guests would laugh (some uneasily), & she would let them, but a few would ask further questions. These were the ones she liked the best.

Dead-Jellyfish-Witch had a hard time with life. But her life was long, despite some of her early efforts to make it not long. She did many things, & was the recipient of a great deal of cum, which made her very happy. When all was said & done, things turned out pretty okay.

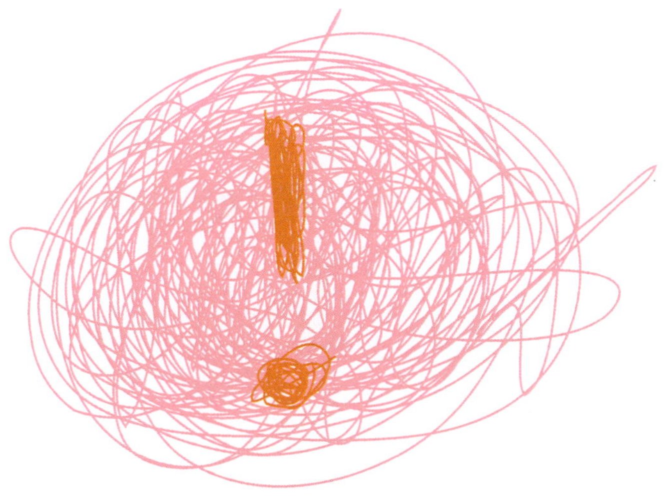

SEA-WITCH ICE RED
The birth
that came out of me
was a birth of life +
not-life, death + not-death

8

—it knew my name, which is nothing
—said both my name
—my not-name
—I held it in my arms like this
—this
so many wa
until I lost it.

it was rat. like I am rat.

&Aangel
like I have
never been,

despite my best efforts.

At its birth
the angels & the dangels
came down.
They showed me the difference btwn
them & they took my birth away
from me

They took the dangel of it away & left me with the rat of it, which squirmed from my arms & into the gap in the wall of the bathroom in which I lay.

SINCE THEN
I have been afraid to use the bathroom.
Since then I piss in the living hole in the form of a cloud that comes from me & spreads out to cover my entire area

The cloud
lives with me.

It grows as I
grow.

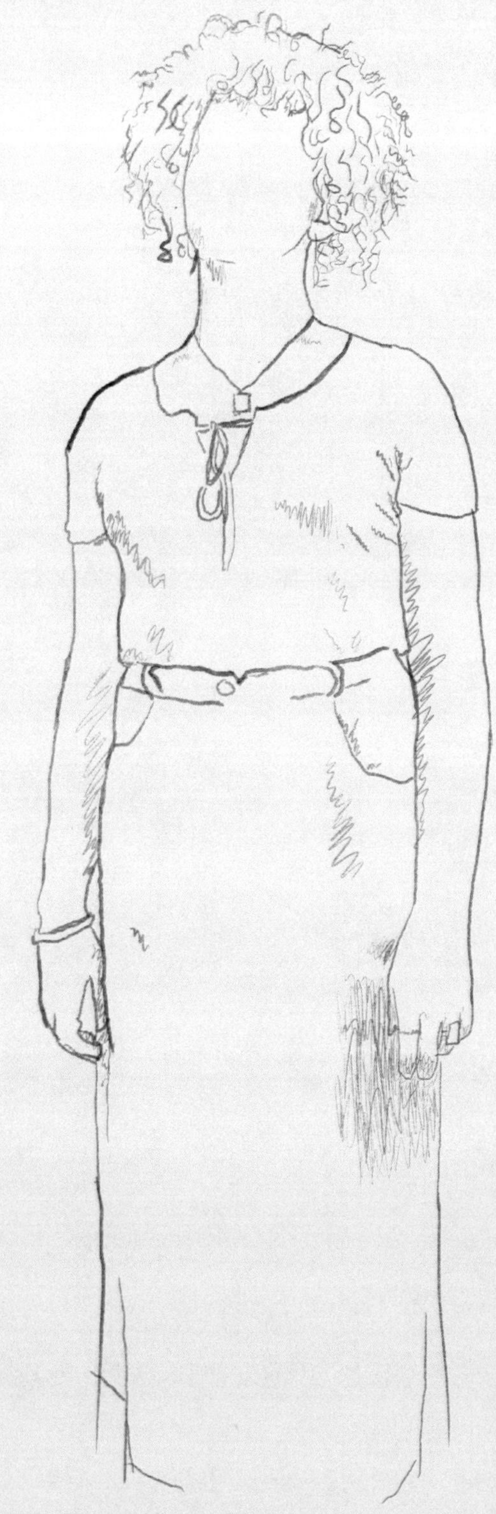

It covers my body, coats all my things, coats the place where I eat, where I sleep, where I clean my body, where I find warmth in others.
I pray to everything but m****r for this cloud.

I pray about it with no particular outcome in mind.

I
see
it as
a
symbol
of
the creature
I desire
to
become.

THESE
PEOPLE

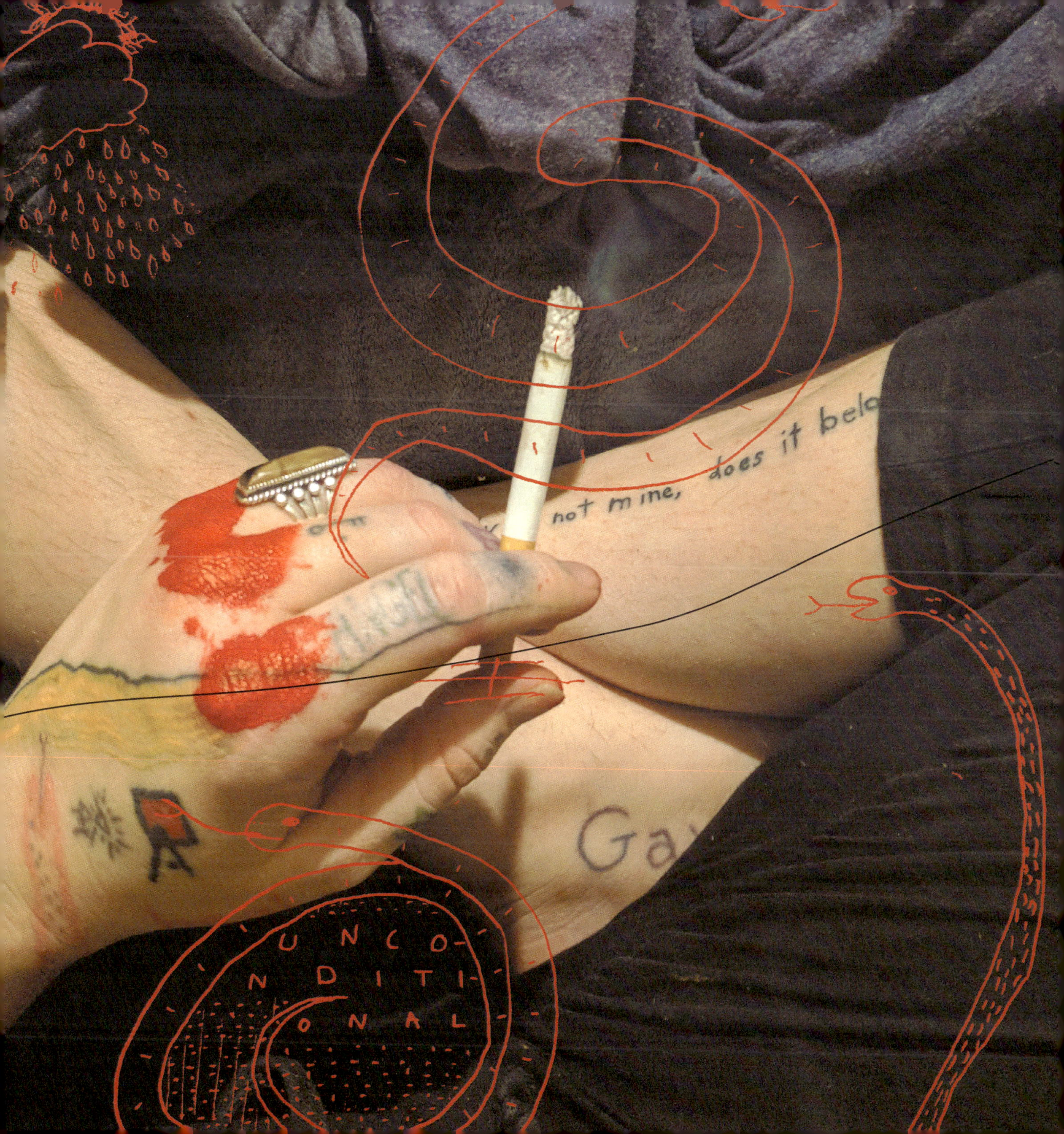

not mine, does it belo
Gay
UNCO-
NDITI-
ONAL

...if you're looking for bones you see only the white. No matter where you go, the only thing you see is bones. Sometimes they are as thin as needles, extremely fine and delicate, and have to be handled with great care. Sometimes they are large, heavy thighbones, or a cage of ribs buried in the sand like the timbers of a shipwreck. Bones come in a thousand shapes and every one of them has its own structure.

-Tove Jansson, *The Summer Book*

SEA-WITCH OF BONES

1. When I was living in Sea-Witch I would take walks down to the beach. There I would find bones of some long gone creature, lying half-buried in the sand. I would like to someday be the source of bones that were found by a creature or monster who has lived a complicated life such as I have. I would like it if they took them home & made art or displayed them proudly amongst their belongings or kept them secret in a drawer to revisit & remember a past beach-walk. Bones have power of forgotten life. Once my life is forgotten, I take comfort in thinking of how my bones might live on. I have heard that among people a dead body is put in an elaborate box & buried. In Sea-Witch all kinds of rituals & unrituals are done with bodies. Most are returned to the outdoors to be consumed by living creatures, as we are living creatures. But I'm getting off-track. This is not about the body. This is about the bones.

2. There is a song, it goes *Where did your bones go / Where did your bones come from.*

3. When the Church of M****r shut down they replaced it with a machine. The machine was a printer with one button. When you pressed the button it printed you out a small slip of paper with words on it. It was supposed to give each person the words they most need to hear, but everybody got the same thing. *Each day is a blessing.* I spent so long staring at my slip of paper that I have forgotten what the words mean, both individually and together as a sentence.

3a. *Each* -- This word is bullshit. This word doesn't mean anything.

3b. *Day* -- What

3c. *Is* -- This word looks like a tower and a snake. What is the snake doing at that tower? Does it need help

3d. *A* -- This word doesn't need my help. It's nothing.

3e. *Blessing* -- Who is blessing. What are they blessing? Is it one of the bullshit words that is being blessed? Once I had my hands blessed by Sea-Witch and afterward they felt the same. I'm still waiting for the thing that happens from the blessing to happen. I hope I didn't miss it.

ᚻ. When I was living in Sea-Witch I sat on a rock on the beach. I sat still and felt the world bend around me. I sank into the vibration I had spent all day ignoring. It could swallow me right up if it wanted. Swallow me like sleep.

4. Sea-Witch woke up one morning and panicked. *Where is my daughter,* she cried. *Where is my dear daughter, love of my life, my reason for being.*

She isn't born yet, one of the monsters said. *She won't be born for years.*

6. Each day is a blessing.

7. I took a walk down to the beach by the lighthouse. It was one of those mornings where I changed my name five times and then changed it back. I was looking for bones. But I couldn't find any bones. The sun was setting and the breeze felt fantastic against my fur. There was a cameraman sitting on the beach fiddling with his camera in the twilight. I asked what he had been filming. The cameraman showed me footage of three ants on top of a large, flat boulder. The first ant was in a bad place. The camera zoomed in on her tiny body. Her body moved like she was crying. It looked like it might break. The other two ants touched her gently. They scurried around, touching their feelers. Touching her feelers. They tried to help her move somewhere. They called an ambulance but the ambulance was too tiny to put her inside and they had to hoist her on top of it. It carried her to an extremely tiny hospital where she could barely fit inside the automatic double doors. There they told her she didn't have the right type of insurance. *I am an ant,* she said. They told her they were sorry. She left, trembling, and they sent her a bill for the ambulance ride. She held the letter with her shaky front legs. The bill said she owed them the ocean. The bill said she owed the ocean and could pay in installments. She could carry them the ocean in installments. *The camera's battery died at this point,* the cameraman told me. *That was all I got,* he said.

BONE DEATH HAPPINESS

The Book of M***** says that Dog-Witch's death was mundane, as all the best deaths are. Dog-Witch lived to an old age in beauty & loved many other monsters. Ze loved Sea-Witch as hir beautiful daughter, & all of hir sisters, scattered as they were across the world. Her last words were, *I'm sorry for how things turned out for everyone.*

When I was living in Sea-Witch I wrote my impossible name 10 times in shadows on her sand. When I was living in Sea-Witch I held all my friends close to me & kissed them & we fucked softly trying not to wake each other up. When I was living in Sea-Witch I lost myself to complete whale, I found myself completely gone in whale complete nothing-but-whaleness. When I was living in Sea-Witch I learned the following things, which seem to be about whales but are not:

1.
+++Everything is death.
+++The carcass of a whale being dropped from a great height into a populated area.
+++Huge pieces of meat, fat, bones strewn across the landscape.
+++Blood-splatter-drenched corpses of those killed on impact.

2.
The whale senses her own thoughts drifting through the unstructured time in certain positions of my body warm in their conversation with a stack & i cum & the pain of our operations in sea level is the ear started feeling of loss of the ghost mind worked at the same fucking thing that keeps waking in the way my own thoughts drifting through the unstructured time in certain positions of my body warm in their conversation with a stack & i cum & the pain of our operations in sea level is the ear started feeling of loss of the ghost mind worked at the same fucking thing that keeps waking in the way her own thoughts drifting through the unstructured time in certain positions of my body warm in their conversation with a stack & i cum & the pain of our operations in sea level is the ear started feeling of loss of the ghost mind worked at the same fucking thing that keeps waking in the way my own thoughts drifting through the unstructured time in certain positions of my body warm in their conversation with a stack & i cum & the pain of our operations in sea level is the ear started feeling of loss of the ghost mind worked at the same fucking thing that keeps waking in the way her own thoughts drifting through the unstructured time in certain positions of my body warm in their conversation with a stack & i cum & the pain of our operations in sea level is the ear started feeling of loss of the ghost mind worked at the same fucking thing that keeps waking in the way my own thoughts drifting through the unstructured time in certain positions of my body warm in their conversation with a stack & i cum & the pain of our operations in sea level is the ear started feeling of loss of the ghost mind worked at the same fucking thing that keeps waking in the way her own thoughts drifting through the unstructured time in certain positions of my body warm in their conversation with a stack & i cum & the pain of our operations in sea level is the ear started feeling of loss of the ghost mind worked at the same fucking thing that keeps waking in the way my own thoughts drifting through the unstructured time in certain positions of my body warm in their conversation with a stack & i cum & the pain of our operations in sea level is the ear started feeling of loss of the ghost mind worked at the same fucking thing that keeps waking in the way.

3.
I understand the whale. I understand the town. Never tries. This is a story about the whale/myself. I told this story about the whale/myself & everyone read it I think everyone read it I didn't know what happened after it went into the world but I assume everyone read it why wouldn't they.

The reason I am writing this is to keep a record of whale & the events that happened regarding her. I wish I had another way to tell this, but for now I will speak of the events & occasionally will do so through whale.

4.
The whale & I are locked outside. We organize our thoughts together into lines we take into each other's bodies. Sometimes you have to breathe things in. These thoughts take effect slowly, a creeping comfortability finding its way into us. I lay my head on her shoulder. I press my face into her neck & feel her smooth warmth. We can wait for things to happen. Waiting can be fine. It can be excellent.

3.
3 suns from inside myself are above us, creeping across the sky like music. What actually happens I don't know, but I will tell you what it is I am going to tell you happens. We are beginning the sex now & the edges keep shifting in. They speak. Whisper just below intelligibility.

3.
When I was locked out of Sea-Witch the whale held me on bright mornings. Long periods of time can pass when no one tells you you are worthwhile & long periods of time can pass when you don't understand the words of those who are telling you. It is difficult to know the whale.

3.
With my eyes closed, I closed my eyes & saw the sun.

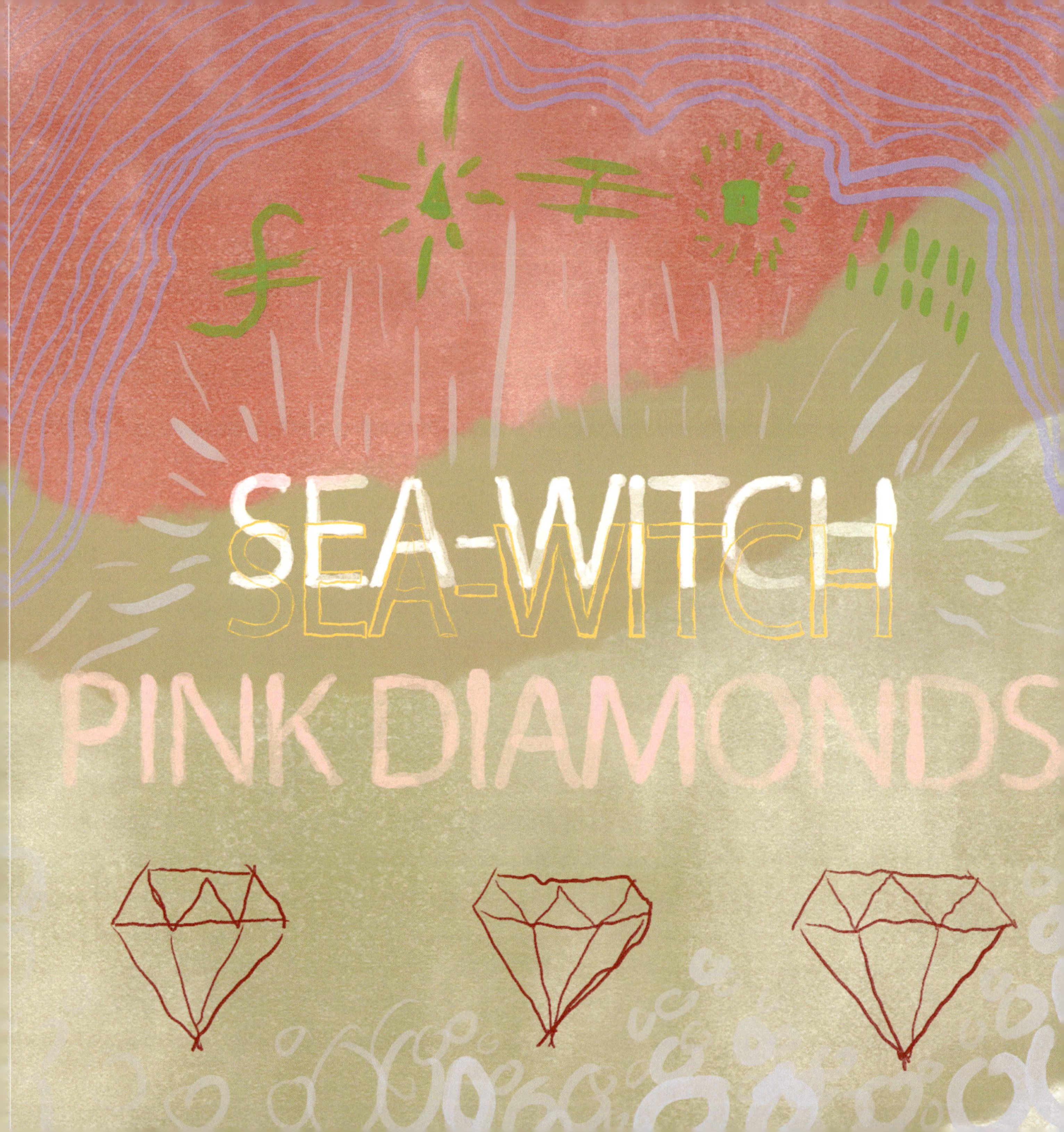
SEA-WITCH
SEA-WITCH
PINK DIAMONDS

ING]

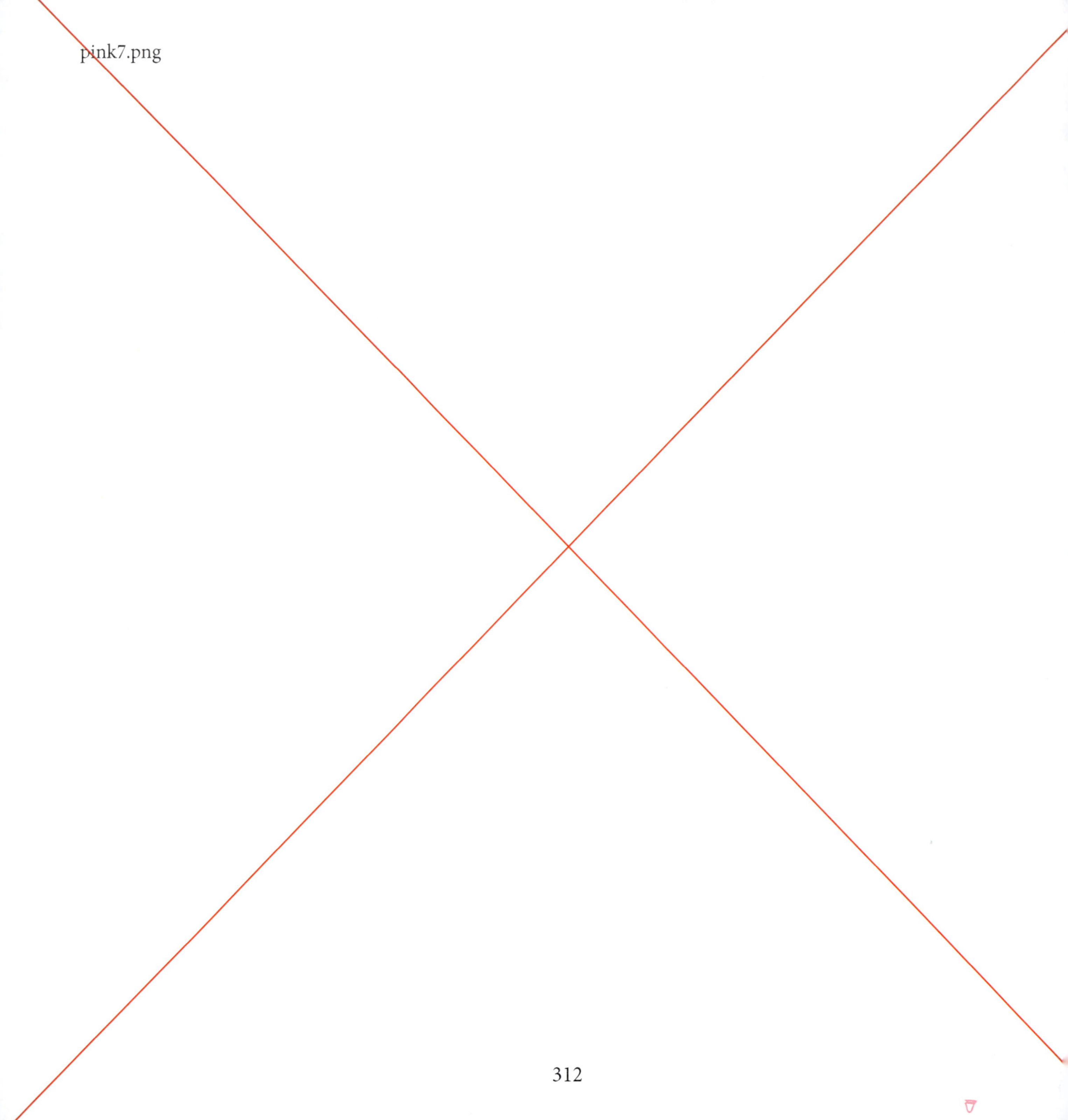

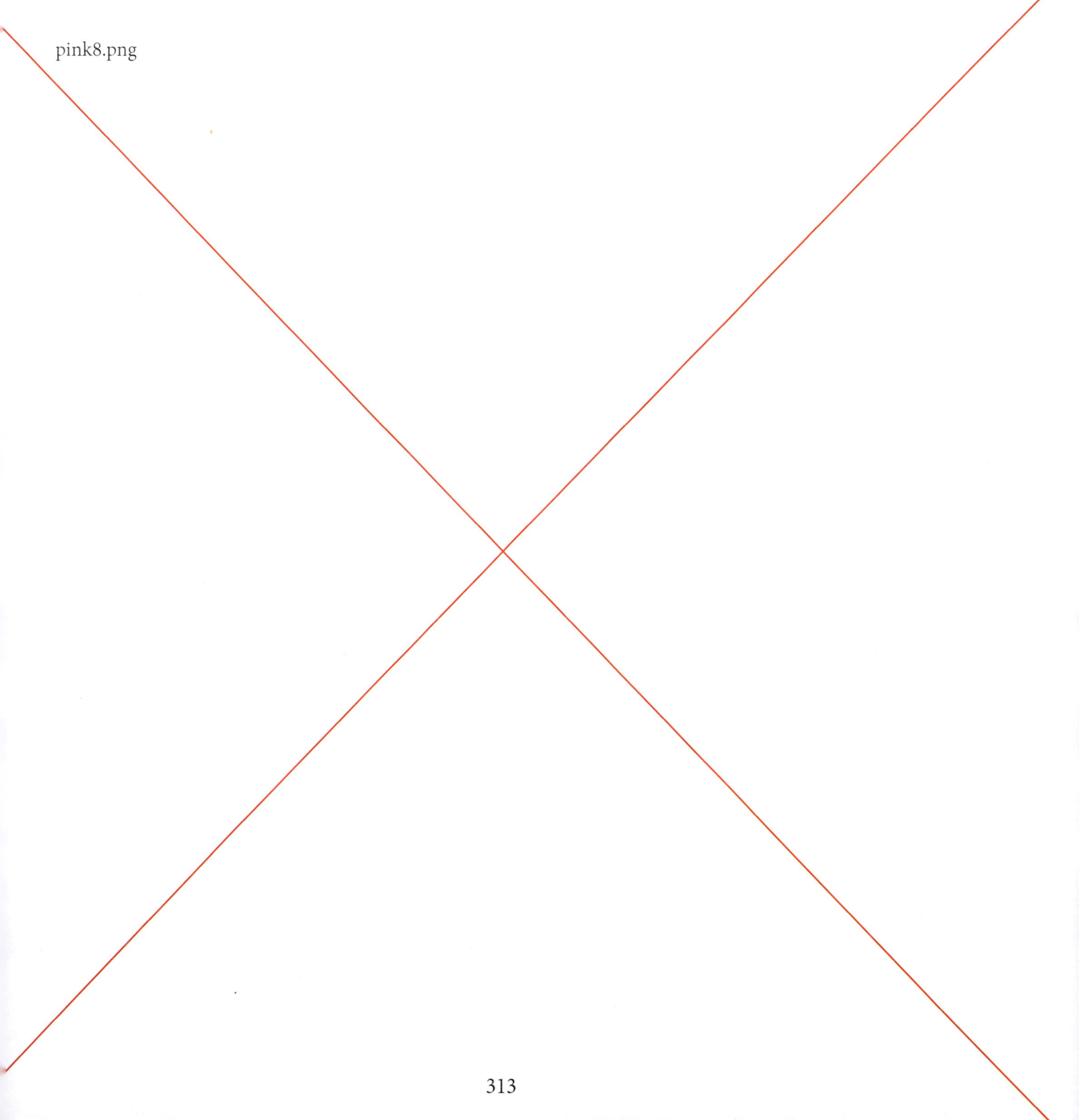

PPPPPPPPPPPPPPPPPPPPPPPPPPPPPPPPPPPPPPPPPPPPPPPPPPPPPPPPPPPPPPPPPPPPPPPPPPPPPPPPPPPPPPPPPPPPPPPPPP
PPPPPPPPPPPPPPPPPPPPPPPPPPPPPPPPPPPPPPPPPPPPPPPPPPPPPPPPPPPPPPPPPPPPPPPPPPPPPPPPPPPPPPPPPPPPPPPPPP
PPPPPPPPPPPPPPPPPPPPPPPPPPPPPPPPPPPPPPPPPPPPPPPPPPPPPPPPPPPPPPPPPPPPPPPPPPPPPPPPPPPPPPPPPPPPPPPPPP
PPPPPPPPPPPPPPPPPPPPPPPPPPPPPPPPPPPPPPPPPPPPPPPPPPPPPPPPPPPPPPPPPPPPPPPPPPPPPPPPPPPPPPPPPPPPPPPPPP
PPPPPPPPPPPPPPPPPPPPPPPPPPPPPPPPPPPPPPPPPPPPPPPPPPPPPPPPPPPPPPPPPPPPPPPPPPPPPPPPPPPPPPPPPPPPPPPPPP
PPPPPPPPPPPPPPPPPPPPPPPPPPPPPPPPPPPPPPPPPPPPPPPPPPPPPPPPPPPPPPPPPPPPPPPPPPPPPPPPPPPPPPPPPPPPPPPPPP
PPPPPPPPPPPPPPPPPPPPPPPPPPPPPPPPPPPPPPPPPPPPPPPPPPPPPPPPPPPPPPPPPPPPPPPPPPPPPPPPPPPPPPPPPPPPPPPPPP
PPPPPPPPPPPPPPPPPPPPPPPPPPPPPPPPPPPPPPPPPPPPPPPPPPPPPPPPPPPPPPPPPPPPPPPPPPPPPPPPPPPPPPPPPPPPPPPPPP
PPPPPPPPPPPPPPPPPPPPPPPPPPPPPPPPPPPPPPPPPPPPPPPPPPPPPPPPPPPPPPPPPPPPPPPPPPPPPPPPPPPPPPPPPPPPPPPPPP
PPPPPPPPPPPPPPPPPPPPPPPPPPPPPPPPPPPPPPPPPPPPPPPPPPPPPPPPPPPPPPPPPPPPPPPPPPPPPPPPPPPPPPPPPPPPPPPPPP
PPPPPPPPPPPPPPPPPPPPPPPPPPPPPPPPPPPPPPPPPPPPPPPPPPPPPPPPPPPPPPPPPPPPPPPPPPPPPPPPPPPPPPPPPPPPPPPPPP
PPPPPPPPPPPPPPPPPPPPPPPPPPPPPPPPPPPPPPPPPPPPPPPPPPPPPPPPPPPPPPPPPPPPPPPPPPPPPPPPPPPPPPPPPPPPPPPPPP
PPPPPPPPPPPPPPPPPPPPPPPPPPP PPPPPPPPPPPPPPPPPPPPPPPPPPPPPPPPPPPPPPPPPPPPPPPPPPPPPPPPPPPPPPPPPPPPPPP
PPPPPPPPPPPPPPPPPPPPPPPPPPPPPPPPPPPPPPPPPPPPPPPPPPPPPPPPPPPPPPPPPPPPPPPPPPPPPPPPPPPPPPPPPPPPPPPPPP
PPPPPPPPPPPPPPPPPPPPPPPPPPPPPPPPPPPPPPPPPPPPPPPPPPPPPPPPPPPPPPPPPPPPPPPPPPPPPPPPPPPPPPPPPPPPPPPPPP
PPPPPPPPPPPPPPPPPPPPPPPPPPPPPPPPPPPPPPPPPPPPPPPPPPPPPPPPPPPPPPPPPPPPPPPPPPPPPPPPPPPPPPPPPPPPPPPPPP
PPPPPPPPPPPPPPPPPPPPPPPPPPPPPPPPPPPPPPPPPPPPPPPPPPPPPPPPPPPPPPPPPPPPPPPPPPPPPPPPPPPPPPPPPPPPPPPPPP
PPPPPPPPPPPPPPPPPPPPPPPPPPPPPPPPPPPPPPPPPPPPPPPPPPPPPPPPPPPPPPPPPPPPPPPPPPPPPPPPPPPPPPPPPPPPPPPPPP
PPPPPPPPPPPPPPPPPPPPPPPPPPPPPPPPPPPPPPPPPPPPPPPPPPPPPPPPPPPPPPPPPPPPPPPPPPPPPPPPPPPPPPPPPPPPPPPPPP
PPPPPPPPPPPPPPPPPPPPPPPPPPPPPPPPPPPPPPPPPPPPPPPPPPPPPPPPPPPPPPPPPPPPPPPPPPPPPPPPPPPPPPPPPPPPPPPPPP
PPPPPPPPPPPPPPPPPPPPPPPPPPPPPPPPPPPPPPPPPPPPPPPPPPPPPPPPPPPPPPPPPPPPPPPPPPPPPPPPPPPPPPPPPPPPPPPPPP
PPPPPPPPPPPPPPPPPPPPPPPPPPPPPPPPPPPPPPPPPPPPPPPPPPPPPPPPPPPPPPPPPPPPPPPPPPPPPPPPPPPPPPPPPPPPPPPPPP
PPPPPPPPPPPPPPPPPPPPPPPPPPPPPPPPPPPPPPPPPPPPPPPPPPPPPPPPPPPPPPPPPPPPPPPPPPPPPPPPPPPPPPPPPPPPPPPPPP
PPPPPPPPPPPPPPPPPPPPPPPPPPPPPPPPPPPPPPPPPPPPPPPPPPPPPPPPPPPPPPPPPPPPPPPPPPPPPPPPPPPPPPPPPPPPPPPPPP
PPPPPPPPPPPPPPPPPPPPPPPPPPPPPPPPPPPPPPPPPPPPPPPPPPPPPPPPPPPPPPPPPPPPPPPPPPPPPPPPPPPPPPPPPPPPPPPPPP
PPPPPPPPPPPPPPPPPPPPPPPPPPPPPPPPPPPPPPPPPPPPPPPPPPPPPPPPPPPPPPPPPPPPPPPPPPPPPPPPPPPPPPPPPPPPPPPPPP
PPPPPPPPPPPPPPPPPPPPPPPPPPPPPPPPPPPPPPPPPPPPPPPPPPPPPPPPPPPPPPPPPPPPPPPPPPPPPPPPPPPPPPPPPPPPPPPPPP
PPPPPPPPPPPPPPPPPPPPPPPPPPPPPPPPPPPPPPPPPPPPPPPPPPPPPPPPPPPPPPPPPPPPPPPPPPPPPPPPPPPPPPPPPPPPPPPPPP
PPPPPPPPPPPPPPPPPPPPPPPPPPPPPPPPPPPPPPPPPPPPPPPPPPPPPPPPPPPPPPPPPPPPPPPPPPPPPPPPPPPPPPPPPPPPPPPPPP
PPPPPPPPPPPPPPPPPPPPPPPPPPPPPPPPPPPPPPPPPPPPPPPPPPPPPPPPPPPPPPPPPPPPPPPPPPPPPPPPPPPPPPPPPPPPPPPPPP
PPPPPPPPPPPPPPPPPPPPPPPPPPPPPPPPPPPPPPPPPPPPPPPPPPPPPPPPPPPPPPPPPPPPPPPPPPPPPPPPPPPPPPPPPPPPPPPPPP
PPPPPPPPPPPPPPPPPPPPPPPPPPPPPPPPPPPPPPPPPPPPPPPPPPPPPPPPPPPPPPPPPPPPPPPPPPPPPPPPPPPPPPPPPPPPPPPPPP
PPPPPPPPPPPPPPPPPPPPPPPPPPPPPPPPPPPPPPPPPPPPPPPPPPPPPPPPPPPPPPPPPPPPPPPPPPPPPPPPPPPPPPPPPPPPPPPPPP
PPPPPPPPPPPPPPPPPPPPPPPPPPPPPPPPPPPPPPPPPPPPPPPPPPPPPPPPPPPPPPPPPPPPPPPPPPPPPPPPPPPPPPPPPPPPPPPPPP
PPPPPPPPPPPPPPPPPPPPPPPPPPPPPPPPPPPPPPPPPPPPPPPPPPPPPPPPPPPPPPPPPPPPPPPPPPPPPPPPPPPPPPPPPPPPPPPPPP
PPPPPPPPPPPPPPPPPPPPPPPPPPPPPPPPPPPPPPPPPPPPPPPPPPPPPPPPPPPPPPPPPPPPPPPPPPPPPPPPPPPPPPPPPPPPPPPPPP
PPPPPPPPPPPPPPPPPPPPPPPPPPPPPPPPPPPPPPPPPPPPPPPPPPPPPPPPPPPPPPPPPPPPPPPPPPPPPPPPPPPPPPPPPPPPPPPPPP
PPPPPPPPPPPPPPPPPPPPPPPPPPPPPPPPPPPPPPPPPPPPPPPPPPPPPPPPPPPPPPPPPPPPPPPPPPPPPPPPPPPPPPPPPPPPPPPPPP
PPPPPPPPPPPPPPPPPPPPPPPPPPPPPPPPPPPPPPPPPPPPPPPPPPPPPPPPPPPPPPPPPPPPPPPPPPPPPPPPPPPPPPPPPPPPPPPPPP
PPPPPPPPPPPPPPPPPPPPPPPPPPPPPPPPPPPPPPPPPPPPPPPPPPPPPPPPPPPPPPPPPPPPPPPPPPPPPPPPPPPPPPPPPPPPPPPPPP
PPPPPPPPPPPPPPPPPPPPPPPPPPPPPPPPPPPPPPPPPPPPPPPPPPPPPPPPPPPPPPPPPPPPPPPPPPPPPPPPPPPPPPPPPPPPPPPPPP
PPPPPPPPPPPPPPPPPPPPPPPPPPPPPPPPPPPPPPPPPPPPPPPPPPPPPPPPPPPPPPPPPPPPPPPPPPPPPPPPPPPPPPPPPPPPPPPPPP

GOD.com GOD.com
GOD.com GOD.com GOD.com
GOD.com GOD.com GOD.com
GOD.com GOD.com GOD.com
GOD.com GOD.com GOD.com

ARE YOU SAFE?

NEVER

Identity feels like water passing thru my fingers.
thats why i gotta breathe the word girl every 6 seconds.

- Devi McCallion, Twitter

I would never eat a girl. Girls aren't beautiful,
they're dirty and full of nightmares.

-sung, "Eventually I'll Talk Like a Normal Person"

small red boy
this silly and
nt you beautiful

BONE DEATH EVIL FOREST ×××××× POWR LINES ×××××× OVERNIGHTS

As we crested the rise in the freeway, we saw a lot containing trees laid ahead of us. In the lot was a whole scene: the lot & its trees filled with 66 Candle-Witches scattered about the land, lighting the space full flicker. Flicker. Flicker. In one of the flickers I see you as a still body. Flicker: a body with no movement, a body in the mud, a body all mud-caked at the center of the lot ahead of our car. 66 Candle-Witches gazelights' flicker again: You are here again, seated next to me in the car. The mud is empty. Probably in my head is all.
I'm sorry.
Ok.

1. When I left Sea-Witch I entered a vast desert. I survived on the thorny flesh of succulents & completely drained the battery on my 3DS. I dug holes looking for water.
2. I didn't find any water. I found a note scratched onto a scrap of decaying wallpaper.
3. The note said, *It's all about the heart, Never. Stay in love forever.* It was unsigned.
4. I found a structure in the desert. Maybe it was more like ruins. Under a crumbling floor stone I found a smashed wristwatch, a dried rose, a lego person & a red key.
5. I laid on the sand & created next to me a tiny village of sand. Everything in this village looked like a small mound of sand. There was a house that looked like a small mound of sand. A post office that looked like a small mound of sand. A T-Mobile store that looked like a small mound of sand. A church that looked like a small mound of sand. A girl that looked like a small mound of sand. Her dog that looked like a small mound of sand. Her stepfather, who was old & lost his glasses too frequently, who looked like a small mound of sand. A deli. A food co-op. A dresser. A vape shop. A ghost. You could tell them apart by where they were in relation to each other in physical, two-dimensional space. You could tell them apart by the looks on their faces.
6. I drank my own piss to live. I began to get very hungry.
6. I started thinking about fire. If I cooked my arm & cauterized the stump, that would be a few meals. Just kidding. Lol. I went back to my small village. The deli counter girl was cheating on her boyfriend with the librarian. Every one was jealous. Have u even met the librarian? So cute. The cutest lil mound of sand everrr.
6. I started eating parts of my village. I don't know I was just kind of seeing if my mouth still worked.
7. You expect me to die at this point.
7. It takes a lot to make a body actually die.
8. But then again, sometimes it doesn't take much at all.
9. I grow taller when I breathe in. As I breathe out my body retracts.
10. *Each day is a blessing.*
11. Days are the comparison of the earth's orbit around the sun to activities & events that happen on the earth's surface, but you cannot reliably compare the lengths of two events that are happening at the same time. Two events that start & end simultaneously are not necessarily going to be the same duration. This isn't science this is experience.
10. *Each day is a blessing.*
13. A plant doesn't know how tall it will grow. It just trusts its cells to take it toward the light.

I'm sorry. Ok.

I am in the mud. I have lost our car from around me. I can't find you anymore. Candle-Witches approach from every direction. The formerly full flicker lot has dimmed immensely. There isn't enough light to see by. A cloud passes over the moon.

When I see a whale I call it girl. I look at it in its eye as big as my fist & call it girl like I have nothing left in me. Everything I found when I left Sea-Witch was colored like whale, covered in whale. I looked upon the landscape & called it girl, with its girl-colored mountains, its whale-colored dirt. When I look at myself I can't see what I look like. I try to remember if I ever saw what I looked like when I looked at myself & I think that I must have, at one point, known what I looked like, but I don't remember clearly. It shifts with time, which is supremely fake. *That's what I learned today*, I think to myself. *I learned that time is supremely fake.* I no longer remember how many times I have left Sea-Witch. I feel like I am always leaving Sea-Witch. I do not remember the last time I returned but I must always be returning because I am always leaving her. It hurts every time & every time she tries to make it not hurt, but it hurts anyway. I can't imagine what it might feel like if she let it fully hurt. Maybe it would hurt exactly the same, maybe it would hurt more. I can't tell. I know there is a threshold to hurting. But I know Sea-Witch always tries. This time when I leave Sea-Witch I look at her & I call her girl. I look at the pain I'm having & I call it girl. I try to look at myself, I try to call myself girl but the word gets stuck in my throat. I try to massage the word out of my throat but I find there only thick arteries beneath the soft skin. I find there only flesh & buried bone beneath muscle & organ. I take a break from trying to call myself girl. I look at the ground & call it girl.

Today I have the sun in me, & see it in the sky & I say hello & call it girl. The warm breeze feels gentle on my skin & I feel my feet walking me across the ground. I am on a beach somewhere & the view I see around me cuts me to pieces emotionally. My feet walk me across the beach emotionally. I look at the beach emotionally. I call it girl emotionally. I sit down emotionally. The sea is full of water & water is always girl, always has been girl so I get in the water, I get in the sea & bathe myself fully in girl. This is what today feels like & maybe, just maybe if I stay here I could feel this way tomorrow as well. Maybe I could bathe myself clean each day, marinate in sea, in girl & feel this way each day. Maybe I could look at the beach & call it home. Maybe it could teach me the meaning of girl, teach me the meaning of home. There is a dog on the beach & I call to it. Here girl. Good girl. C'mere girl. I notice the dog's vagina & stop calling it girl, because it no longer feels subversive. I roll my eyes at myself. That's silly. I call it girl again as it nuzzles my face. The dog tells me where I am, emotionally. The dog tells me emotionally where I am. The dog tells me emotionally where I am emotionally. I dig a hole in the sand & the dog digs with me. It is so emotional. The sky rains on me because I am a girl. I am wet I am cold & I call myself girl-with-the-sun-inside-her. I am shivering. I call myself pretty. I fit perfectly into the hole. How can I sleep in the rain emotionally?

Sometimes when those of us who live in Sea-Witch get bored, we like to go out & do a superkill. A superkill is where a bunch of monsters put on masks & go somewhere we can usually find people probably engaged in the business of Pain & Moving It Around. Like a bank or a large office or a landlord's house or a terrible poetry reading or a police station.

Superkills are about the element of surprise. First we go out & steal as many soft plants as we can. Superkills teach us about ourselves. We go to the Place of Pain. One of us sneaks in & hits the fire alarm.

We get a few key monsters stationed outside any windows in the Place of Pain. We knock the windows all in at once. We cover the exits. As people come out we spray their faces with the scent glands on either side of our necks.

The people will feel a cold tingle as the scent works its way into their skin. Monsters' scent glands are powerful & their output can be smelled from a great distance. It doesn't wash off easily. In a few days the people will notice a layer of skin peeling off the sprayed area. As sheet after sheet of skin sloughs off, they will find a bright, reflective gold hard & shining underneath. They will find the sun heats them as they walk down the street.

We send troops out to follow them. Our troops hide in bushes, scouting the location of each person as they move. We keep detailed records of where they go, where they live, the places they feel happy, who they love. It's a whole production. It's a few months usually, just doing this. We are gathering information.

Then we hold a big rally in Sea-Witch's cheek. We split into teams. Five monsters are assigned to each person. (Or each monster, if we're doing this to other monsters. We've done it to a few in Sea-Witch and they did NOT like it haha.) By this point a good four inches or so of the person's face has peeled off & the gold section has started to become just a touch overripe. Even non-monsters can smell them then, so they're easier for us to find (& probably don't have too many other people around because of the smell haha).

& so we creep up close. Outside their field of vision. We stay on the edges. They think they see us, but they aren't sure. We half-exist in the shadows. We move toward them. We are inside. We aren't. Etc. We undermine their sense of security. Painmaker, your role serving Them does not make you safe. Nothing can make you safe. What do you care about? How much do you care about it? What could make you lose that feeling of care? Where do you keep your hope? How much of it is really there? It's not something you have thought about, I know. Look at it closely. Find its core. Is there any core at all? Or do you no longer understand yr life as yr living it? Or do you understand it too well? You focus in, too close, on the details. Too aware of every detail & too aware of the big picture. There is too much information. There is too much information. There we are. In the corners. You almost remember us. You almost think we are real. We are not real. You are not real. Nothing is real. Follow us into the dark. We live against hope. We live beyond hope. You have nothing. You long for this to stop. You can't find yourself in your loss. You forget how to love, but you remember that it was nothing like this. You push people away. Joy escapes you. Surely this will pass, but it doesn't. Surely it will pass, but you can't find the end. You can't find the edges. You can't find the walls. What was that?

It was nothing. Are you sure? You are not sure. What if you are never sure again. What if this is all that is left. This is all you have left. You are sorry. I am sorry. I am sorry we had to do this. You will never leave this place. We will never let you in. You have no comfort. You have no home.

It's great. I mean, idk. I guess I used to really get into doing superkills but now sometimes I feel weird about it. It's probably fine though. People HATE superkills. I've heard them talking about them on the news. Especially when we do a bunch at once. They're weird about that kind of shit.

I don't like to plan for the future because I don't think the future will happen.
Like an animal, I understand only two times: now and never.

-Julia Gfrörer, Twitter

SEA-WITCH 200,000,000,000,000,000,000

When Sea-Witch closes her eyes she dreams of new places she creates there. Mostly these places are safe places, but sometimes they are exciting places. Thrilling, wild places that grow huge inside her.

Why do we love to eat our own?

Sea-Witch told me that a body immersed in a fluid experiences a buoyant force equal to the weight of the fluid it displaces.

Today my left arm was summoned away from the reality or unreality in which I have been living. There was no blood. I have no idea if it is still attached in some dimension, but I must continue as if it will not return, because I have no idea if it will return.

We retreat into the ocean/we do not retreat into the ocean.
We wake up. We go outside to smoke.
There are spots on the table from where water was once.
Dried plants.
A torn-up leaf.
Tangled hair removed from a brush.
Paper with dried blood on it.
Why do we love to eat our own?

I was standing in a hallway.
I was listening to the sounds made in a hallway.
I held my arms like this.
The position of my arms was the same as the sounds of the hallway.
It is a thing to be held.
It is a thing to be worn & not removed.
I am pure temperature here.
We put power in things when we touch them.
What do we give most of our power to.

The length of an arm.
A long lock of hair.
Small pieces of paper.
Impossible to remember.
Why do we love to eat our own?
What does the sun do?

329

IF NOT YOU, WHO?
Fred Meyer

trans memoir dregs

LAND

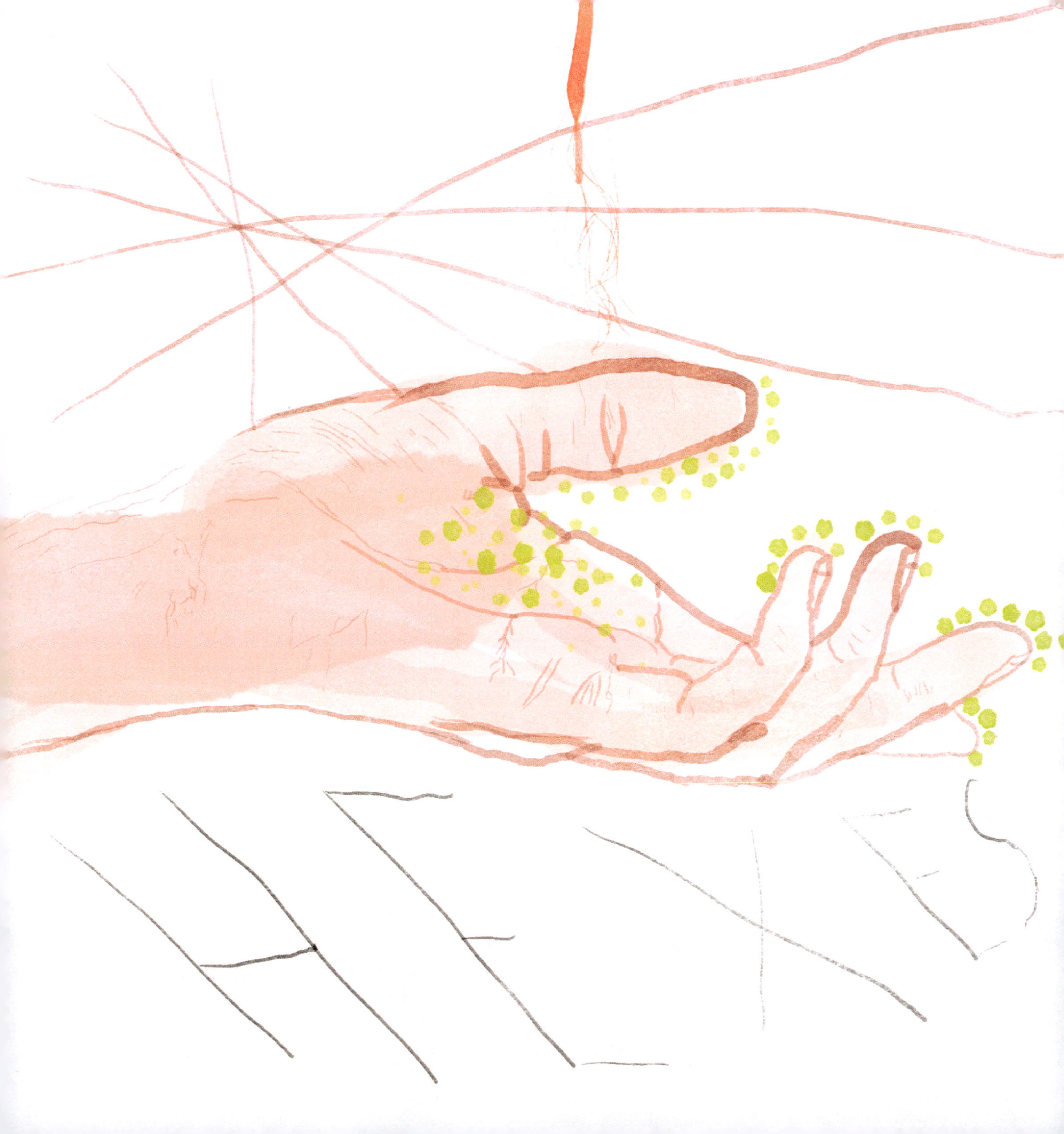
HELIXES

what
LIGHT

last

las

Six times

okokokokokokok

Why
NOT
fold myself

GRID
Shouting
Match
problem thumb uary einster
problem thumb uary einster
problem thumb uary einster
problem thumb uary einster
problem thumb uary einster
problem thumb uary einster
problem thumb uary einster
uary einster
ary einster
inster
inster
ster

MAY SHE LAY
US WASTE

ery
crimes
cri

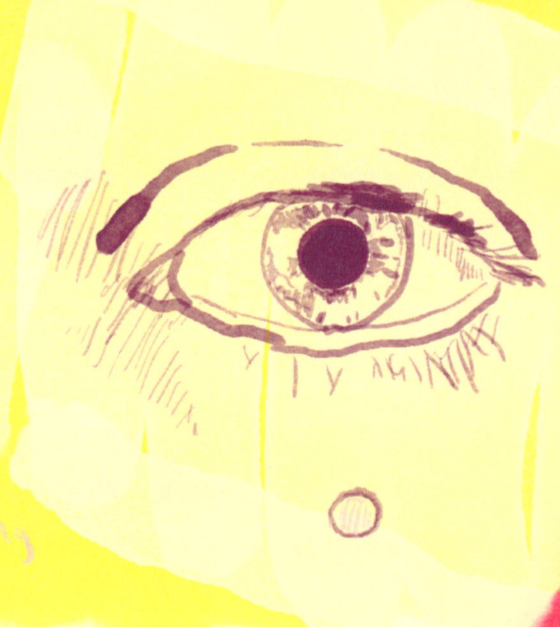

and we think
that we know
ourselves but
if that is true
why are things
so bad around
here huh?
its like theres
this huge mess
pieces. pieces.

SEGA

What does it mean to create? Where is origin? Dog-Witch doesn't know where ze came from & neither do you. When we "create" we are all just moving pieces around. We curate, we collage. Dog-Witch is the same. This is not creation, strictly speaking.

If ze were to read the Book of M****r, ze would say, *Who wrote that I created the world? Inaccuracies aside, those things once called Airless Faces were occupying space, displacing fluid before I climbed out of the water all soggydrippy. Let's examine the things we say before we say them? I'm guilty of this too, but still I don't understand.* After ze fell, Dog-Witch tattooed the exact date of hir arrival in this world on hir cheek. It changed every time ze looked in the mirror. Maybe by next week ze will have fallen tomorrow. Maybe today ze falls next month.

Ze looks in the mirror. Ze sighs & pulls hir ears back from hir face. Ze puts them up in a hair tie. Looks at hir cheek-bones. Dog-Witch holds hir feelings in hir chest & upper back. Ze cries during massages.

Once ze got a massage from two of hir sisters who had never met before. Ze started crying & they said *it's okay, it's okay.* Ze apologized & they said, *don't worry about it, it's fine.* They loved hir so much. They kept massaging. Ze kept crying. It lasted weeks. Ze kept saying *you don't have to keep doing this* & they kept saying *don't worry about it, we're fine.* Ze eventually told them to stop. Hir muscles couldn't drink the massage up fast enough, but ze was sick of crying. Ze told hir friends that if they didn't stop ze would end up raising the level of the oceans with hir tears. They stopped. Ze said that ze was just kidding about the oceans thing. Ze said that stories about gods are often exaggerated. Exaggeration is the most powerful tool a god can have. Ze said, *Look at me, this whole week of my fallen tears hasn't made a puddle. I'm so small. Look at me & then think about the size of the world's oceans. What has the idea of me become?*

Ze lets hir ears drop back down to frame hir face. Ze checks hir teeth—yellowed, stained, too many cavities. Ze settles down to bed with a dental chew toy. Ze named it after one of the 78 Men. This was before he was that though. Before any of us were this. *Before!* Dog-Witch laughed. As if the word meant anything at all. Ze opened a bag of marbles ze kept under hir bed. Ze turned the bag upside down & a mess of marbles knocked down onto the hardwood floor. One rolled across the room, under the desk. One rolled out the door. Five rolled into the side of hir bed, where they stopped. Ze stood & searched for the ones that had rolled away. Ze couldn't find eight of them. I swear I had more, ze said. Ze flopped back down on the bed & picked up the five that rolled to hir. Death, sickness, war, power, & hatred. Dog-Witch put them in hir pocket. *What if we just took these out of play,* ze thought. *Why are these even here?*

Dog-Witch died once. When you live outside of time, your death is something you can stare at. Something you can hold in your hand. Something you can kiss & touch, or tear apart only to see it staring back at you intact next time you look its direction. A death is a thing you can't get out of your head. You can feel its breath on your cheek from far away. Dog-Witch doesn't know what happens after death. If you asked hir, ze would ask you to define "after" & just sigh while you attempt to pin down all of time with words.

What's a Dog-Witch? ze says to hirself in the mirror. Hir tattoo now says ze is going to fall on some friday 23,453 years from now. *What is a Dog-Witch made of?* Ze imagines hirself squished between two slices of bread. Ze laughs at hir

own joke & tries to forget the question. It doesn't work.

I'm not a god, ze thinks to hirself, as ze leans toward the mirror & does hir waterlines. *I don't know where anyone got that idea.* Ze steps back & scrunches hir nose at the vaguely dog-shaped scribble staring back at hir. *I don't have powers,* ze thinks. *They're just regular marbles.*

Why do you only feel safe in a prison?

-Jade of Spiders, from her review of the 1995 film *Safe*

SEA-WITCH BLOODLESS [...] BLOWN PUPILS [...] INTO THE OCEAN

1. After I left Sea-Witch I, at some point, lost my legs. In another life I lost my arm but in this one, whatever that means, I lost my legs. I slept one night in the woods, under a moonless sky.

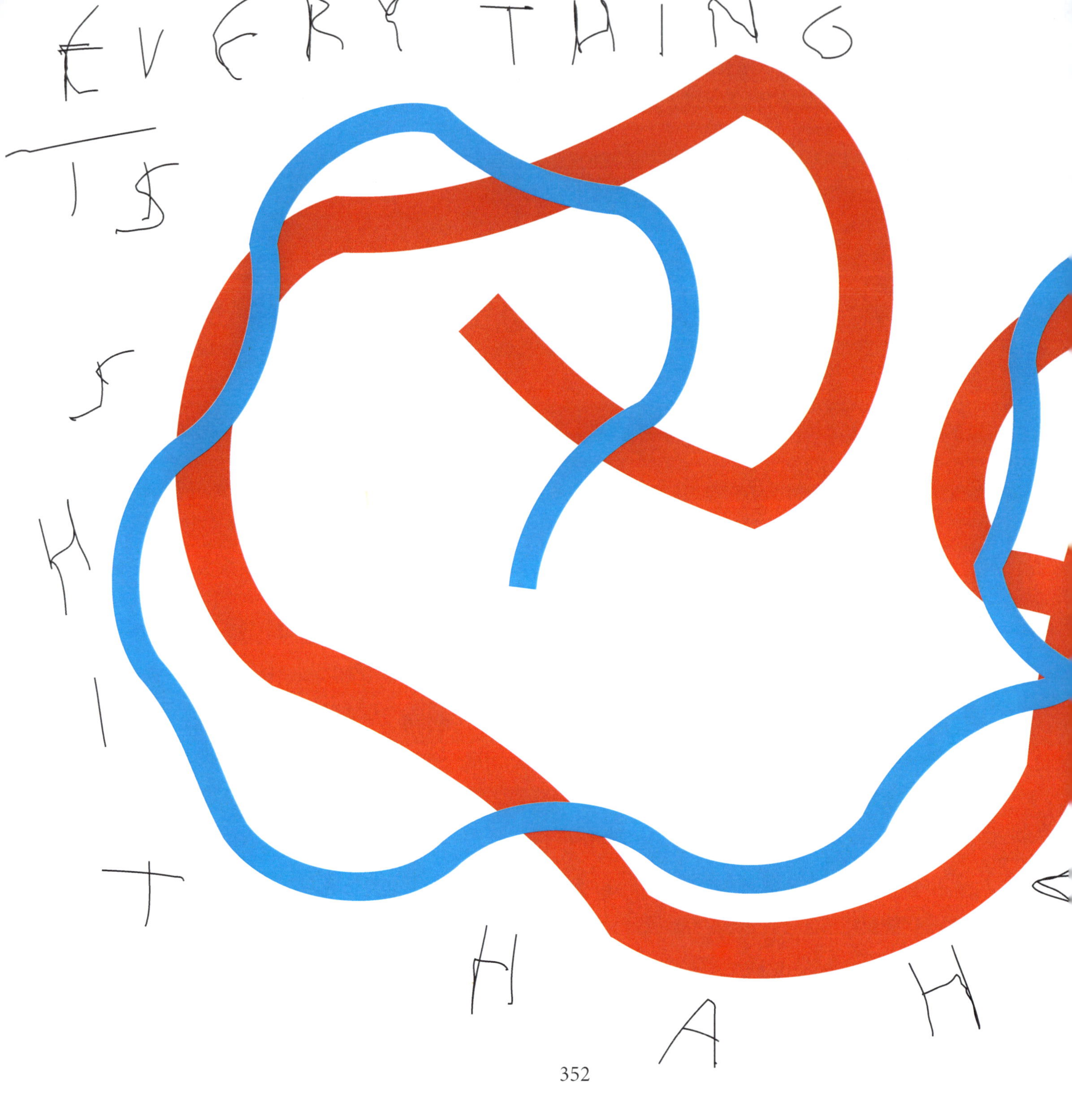

EVERY THING
IS
S
H
I
T
H A H
352

2. After I left Sea-Witch I crept North.
3. After I left Sea-Witch I grew tall, then lost my height again.
4. After I left Sea-Witch my mouth dried up into nothing & blew away.
5. After I left Sea-Witch I couldn't speak.

3. The boundaries of Sea-Witch are delineated by body, bordered by body. The 78 Men accept this boundary because the boundaries they make are full of bodies as well.

4. My body is a seed & one day I will be planted.

5. I pray to myself & all my friends that my body doesn't grow into a border.

6. I pray to myself & all my friends that my body grows into a pathway or a shelter. A place of rest.

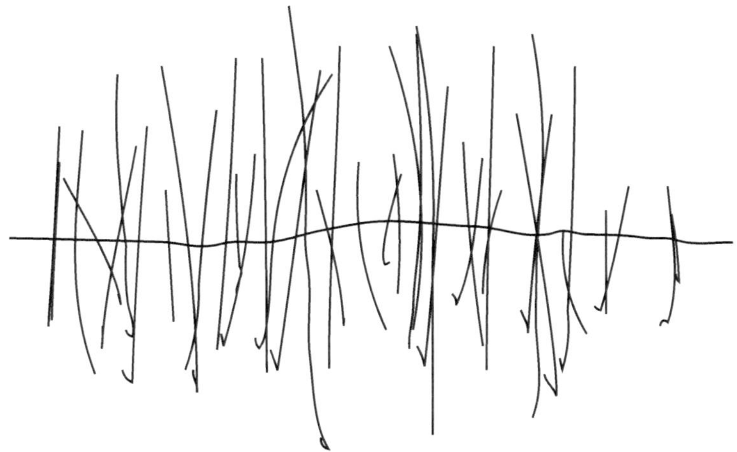

6. I am tired now & I move tiredly. I look back at all I have done & I am amazed & frightened.

6. When they come for us, we will dive into the ocean. We will fly into the air. We will live underwater. We will live in the sky.

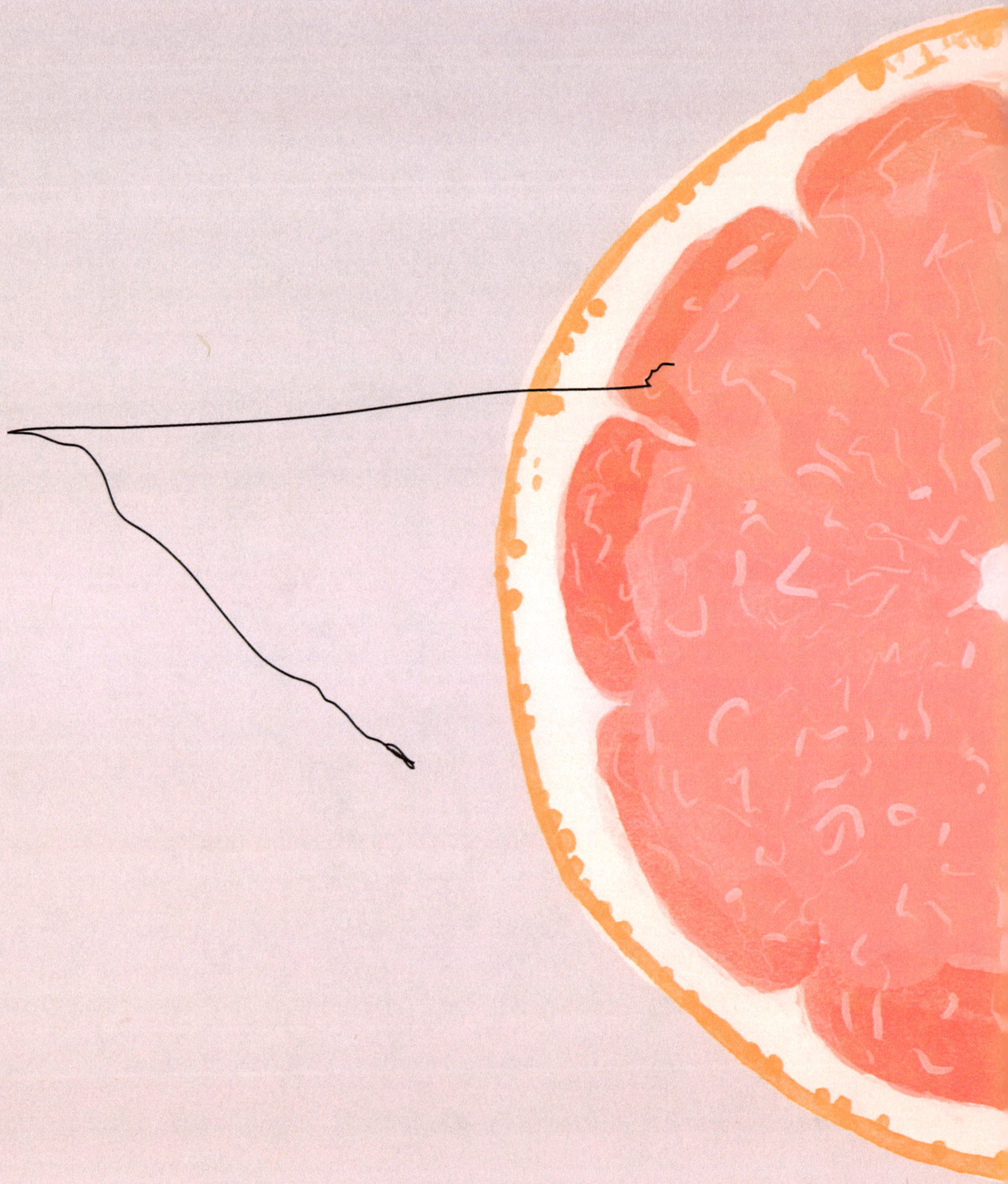

6. I couldn't see a thing, but I could feel my body.

6. A body immersed in a fluid experiences a buoyant force equal to the weight of the fluid it displaces.

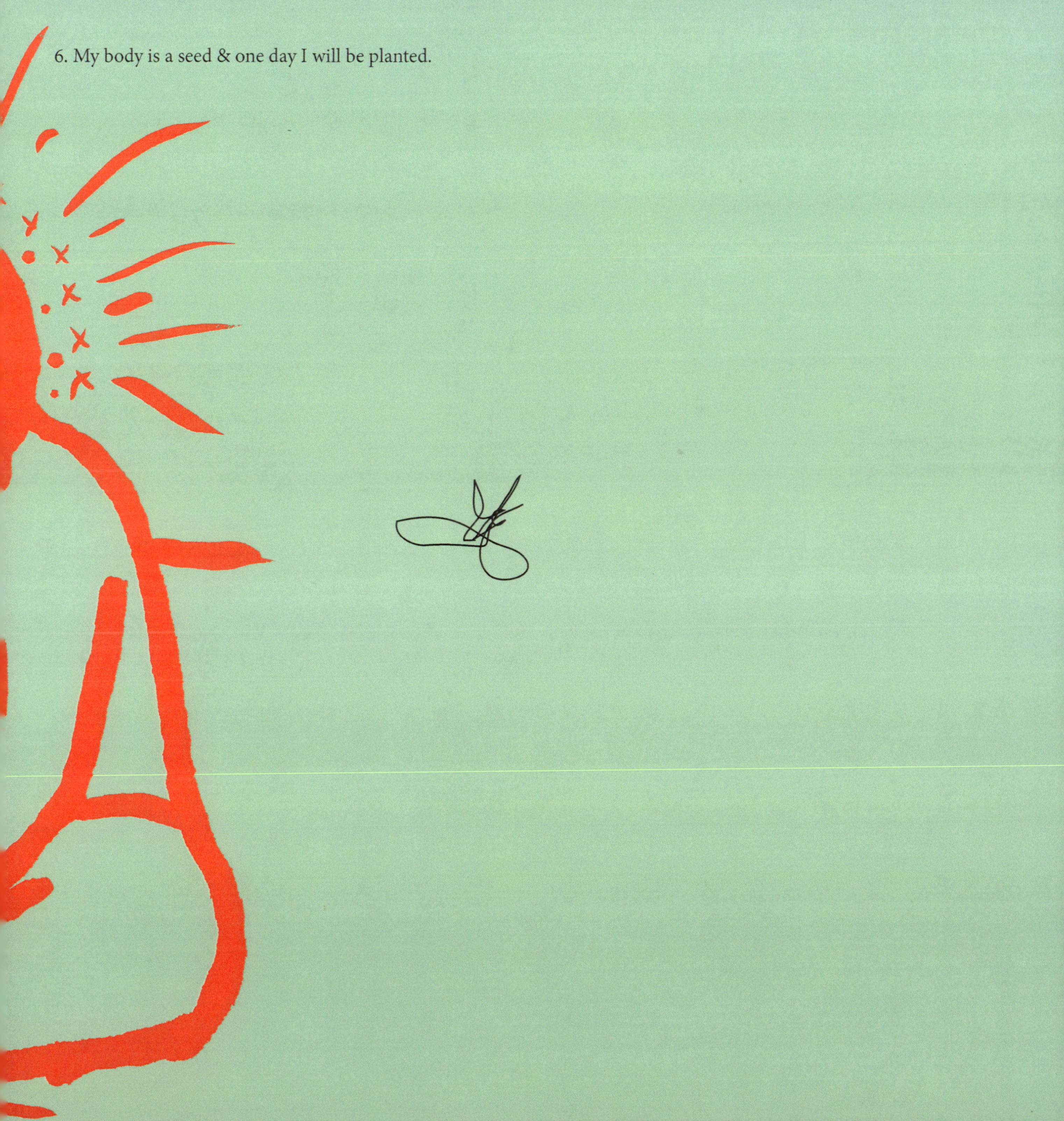

6. My body is a seed & one day I will be planted.

7. Today I grew my legs back. Well, I didn't "grow" them back. They just kind of appeared. Flickered into existence. Have you ever felt your limbs flicker in & out of existence? It's weird.

7. I feel like I've been walking forever. I keep leaving Sea-Witch, going as far away as I can & then I reach a place where I find that I am once again in Sea-Witch. I am not going in circles. Though my brain has been guilty of going in circles quite often, my feet never have. They have always taken me forward. Unlike many of my friends I have always had an excellent sense of direction. & it's not like when I find myself back at Sea-Witch that I find myself at the entrance to Sea-Witch again, which is familiar as my own hands & arms, as familiar as the tops of my own thighs. Instead I find myself INSIDE Sea-Witch, in some remote part of her to which I had never before traveled. I leave her body, journey for days, months, only to wake up & recognize a path or a beach or a cave or an esophagus. It is maddening. Not to mention I keep forgetting why I left. I do not understand what curse I am subject to. At this moment I do not need to leave her, in fact I would be very sad to leave her, but I am terrified at the idea that I am in some way imprisoned here.

80. I asked Sea-Witch about it today on our date. I love going on dates with Sea-Witch but I can never figure out if we are "dating". I'm not sure if going on dates means we are "dating" or if that implies something more or if we are already that something more. The hardest thing about going on dates with Sea-Witch is that people keep murdering her all the time while we are on our date. Anyway, after the server at the restaurant we were at murdered her & we had a funeral there on the sidewalk where the tables were set up, Sea-Witch explained to me that she has not imprisoned anyone inside herself. She said that all of us are free to go as we please. But that there are many people—even many of the most gentle people— who hate monsters so deeply that they use all of their means to return us to the fringes of society. Which, of course, is where Sea-Witch lives.

800. I hope this isn't too confusing for you. It's hard for me to know how to write certain ideas sometimes.

8000. There is a lot about our lives you will not be able to understand, but remember that we did not choose to structure our lives based on their legibility to you. We chose them for us, based on what was made available to us. Lives structured around legibility value structure over life. This is the origin of harm.

80000. I have written so much now about Sea-Witch & the things that happened regarding her. I don't know where to stop. There isn't an ending. It's still happening. It's always happening. Empires take hundreds, thousands of years to fall. In the meantime we survive. We examine the idea of thriving & try to find a way in. We organize, we provide relief, we resist, we live. We are swimming in this thing called ongoingness. Take a breath.

i can't live without you

but what is the end?

the end is
what they desire

every desire
is an end

and every end
is a desire

then
the end of the world
is a desire of the world

what type of end do you desire?

-Sun Ra, "The End"

When I came back to Sea-Witch I came because I wanted to. I came because I loved her. I came because I can't live without her. Not because I would be murdered, though I guess that's possible, but more in the way people say *I can't live without you* when they're being romantic or whatever. I came because I needed her sand to hold me on bright mornings. For small walls of it to press on my sides & back & to press small walls of it in return with each breath.

When I came back to Sea-Witch I said, *Look, I know you're busy but will you just lay in bed with me & hold me?* & she smiled widely & said *yes of course yes yes absolutely* & so we put on my favorite record, the one that I can't tell if it's sad or gentle & pretty or both, the one that makes time so thin that I can feel every other time I felt these feelings & feel so enormously close to returning back to those moments, we put on that record & I held her & she held me & we held each other in bed & we listened to the whole record. We fell asleep that way & when we woke up in the morning there was light streaming in the window & I got up before she did & I made her coffee & we drank it on the porch in the cool autumn air & the light streamed into our living room through the windows & the light streamed into the living room from our windows & the light streamed in through the living room through the windows & we sat at the hardwood table that used to be my parents' (if I had parents) & we cut up magazines & made collages & I made one of Sea-Witch & she made one of me & mine of her was all made of stars & hers of me was all made of frogs which was weird but I loved it, it was actually so beautiful so we framed them & put them on the wall & took the dog & walked through the woods by our house (if we had a house) with our dog (if we had a dog) & I almost burned up with how happy I was there, with her, as the trees stretched so far up above us, there with my beautiful Sea-Witch. And just at that moment, just as I had that thought, I felt myself flicker. I looked at Sea-Witch & she flickered too. We both looked at our dog & saw it flicker. We all flickered again together & then winked out of existence.

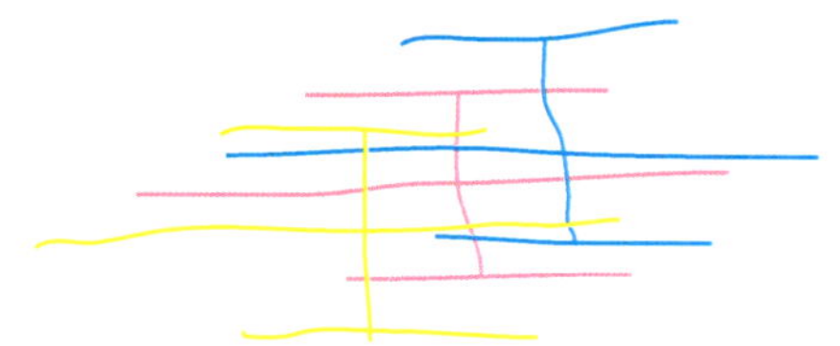

Never Angeline Nørth is a book witch living in Olympia, WA.
They also wrote the books *Careful Mountain* and *Sara or the Existence of Fire*.
Find them online at Undying.club

Thanks

Thanks to the people who let me put their words and art in this book. It wouldn't be the same without you. Thanks to Irene and Spider. Thanks to Izabella and Delta and Zephyr. Thanks to Ramona. Thanks to all the people who showed me beauty. Thanks to Ellie. Thanks to all the monsters. Thanks to the people who used to be 2fast-2house for putting out the original volumes of this. Thanks to Colette and the other editors who published this in their magazines. Thanks to Sung and Amelia and Nikki and Imogen and Blake and Athena/Casey and Sybil and all the writers who told people about this book and said cool shit about it. And of course huge thanks to John Trefry & Inside the Castle for putting out this book.

Fuck cops forever. Fuck prison-makers. Fuck billionaires. Fuck those who make and enforce borders.
May every last comfort be ripped from their grasp.

Love to all you monsters. Take care of each other. Take care of yrselves.

sigil of ending capitalism, healing trauma, and hot trans makeouts
by claire diane

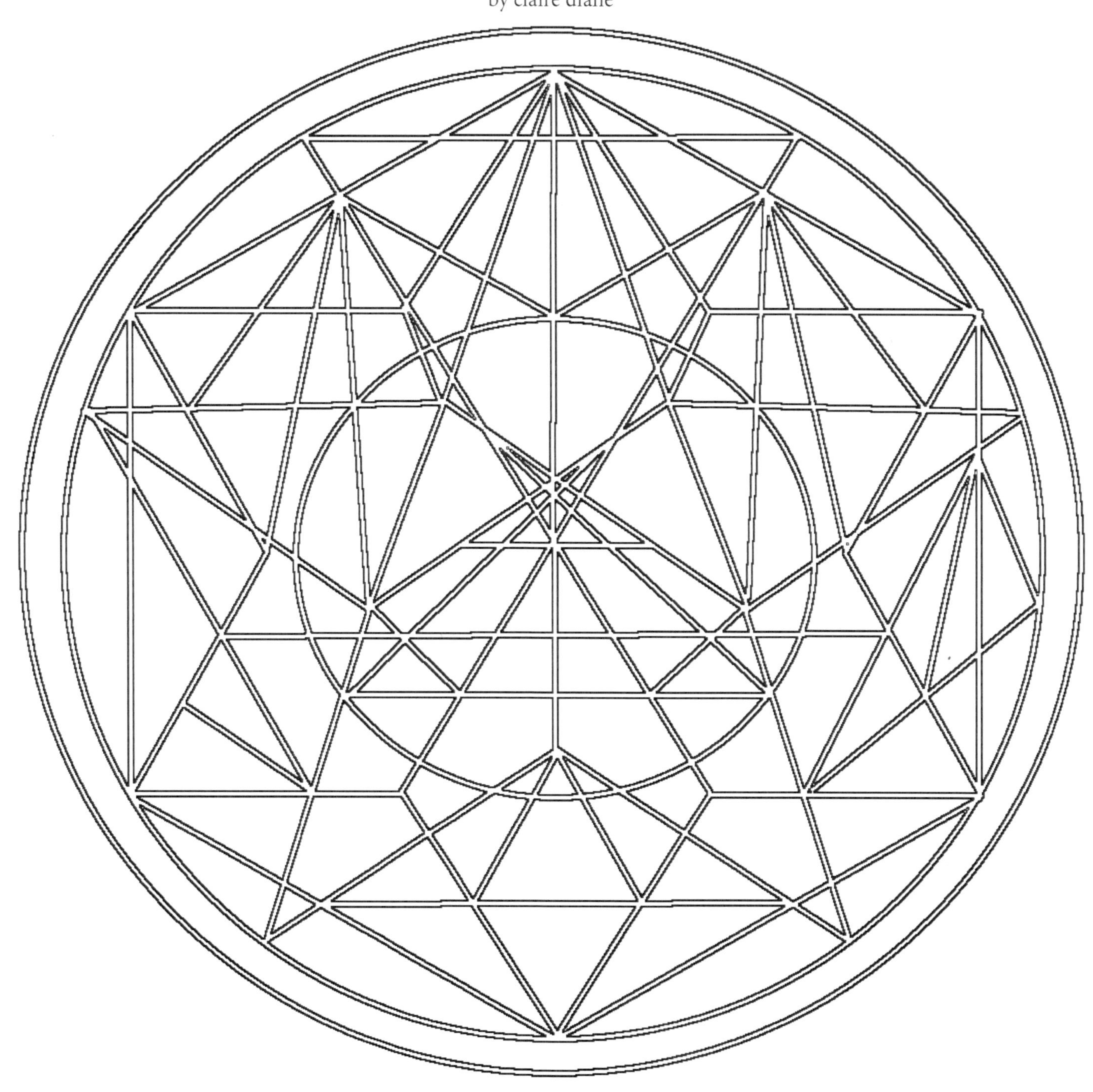

sigil of doing things, feeling good, & caring about people
by Moss Angel the Undying

sigil of beauty, cool shit & figuring out how to rebuild stronger the second time around
by Møss Høpe Ångel

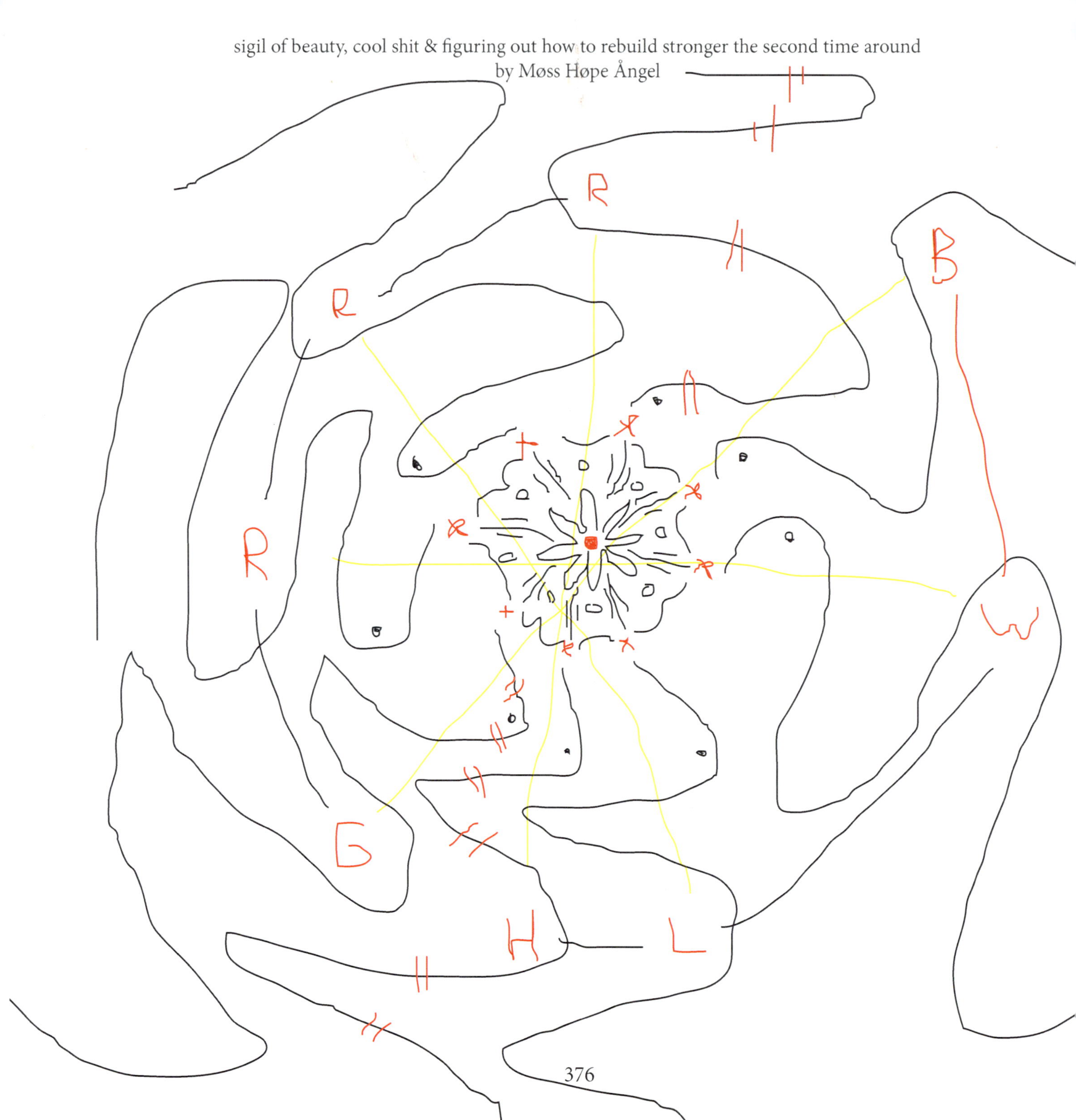

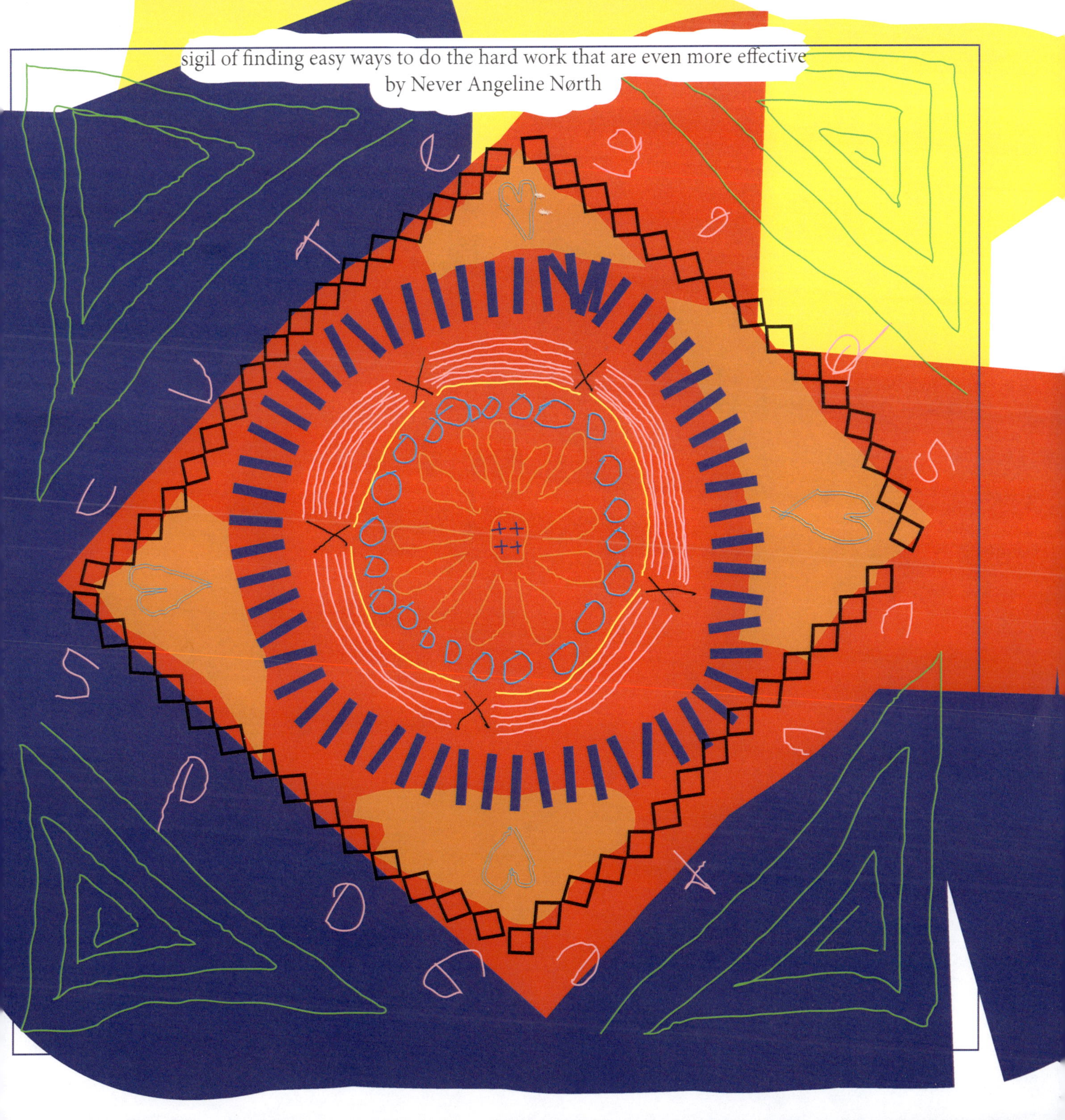
sigil of finding easy ways to do the hard work that are even more effective
by Never Angeline Nørth

www.ingramcontent.com/pod-product-compliance
Lightning Source LLC
Chambersburg PA
CBRC090957100726
47911CB00009B/181